PROLOGUE

THE RED THREE-INCH HARD BOUND book lay open on my counsel table. The *Manual for Courts-Martial* was the military's bible. It was heavy, its pages well-worn and dog-eared. How many editions had there been in the last twenty years? I still had my original from Military Justice School in Newport, Rhode Island. Trial Counsel was making her initial sentencing argument to the jury; I was half-listening.

I stared at the page, looking at the words I knew all too well. They were highlighted in yellow marker:

> The sources of military jurisdiction include the Constitution and international law, including the law of war… The agencies through which military jurisdiction is exercised include Court-Martials for the trial of offences against military law and, in the case of a General Court-Martial, of persons who by the law of war are subject to trial by military tribunals.

A General Court-Martial is a felony-level trial where the jurors could award any punishment they so choose, from a letter of reprimand to the death penalty. My gaze drifted to a paragraph on the next page, one I had reminded juries of so many times in the past:

The purpose of military law is to promote justice, to assist in maintaining good order and discipline in the Armed Forces, to promote efficiency and effectiveness in the military establishment, and thereby to strengthen the national security of the United States.

I picked up the book and flipped through the pages until I found the "Punitive Articles," the listed offenses for which a military member, regardless of rank, could be charged. I stopped at Article 133, -Conduct Unbecoming an Officer and Gentlemen. It read,

Conduct which violates this article is action or behavior in an official capacity which, in dishonoring or disgracing the person as an officer, seriously compromises the officer's character as a gentleman... There are certain moral attributes common to the ideal officer and the perfect gentleman, a lack of which is indicated by acts of dishonesty, unfair dealing, indecency, indecorum, lawlessness, injustice, or cruelty. Not everyone is or can be expected to meet unrealistically high moral standards, but there is a limit of tolerance based on customs of the service and military necessity below which the personal standards of an officer cannot fall without seriously compromising the person's standing as an officer, or the person's character as a gentleman. This article prohibits conduct by a commissioned officer, which, taking all the circumstances into consideration is thus compromising.

The maximum punishment for violation of this article is dismissal, forfeiture of all pay and allowances, and confinement.

And I thought to myself, disbarment if you're a lawyer. There goes my reenlistment bonus!

I moved the thick book to the side and picked up the thinner one underneath; a nearly new copy of *The Rules of Professional Conduct* published by the Virginia State Bar Association. I found Rule 8.4, which defined lawyer misconduct:

> It is professional misconduct for a lawyer to commit... a deliberately wrongful act that reflects adversely on the lawyer's honesty, trustworthiness or fitness to practice law... or engage in conduct involving... misrepresentation.

It had been ten days since the trial began. Much had changed. I thought of my client seated next to me, his head slightly bowed. A military lawyer was both a military officer, who was supposed to obey his superior's orders, as well as an attorney, who was supposed to obey his client's instructions. So if a conflict arose between the two, which one wins out? In advocating your client's cause, nothing was supposed to stand in your way. It had led to some interesting situations over the years. Was it the Admiral or the Seaman who was your boss?

Trial Counsel was concluding her initial argument. She was good. The jury was hanging on her every word. It was nice to try a case against a worthy opponent. It kept you on your toes and sharpened your courtroom skills. Lately the quality of the newly appointed Judge Advocates was declining. I guess if you sweated it out for three years in law school, you didn't want to sweat it out for six more months on an aircraft carrier in the middle of an ocean.

Since the Government had the burden of proof in a criminal case, she would get to speak to the jury again, a fact I always reminded them of. Several times in fact. I finished each of my closing arguments with a few questions that I asked the jurors to pose to the prosecutor when they rose to speak again—questions I knew they couldn't answer. Most took the bait; the experienced ones usually didn't.

Commander Dempsey had finished. The Military Judge looked at me and nodded.

"May it please the court?" I rose and walked toward the jury box. How many times in my career had I stood there? How many times had my words made a difference? They needed to today.

It was comforting being back in the old courtroom where I first started trying cases. Almost two decades' worth of representing every type of criminal. It was hot even for June. The window air conditioner units still didn't work very well. The carpet was threadbare after so many years of use. Pictures of two of the oldest sailing vessels, the USS *Constitution*, or Old Ironsides, one of the six original Navy frigates and the world's oldest commissioned warship afloat, and the USS *Bon Homme Richard*, named to honor Benjamin Franklin after he authored *Poor Richard's Almanac* and captained by John Paul Jones, still hung in the same place on either side of the jury box. I started to sweat.

"We have been through an emotional few days. I recognize the tremendous loss the Williams family must feel. I had hoped to spare this family any more grief by having to review the tragic circumstances that bring us, total strangers, together in this courtroom. But justice demands that I ask you, one last time, to examine the reasons we are here."

The family stared back at me. What were they thinking? I was often asked how I could defend the people I did. They seemed like decent people. I imagined the father going off to work each day; the mother keeping the house clean, having dinner on the table when her husband arrived home, proud their only son was—had been—a Marine. And then there was the wife. She sat there quietly, cradling the baby close to her chest, gently rocking him back and forth—a child that would never get to know his father.

I continued. "Something the Sergeant said during his testimony was particularly poignant to me. He said that he could have accepted Lance Corporal Williams's death if it had occurred in battle; that would have been a 'good death.' That's the marine mentality—that if a marine is lost in battle, then that's okay. My father was a marine. His brother, my uncle, was a marine. My brother-in-law was a marine. I

8

understand that thinking. However, I respectfully disagree with the Sergeant in one respect: the death of a young person is always tragic, whether it's in wartime, whether it's from an automobile accident, whether it's by an event such as this."

Was I getting through to them? The twelve jurors, eight males and four females, while all wearing the same uniform, were from different walks of life. Two were from the North, four Midwesterners, three from the West Coast, and three from the South. The military brought together people from all across the country. Six had children, two were divorced, seven were officers, and five were senior enlisted. I liked enlisted members. They knew what the real world was like. They dealt with the daily struggles of their sailors and marines. They had experienced the loneliness of a six-month deployment being away from family and friends—the bone-weary twenty-hour days sweating away in the bowels of a ship or standing watch at lonely duty stations. They knew how demeaning it was getting yelled at for some imagined infraction by a young JO, junior officer, who had just graduated from the Naval Academy, or ROTC (Reserve Officers' Training Corps), whose only previous "real" job had been as a summer lifeguard at their daddy's country club and who usually didn't know his ass from a hole in the ground.

I walked from one end of the jury box to the other.

"But first let's talk about some of the realities of which you are already aware." I looked intently into each face. "Whatever happens here today, you cannot give back to the Williams family that which they truly want the most. And I understand their desire that Petty Officer Miller suffer the ultimate penalty—the same fate their son suffered. I hope you can also understand the Miller family's desire that Joshua's life be spared, that he be allowed to live, if you can call what he has facing him, living. You have to balance those two needs." I paused for a moment. "But you also have another need to balance, maybe not as great, but certainly important." I paused again. "And that is the need of society as a whole. Ask yourself: What type of world do you want to live in? A world of vengeance and retribution? Or a world of understanding and forgiveness? When you get back to the deliberation room in a few minutes, think about that and how your vote today will affect us all. Winston Churchill said, 'A society is measured by how it treats its weakest members.' Weakness can be defined in many ways. In this case, as you've seen, there is no greater weakness than that of the heart."

I walked over to my client and placed a hand on his shoulder. He looked up at me with sadness in his eyes. "What you are being called upon to do today is not easy. The moment you return to the courtroom with your verdict, there will be much emotion. But your duty requires you to do what is right. What is just. That is why you were chosen to sit on this jury. You were selected for your maturity, for your experience, for your understanding of human nature, and"—I paused once again—"for your compassion."

Again, I took several seconds to look each one of the members in the eye. Even though I was tired, I was in no hurry. Some looked away, perhaps not yet willing to face the decision they would shortly have to make.

"The Government's case showed you a snapshot of a few hours of time in a troubled young man's life. He acted out of fear for a loved one. Were his actions irrational? Probably so. And if you believe that he has no heart, that he has no soul, that he has no good in him, put him to death." From the corner of my eye I saw Miller's mother, who was seated on the front row behind us, jerk her head up. "However, I also ask you to examine the other twenty years of this young man's life. If you see any redeeming value in those years, then you must vote to spare him."

Trial Counsel asked rhetorically, "What is a life worth? There is no price you can put on a life. A life is priceless, everyone's life. There's no justification for what happened that night in those woods in eastern North Carolina—but there is a reason. And you've seen that reason. She took the stand. You heard her testimony. Think back to the first time you were in love. In today's world 'love' is very different concept than when you and I were growing up. The Internet has changed the rules of the game. It brings us closer yet keeps us further away. You met someone... but do you really get to know them?"

Now all twelve faces were staring back at me. Were they listening? Did they care? In a few hours, my client would know if he was going to live or die.

It had been a long six months.

CHAPTER ONE

He slowed as he pulled his car up to the security checkpoint on base and rolled down his window. He had been driving for over seven hours. Joshua Miller loved his 1987 El Camino, the last year Chevrolet made the half-car, half-truck. The 350-cubic-inch V8 engine delivered 170 horsepower and was the fastest car in Lee County. Miller had spent hours in the barn customizing the vehicle. When he was finished, he painted it black and named it "The Shadow." But it was not very comfortable, especially on long drives. He needed to get out and stretch.

Joshua got a late start because he really didn't want to leave. It was the first of November; fall in the mountains was his favorite time of year. He loved to watch the leaves change colors while he sat beside the creek not far from the farm where he grew up. The sound of the water gently cascading over the rocks and pebbles in the stream comforted him. In Lee County, Virginia, the western-most part of the state named after revolutionary war hero Henry "Light-Horse Harry" Lee, who was also the father of confederate war General Robert E. Lee, there wasn't much to do. In a county of only twenty-five thousand people you could get lost in your thoughts for hours and no one would miss you.

Tidewater, Virginia, was the furthest from home he had been since he was a seaman recruit at Great Lakes, one of the Navy's largest boot camps. Forty thousand newbies passed through there each year. That was ten times the number of people in his hometown. He had flown to Illinois, his first time on a plane, so it didn't seem so far away. He didn't like to fly; it made him feel helpless, a feeling he didn't like.

His eight weeks at boot camp passed quickly. He was exposed to the basic essentials of Navy life, learning military drills, basic seamanship, shipboard damage control, and firefighting. He easily passed the confidence chamber (where they pipe in tear gas to determine how you respond to adversity) and the swimming test (where they tie your hands behind your back and throw you in the pool). Growing up in the woods kept him in good shape and endowed him with certain toughness.

A marine dressed in his utility uniform came out of the guard shack. He was wearing body armor with a Beretta M9 attached to his black riggers belt—a belt worn by those who were proficient in the martial arts. Even though this was a Navy base, marines still provided the perimeter security.

"Joshua Miller reporting for duty," his voice cracked. He still had trouble with authority.

"ID and orders, Sailor." Guess he didn't look like a marine. He was self-conscious in his civilian clothes.

Miller had enlisted in the Navy's Delayed Entry Program while still in high school. His mother thought the military would be good for him since he had grown up without a father. After attending boot camp, he was sent to A school, the Navy's basic training school for a particular rate or job specialty. He then reported to a ship for a year tour and now, after two weeks leave, was reporting to Fleet Combat Training Center Atlantic, or FCTC, located at Dam Neck Naval Base in Virginia Beach, Virginia, for C school, part of the Navy's advanced training program.

The base was located on the site of the nineteenth-century Dam Neck Mills Lifesaving Service. This part of the coast, from the Outer Banks of North Carolina to the Chesapeake Bay where the base was located, was called the Graveyard of the Atlantic. The United States Lifesaving Service merged with other agencies to form the United States Coast Guard in 1915. FCTC was also home to the Navy and Marine Corps Intelligence Training Center, or NMITC.

Miller wanted to be an Intelligence Specialist. He loved the idea of the solitude he would have working in the intelligence field. Of the three hundred thousand–plus active-duty sailors there were less than two thousand ISs whose job it was to analyze data and break it down to determine its military usefulness. Joshua could study an issue for hours. It reminded him of the complex jigsaw puzzles he put together growing up. Besides, he never really liked the ocean.

Joshua moved the brown paper bag his mother had used to pack his lunch, a peanut butter and jelly sandwich and barbecue potato chips, and handed his orders out the window.

The marine looked at them briefly and said, "Barracks 508. Straight ahead, take a left at the second light. It's the first building on the right after that." He turned sharply and went back inside the guard shack.

Miller drove the half mile down the black asphalt road that had been patched numerous times and turned into a large parking lot with few vacant spaces. Five large red brick buildings loomed in a semicircle in front of him. They all looked alike. Eight stories tall, twenty-five double-bunked rooms on each floor. A tall flagpole stood in the center of the compound with an enormous American flag flying. Military custom required that the flag be flown from sunrise to sunset. It was to be raised quickly but lowered slowly and ceremoniously. The color guard was forming outside and getting ready to play "Retreat." Miller had to hurry and get inside. If you were outside when the bugle call began, you had to stop, turn toward the flag, and salute, if in uniform, or place your hand over your heart if you weren't, until the colors were struck.

Miller parked in one of the last available spaces. There were vehicles of every make, model, and kind. New BMWs to beat up old clunkers. He hurriedly put on his windbreaker, threw his bag over his shoulder, and started to jog between the cars across the huge parking lot. It was getting cold outside.

Joshua opened one of the double doors to building and stopped at the front desk to check in. A Petty Officer not much older than him handed Miller several forms to fill out and sign. It didn't take long. Luckily, his assigned room was on the second floor, not too many steps to walk up or down. Trying to catch an elevator in the morning when four hundred sailors were hurrying to get to class was a pain. You couldn't be late.

Joshua turned to the left and found the stairwell. He climbed the stairs quickly and entered the second floor. The hallway was long with identical rooms on either side. The linoleum floors were polished to a high gloss. The smell of disinfectant was strong. There were small placards on the doors with the floor and room number; he was assigned to room 2-17. As he began looking for his room, he noticed some of the doors were open revealing young men in various stages of activity. Some lying on their bunks reading, others playing cards, a few on the phone. At the far end of the hallway was the bathroom with one big bay where everyone showered, along with four sinks and three "crappers."

Miller was told he wouldn't have a roommate for several weeks. He knew he might get lucky and not have one at all. Sailors unexpectedly got transferred to other units, were suddenly shipped out to sea to fill an empty billet, or even went AWOL (absent without leave) when the pressure got to be too much or a girlfriend threatened to leave.

Joshua found his room and went inside. He closed the door behind him as he didn't want to be bothered by strangers asking him questions about where he was from or what classes he was taking. He threw his bag on the cot closest to the window. On his side of the room was a wooden desk with a metal chair. He opened the small closet; it was just large enough for a few uniforms. The cinderblock walls were cool to the touch.

Joshua was hungry. He had only eaten the one sandwich and bag of chips his mom gave him. The chow hall couldn't be far away. He didn't know what time it closed, but he didn't want to drive into town. Virginia Beach seemed like a big place and he knew he would get lost. Besides, he had get up early and be ready for his first day of class tomorrow.

Joshua turned to head out the door. Unexpectedly, his room phone rang. He never understood why the barracks room had telephones; everyone carried a cell phone these days. At Great Lakes, he never used the room phone. Besides, he hated talking on the phone. The phone rang again.

Miller hesitated. He was new here and didn't know anyone. He knew it couldn't be the CDO, Command Duty Officer; he wasn't even assigned a watch section yet. Let it ring, he thought. I'm really hungry. He reached for the doorknob and opened the door to leave. He walked into the hallway. The telephone continued to ring. He really didn't want to answer it but something made him hesitate.

He turned and walked back inside.

CHAPTER TWO

I WAS SITTING IN MY office staring out the window at the new fallen snow. It didn't snow often in Norfolk, Virginia, not even in late January. I was lost in my thoughts. I heard the telephone in the outer office ring.

"Commander, you have a phone call."

It was 1800, late to be in the office by Navy standards. It was already dark outside. I hated daylight saving time. Three of the eleven aircraft carrier groups were making preparations to get underway: the USS *John F. Kennedy* CV-67, USS *Nimitz* CVN-68, and USS *Theodore Roosevelt* CVN-71. Each had over 5,600 sailors onboard—3,200 ship's company and 2,400 with the air wing. To get a decent parking spot, you needed to be on the base by 0600, which meant most everyone left work between 1500 and 1700.

"Who is it?" I yelled to the LN1 (Legalman First Class) Jeff Leonard, who was seated in a cubicle outside my door. Anyone of importance was already gone for the day.

"Sir, it's a Mrs. Anne Davis, Petty Officer Miller's mom."

Miller? That was the name of the newest prisoner charged with murdering a marine. As Senior Defense Counsel, I was given a daily report from the brig of all new inmates so I could assign them counsel. A synopsis of the NCIS investigation showed a shaky eyewitness linking the two together and an inconclusive surveillance video. The evidence seemed pretty thin. More importantly, a body hadn't been found.

"Tell her I have already assigned him a lawyer."

As the most experienced defense attorney at the largest Naval Legal Service Office in the Navy, I was in charge of twenty-two attorneys. It was not the most sought-after billet in the Judge Advocate General Corps, which were now almost seven hundred strong. To advance in rank you needed to provide "Service to the Fleet." The "tickets" you had to punch to get promoted to Captain or Admiral were almost preordained. You started off in Legal Assistance or as a criminal defense counsel; after getting some experience as a litigator you moved into a trial counsel slot (the civilian equivalent of a prosecutor) and then to a Staff Judge Advocate job. There you were on some "Four Striper's" staff giving general legal advice on a variety of subjects to someone who really didn't want to listen to a word you said. You needed some sea time, preferably on an aircraft carrier, and then a tour of duty at the Pentagon. It was a very predictable, and boring, career path. Along the way, you must remember not to piss off anyone senior to you because you never knew who would be on the next promotion board.

I continued to look out the window. I missed the days as a young lawyer when my only worry was defending my client. Now I had all these administrative duties and command functions I had to attend to. Once in a while, I got to try a case.

I thought of the new group of young defense counsel who had just reported for duty. During my morning indoctrination session, I reminded them that even though they wore a uniform they swore an oath to their client first. Not all JAGs thought that way. Being a lawyer in the military created its conflicts. You had a Commanding Officer referring a sailor to trial—a shitbag who was hindering the commands "mission." Your CO didn't want to tick off that CO, so the young JOs, junior officers, had quite a balancing act. How hard should they fight back? Would putting a senior officer on the stand and subjecting him to a vigorous cross-examination hurt their career? They needed someone in their corner. I was—at least for a while. I was growing more and more tired of all the BS. I was thinking of getting out and seeing what the civilian world had to offer.

"Yes, Sir, but she insists on speaking with you."

I paused, then said, "Put her through."

The quality of sailors entering the Armed Forces had improved greatly over the last twenty years. There was a time when young criminals were told by the local Judge that they could either go to jail or go into the Navy. Early in my career, I represented a Master Chief, the Navy's highest enlisted rank, onboard the USS *Nimitz*, who had nineteen nonjudicial punishments. In the old days multiple NJPs were considered a "badge of honor." Not in today's Navy. If you didn't get into trouble during your enlistment, you were entitled to wear a gold hash mark on your sleeve; if there were any NJPs on your record, the hash mark was red. Real sailors wore red, they used to say.

Today's sailor was more brains than brawn. There was less violent crime. With the economy the way it was, it was tough finding a job, particularly in the rural areas. So the military had its pick of recruits. Most of the ratings required that you undergo a fairly rigorous screening process and usually required you to be computer literate.

I sighed as I picked up the telephone that sat at the corner of my desk. "Commander DeMarco, how may I help you?"

"Commander, my name is Anne Davis. My son is Joshua Miller."

"Yes, Ma'am, I'm sorry to learn of your son's situation." I thought, another mother whose child had been sent off, perhaps too early, to the Navy. Kids today just didn't grow up as quickly as in the past. They were sheltered. The days in the Navy were long, and while underway, there were no weekends and very little downtime. It was a tough life.

"Sir, I really need to talk to you," she said.

"Ma'am, I really can't speak to you about your son's case. He has already been assigned a defense counsel." Besides, what do you tell a mother whose son has been charged with capital murder and is facing the death penalty? The military has several levels of punishment, from NJP, nonjudicial punishment, where the CO is judge, jury, and executioner but the punishment is limited, all the way up to a General Court-Martial, where the ultimate penalty is death. The armed services had only fifteen sailors on Death Row. The last time the military executed someone was during the Kennedy administration, but that doesn't mean they weren't trying. Most of the condemned spend decades going through the appeals process.

"Yes, Sir, I know that, but he's a good boy." Her voice sounded small through the telephone.

"Yes, Ma'am, I'm sure he is." What else could I say?

"Commander, he needs a good attorney."

"Ma'am, we have plenty of good attorneys in this office." I didn't want to tell her that half the staff had never tried a major felony.

"Commander, I'm concerned about him." She paused. "And I don't think he did this."

How would I respond to that? I was sure every mother thought her son was innocent. The motherly instinct wouldn't allow them to accept that fact that no matter how good a job they did raising their child, somewhere along the way he changed or circumstances and experiences changed him.

"Yes, Ma'am. Well, I'm sure he'll have his day in court," was all I could manage to say.

"May I come right to the point?" Oh no. I always worried when I heard someone ask me that.

"Sure," I responded.

"My psychic told me you are the only one that can save my boy's life."

I hate it when that happens.

CHAPTER THREE

It was Monday morning, the start of the third week of class. The first text message arrived at 6:00 a.m. It was a good way to start the day, Joshua thought. He read it quickly and sent a short response back. He had to shower, get dressed in his uniform, get to the mess hall for a quick breakfast, and be in class by 7:00 a.m. He laid the cell phone on his desk and hurried down the hallway to the bathroom. When he returned, he quickly dressed and shoved the phone into his pocket as he hurried out the door. As he ran across the courtyard, he barely noticed the cold.

Ever since that first telephone call the day he arrived two weeks ago, he and Samantha had been talking and texting every day—many times every day. She originally said she had the wrong number. But she called back. He was glad she did. He couldn't wait to meet her.

At C school, where the Navy taught its most advanced classes, students weren't allowed to have cell phones in class; he brought his in anyway. His first class was "Analyst Training: Writing, Analysis, and Preparing Briefings." He sat in the back of the classroom on a hard wooden chair that felt like it might collapse at any minute. He was at the end of a long table where six young sailors were busy taking notes.

The phone in his pocket began vibrating. It was her. Joshua had never felt this way before. A girl, a beautiful girl, was paying attention to him. He wasn't bad looking, perhaps a little on the short side. Joshua just didn't know what to say or how to act around girls, especially pretty ones. In Southwest Virginia, there weren't many pretty girls. The ones that were never paid him much attention. He wasn't listening to the instructor.

Joshua grew up in a farming community at the foothills of the Appalachian mountain range. When he was ten years old, his dad died. The ensuing years were rough on his mom and older brother, but they were particularly hard on him. His father was twenty-five years older than his mom and semiretired. He and his dad did everything together; he even took Joshua to his fiftieth high school reunion. In the evenings, his father sat in his chair by the fireplace, smoking his pipe, with Joshua on his lap. There was a lot of love in his home back then. After his dad died, his mom withdrew from the world, and there wasn't much of a world in rural Virginia. He guessed she did the best she could. But he was lonely.

The cell phone buzzed again. He glanced down and tried to read what she said but the screen was too small. Joshua thought about trying to text her back but didn't want to get caught. He really needed to concentrate, but he couldn't. At the first break, he would run into the hallway to call her. He just needed to hear her voice.

"Sam" lived in the Outer Banks of North Carolina, only a few hours' drive from the base. She said her family was originally from Texas and was rich. He wondered how she got to the Outer Banks. He'd have to remember to ask her. They would have plenty of time to talk about such things. Joshua had Thanksgiving leave coming up in a few weeks. Then they could finally meet in person. He tried to convince himself the time would pass quickly. The thought of her was driving him crazy.

Joshua tried to call during the short ten-minute break but she didn't answer. He returned to class disappointed. However, shortly before the lecture started a text message arrived. He read it and blushed. The messages were getting more and more sexual. Samantha was 5'1", 105 pounds, with long blond hair. The photos she sent were unbelievable. He printed the one she sent from the Halloween party she went to a few weeks ago and put it in his wallet. Damn, she looked good in that devil outfit! Shortly thereafter, she began sending partially naked pictures. They were usually a little distorted but he didn't care. Her hand must have been shaking as much as his.

During the half-hour lunch break, they would try to talk to each other again. Joshua could barely find time to eat. He loved the sound of her voice. It soothed him. Then it was back to class until 1600. Afterward, he would rush back to the barracks, change, and head to the gym for a quick workout. Keeping in shape was important, particularly now.

Miller wondered what he would say to her when they finally met. Samantha told him she had a college degree in art history from Old Dominion University. He wasn't really sure what that was. But she didn't talk to him in that "uppity" manner the way some of the college girls he had met did. When he first arrived at the base, he went to several bars near the local university or on the strip but never stayed too long. Sam was not like those girls; she was a regular person.

At evening chow, he found himself sitting alone in the mess hall texting her. When classes first began, he made a few friends. Everyone was from somewhere else and lonely, whether they admitted it or not. The guys from up North talked tough, the West Coast ones were laid-back, the Midwesterners kind of shy, and all the Southern guys talked about was hunting, He really didn't fit in with any group, but that didn't bother him. He had been alone most of his life.

Now the few friends he did have quit talking to him because he was spending all his time on the phone with Samantha. No more touch football games on the quad or late-night card games. The guys kidded him about it, but they were just jealous! He didn't care. He had waited for something like this his whole life. He wasn't sure what being in love felt like, but this had to be it.

The texting and phone calls continued throughout the evening except when he was at the mandatory two-hour study hall. The proctors roamed the room, and there was no way you could pull your phone out. Joshua found his mind drifting off to thoughts of her.

Lights out was 10:00 p.m. How many times did they talk today? He lost count. Joshua needed to get some sleep. His grades were slipping and the competition was tough in C school. If he washed out, he was going to be a deckhand chipping paint on a destroyer. She wouldn't like that, would she? Or maybe she wouldn't care. Maybe she would love him for who he was. He could take college courses online and get his degree. He could apply for Officer Candidate School. She would probably like being an officer's wife. He tried to close his eyes but couldn't sleep.

Joshua made one more call. Her voice was the last one he needed to hear.

CHAPTER FOUR

JOSHUA WAS MAD AT HER—AT least as mad as you could be at your true love. He threw his hooded sweatshirt on the bunk. He had gotten back to his barracks room two minutes before curfew. He called her immediately. "Where were you?"

"You said we were going to meet at five o'clock," replied Samantha. He still loved the sound of her voice.

"No, I didn't. I said six o'clock. You know I don't get out of class until four. I waited for over two hours. Why didn't you stay until I got there?"

"I waited until five forty-five. I didn't know if you were going to show up or if you were at the wrong place like last time, so I left."

"You didn't even answer your phone." His anger was starting to go away.

"I told you there is bad reception down here."

Joshua was frustrated. He couldn't wait until he was on leave to meet her, so he convinced Samantha to meet him for a few hours after class. This was the second time in a week he had driven down the North Carolina and they still hadn't met face to face. First, it was the wrong place; now it was the wrong time. They were never going to get together! He wanted so badly to see her, to hold her, to look into her eyes.

"You know I have to be up at six in the morning. I have class all day and I have to study. I'm really falling far behind. They may kick me out. Then what am I going to do? I'll be back onboard a ship!"

He didn't want to sound like he was whining, but he was getting desperate.

"Joshua, I'm really sorry." Her voice was soft and low.

"That's what you always say." He was trying to stay mad at her but couldn't. "I drove almost two hours to see you and two hours back." There was silence on the other end of the phone. "I'm beginning to think you don't want to see me." Now he was whining.

"Joshua, don't say that."

"Well, what am I to think? It's been almost a month now. We talk twenty times a day, we text, you sent me those pictures." He had to compose himself.

"I do want to see you."

"Well, look what happened last time—you didn't show up."

"Joshua, we just got our signals crossed."

"But you didn't even give me the right address. I looked. I drove all over the place looking for you. I was worried about you. I looked everywhere for you. And when you were in that car accident, I thought I would die. You didn't call." He lay on his bed, looking up at the ceiling, while they talked.

"I guess I was just upset about my car. And we weren't far from the base hospital, so we drove there. I did try to have my friend leave you a message, but the reception down here is so bad." She was bringing her best friend Susan with her so that he could also meet her; maybe she really did care about him. "And you really didn't need to get law enforcement involved."

Joshua started to feel guilty. "You could have at least told me where you were so I could have come see you."

"We weren't thinking."

What was he to do? "It's just that I love you." There, he finally said it. There was silence on the other end of the phone. "You don't have to say anything. I just wanted you to know."

"Joshua, you don't even really know me yet," she breathed softly.

"Yes, I do. I do know you," he insisted. "We talk about things I've never talked to anyone else about before." Then he blurted out, "Let's try to meet again. I can't wait until Thanksgiving."

"I don't know. Can you get off the base again?"

"I can leave right after chow tomorrow. I just have to be back before curfew and lights out. So I can't stay long." A few minutes, anything was better than nothing. He would get in trouble for missing study hall again, but he was going crazy. "Can you meet me halfway?"

"I don't know. And I think I have to go out of town for Thanksgiving."

"Where are you going?"

"I have that project I've been working on in Atlanta. You know, the one I told you about, that historic building." Samantha led such an exciting life. What did she see in him? He was just a sailor, a farm boy from the country. He had never left the county he was born in until he joined the Navy. What did this wonderful girl see in him?

"Are they going to fly you down in that jet again?" A private jet. He could only imagine what that must be like. He thought only famous people flew on their own jet. But she did.

"I think so."

"You going to stay at that fancy hotel you told me about, the St. Regis?" Joshua was proud of himself that he had remembered the name. He tried to remember every conversation they had, every word they spoke. After they were through talking for the night, he tried to commit every detail to memory. She said the St. Regis was a five-star hotel. He didn't exactly know what that meant. She explained to him it was how comfortable the beds were, whether they had enough parking and if the guests liked the food. Samantha patiently explained a lot of things to him. Joshua had never stayed in a hotel. At boot camp at Great Lakes, it was a dorm. There were fifty sailors in a big open area in bunk beds. On ship, he stayed in berthing with twenty other sailors. It wasn't that bad.

"Maybe in a few days we can try again." Joshua's heart sank. It had been a month of phone calls, text messages, and dreams. Thanksgiving wasn't looking good and Christmas was fast approaching. He wanted her to meet his family. His mom would like her. He would show his brother that he could indeed get a girl—one that knew things, one that traveled, one that was sophisticated, not like those county bumpkins he brought home.

Joshua wondered if Samantha would like the small town he was from. Would she like the woods? There wasn't much to do, but the people were nice. They had recently got a Walmart and a McDonald's. They could go bowling. There wasn't a movie theater in town yet. You had to drive into Tennessee if you wanted to see a movie. I bet she would like something different; she liked adventure.

Joshua wanted to buy her a special gift. He had been saving all his pay. Would it be a ring, a bracelet, or a necklace? He had never bought a girl anything. One time he bought his mom a bottle of perfume she seemed to like. It sat on her bureau dresser in her bedroom. He didn't think she used it much.

"I don't think I can wait much longer," Joshua pleaded.

"I promise we'll see each other soon."

"Okay, then let's make a plan right now," he said.

"Joshua, not now. I'm getting tired." Samantha yawned.

"Just a couple more minutes." He was begging now.

"What do you want to talk about?"

"Anything you want. Tell me some more about your travels."

Samantha could take him to places he had never been.

CHAPTER FIVE

I WAS TRAVELING ON HAMPTON Boulevard, the four-lane road leading into the Navy base. Recognizing the importance of the Norfolk harbor the Navy established the US Naval Operating Base and Training Station on 474 acres in 1917. Naval Station Norfolk is now homeport to 186 ships, 1,300 aircraft, and 118,000 sailors and marines.

At one end of the thoroughfare sat Old Dominion University, the local college with almost twenty-five thousand students; at the other, the world's largest Naval Base. And Virginia Beach, a sailor's paradise with all kinds of mischief, was only ten miles away. I tell the young female officers, "No sailors, no surfers."

Along the way, I marveled at the number of tattoo parlors, used car dealerships, and 7-Elevens. How could they all stay so busy? I passed the Destroyers and Submarines (D&S) piers. I thought about the different types of sailors in our Navy: submariners, a strange breed; the pilots, or brown shoes; and the surface guys, or black shoes. All the different commands of the Navy were located within a twenty-five-mile radius. Although several of the carrier battle groups had left for replenishment training or deployment, the roadways were crowded with sailors coming and going. All short hair and jacked-up cars.

I turned right onto Arleigh Burke Way the long, winding, pot-filled road that led to the Norfolk Naval Brig. It surprised me that you had to drive through Navy housing to get to a prison. Guess the Government wasn't going to pay top dollar for prime real estate to house our criminals. Half-dressed children played in the cold ignorant to the suffering that went on in the back of their neighborhood. The sun never seemed to shine there.

I had been going to the brig for many years. The parking lot was always crowded, yet you never saw anyone. Cars were parked haphazardly as if their owners didn't care—or maybe they were just in a hurry to get inside. Sailors joked that the Navy's real motto was "Hurry up and wait" or that the acronym for NAVY was "Never Again Volunteer Yourself." Where was the "Good Order and Discipline" that we heard about every day? The punitive articles in the *Uniform Code of Military Justice*, the *UCMJ*, even made a violation of "good order and discipline," an element of many criminal offenses. Yet Senior Petty Officers and Chiefs—the backbone of the Navy—couldn't even park their cars within the lines. What was this world coming to? Barbed wire was everywhere. So were the weeds, even in the colder months. Time stood still here.

The brig always had the same smell, as if the entire building was bleached daily. The linoleum floors shined brightly in the florescent lighting. There was the constant sound of buzzing as the doors opened and closed. The worst was the slamming of the metal jail doors. That always made me jump; the feeling of uneasiness when they closed had never left me even after all these years.

As I entered the front door, I was greeted with, "Good morning, Commander DeMarco."

"Morning, Petty Officer." Damn, they get younger every year.

"You know the routine, Sir."

I pushed my keys, wallet, and cell phone through the small opening at the bottom of the Plexiglas window. I grabbed the clipboard and printed my name, rank, command, make of vehicle, license plate number, time, and my newly assigned client's name on the legal pad. With all the identity theft, you no longer needed to give your social security number. The guard took the pad but never looked at the information. I wondered if anyone ever checked. Just once, I'd like write something humorous, although there wasn't much to laugh about here.

"Looks like a slow day," I said, noting I was only the second lawyer to sign in. Many of the attorneys liked to visit their client on their way into work. Not a great way to start the day, I thought. Besides, if you arrived too early, you had to wait until the inmates were checked back in after breakfast and all the silverware was counted. Several years ago, one of my clients hid his fork in the scrambled eggs; the inmates sat back and enjoyed watching the guards dig through the Dumpsters for several hours until it was found. I understood the payback was not good.

"Yes, Sir, not many of you legal types visiting today."

"Crime must have taken a holiday." The young Master-at-Arms just looked at me. Guess you can't have a sense of humor and work here. The Navy, it's not just a Job; it's an Adventure! Guess the recruiters didn't tell him.

The guards all looked the same. I wondered if that was by design. Did the detailers assign the master-at-arms by the picture on their service jacket? Haircuts were shorter than normal. All were decked out in camouflage with biceps bulging. Caps pulled down low over blank stares. Sidearms, batons, handcuffs, and a myriad of other items swung back and forth from their belts. None of them smiled.

The Norfolk Brig was a long-term detention facility where prisoners could be housed for several days or many years. The really bad actors were eventually transported to the federal penitentiaries, like the US Disciplinary Barracks in Leavenworth, Kanas. This brig had been around forever. The mattresses on the cots were less than an inch thick and stained. They sagged in more than one place. I don't recall seeing a blanket. I seemed to remember learning as a law student that cruel and unusual punishment was banned by the Constitution. But that was a lifetime ago.

"Here to see Miller." It wasn't a question. "We'll bring him right in."

I was buzzed inside through the thick metal door. Procedure required that visitors, including attorneys, stand against the hallway wall so the guards could pass. I think the enlisted guards took perverse pleasure in seeing an officer pressed against the cinder block wall. There was a constant give and take between the guards, inmates, prison counselors, and attorneys—all playing within the rules but each seeing what they could get away with. It helped pass the time.

I waited outside the client meeting room. I hated going in there and usually waited until the last minute to enter. The room was small, no bigger than five by seven, with two chairs and a metal table. Opening your briefcase was difficult. There were no windows or ventilation. The CO wanted the attorneys out of his brig as quickly as possible.

I stood watching the outside common area through a double-paned window. My breath fogged it up. Several marines were escorting a young boy from the dormitory across the yard. It had to be Miller. High barbed-wire fences were all around. Even though it was cold, the marines were in short sleeves.

The prisoner couldn't have been older than twenty years old. He was wearing an orange jumpsuit; the bottoms of his pants were cuffed several times. He was led along in leg shackles and handcuffs, head down. Two marines, one on either side, held onto his belt as he shuffled forward. Another marine was in the rear, several feet behind, in case the prisoner tried to escape, M16 rifle at the ready.

The boy was short, about 5'9" with a medium but athletic build and close cropped blond hair. No evidence of a beard or that he even needed to shave. Angular, good-looking face, with traces of acne even at this distance.

I continued to stare at him. So this is the monster the Navy wants to execute.

CHAPTER SIX

IT WAS LATE FRIDAY NIGHT and he was tired. It had been a long week. Joshua was spending too much time thinking about her. There were two exams left before the Christmas break. His grades weren't good. Joshua needed a 75 average to remain in school; he had a 75.3. He was barely hanging on. He didn't want to go back to the fleet and swab decks.

Joshua had made two failed trips to see her. Each time there was a different excuse: wrong place, wrong time, car accident. It was a two-hour drive to the Outer Banks and two hours back. He could have used that time to study. Now she says she's too busy, traveling for work and all that. He felt like such an idiot!

Most of the guys had gone out. He heard they were heading to Headlight's, a club on the strip. They had long ago stopped asking him to join them. Joshua saw the commotion from his open door, guys with no shirts on running up and down the hallway asking to borrow shaving cream or cologne. After a few drinks at the club, they were going to a Kenny Chesney concert at the Virginia Beach Amphitheater. Damn, he would have liked to go to that. Most sailors couldn't afford the covered seats under the outdoor awning, so they would sit on the grass. It would be a great time even if it was getting cold outside. But he couldn't go even if they had asked. He had to get caught up on his schoolwork; there was a paper due on Monday that he had to "Ace."

Joshua was seated at his desk. The telephone on the table rang again. Joshua tried to ignore it; he knew it was her. She was the only one that ever called his barracks room. He let it ring. For the first time he was beginning to have his doubts. It had been over a month since they first started talking, ten, twenty, sometimes thirty times a day. They talked about everything. But he hadn't actually met her. Samantha had sent him pictures, but it wasn't the same. And they had said all those things to each other. He wanted—he needed—to hold her.

Joshua put his head in his hands. His thoughts were all jumbled. Maybe he was spending too much time on this. He had never really gotten close to a girl before. Relationships never worked out. Either you end up breaking up, like his brother and all his girlfriends, or someone died, like his dad. Besides, no one in his life ever really appreciated him.

Joshua got up from his desk and walked to the mirror hanging inside his closet. He looked at himself. He studied his forehead and the shape of his mouth. He was a good-looking guy; he kept himself in good physical shape. Maybe he was a little awkward around people he didn't know and he didn't let them get close. So what? He hadn't really traveled much—well, not at all except where he went with the Navy. But he had a lot to offer.

The cell phone in his pocket rang. Why does she keep calling every few minutes? Joshua told her an hour ago he didn't want to talk to her anymore. He was done. He told her he thought she didn't exist, that she was a dream, that this was all a lie. He was pretty mean to her. So why did he feel so terrible? Samantha said she didn't want it to end. Joshua wanted to believe her. He let the call go to voice mail again.

Joshua sat back down at his desk and opened one of his textbooks. He just stared at the pages. He couldn't focus. He was so tired. All the weeks of very little sleep were getting to him. The cell phone rang again. He grabbed it from his pocket. He would tell her once and for all to stop calling.

"Joshua, this is Samantha. Please don't hang up."

There was a lot of noise in the background. "Samantha, I can barely hear you."

"Joshua, we need to talk." She was slurring her words.

"No, Samantha, we're done. Don't call me anymore," he started to hang up the phone.

"I have something to tell you," she said in a desperate voice.

Joshua felt his anger rising. "Samantha, I said we're done. Are you deaf? We're finished. It's all been a lie and I can't take it anymore."

"Joshua, please listen to me," she blurted out.

"I'm done listening—" Samantha cut him off.

"Joshua, I've been raped."

"What?" Miller shot out of his chair almost dropping the phone. "Are you okay?"

"I'll be all right. I'm not hurt." Her voice sounded small, her words unclear.

"You have to go to the police."

"No, Joshua, I'll be fine."

"I'll come get you right now. Where are you?"

"Joshua, you can't. I'm with my girlfriends. We're trying to figure out what to do."

"Figure out what to do? You need to go to the police. I'll take you."

"Joshua, I just can't do that. I'll explain it to you more later. I just wanted you to know."

"Samantha, it's okay if you've been drinking. That doesn't matter. No one has a right to do that to you." He was starting to get angry again.

"It's not that. I just have to talk to you about it later."

Joshua was confused. It sounded like Samantha was at a party; apparently, she was drinking. She said she was raped and was now with her girlfriends but she wouldn't tell him where. Something strange was going on. Maybe she knew the person. Maybe it was an old boyfriend.

"Do you know who did this to you?" There was silence on the other end of the phone. The only sound Joshua could hear was the laughter and loud noise in the background. Where was she he wondered? "Samantha?"

"There were three of them. Three marines. Two held me down and one raped me. I can't tell you who they are."

"Why not?" Joshua demanded.

"Because they go to school with you on base."

Joshua just stared at the phone.

CHAPTER SEVEN

THE NCIS FIELD OFFICE WAS in a small building onboard Naval Air Station Oceana, the adjoining Master Jet Base a few miles down the road from Dam Neck. If you were driving faster than the base speed limit of twenty-five miles per hour, you would probably miss the small sign out front. The furniture hadn't changed in twenty years. The technology had improved.

The newest member of the NCIS staff, Special Agent Cole Hansen, was searching through a stack of telephone records. You obtained arrests by evidence not through accusations, he thought. There was a hiring freeze on and everyone had more work to do than they could handle. His unit was now divided into two sections—investigators who were in the field or those that stayed behind in the office examining documents or doing computer enhancements. The later was boring as hell. Currently, he was office bound and hated it. Hansen had to do something to change the situation.

Cole learned that Commander DeMarco had taken over the handling of the marine murder case. He thought back to his first trial over two years ago when he had been an agent for only a few months. DeMarco was the defense counsel on a case for which he had long forgotten the details. He hadn't forgotten the Commander. On cross-examination, DeMarco was parsing through Hansen's limited credentials. When he was finished, he concluded by asking Hansen if all agents of the Naval Criminal Investigative Service were called "Special Agents". When Hansen proudly acknowledged they were,

DeMarco hesitated, gave him a brief smile, and asked, "Well, Agent Hansen, would you agree with me then that there is nothing special about being a "Special" Agent, is there?" That got a good laugh from the jury. And DeMarco made his point. Cole liked the Commander. He was tough but played by the rules of the game, and oftentimes it was a game. DeMarco was successful because he was always prepared. Hansen wanted to be like that—be thorough and don't take short-cuts. But damn all these files!

Being the newest agent wasn't easy. Hansen had fifty active cases with hundreds of records to review; he hadn't closed a case in months. If he wanted to get out into the field, he had to produce. He looked at the stack of drug cases on the corner of his desk. Maybe he could close a few of them.

In the old days, urinalysis cases took up most of the new agents' time. The Navy had a zero-tolerance policy for drugs; if you popped positive on a piss test, you were sent to a court-martial. As the Navy's police force, part of the agent's job was to interview the expert at the drug-screening lab to make sure none of the dozens of techni-cians who examined the defendant's sample had problems. There was nothing worse than going to court with a case where a tech had been disciplined for mixing up or contaminating prior samples. In addition, you had to verify any story the defense came up with and run down those witnesses. The "someone put pot in my brownies" or "passive inhalation—everyone else in the car was smoking but me" defenses were long gone. The testing was too precise; in cocaine cases, you could test down to the nanogram level (one billionth of a gram) or even a picogram (one trillionth of a gram). But sailors, as they have done throughout the ages, always seem to adapt; defen-dants then started claiming that the drugs in their system came from handling contaminated dollar bills from the Washington, DC, area, the cocaine capital of the East Coast.

As a cost-saving measure many Commands were now just administratively separating the sailors with an OTH (other-than-hon-orable) discharge instead of taking them to court. No judge, no jury. Not much due process, but who had the time and resources? That still meant that the service member had a "bad" discharge on his record, so sailors were coming up with new ways to beat the system. Recently, the drug of choice was "spice," a synthetic form of marijuana that didn't show up on the drug tests. Hansen was waiting for return phone calls from a few of the local head shops to check on what products they were selling.

A few of the files dealt with performance enhancing drugs. PEDs were really popular with the SEAL teams and dive units who used them to recover quickly from the beating their bodies took. Hansen could hardly blame them; those guys were true warriors. He put those files at the bottom of the stack.

Senior agents told Hansen that in their time sailors who committed crimes were just ordinary thugs. Now, with the "New Navy," the quality of sailor was better and the crimes, while less frequent, were getting more sophisticated. Today's agent had to be smarter to keep up. He yearned to get out from behind his desk.

The SAC, or Special Agent in Charge, poked his head into Hansen's office, startling him. "Come on, Cole, I need something more on that surveillance video."

Headquarters was getting a lot of pressure to gather more evidence in the marine case. There was increasing tension lately between the Commandant of the Marine Corps and the Chief of Naval Operations. With the reduction in the number of ships in the fleet and the increase in the number of marine ground troops, everyone was fighting for their fair share of the budget. Resources were scarce. Now a marine, a war hero just back from Afghanistan, went missing from a Navy base and was suspected dead.

The press was having a field day. It was the lead story on the news every night. That sexy blonde anchorwoman was getting all the attention she wanted. Hansen questioned whether their prime suspect, IS3 Joshua Miller, a young sailor assigned to Dam Neck, was really involved at all.

After all the news reports came out, an eyewitness showed up at the office—a Petty Officer who said he was manning the front desk at the marine barracks when Miller came asking for Williams a few days before he went missing. But Hansen knew that eyewitness testimony was inherently unreliable. In fact, the witness acknowledged to Hansen that he only got a brief look at the person.

Hansen had obtained the surveillance video from the parking lot of Williams's barracks for the week he went missing. It didn't reveal much. In the early morning hours of New Year's Day, Williams was seen voluntarily getting into a vehicle that left the base. Recent weather had caused the temperature near ground level to fall under the dew point, creating a dense fog that made it difficult to make out any detail. Plus the vehicle was at the edge of the dimly lit parking lot and was traveling away from the camera. The license plate was tinted and almost impossible to read. Hansen was able to enhance the video and make out two of the seven characters, the letter B and the number 1, which matched the license plate on Miller vehicle but also happened to be the two most common characteristics on license plates. He couldn't even be sure of the type vehicle.

Hansen looked back at the stack of Miller's cell phone records. Most of them were to a 252 area code in eastern North Carolina. Probably some bimbo he met on leave. Young sailors were all alike. Williams's cell phone had a 712 area code—Iowa. There were no calls made within several states of there in Miller's records. A telephone call was made to Williams's room the night he disappeared from a phone stand outside the training barracks, where Miller lived along with four hundred other recruits. There were too many uncertainties. Any halfway-decent defense counsel, and Commander DeMarco was more than halfway decent, would have a field day with this evidence.

Hansen would have liked to review Miller's credit card or bank statements but there were none. The kid must have paid for everything in cash. What does an E-4 make anyway? Sailors were given Base Pay, Basic Allowance for Housing (BAH), and Basic Allowance for Subsistence (BAS), a misnomer if there ever was one—most of these kids were barely getting by. Yet they all had brand-new cars or motorcycles and girlfriends in every port.

There was just no evidence linking Miller and Williams together, not even a bar fight. Field agents had canvassed all the local hangouts and no one recognized a picture of either Miller or Williams.

Yet Hansen had an uneasy feeling. What was it? Either Miller was innocent, a distinct possibility at this point, or they had missed something. What do a Marine war hero and a Navy intelligence specialist have in common? One was a stud, one a nerd. Like the jock and geek in high school. Cole knew better than to have preconceived notions. Labels distracted you. He remembered what Sherlock Holmes used to say in the books he read growing up: "When you have eliminated the impossible, whatever remains, however improbable, must be the truth." What was the connection?

"Sir, the video is as good as it's going to get. The letter B and the number 1 on the license plate is all I can make out, everything else is a blur," Hansen responded.

"Jesus Christ! What are we supposed to do with that!" the SAC lamented.

"Yup," was all Hansen could respond.

The SAC said, "Anything more on the identification of the vehicle?"

"Nope. I'm not even sure what type it is." The SAC glared at him before turning and storming out of the building.

Hansen got up from his chair. His gut told him there was something more to this case and he wasn't going to find out what it was sitting behind a desk.

CHAPTER EIGHT

SERGEANT FRANK MINEO OF THE Currituck County Sheriff's Department sat with his feet up on his desk. He was admiring the new cowboy boots he had recently purchased. It was Saturday. All was quiet. He had just finished lunch and was getting ready to start his shift.

After working for thirty years as a policeman in New York City, he enjoyed the leisurely pace of law enforcement in the South. Currituck County was the northeastern-most county in North Carolina, bordered by the Atlantic Ocean and the Currituck Sound. Mineo moved to the Outer Banks region five years ago. He loved it here. Even in the late fall you didn't need to wear anything warmer than a light jacket. He bought an acre of land inland and had planted a garden. He grew tomatoes, cucumbers, and zucchini. He got to know his neighbors. He didn't have to lock his doors. Tourist season from June through September was hectic, but otherwise it was just how he envisioned semiretirement.

Mineo's duties included supervising the detective division, which consisted of two officers, and the investigation of felonies, few as they were. He spent many of his days chasing teenagers drag racing four-wheelers on the beach or investigating traffic accidents after a motorist hit one of the wild horses that roamed from the dunes.

Mineo heard a knock on his door. He looked through the pane of glass and saw a young man with closely cropped hair standing

43

there. A sailor from the Tidewater area, Mineo thought. The boy looked familiar. He motioned him in.

"How may I help you, son?" Mineo asked.

Joshua stood in the doorway. He hesitated then the words rushed out. "Sir, my name is Joshua Miller. I'm trying to find my girlfriend, but I can't seem to find the address she gave me. I have her cell phone number. When I call and ask for her, the person who answers says 'Yes' and then the phone cuts off. It's important that I find her."

Even though the request seemed odd to Mineo, he had a few minutes and the young man looked desperate. Then it came to him. "I remember you. Didn't we meet a few weeks?"

Joshua paused and then said, "Yes, Sir, we did."

Mineo remembered Miller pulling up beside his patrol car while Mineo was parked at the local 7-Eleven filling out a report. Miller had asked for help in trying to locate his girlfriend; he recalled her name was Samantha. Mineo called central communications trying to locate the address the young man had given him as well as calling the cell phone number Miller provided. When a young female answered, Mineo asked for her name and identified himself. He remembered the young lady seemed agitated. Mineo handed his phone to the young man and walked away. When the young man returned a few minutes later, he looked dejected. He handed Mineo his phone back, thanked him, got into his car, and left. A lovers' quarrel, Mineo thought at the time.

"Son, didn't I help you try to find her then? Mineo said.

Miller looked embarrassed "Yes, Sir." Then he blurted out, "I think she has been sexual assaulted, Sir."

That got Mineo's attention. He took his feet off the desk and straightened up in his chair. "Why? What do you think has happened?"

"My girlfriend and I had a fight last night. We broke up. Then she called me later that evening and told me that she had been raped. I need to find her."

Mineo was suspicious. He'd heard many crazy stories over his long career. "Let's start from the beginning. Did you two ever get together the last time you were here?"

"No."

"Why didn't she report this incident?" Mineo questioned. Miller was silent.

"Did you tell her you were going to the police?"

"Yes."

"What did she say about that?"

"Well, not much."

"Tell me her name again."

"Samantha Stevens."

Mineo had been living in this small county for a number of years, he knew everyone. The name didn't ring a bell. Maybe he would recognize her if he saw her. "Do you happen to have a picture of your girlfriend?"

Miller took out his cell phone. He showed Mineo a picture of a pretty blond young woman. He had other photos on the phone that he insinuated to the sheriff might be of a sexual nature, so Mineo only asked to see the one.

Mineo looked in his field book. "The address that you gave me last time, Sea Haven Lane, doesn't exist. Is that the only address you have for her?"

Miller said, "Yes, Sir."

"Do you have any other information about her?"

"She's a student at Old Dominion University."

Mineo looked up the number to the university and called the security office. He was told there was no Samantha Stevens enrolled at the school. Mineo then conducted a statewide search in the Department of Motor Vehicle records with no match. He was now late for his shift but wanted to help the young man. "Anything else you can tell me?"

Miller said he thought Stevens's mom was from Corpus Christi. Mineo checked the Texas land records and telephone book but again could find nothing.

"Mr. Miller, I gotta say it's pretty strange to have a girlfriend that we can't find anything about. I don't mean any disrespect, but are you sure she's real? Maybe she's a dancer or something?"

Miller didn't seem offended by this and only shook his head. "No." He paused. "I can see how you might find this strange, but I know she's in trouble."

"Son, I think there is more to this than you realize."

CHAPTER NINE

JOSHUA JUMPED FROM HIS CHAIR and ran out of the classroom. Even though the base cafeteria was only a short walk away, he only had a half hour for lunch. With hundreds of students tying to eat at one time, it was a challenge to get in, get some food, and get back to class on time. Final exams would be starting in a few days and everyone was in a rush.

As he entered the large cafeteria, there was a cacophony of sounds—trays being dropped, silverware clanking, loud laughter, and jumbled conversation you couldn't understand.

Miller went to the end of the line, picked up his tray, and waited as he inched forward. As he reached the first server, he put the tray down on the metal railing, picked up a fork and spoon, and began to make his choices.

"Macaroni and cheese, mashed potatoes, and a grilled cheese sandwich, please," he said to the young mess cook wearing a hairnet behind the stainless steel counter.

His mother would have a fit if she knew he was eating all these carbohydrates. But he had to keep his strength up. Joshua was worried about Samantha and wasn't getting much sleep. He had to do well on his finals and then maybe they could be together during the Christmas break. He picked up a sweetened ice tea from the large stack next to the cash register. The glass was sweating, the ice almost totally melted. It didn't taste like his mother's; she would put four scoops of sugar in every half gallon, but it would have to do.

Joshua paid the cashier and stuffed the change in his pocket. He began looking for an empty seat. Many of his classmates were saving seats for their buddies. Since he had no one to sit with, it was only a matter of finding a solitary space, which was usually at the far end of the room. He began walking that way. He wanted to be alone with his thoughts anyway.

As he walked between the tables, a marine two tables over suddenly turned in his chair and stared at him. "Wonder what he's looking at," Joshua thought to himself. He felt a strange sensation, a connection to this person. He didn't understand why.

The marine was tall, as most of them seem to be, muscular with short cropped hair and dressed in camouflage. Joshua tried to ignore him but the marine's gaze seemed to follow him as he walked by.

Joshua walked around several more tables until he spotted an empty seat at a table in the far corner. He hurried over, put his tray down, and slid into the vacant spot. He picked up his fork and tried to eat some of his mashed potatoes; the strange feeling wouldn't leave him. He stood up to see if the marine was still looking at him; he wasn't. Joshua squinted his eyes and tried to read the marine's name tag, but it was too difficult to see at this distance. He thought the marine looked his way once or twice.

Joshua took a bite of his grilled cheese sandwich but the food didn't taste right. He wanted to get back to class but remained curious about the marine. Why was he looking at him? Joshua got up, picked up his tray, and took a route between the tables, which would bring him right in front of the marine.

As Joshua walked by, the marine kept eating his food with his head down. He looked at the name tag above the left chest; it read, "Williams."

CHAPTER TEN

"ALL RISE."

The main courtroom had not changed much in the last twenty years. Neither did the building. Building A-50, the Navy Legal Service Office, NLSO, was on the corner of Midway Drive and Farragut Way. It was situated next to the Bachelor Officer Quarters, BOQ, and across from the Enlisted Men's Club. An odd placement. Many lives had been inalterably changed in this building.

After you entered the front doors, you had to pass through a metal detector. There was a time not so long ago when you could just walk right in; nowadays security concerns were becoming more common in the courtrooms.

On the wall to the left was a picture of the President. I had seen more than a few presidential portraits hung there in my years. The first, Ronald Reagan, was the mastermind of the 600-Ship Navy, a strategic plan to rebuild the fleet after the cutbacks that followed the Vietnam "conflict"—it was only a *war* if they let you win it. Next was George H. W. Bush, "41", an enlisted man who completed flight training and became one of the Navy's youngest pilots. Bush flew with torpedo squadron VT-51 on board the aircraft carrier USS *San Jacinto* and received the Distinguished Flying Cross. There was Bill Clinton, a "Yalie" lawyer and, as many of my clients often told me, "our first black President." He took office at the end of the Cold War; his "don't ask, don't tell" policies didn't endear him to many in the service at that time. Then came George Bush, the younger, whose preferential treatment while with the Texas and Alabama Air National Guard didn't allow him the popularity his dad had, although his Global War on Terror after the 9/11 attacks made up for it somewhat. Currently, there was Barack Obama; the jury was still out on him. Even though the military was made up of over 30 percent minorities, sailors still voted with their pocketbook and the economy was in shambles.

Next to the President's picture was that of the Secretary of Defense, the person sixth in line to presidential succession, second only to the President in the military hierarchy, the de facto Deputy Commander in Chief and boss of the Chairman of the Joint Chiefs of Staff. The first Secretary of Defense was a Navy man, James Forrestal, who served under Harry Truman and didn't really want the job; we named an aircraft carrier after him. You would think the SecDefs would be more memorable: Caspar Weinberger (who, despite the nickname "Cap the Knife", vigorously lobbied to increase defense spending); Frank Carlucci and Leon Panetta (the Italians); Dick Cheney (one of the most powerful Vice Presidents while serving under the younger Bush); then Aspin, Perry, Cohen, Rumsfeld (the second longest serving SecDef), Gates, Nagel, and Cohen.

I had gotten into the elevator and pushed the button for the third floor where all the courtrooms were located. I was surprised the damned thing still worked. The doors took forever to close. The numbered buttons for the floors were rubbed off and almost illegible. It creaked as it rose. I could have climbed the stairs faster. When I was younger, I did. Now my knees were getting a bit stiff.

I entered the JAG Corps after law school and was assigned to the Washington Navy Yard as a defense counsel. After gaining some experience, particularly that case in Guantanamo Bay, Cuba, where I defended a marine accused of murder while performing a "Code Red", a form of unit discipline sanctioned by the chain of command, I was transferred to the Mobile Trial Team out of Norfolk. With MOJAG, we would fly all over the world trying cases. The Navy didn't want the need for witnesses in the criminal justice system to interfere with the mission of the fleet; they decided it would be more economical to fly a Judge, Prosecutor, and Defense Counsel to the ships rather than fly crucial sailors to courtrooms around the world where they would be sitting around for days doing nothing. Makeshift courtrooms were erected and we'd try cases well into the morning hours. It was exciting.

After turning left out of the elevator, I walked a few paces and entered my code into the keypad next to the door, which allowed access to the hallway where the Judge's chambers and courtrooms were located. Why the need for all this security? Weren't the bad guys already locked up? It was difficult getting used to all these changes.

After MOJAG, I was transferred to the Trial Counsel shop, the civilian equivalent of a prosecutor. I fought the assignment. To be a good prosecutor, you needed to see events in black and white—I saw too many grays. Plus Trial Counsel had to kiss the command's ass. They had to get the witnesses to court (no small task as sailors could be stationed anywhere in the world), make sure you had enough copies of all the evidence, and handle many other mundane matters. You worried about getting defendants arraigned so you didn't miss any speedy trial deadlines. A good defense counsel had to be dragged into court; time is on the defendant's side—witnesses die, evidence gets lost—it's a fact of life.

I entered the main courtroom and walked to the table on the right. I placed my briefcase behind the railing, separating the participants from the spectators. Defense Counsel table, by tradition, is the one furthest from the jury box. You usually wanted it that way. It wasn't good having the jurors closely scrutinizing the accused for days on end. You never knew what they might see your client doing.

The Trial Counsel assigned to the case, Alfred Mays, a young Lieutenant Commander, was already seated at his table on the left. I didn't know Mays very well. If I had gotten to the courtroom first, I would have sat at his table and started the fireworks a little early. I nodded at him.

"The court will now come to order. Captain Christopher Johnson presiding." The bailiff continued to stand at attention.

Captain Johnson was the Chief Judge of the Navy-Marine Corps Trial Judiciary. I have known Johnson since we were classmates at Officer Indoctrination School, OIS, in Newport, Rhode Island.

Unlike Officer Candidate School, OCS, where all the "real" officers go, OIS was for the Staff Corps—the nurses, doctors, dentists, lawyers, and ministers. It was the first experience with military life for many of us. We learned to march, wear our uniforms correctly, and become physically fit and morally straight! Johnson couldn't even make the one-and-half-mile morning run without complaining. I was the company commander back then and rode his ass every day. It had been payback time for him for the last few years.

I knew Johnson would assign himself this case. He loved the publicity; the courtroom sketch artist drawing pictures of him for the local newspaper was right up his alley. Captain Johnson and I were not friends. He was smart and got promoted faster than me but only because he was an "ass kisser"—a fat-ass ass kisser! Within each military unit, only one person can be ranked first. If you were an aggressive defense attorney who did his job, you tended to piss people off. In my experience, most Trial Counsel told the Commands whatever they wanted to hear, justice be damned. Johnson never cared too much about justice.

As the judge took his seat, I wondered why I was still here. I thought about all the guys I came through the ranks with but were no longer around. My "buds" Donnie Redford, now a famous personal injury attorney with offices in several states; Tyrone Hughes, a successful real estate lawyer in Louisiana; and Jimmy Anderson, a civilian judge. We worked hard during the day and played even harder at night. Who could forget the Green Wheel Inn, redneck heaven! Right next door to the Foxy Lady, the bar where all the "brothers" hung out. We staggered between the two without a care. I understand we are still famous for our drunken rendition of "Once, Twice, Three Times a Lady." We always had each other's back, whether it was in the courtroom or on the softball field. It was the second deck, where our offices were located, against the world!

After my first four-year tour, I could have gotten out. The case in GITMO made me stay. Our defense was that my client was only following orders. The jury found that an "implied" order was indeed given and acquitted my clients of murder but still discharged them. That case haunted me ever since. Certain cases will do that to you.

You wake up in the early morning hours wondering what you could have done differently. Sleep had been hard to come by lately.

After Norfolk, it was a teaching position at the Naval Academy in Annapolis, Maryland, a beautiful campus with much history. Then postgraduate school for a master's degree in criminal law. By then I had twelve years in the military, and while my peers were making more money, I was having too much fun traveling the world trying cases. Now all that had changed.

Trial work was becoming tedious. Justice was seldom served. I had been in the military over eighteen years; I was forty-three years old. Decisions had to be made—stay in, maybe get promoted to Captain, and eventually retire with a military pension, or get out now and make some real money.

I was offered a position at the Pentagon. The Pentagon is an amazing place with almost thirty thousand employees. It has seven floors, two underground, consisting of six and half million square feet. Five concentric pentagonal rings are intersected by ten radial corridors that, if laid out end to end, would stretch seventeen and half miles. Yet it only took seven minutes to travel between any two points. Two- and Three-Star Admirals were a dime a dozen. I didn't know if I could fight the daily grind and kiss that many asses in one day. Maybe it was time to leave. I thought more and more about the upcoming interview I had for a civilian job in Charlotte. I was told being a Harvard graduate on the outside pays well.

"Will counsel please identify themselves, state by whom you've been detailed, your qualifications, your status as to oath, and whether you've acted in any disqualifying capacity," Captain Johnson's intoned in his baritone voice.

Rising from my chair, I began, "Sir, Commander Mike DeMarco, Judge Advocate General Corps, United States Navy. I am qualified and certified in accordance with Article 27(b), and sworn under Article 42(a) of the *Uniform Code of Military Justice*. I have not acted in any disqualifying manner." I paused. "And, ah, by the way, I have detailed myself to this Court-Martial under my authority as the Senior Defense Counsel of the Navy Legal Service Office Norfolk."

The judge and I stared at each other. "By the way"—Captain Johnson paused for effect—"*Commander*"—he emphasized our difference in rank—"what is this 'Substitution of Counsel' motion you filed? I thought Lieutenant Commander Malone was assigned to this case."

"Sir, the accused has released his Detailed Defense Counsel and requested that I be assigned to represent him."

With a sarcastic grin, Captain Johnson said, "I thought you were finished trying cases, Commander?" Word travels quickly throughout the halls of the NLSO.

I could feel my temper beginning to rise and was reminded again why it was going to be difficult for me to be promoted to O-6. "Captain," I said, smiling, "I always try to accommodate our sailors."

He stared back at me. "Commander, you do realize that the accused will be arraigned shortly and a trial date set within the next one hundred twenty days?"

"Yes, Sir, I do."

"And knowing that you still detailed yourself to this Court-Martial?"

"Yes, Sir, I did. I thought that would be my right as Senior Defense Counsel at the largest Naval Base in the world."

Captain Johnson continued to glare at me from the bench. "And you gave no consideration to the approaching deadlines?"

I tried, but couldn't help myself. "Well, Captain, I figured my client's right to counsel was more important than your processing times."

We were not off to a good start.

Captain Johnson paused as he tried to get himself under control. "Commander, I am well aware of your prior tactics." He was getting worked up now. "You don't intend to ask for any extra time now, do you?"

"Captain, with the Government's evidence, being what it is, I don't think I'm going to need to." With a slight grin, I shot a sideways glance over at Trial Counsel. I was going to have some fun with this guy.

Lieutenant Commander Mays shot out of his chair. At least he was showing some life. "Captain, I object."

Johnson slammed both hands down on his bench and leaned forward. "Sit down both of you. Let's go off the record for a moment," the judge said, nodding at the court reporter. Then glaring at me, he said, "Commander, as you well know, I run a tight ship." Who was he, Admiral Nimitz? "You and I go back a long way. I am not going to let you push this court around." I was flattered. "We are going to conduct this trial in an orderly fashion. The press will be here every day and we are going to march forward smartly and do the Navy proud." It would have been nice to mention that we were also going to ensure that justice would be served. "I expect you both to get together by Friday and agree to a Case Management Order. The deadlines set out therein will be strictly adhered to and there will be no continuances or delays."

I started to rise. The Judge just shook his head, his face beginning to redden. He motioned for me to sit back down. "Gentlemen, here's how it's going to work." Again, he stared at me. "If the good Commander wants to get involved in this case at this late date—a capital murder case, I might add—then I am going to let him. But I expect him, and you, Lieutenant Commander Mays, to be prepared and present your cases in an orderly fashion." He paused to take a deep breath. I was beginning to worry about him. Well, not really. "I want the pleas to the charges entered and forum selection made within three weeks. I want witness requests along with subpoenas issued within ninety days; any motions to be heard exchanged ten days after that with a motion session to hear those motions five days later. Trial will be one hundred and twenty days from today."

Having said that he got up, turned and quickly hurried off the bench and into his chambers never going back on the record. He was pissed!

Wonder if it was something I did?

CHAPTER ELEVEN

HANSEN GRABBED HIS JACKET AND rushed out the door. It was almost 6:00 p.m.

"Where you going?" the SAC inquired, looking at him suspiciously. Most of the other agents had already left the office heading for the base gym to work off some steam or to get ready for the physical readiness test held annually each March. No agent had ever failed the PRT.

"Got somewhere to go, boss," Hansen yelled back over his shoulder and kept on going.

"Keep your cell phone on. Maybe we can catch a break in that damn murder case." That last sentence was more to himself than to his agent. He didn't have to specify which case.

Once outside, Hansen wondered if he was doing the right thing. He estimated it was a two-hour drive to the Outer Banks. He had never been there before. Many of his fellow agents went there for vacation or at least long weekends. He heard the beaches were nice and secluded. Hansen wasn't really a beach guy. Since most of the Navy installations were located on water, a majority of the agents took up water sports. Hansen liked to snow ski. He didn't look forward to his required afloat tour on one of the carriers. An overseas tour, perhaps Rota, Spain, on the Bay of Cadiz halfway between Portugal and Gibraltar, might be nice. Not too far from the Alps. At least he didn't think it was.

Hansen concluded that what he did on his own time was up to him, wasn't it? It's not like he was on active duty where the military owned you twenty-four hours a day. But he knew he was only trying to justify his actions. Hansen had a hunch. And if he had a hunch, protocol required he pass it along to his SAC or at least to a field agent.

Since it was the off-season, Hansen knew there wouldn't be much traffic. It couldn't be that hard to find the Sea Ranch Motel. Many of Miller's calls were made to that location. Maybe he was just shacking up with some girl; if so, why travel that far? There were plenty of dives in the Tidewater area. Just drive down to East Ocean View. You could rent a room by the hour. The forerunner of the NCIS, the Naval Investigative Service, NIS, regularly conducted stings at the local hotels getting female agents to pose as prostitutes and proposition the young sailors—kind of like shooting fish in a barrel. The local cops run that operation now.

Hansen stopped in front of his government issued Crown Victoria. He looked at the Government license plate and two antennas. Not too conspicuous! he thought. Real "perps", and probably even those that weren't, would spot him a mile away. He would drive it anyway.

Hansen decided to take the expressway since he was leaving after rush hour. From 3:00 p.m. to 6:00 p.m., you didn't want to travel on the local interstate. The HOV lanes only made traffic worse. He could take the back roads through the Dismissal Swamp, but you never knew when there might be a bridge lift and you'd be stuck for an hour waiting for some pleasure cruiser heading down the inter-coastal waterway to get through the locks.

After driving for twenty miles, he got off at Exit 291, Highway 168, which would take him directly to the Outer Banks. After the exit, he forked left away from Elizabeth City, NC. The roadway was vacant. Hansen thoughts began to wander.

What connection did the motel have? Probably none. There was no evidence that Miller had visited there and no evidence Williams had been there. It was too far away from where they were stationed.

But when Hansen looked at the cell phone records, he had a gut feeling. All those phone calls and text messages had to mean something.

Was it normal for kids nowadays to call or text one another ten, fifteen, twenty times a day? The telephone numbers Miller called the first few weeks he was on base were to numbers that had now been disconnected or were to a burner phone, a temporary and disposable phone number. Plenty of young kids purchased them because they were cheap and didn't require long-term plans.

Hansen looked at the dashboard clock. He had another hour-and-a-half drive. Damn, he had almost forgotten the three dollars for the toll. Shouldn't they let government vehicles just pass on through? In this area, they'd lose a lot of money if they did. He stopped at the booth and rolled down his window.

"How y'all doing this evening, sweetie?" The elderly lady sitting inside the booth was bundled up. A yellow sign was posted in the window that read, "Please turn off your windshield wipers." If someone was reading that now, it was too late to do any good, Hansen thought.

"Fine, Ma'am." Hansen politely smiled back.

"You on official business, young man?" she said, looking inside the car.

"Ah… No, Ma'am. Just taking a little trip to the Outer Banks," he managed to say. He handed her the dollar bills.

"At this time of year? You won't find much to do," she offered helpfully as she handed him a receipt.

Hansen gave her a polite wave as he drove off. Gotta love the locals. He didn't roll the window all the way back up. He liked the smell of the cool country air.

In less than ten minutes, Hansen crossed over the North Carolina border. He smelled the cooked barbeque coming from the outdoor fire pits of the Border Station restaurant. He continued driving through Moyock, Coinjock, and Grandy—small towns or hamlets with Native American Indian names that were separated every ten miles or so by barren stretches of roadway. What did these people do all year? He imagined they hunted and fished, that is until the tourists came, swelling their ranks from under twenty thousand to over two hundred thousand. Then they sold trinkets much like their ancestors.

It was almost 7:30 p.m. when Hansen reached the Wright Brothers Memorial Bridge. It didn't look like much had changed since Orville and Wilbur arrived in the Outer Banks in 1903. A mile after crossing the bridge, the roadway split. Hansen turned south; the road north would take you to Duck, Corolla, then Whalehead, where the roadway ended shortly before it met the Virginia border. The roadway south was marked every mile by a white signpost. At milepost 12, he turned left toward the beach road until he located the Sea Ranch Motel.

The Sea Ranch was an old two-story wood frame building squeezed in between two more modern hotels. What was the difference between a hotel and a motel? Hansen seemed to remember motels had fewer amenities, were cheaper, and had exterior entrances for easier accessibility. A lot could go on without anyone noticing. Hansen pulled into the gravel parking lot.

There was only one car parked out front. Hansen pulled to the left of the building so he couldn't be seen through the front glass window. He backed in, an old police habit in case one had to leave quickly. He couldn't imagine that happening tonight.

He got out of his car. There was a cold breeze blowing from the Atlantic Ocean. A light dusting of sand was covering the parking lot. Hansen could see his breath. He was dressed in khaki pants and a white button-downed dress shirt. He was cold without his jacket on.

The neon sign in the office window read, "Open—Winter Rates." Hansen opened the front door. It creaked, the hinges rusted from the salt air. He went inside. A heavyset young girl was talking on her cell phone behind the counter. She didn't look up; she was engrossed in her conversation. She was turned sideways in the desk chair. Well, maybe it wasn't sideways; she just couldn't fit any other way. Hansen cleared his throat.

"Oh, I'm sorry. I didn't hear you come in." She had a sweet, soft voice. Her name tag read, "Susan."

"My name is Special Agent Hansen from the NCIS." He flipped open his badge. She stiffened, a not too common reaction. "I'm investigating a missing person report. I just need to ask you some questions if you have a minute." She nodded. "How long have you worked here?"

"I guess, maybe three years now."

"Do you know this man?" He showed her a picture of Joshua Miller. There was something about the way she hesitated.

"No, I've never seen him before. Why?"

"Well, he placed several calls to this motel."

"No, Sir. I've never seen him." What was it about her? The way she answered? He felt sure she was hiding something.

"Are you the manager?"

"I only work the night desk. There isn't anyone else here in the wintertime. It's very slow."

"Does each room have a telephone?" Hansen inquired.

"Yes," she responded, "a TV and a microwave too."

Hansen looked at her. "Do you have a guest register?"

Again she nodded. With great effort, she slid from the chair. She reached under the counter. Perspiration was showing on her forehead. Physical activity must be hard for someone that size, he thought. "Here you go," she said, slightly out of breath.

Hansen thumbed through the first several pages, which noted the guests' names over the past several months. There wasn't much activity in the winter. He didn't see Miller's name.

"Oh well, sorry to bother you," Hansen said, closing the book and passing it back to her.

"It's no bother," she said sweetly.

Something wasn't right. He could feel it. Hansen left his card on the desk, turned, and walked out the door.

CHAPTER TWELVE

JOSHUA RETURNED TO HIS BARRACKS' room after a long day. The phone rang. It was her. He had been waiting to hear her voice. Samantha hadn't been calling as much the last several days. He figured she needed some time.

"Hey," she said quietly.

He knew right away something was wrong. "What's the matter, Sam?"

"Joshua," she hesitated, "they broke into my house." It sounded as if she was going to cry.

He was confused, "Who did?"

"The marines."

"How did they know where you lived?"

"I don't know."

"How do you know it was them, did you see them?"

"No, but my parakeet is dead." He thought that was odd but before he could say anything she continued. "And my cat is missing."

"Maybe he just ran away," Joshua stated, thinking to himself, why would the marines break into her house?

As if she knew what he was thinking she responded, "I think they are trying to intimidate me."

"Samantha, it's time you reported this to the police," he said forcefully.

"No, I told you I can't do that," Samantha said quietly.

Joshua paused. He thought back to his lunchroom encounter earlier that day. "Samantha, was a guy named Williams involved?"

She hesitated again and then said, "Why do you ask that?"

"It was strange. I was in the cafeteria today and this marine kept looking at me kind of funny. I just had a strange vibe."

"No. No, it wasn't him," she said quickly.

"Are you sure?"

"Yes."

"Do you want me to come and get you?"

"No, Joshua. We've been through this before. We'll meet soon."

"Well, I'm worried about you. Do you want me to buy you a gun?"

"Joshua, that's crazy."

"Samantha, you have to let me protect you."

There was silence at the other end of the phone. Neither spoke. Joshua's mind wandered back to his school days. After the dismissal bell, he would wait outside the rear cafeteria door until all the other kids had left the building. He was self-conscious about the way he looked. He wore his brother's jeans, which had to be cuffed several times so they wouldn't drag along the ground. He didn't have many friends. The girls ignored him, and the boys talked about things, mostly sports, that didn't interest him. It was a mile-and-a-half walk to the farm where he lived.

Joshua thought back to the day the fire trucks shot past him, almost running him off the road. Their sirens were deafening. From a distance, he could see old man Sizemore's farmhouse ablaze with flames shooting out of the roof. He ran to catch up with the trucks. When he arrived at the property out of breath, the firemen had already place a ladder against the wood frame house. It was now totally engulfed in flames. A border collie was staring out from a second-story window.

Joshua remembered standing just outside the wooden fence, staring in amazement, as a fireman ran up the ladder. He busted the window with his axe and dove in. It seemed forever before the firemen came out holding the fifty-pound dog across his shoulders while he tried to find his footing back down the ladder.

Joshua had tears in his eyes when the firemen reached the ground and released the dog into the arms of its owner. The newspaper the next day showed a picture of the firemen getting an award from the mayor. Ever since that day, Joshua liked uniforms. All who wore them were heroes. He wanted to protect people just like the firemen did.

Joshua came back to reality. "Samantha, are you sure that Williams wasn't involved?"

"I don't know, maybe that was his name."

"Are you sure?"

He could hear her take a deep breath. "I guess so. I think so. I think he was one of the ones who held me down."

"Was he tall, what did he look like?" Joshua questioned.

"Well, he was tall, muscular with short hair."

"And he was a marine?"

"Yes."

Joshua had his first suspect.

CHAPTER THIRTEEN

MILLER WALKED UP TO THE barracks where most of the marines resided. He felt self-conscious in the thrift store suit he had purchased earlier that morning. Did all NCIS agents wear a suit and tie? He wasn't sure. He didn't buy a tie.

It was Tuesday, December 21, 4:20 p.m., almost time for chow. The florescent light over the front doorway cast a late afternoon shadow. It was starting to get dark early. He hoped a senior petty officer was working the front desk. The upperclassmen were nearing the end of their final exams. They would be studying, and hopefully, no one would pay him much attention. He had tinted his hair and was wearing glasses in an effort to disguise himself. He didn't know what he would do if someone asked him to show a badge.

As he walked through the door, the First Class Petty Officer glanced up from his books. He didn't put down his pencil.

"May I help you, Sir?"

"I am Special Agent John Montgomery," Miller said, trying to deepen his voice. The Petty Officer only nodded as he turned the page of the propulsion systems textbook.

"Here to see someone, Sir?"

"Lance Corporal Williams."

"One moment, Sir, I'll check the roster." The petty officer grabbed the notepad with the resident's names listed in alphabetical order. He went directly to the last page and again, without looking up, said, "Lance Corporal Jonathan Williams is in room 104, Sir. Go back out the front door, make a left, it's the fourth room."

"Thank you, Petty Officer." Miller quickly left the way he came. That went well, he thought. He doubted the petty officer saw him for more than a few seconds.

Even though he rehearsed the scene many times in his head, Joshua wasn't sure he would know what to say the first time he confronted Williams. All he cared about was that Samantha told him Williams was one of the Marines involved. He had to find out what actually happened. Miller tried to walk confidently down the passageway. He was anxious and his hands were shaking. He shoved them in his front pockets.

Miller was almost to Williams's room when the door unexpectedly opened. Out stepped a six feet four, well-muscled marine wearing his bravo fatigues. Miller recognized the marine as the one he had seen in the cafeteria. He stopped short, still several feet away. Too far away for a real policeman, Joshua thought. For some reason he didn't want to get too close. Williams shut his door, turned, and hesitated as he saw Miller staring at him. Joshua tried to meet Williams's gaze but couldn't. He was nervous as hell.

"Lance Corporal Williams?"

Williams came to attention, elbows slightly bend, hands at his side, back straight, gaze looking straight ahead. "Sir, yes, Sir."

"Corporal Williams," Miller's voice cracked, "my name is Special Agent John Montgomery."

"Sir, yes, Sir." There was silence. Finally, Williams looked down at Miller as they both continued to stare at each other. Williams spoke, "Sir, you're with the NCIS?" He looked puzzled.

"Yes." Miller couldn't find the words to say more.

"Sir, how can I help you, Sir?" Williams was still at attention.

Miller willed himself to speak. "Lance Corporal, I am investigating the rape of a young girl from North Carolina." His voice now sounded squeaky. Williams stared at him with a wide-eyed expression. "Your name was mentioned."

Williams stammered, "Sir, there must be some mistake. I just returned from two tours in Afghanistan. I'm recently married and have a child on the way. I don't even drink. The most exciting thing I do is go bowling. I'm not exactly sure what you're talking about, Sir." Williams appeared sincere. Wasn't someone involved in a crime supposed to look guilty? How do you interrogate someone? Miller thought. He continued to stare at Williams without responding.

Williams broke the silence, "Sir, when did this occur?" Miller had to think quickly. He was becoming confused. What would happen if Williams got mad? He was at least seven inches taller and fifty pounds heavier. Next time he would carry a gun.

"Lance Corporal, all I know is what I've been told. Do you know a Samantha Stevens?"

"No, Sir, I've never heard of her, Sir."

"She's blonde, approximately five feet tall, weighs one hundred pounds, more or less?"

"No, Sir, I'm sorry."

"She's from the Outer Banks of North Carolina."

"No, Sir, doesn't sound familiar at all."

Miller couldn't think of any other questions. He continued to stare at Williams. Finally he stammered, "Corporal, just don't leave the area."

"No, Sir, thank you, Sir. May I leave now, Sir?"

Miller didn't respond. Instead he turned and quickly hurried away.

CHAPTER FOURTEEN

HIS TELEPHONE WAS RINGING; WILLIAMS looked at the clock on the nightstand. It was 3:10 a.m. Maybe his wife was having difficulty with the pregnancy. They say the last trimester is the worst. He rolled over and reached for the phone. "Hello."

"Lance Corporal Williams, this is Special Agent Montgomery. We spoke a week or so ago about the rape of Samantha Stevens." The caller was hard to hear.

"Oh... Yes, Sir." Williams sat up in bed, still slightly groggy. Since being back in the States, he wasn't used to getting up this early anymore. In Afghanistan, the firefights usually started in the early morning hours when the human body was in its deepest sleep cycle. "But I'm sorry. I still not quite sure how I can help you."

"Lance Corporal Williams, Ms. Stevens has taken a turn for the worst. She is in the hospital. If you want to clear your name, you need to come with me right now."

This was not making any sense, Williams thought to himself. How could anyone think he was involved in a rape? It was all a mistake. Rape? He was brought up to respect women.

"Well, okay, Sir. Sure. What do you need me to do?"

"I'll be outside your barracks in fifteen minutes. Meet me in the parking lot."

Williams tried to clear his head as he pulled on his fatigues. He thought for a moment about calling his wife but didn't want to wake her. And he certainly didn't want to worry her, not in her condition.

He would go with this NCIS agent, clear his name once and for all, and then this would all be over.

Williams walked briskly past the front desk, startling the security guard who was half-asleep. He exited the front door. Once outside he could see his breath. Because of the fog, he could barely make out the NCIS agent standing across the parking lot beside what he thought was a pickup truck. An odd-looking vehicle. He thought most government agents drove sedans. He hurriedly crossed the large lot.

When he reached the vehicle, Miller was already behind the wheel. Williams climbed into the passenger seat. His knees touched the dashboard. "Okay, Sir. I'm ready. Where are we going, Sir?"

"To Elizabeth City, North Carolina," Miller responded. Williams wasn't sure where that was, but at this point he just wanted this misunderstanding to be over.

They were both silent as Miller drove through the gates of the base heading south. Highway 168 was a lonely road with few streetlights. Miller was nervous. He was again wearing his ill-fitting suit, this time armed with a nine-millimeter pistol, a knife, and handcuffs. He wondered if the gun made a bulge in his suit. He didn't have a plan; he just wanted to get Williams alone, maybe scare him a little, and get him talking. He had to get to the bottom of what happened to Samantha.

Miller tried to remain calm. He tried quietly to take in several deep breaths. If he focused too long on what he was doing, kidnapping a United States marine, one who is 6'4", 190 pounds of pure muscle, he probably would have turned back. Then an idea struck him.

He pretended to get a telephone call. After a moment he said, "Lance Corporal Williams, that was my supervisor. As much as I don't want to, since you've been so cooperative, I'm going to have to handcuff you." Williams thought that was unnecessary and was going to say so, but he was used to following orders. He nodded.

Miller pulled his vehicle over to the side of the road. Williams got out, stood beside the door, and put his hands behind his back. Miller came around the back of his car and put the handcuffs on

Williams but not too snug. They both got back in the truck and continued driving past the scrub brush and scrawny pines. It was early January. There were no stars out. The temperature had dropped below thirty degrees. The windshield continued to fog.

After approximately forty-five minutes, Miller saw a dirt road up ahead. He needed to find a secluded area. "Lance Corporal Williams, do you need to use the bathroom?"

"Yes, Sir, that would be great."

"Let's pull off here." Joshua turned onto the dark dirt road which apparently the local power company used to access its transmission lines. It was full of potholes. Joshua had a difficult time making out the edges of the roadway even with the high beams on. After a short distance, they passed a transformer station surrounded by a chain-link fence. This was a good a place as any to interrogate someone—lonely and desolate. They wouldn't be interrupted.

Joshua stopped the vehicle in the middle of the road. They both just sat there neither one knowing quite what to do. Neither spoke. Finally, Miller finally got out. He walked around to the side of the truck and opened the door. Williams stepped out expecting the handcuffs to be released.

Suddenly, Miller threw Williams to the ground. Despite the difference in size, Miller was quickly on top of him with his knee in the middle of Williams back, pistol to his head. Williams lay on the cold ground stunned.

"You raped my girlfriend," Miller growled.

"What do you mean?" gasped Williams, his face lying in a mound of dirt and decaying leaves.

"My name is Joshua Miller. I'm not an NCIS agent, and you raped my girlfriend," breathlessly shouted Miller.

Williams's head was swirling; he felt like he was back in combat. He remembered, try to breathe, assess the situation, assess the threat. He needed time to think. "I don't know what you're talking about."

"Samantha Stevens, you held her down," Joshua again shouted at him. Adrenaline coursed through his body.

"I don't know anything about a rape," Jonathan pleaded. He hesitated and almost without thinking blurred out, "I swear on my unborn son, I had nothing to do with it."

Miller stopped breathing. What did he just say? An unborn son? His anger started to subside. He was confused. Suddenly a part of him was starting to believe Williams. It was the mention of a son. Joshua had once been a son.

Miller looked around. It was dark. There was no movement in the woods. The only sound he could hear was his own breathing.

Williams yelled out again, "I swear on my unborn son I had nothing to do with any rape."

Miller hesitated; then he slowly holstered his gun. It was starting to make sense to him now. He removed the handcuff key from his front pants pocket. He started to put it into the handcuffs. What have I done? he thought. All this over a girl he never met? He'd kidnapped a Marine. He turned the key a quarter turn. He again paused. If he let him go, was he going to kick his ass? Was he really telling the truth?

Joshua's thoughts shifted. What about Samantha? He loved her, didn't he? He saw a thin silver band on Williams's left ring finger. Would he ever get married? Williams was going to have a son—a newborn with no troubles, no worries. Joshua didn't have a father anymore.

He felt himself becoming angry again. His thoughts became more jumbled. He felt as if his head was going to explode. How can I make this all go away? He should just get back in his truck and drive away. He could drive back to the mountains and hide. He would set Williams free so he could walk back to the roadway and hitch a ride back to base. This would all be over. No one would have to die.

Williams moved beneath him. "Please," he begged.

Joshua looked down at Williams, whose face was covered with dirt. He dropped the key and looked away. Then suddenly with his right hand, he pulled the knife from its scabbard. He grabbed Williams by the back of his head, pulling it up to expose his throat, as he ran the knife across it.

CHAPTER FIFTEEN

CHARLOTTE, NORTH CAROLINA, WAS A six-hour drive from Norfolk. An hour and one-half drive west to Emporia, Virginia on US Highway 158 (informally known as Suicide Strip due to having only two lanes of roadway traveled mostly by eighteen-wheelers), then 250 miles south on three different interstate highways.

The "Queen City", as she is known, is the largest city in North Carolina. In 1762 she was named in honor of the British Queen Charlotte Sophia. The county, Mecklenburg, was named for the region in Germany where Charlotte was born. During the American Revolution, the British Commander Cornwallis briefly occupied the city before being driven out by hostile residents, prompting him to write that Charlotte was a "hornet's nest" of rebellion—hence the name of the local NBA team that plays there.

After Washington, DC, Charlotte was the closet metropolitan area to Tidewater Virginia where a criminal lawyer could be paid as well as one that handled civil litigation. Criminal work was all I knew. And I was done with all things Washington. The South might be a welcome change.

Charlotte had a population of three quarters of a million people, with 2.3 million in the surrounding area. She was the second largest financial center after New York. The crime rate was almost double the national average. The FBI ranked Charlotte in the top twenty-five American cities with the highest occurrences of crime. With the proliferation of new lawyers flooding the market—there were fifteen law schools in Virginia and North Carolina alone—entrepreneurial law firms were looking for ways to expand into new practice areas.

The law firm of Crabtree and Scott, Charlotte's largest with 227 attorneys, had called. They wanted someone to head up their new "white-collar" criminal division, which would defend those charged with financially motivated nonviolent crimes such as fraud, bribery, Ponzi schemes, insider trading, embezzlement, money laundering, and identify theft. In 1939, sociologist Edwin Sutherland first defined white-collar crimes as those crimes "committed by a person of respectability and high social status in the course of his occupation." One of the law firm partners who served on the search committee had graduated from law school with a Reservist Judge I had tried several cases in front of. He mentioned that I may be getting out of the military shortly and would be a good candidate. Word does travel fast.

I decided to drive to the interview rather than fly. I needed to clear my head. Driving always did that for me. This new murder case was troubling me; I wasn't sure why. I had had many difficult cases in the past. But this Miller case was different. It just didn't make sense. I was missing something.

My appointment was scheduled for 11:00 a.m. There would be a one-hour "get to know you" session with the five members on the search committee. Then we would go to lunch. When we returned, the tough questions would be handled by the managing partner as well as one of the named partners. I hadn't been on a job interview in almost twenty years. I didn't feel comfortable in a suit. Uniforms were easy; you didn't have to worry about what color shirt to wear or whether your tie matched.

I pulled into the parking lot of the eight-story tan brick building at 10:45 a.m. Military habits were hard to break; if you were five minutes early, you were late. I rolled down my window and felt a warm breeze blowing in from the west. Spring had arrived early. I pushed the buzzer. I waited while the security arm rose and allowed me in. There were several reserved parking spot in the front of the building for visitors and, I imagined, well-paying clients. I parked there.

Italian cypress trees adorned the front and sides of the large building. I walked up the paved walkway and stopped in front of the double doors with floor to ceiling glass. I straighten my tie and buttoned my jacket. I had a recent haircut from the base barbershop.

I entered into a well-appointed lobby with highly polished floors, Carrara marble statues, and tapestries hung on the wall. The receptionist desk, if you could call it that, stood alone in the center. "Minimalist," I think the term was. It was long and thin and made of glass. On top was a small computer and single telephone. The firm's name was prominently displayed in bold letters behind the pretty young receptionist.

As I approached, she came around the desk to meet me. Her knit skirt was tight and short. She had athletic legs; maybe she played a lot of tennis. Her hair was blond and full. She greeted me with a big smile. Nice teeth. Her name tag read, "Kim."

"Good morning, you must be Commander DeMarco," Kim said in a Southern drawl. She extended her hand. Her grip was firm. Definitely a tennis player. "I hope you had a nice trip." Southern hospitality.

"Good morning, Ma'am. I did. Thank you," I responded.

"Please take the elevator to the top floor. Mr. Epps and the rest of the committee are waiting for you in the conference room." Kim pointed the way to the elevator, smiled again, and returned to her desk. Very efficient. And good-looking.

I nodded and walked to the elevator, which was also made of glass, bordered by dark wood and a brass bar to hold on to. The doors opened slowly. When I stepped inside, it smelled like old money. It was a quiet ride to the eighth floor. When I exited, James "Jimmy" W. Epps, the attorney I had been speaking with, greeted me warmly.

"Welcome to Charlotte, Commander. I have heard a lot of good things about you from Judge Thompson. He and I were law school buddies at the University of South Carolina. He tells me you are quite the litigator."

"Thank you, Sir," I said, somewhat embarrassed.

"Please call me, Jimmy," he responded as he put his hand in the small of my back and began directing me to the conference room.

"Yes, Sir." It was hard to change habits that had been ingrained in you for decades.

The conference room took up almost the entire floor. The outside walls were floor to ceiling glass like the rest of the building. The view took in the entire city, the area the locals call "Uptown". I could see the Carolina Panthers Football Stadium in the background. There were twelve thick tufted black leather chairs arranged around a long conference table. At one end of the room was a bar filled with decorative bottles of scotch, bourbon, whiskey, and other dark liquors along with Waterford cut crystal glasses; at the other end were a huge TV screen and other trial presentation devices.

As I entered the conference room, they all stood. "Let me introduce you to everyone. This is Tommy Scott, our founding partner." Scott was in his seventies and was a large man weighing over 250 pounds. He rose easily from his chair at the head of the table and extended his hand. I read his biography before I came: star running back at Wake Forest University and editor of the *Duke Law Review* before starting his own firm and making millions handling plaintiffs' medical malpractice cases. He had a drink in his hand that didn't look like ice tea. His hand engulfed mine.

"It's a pleasure to meet you, young man."

"Yes, Sir."

The introductions continued. "This is Rich Turbeville, Jay Prentiss, and Tim Nettles." Each was dressed in an immaculate custom-made suit with French cuffs. Prentiss was the head of all litigation; Turbeville, the head of the criminal division. I didn't know much about Nettles. He was sporting a bow tie and appeared the youngest of the group at age fifty. They each nodded politely.

The lawyers sat back down indicating that I should be seated across from them. They began with some small talk about where I grew up, where I went to law school, and why I decided to join the military. The conversation quickly turned to my career.

"How many jury trials have you had?" asked Prentiss.

I thought for a moment wanting to be accurate. "I don't know exactly, Sir... Hundreds probably." They all looked at each other.

"But they were all military trials?" Turbeville questioned, not sure if that made a difference but thinking it must, given what to them was apparently a large number.

"Yes, Sir." Knowing that most civilian attorneys had no idea about how the military criminal justice system worked, I thought I should educate them. "In the military an accused can request a trial before either a Military Judge alone or a jury. The jurors are usually officers unless the accused requests a portion of the jury be made up of enlisted personnel who must be senior in rank to the accused. Personally, I prefer juries with enlisted members. And unlike the civilian world, the verdict is by majority vote, not unanimous. All officers and most senior enlisted have college degrees, so it's tough to pull anything over on them." That seemed to impress the group.

But the next question made me think I hadn't educated them enough. "Are your clients officers or enlisted?" asked Prentiss.

"Both, Sir. I've represented E-1s to O-6s." Seeing their blank stares, I continued, "Seamen Recruits to Captains."

"And they don't have to pay you?" questioned Epps.

"No, Sir. I come free of charge." I smiled, hoping they would appreciate my humor. No one seemed to think that was funny; they stared back at me. I continued, "The accused also has the right to hire a civilian counsel to work with me." And I quickly added, "They have to pay him." Maybe that would make them feel better.

There was a moment of silence while they digested that information. Then came the question: "Do you have investigators and paralegals to work up the case for you?" That came from Nettles, who was probably used to having a team of young lawyers working behind the scenes, doing all the grunt work, while he walked into the courtroom and got all the glory.

"Sir, I have a Legalman, but he handles most of the administrative work around the office. I do most of my own investigative work and trial prep. It helps me get to know my case better." I'm not sure that impressed them.

Finally, Scott, who had been sitting silent, jumped in. "Commander," he said, drawing out the three syllables in his Southern drawl, "I checked online to see what the Government pays you." I fidgeted in my chair. "With all due respect, we pay our senior associates more than what you make."

Not knowing quite what to say, I responded with the first thing that came to my mind. "Well, Sir, sometimes it's not always about the money."

Scott leaned back in his chair, put his arms behind his head, and with a big smile said, "Son, my daddy always told me never to trust anyone who doesn't like money."

I was ready for lunch.

CHAPTER SIXTEEN

MASTER SERGEANT PHIL BURTON WAS the Navy Marine Corps Intelligence Training Center Class Coordinator for class 0939. He had 60 students in his class. Lance Corporal Jonathan Williams was one.

It was Tuesday, January 4, 8:00 a.m. He had just been handed an attendance report that showed Williams had not shown up for class that morning, the second day of classes after the New Year break. Missing two days of class without an excuse was grounds for dismissal from the program.

Burton was a good evaluator of men; a senior enlisted in the Marine Corps had to be. In the short period of time Burton had observed Williams, he thought he was an excellent marine—good PT habits, good study habits, good leadership skills. Williams knew how to follow orders. If he was told to "take that hill," he would take that hill. That's why Burton loved the Corps. It was pretty simple— you were given an order and you followed it.

Burton had been around the training compound for fourteen years. It happened occasionally at the schoolhouse. Marines just didn't show up: they got into accidents over the holidays, they drank too much and were hung over, they got locked up, they fell in love and run off with a girl, or their raggedy-ass car broke down. Marines were the best the military had to offer but most were still teenage boys filled with too much testosterone.

Burton leaned back in his chair. Maybe it was something more serious this time. Burton had reviewed Williams's service jacket and knew Williams had served two tours in Afghanistan. More and more soldiers were coming back from the war with mental issues. The physical wounds the Corps could handle; the emotional ones they didn't deal with quite as well. Burton's father had been a marine in the South Pacific during World War II. After he enlisted in the Corps, he learned that his dad had been involved in some of the worst fighting in the Marshall Islands where Japanese soldiers, wearing soft-soled shoes, would sneak up on the marines in their foxholes and cut off their genitals. Burton remembered hearing his Dad in his bedroom late at night yelling out until he woke himself up. His mother would tell Burton to go back to sleep; his father was just having a bad dream. His dad never talked about it. Today, they call it post-traumatic stress disorder.

But Williams had never shown any signs of having problems. Burton thought that as he got older maybe he was getting soft and making too many excuses for his troops.

From long experience, Burton knew that someone in Williams's class might know something about the marine's whereabouts. The Corps motto was "Unit, Corps, God, Country," in that order. If there was a problem, your squad mates knew about it first. But before Burton distracted them from their classwork, he wanted to conduct his own investigation. He got up from his chair and called two of his senior NCOs into his office.

"Sergeant Brumbles, Corporal Williams hasn't showed up for class the last two days. He's not the type of marine to get into trouble. Take Lowder with you and check Williams barracks room, check the base police and shore patrol blotters, call the local hospitals, the local cops. Call his wife. Find out what happened to my marine."

"Yes, Master Sergeant," they both said in unison. They saluted, executed an about face, and were gone.

At 3:30 p.m. the two marines returned. Burton looked up from his paperwork. "Did you find my marine?"

"Negative, Master Sergeant," said Brumbles. "Of everyone we spoke to, no one has seen Williams or have any idea where he is."

Burton leaned back and ran his hand over his nearly bald head. He blew out a long breath.

"Okay, tell the class to remain after their instruction period is over today so I can talk with them and find out what the hell is going on."

Burton entered the lecture hall at exactly 4:00 p.m. All eyes were upon him. "Men, one of your classmates, Lance Corporal Jonathan Williams, hasn't shown up for class the last two days. He appeared to me to be a pretty squared-away marine. We talked to the local authorities, checked the hospitals, called his wife. No one had seen or heard from him. If anyone knows anything regarding his whereabouts, I need to know."

Corporal's Keith Richards, Lewis Martinez, and Bob Cox were sitting in the front row. Williams regularly ate with them and went bowling with the group on Thursday nights.

Martinez rose. "Master Sergeant, Williams told me he thought he was involved in an investigation."

"Martinez, how the hell can you *think* you are involved in an investigation? Either you are or you aren't."

"Yes, Master Sergeant, that's what I told him. But he said a few weeks ago he had been approached by an NCIS agent regarding a rape case. Williams said he didn't know nothing about it. Williams said the NCIS agent was kind of young and nervous, which he thought was strange. Williams was concerned that someone might have wrongly accused him of something he didn't do or it was just a case of mistaken identity. He didn't seem overly concerned," Martinez concluded.

"Anyone else?" Richards and Cox both stood at the same time. Each looked at each other expecting the other to go first. When neither did, Burton said, "Okay, Richards, what do you know?"

"Well, Master Sergeant, Williams appeared normal to me. He was all excited about the upcoming birth of his first child. Nothing unusual." Cox nodded in agreement.

"Anyone got anything else to add?" The class remained silent. "If you think of anything else important, contact me immediately. Dismissed."

Burton went back to his office and called the base Provost Marshal. He faxed over a missing-persons report. Next, he drove over to the local NCIS office to see if any of their agents were involved in a rape investigation. The senior agent in charge thought his request odd. He informed Burton that while he couldn't comment on any investigations, they had no active rape investigation ongoing.

Burton returned to his office and filed a report summarizing his finding and hesitantly recommending that when Williams returned he be charged with being AWOL.

Just another day at the Marine Corps barracks, he thought.

CHAPTER SEVENTEEN

THE AGENTS WERE STACKED BEHIND each other on either side of the doorway. Eight well-muscled men evenly divided. They had practiced this countless times. The areas they breached were usually larger—an office building, a warehouse, or even the bridge of a ship, never a dorm room. It wasn't often you made an armed assault in the barracks, the training barracks no less.

Every agent's heart was racing; however, they had long ago learned to control their breathing. Breathe in through your nostrils, out through your mouth. Quietly. Each agent wore body armor under black jackets stenciled with the words *NCIS* boldly in yellow. They wore black assault pants held up by a web belt with a full complement of ammo, handcuffs, batons, and various other items that they probably wouldn't need. Their boots were rubber-soled so as not to make a sound as they glided across the polished linoleum floor. The senior agent in charge had ordered night-vision goggles in case they needed to cut the power to the building.

Even though they had only walked up one flight of stairs, Hansen was drenched in sweat. He was in the assault party because one of the regular field agents had taken an extra vacation day for the Martin Luther King Jr. holiday and they needed a fill in. Once the arrest was made, his job would be to tag and catalog any evidence they might find in the room. He was at the end of the line.

The building superintendent had given them a key. They knew Miller was inside. The sailor at the front desk was instructed to call when Miller returned from study hall. They could hear him talking on the telephone.

The first agent would enter the room low and to the right. Each subsequent agent would hurry through the doorway in the opposite direction to the one before him. If the suspect was armed and right-handed, he would normally swing his firearm to his left giving the second agent, who entered in the opposite direction, time to fire his weapon. Each agent carried a SIG Sauer P229 .40 S&W semiautomatic pistol with ten hollow point rounds.

It was mid-January. The marine had been missing for almost two weeks. The top brass couldn't wait any longer. The order had come down to arrest Miller as the prime suspect. They were told he was armed and dangerous and that they were to apprehend Miller by any means necessary. Deadly force was authorized. Hansen was concerned because he knew the evidence they had so far wasn't that strong. To the field agents, Miller was just another criminal, another sailor that had made it through the screening but was evil at heart. Hansen wasn't convinced Miller was guilty. He hoped the young sailor wouldn't resist or that one of the newer agents didn't get trigger-happy. All agents were required to go to the firing range weekly, but when you were in the field and the adrenaline started flowing, you never knew what might happen. A sudden unexpected movement by a suspect could set off a gun fight.

The lead agent signaled he was ready. He counted down with his left hand. The agent to his left was standing tall with the key to the door already in the lock. "Go!"

The agents stormed into the small room all yelling at the same time. It was chaos. Quickly, four agents formed a half circle around Miller who was seated at his desk. Each had his pistol drawn and pointed at Miller's head. The other four agents spread out and covered all corners of the room. The smell of perspiration was strong. For a brief second Hansen thought how comical they all looked. Eight agents all pointing their weapons at a young sailor seated at his desk on the telephone in a room that could barely contain them all. But then he remembered that this sailor was accused of killing a battle-tested marine.

Thankfully, Miller didn't move. He looked at them calmly, almost as if he was expecting them. He slowly closed his cell phone and placed it on the desk. The noise ceased. Miller continued to sit looking at the agents. Two holstered their pistols and hurried over to him. They stood him up, brusquely turned him around, and handcuffed his hands behind his back. They spun Miller back around and pushed him against a wall. Hansen began searching the room.

The senior agent stepped forward. "Petty Officer Miller, you are under arrest for the murder of Lance Corporal Jonathan Williams. Under *UCMJ*, Article 31, you have the right against self-incrimination. You have the right to remain silent. You do not have to answer questions or make a statement. However, if you do anything you say can, and will, be used against you in a court of law. You have the right to an attorney. Under the *UCMJ*, an independent military attorney will be appointed to you. Do you understand these rights I have just explained to you?"

Miller looked at him with a blank expression. "With these rights in mind, do you wish to speak to me?" Miller looked from face to face. He was in no hurry. The room remained silent as did he.

Meanwhile Hansen had opened and quickly searched Miller's locker. He found nothing unusual. He moved to the desk where Miller had been sitting. As he opened the empty desk drawer, everyone could hear a small metal object sliding toward the rear. When it stopped, Hansen reached in and pulled out a thin silver ring, which appeared to be a wedding band. He held it up as he looked into Miller eyes. They were only a few feet apart.

Hansen and Miller stared at one another for a long minute. Perhaps it was the nearness in age. Perhaps something more. Hansen was slightly unnerved. What did he see? Something imperceptible passed between them.

"Sailor, do you wish to speak with me now?" the senior agent barked. Miller's gaze never left Hansen's. He didn't seem to be afraid.

"No, Sir, I do not."

Frustrated, the agents grabbed Miller by the elbows and rushed him out the door.

CHAPTER EIGHTEEN

WE WERE BACK IN THE same small room where I had met Miller several weeks ago. We sat across from each other, so close I could feel his breath. The table was barely large enough for my briefcase, which sat open. The air inside the small space was stuffy; a single lightbulb scarcely illuminated the room.

The first visit hadn't gone well. Miller told me little more than his name, rank, and duty station. Today I was making a little progress. I think he finally realized I was there to help.

Miller sat upright in the metal chair. He looked me directly in the eye. Whether you were innocent or guilty, most would look away at some point. Miller didn't. There were studies that showed that if someone was answering and looked right, they were remembering; if they looked left, they were creating or lying. There was a whole subculture of experts evolving in the criminal justice system—jury consultants, body language experts. Neurolinguistic behavior, I think they called it in law school. I usually went with my gut. Miller was different than most of the clients I had represented. He didn't want to talk.

I went through his background, where he grew up, his relationship with his parents, his father's death, family life, school, extracurricular activities, few as they were, brief employment history, essentially every aspect of life growing up in a small town.

"So why did you join the Navy?" I asked.

"Because I couldn't find a job back home, Sir." He would answer directly but gave me no more or less than the question asked for.

"So what was it like growing up in your hometown?" I was trying to build some rapport with him.

"Well, Sir, like I said, not a lot of jobs. Seems as if everyone was getting some type of government paycheck, but they was good people, always helping each other out. George would come by and cut our grass when the tractor broke down. Franco would help Mom with the chores. Everyone just pitched in." He was loosening up.

"Why did you decide to become an Intelligent Specialist?"

"I took some tests and that's where they said I would fit in." He stopped talking for a minute then. "Also I like to play video war games." He looked embarrassed. "I used to work at a video store and got them cheap." He sat back quietly waiting for the next question. If we both just sat there, I wondered who would feel the need to speak first. Sometimes, particularly when I knew a person was lying, I would pause after they answered my question. People feel the need to fill the silence by saying something—that's when they get into trouble.

"You advanced pretty quickly."

"I guess… Sir." He remembered his military courtesies. I could tell he was smart.

"Did you like C school?" This time there was no answer. I sensed we were getting into a sensitive area. His body tensed but he didn't look away.

"Did you make many friends in school?" I leaned forward.

"Not many," he answered more cautiously.

"What barracks did you live in?"

"508." Miller started to fidget slightly in his chair. For the first time perspiration was beginning to show on his forehead. His breathing was the same but I knew that would change shortly.

"Did you have any roommates?"

"No."

"What type car do you drive?" No response. I already knew the answer. "Do you remember your license plate number?"

Suddenly, for the first time, he leaned forward and asked me a question. "Sir, you are a Naval Officer, right?"

"Yes." I knew where this was going. Enlisted men had been shit on by officers ever since there was a military. He was worried whether someone with some rank would be more concerned with getting promoted than seeing that justice was done. He was wondering if one day I'd cave and serve him up on a platter to the command.

"So isn't your obligation to the Navy?"

"Well, while it's true I am a United States Naval Officer, I am also a lawyer and you are my client."

"But I'm just an E-4, a nobody."

I dropped my pen on the table and leaned toward him. "Petty Officer Miller, I took an oath to support and defend the Constitution of the United States and to follow the orders of my superiors, but that Constitution also requires me to represent my client to the best of my ability."

He didn't back away. "So which comes first?"

"They are both equally important," I said quickly.

"But don't you want to get promoted?"

Good question. I paused. "Sure I do, but I figure if I do my job that it will all work out."

"Well, no disrespect, Sir, but if you defend an enlisted man against an admiral, you won't get very far." Miller looked at the three stripes on my sleeves. I thought his comment was pretty clever; he didn't seem to appreciate the humor.

I felt I was finally getting close to him. He had to trust me if he was going to eventually take my advice. I tell my clients it's their life; I go home at the end of the day, they may go to jail. It's in their best interest to tell me everything and to listen to what I say. "Petty Officer Miller, what are you concerned about?"

He hesitated. "Do I have to testify, Sir?"

"Well… the burden of proof is on the Government, but realistically the jury usually wants to hear what the accused has to say. But this case is a little unusual as they don't have a body. All the Government's evidence is circumstantial. So at this point I would recommend that you don't take the stand." He stared at me. I could tell he was thinking about something troubling.

I continued, "Remember, everything you tell me is in confidence, but if you don't tell me the entire story, I don't know how best to defend you."

He shifted slightly in his chair. "So that means you can't tell anyone what I say?"

"I can't if you don't want me to." Where was he going with this? I pressed. "Where were you on New Year's Eve?" Silence.

"Did you know Lance Corporal Williams?" Miller looked down and clasped his hands together.

Softly he answered, "I didn't know him personally." That sounded strange. Then he blurted out, "I think I'm tired. Can we stop now?" Before I could respond, he got up quickly, turned, and walked to the door.

"Joshua, remember, if you need me, just ask the guard's to call me. We have a lot more to go over."

The guard opened the door, and before I could say anything more, Miller was gone.

Why was everyone walking out on me lately?

CHAPTER NINETEEN

I SAT IN MY HOME office staring at a picture of a ship; her name was *Palatia*. The ocean had always been a part of me. It calmed me during difficult times. The *Palatia* was built by A/G Vulcan shipyard in Stettin, Germany, in 1894. It carried my grandfather Angelo from the town of Bitetto in the province of Bari, Italy, to Ellis Island. The year was 1904; he was sixteen.

The *Palatia* was only four hundred feet long and weighed just 7,326 tons; it was not a large vessel. Top speed was thirteen knots. It carried 2,060 passengers; sixty in first class, the remainder in steerage. "Steerage", or between decks, originally described the deck below the main deck. The ships that were used to transport immigrants were initially cargo ships. The cargo holds, where as many human beings as possible, men, women, and children were crowded into, were only accessible by ladders. Ceiling heights were eighty inches. Multiple bunks with straw mattresses were stacked up along the bulkheads. The immigrants had to bring their own pillow and blankets or they did without. There was little ventilation. Sanitation was nil. To maximize their profits, the shipping lines, as soon as the passengers were discharged, returned the ship to Europe filled with cargo.

My "Nonno's" desire to leave the place of his birth, and thereby his family and way of life, was fueled by dire poverty. Life in southern Italy offered landless peasants, or those that fished as his family did, little more than hardship, exploitation, and violence. From 1900 to 1911, almost two million Italian immigrants made the journey to the United States. When my grandfather arrived at Ellis Island after a month long journey at sea, he knew he had reached the promised land.

The marriage to my grandmother Domenica was arranged by their families back in Italy. The first time they met was when she arrived in New York in 1911. Neither of my grandparents spoke English, nor could they read or write. With nine children, two boys and seven girls, putting food on the table was more important than education. They tried hard to blend in and become Americans. Both were extremely proud when they became US citizens in 1924.

Only one of the children, the youngest son, Dante, graduated from high school. My father, Dominick, the fifth born and oldest boy, had the most promise, but growing up during the Depression to an immigrant family required that he work to help support the family. However, he knew that education was the best way to get ahead in this country. He went to school at night to earn his GED, enlisted in the military during the war, and after his discharge January 31, 1946, he went to work at a manufacturing plant, working sixteen-hour days.

I grew up in a loving household; each of my parents had their role to play. It worked. From any early age, I knew that I was going to college. It didn't matter what I got my degree in but I was going. My father craved knowledge and loved to read. One of his favorites was a poem by Rudyard Kipling titled "If—." I can still hear him quoting his favorite stanzas to me:

> If you can keep your head when all about you
> Are losing theirs and blaming it on you...
> If you can talk with crowds and keep your virtue,
> or walk with Kings—nor lose the common touch...

Another favorite was "The Man in the Mirror." He would remind me that whatever you did, you had to look yourself in the mirror the next day. When he died, he left me something more valuable than money—a sense of integrity.

So what was I to do with Petty Officer Joshua Miller? I never had a client that refused to cooperate. Most loved to talk—that's usually how they got caught. I could threaten that I was going to withdraw from his case. But who was qualified enough at the NLSO to take over the defense? A good prosecutor would eat them alive. Even though the evidence was circumstantial, there was a missing, and presumably dead, marine war hero.

I continued to stare at the picture. Maybe I should get out and take that job in Charlotte. Miller would then have to get another attorney. Could I walk away? Did he really need me? I had represented hundreds of defendants from all backgrounds. If they were guilty, as most were, they either wanted to cop a plea or tried to bullshit you until you finally made them see the light. Some you had to gently lead to the realization of their circumstances; others you had to bludgeon over the head. Miller was going to be a challenge. I couldn't leave him in the hands of a rookie.

I told every client it wasn't my job to judge them, that I was on their side. I don't know if that made them feel any more comfortable, but we usually ended up where we needed to be. But I wasn't getting through to this guy.

Did I really need his cooperation? I leaned back in my chair going over the Government's evidence in my mind. The most important piece of evidence—a body—hadn't been found. Granted Williams was a stellar marine and it was highly unlikely that he just walked off post leaving a pregnant wife behind. But people do strange things all the time. Maybe he was suffering from PTSD—two tours in Afghanistan could do that to you. Maybe Williams was fed up with the Marine Corps; some gunny sergeant was up his ass all the time and he snapped. Maybe he was scared of being a new father; maybe he found another girl. Maybe, maybe, maybe. There were a number of possibilities I could point out to the jury.

The rest of the evidence was just as weak. A shaky identification by a barracks petty officer who was immersed in his studies and had only a few seconds to observe Miller; I could get an eyewitness identification expect to testify that eyewitness testimony is the weakest form of evidence. Put several people in a room and ask them to witness an event and all will describe it differently, especially if it's a common occurrence and they're trying to recall it after a lapse in time of several weeks. Next, a telephone call to Williams's barracks room that was placed from outside the training recruits' barracks where hundreds of students had access. That would be easy to deal with. Then a surveillance video that was blurry. NCIS was able to identify a partial license plate number. But only one letter and one number matched my client's car. That wasn't enough, was it? They couldn't even identity the car. I'd make a motion to suppress that evidence.

But I was worried about that damned ring. Why would it be in Miller's desk drawer? Sure, there had been several residents in that room each year and scores of recruits visiting each other in their rooms. Anyone of them could have left it. And there weren't any identifying marks on the ring which was frequently sold at mall kiosks. And if Miller did it, why keep a ring?

So while the evidence in total might be concerning this was a capital murder case. The jury would scrutinize everything closely. And I'd won hundreds of cases with the Government having more evidence than this. I just had to keep emphasizing "beyond a reasonable doubt," the highest standard known to the law, a criminal defense lawyer's best friend.

So why was I concerned?

There wasn't any evidence or circumstances connecting Miller and Williams. I realized that some murders were random acts of killing, but usually there was something linking the parties. Here there was no grudge, two totally different types of personalities from two different branches of the service. There was no common link. There was no motive.

So what was bothering me? I couldn't put my finger on it, but I felt it in my gut. What was it?

I got up and looked out the window. After a few seconds, I pushed all the doubt from my mind. My trial strategy would be to keep out as much of the evidence as I could; whatever came in I would cross-exam the hell out of it. I'd give the jury alternative explanations for what the evidence meant. A good trial lawyer can take any fact and spin it in his favor. I would not have Miller testify.

During voir dire, I would ask the jury if they understood that a criminal defendant had a constitutional right not to testify and that it was the Government who had the burden of proof. I would remind them of that during the entire trial. No body. No links. No motive. That should be enough. I would finish my naval career with a major win.

So what was the problem?

I wouldn't sleep much that night.

CHAPTER TWENTY

SHE TURNED TO LOOK AT me as I walked into the courtroom. Son of a bitch! Commander Nora Dempsey was seated beside Lieutenant Commander Mays at the prosecutors' table. I hadn't seen Nora in years. She and I first met when we were classmates at Naval Justice School in Newport, Rhode Island, twenty years ago. She finished second in our class; I finished third, by less than half a point. I used to kid her that she cheated by looking at my exams. Being the smart-ass she was, she reminded me that she had the better grades. Nora still looked good in a skirt, even a polyester/nylon blend.

Nora and I quickly figured out that we would be better friends than lovers. There was too much testosterone between us. Even so, we spent many nights together at the local bars drinking Drambuie and scotch, a "rusty nail," to warm us from the Newport cold. Newport is known as the sailing capital of the world. When the wind blew off the Narragansett Bay, it would cut right through you. I had missed her.

Nora came from a military family, a good Catholic family. All six brothers and sisters had served in the armed forces. At Newport she gave as good as she got. On the ten-mile runs with the marines along the Newport mansions, the cliff walks, she never finished lower than third. And when she won, she let you know it. One time the line officers at Officer Candidate School, OCS, challenged the staff guys to an arm-wrestling contest; Nora easily beat the female Marine

Corps instructor and became a local legend. She was tough, smart, and pretty.

"Good morning, Michael." Nora rose as she extended her hand.

Michael? No one calls me that, except my mother. "Commander Dempsey, to what do I owe the pleasure?" I said as I took her hand in mine.

"OJAG said you weren't playing nice again."

"Me?" I feigned an insulted look and stepped back slightly.

"So tell me what you got?" I just looked at her, both of us knowing that I wouldn't tell her anything about my case. "Any plea discussions?" she continued.

"Not unless you want to drop the charges."

Our conversation was interrupted as the bailiff abruptly stood. He called the court to order as Captain Johnson entered from his chambers. I winked at Nora as I went over to my counsel table; she gave me a nod and a smile as she sat down.

"This General Court-Martial is called to order at Naval Station, Norfolk, Virginia, in the case of *United States versus Intelligence Specialist Third Class Joshua Miller, United States Navy*. Trial Counsel, would you please state the jurisdictional data for this General Court-Martial?"

Commander Dempsey stood. "This court-martial is convened by Commander, Navy Regional Mid-Atlantic, by General Court-Martial convening order 1-06, and referred as a capital case as recommended by the Staff Judge Advocate, copies of which have been furnished to the Military Judge, the counsel, and the accused, and which are to be inserted into the record at this time.

"The accused and the following persons detailed to this court-martial are present: Captain Christopher Johnson, JAGC, US Navy, Military Judge; Commander Nora Dempsey, JAGC, US Navy, Trial Counsel; Lieutenant Commander Alfred Mays, JAGC, US Navy, Assistant Trial Counsel; and Commander Michael DeMarco, JAGC, US Navy, Detailed Defense Counsel. Mrs. Cindy Spainhour has been detailed as court reporter. The members assigned to this court-martial are currently absent."

Commander Dempsey continued. "All members of the prosecution have been detailed to this court-martial by the Senior Trial Counsel of the Regional Legal Service Office Mid-Atlantic, pursuant to the authority delegated to him by the Commanding Officer of the same command. All members of the prosecution team are qualified and certified under Article 27(b) and sworn under Article 42(a) of the *Uniform Code of Military Justice*. No member of the prosecution has acted in any manner that might tend to disqualify them from this court-martial."

The Military Judge smiled sweetly at her. "Thank you, Commander." Dempsey took a seat. Looking sternly at my client, Captain Johnson said, "Are you, Intelligence Specialist Joshua Miller, United States Navy?"

"Yes, Sir," answered Miller jumping up and standing at attention as I had instructed him.

"And you are the accused in this matter?" I wanted to ask who the hell else would be sitting next to me?

"Yes, Sir."

"Now, Intelligence Specialist Miller, you have the right to be represented by Commander Mike DeMarco, JAG Corps, United States Navy, as your Detailed Defense Counsel and he is provided to you at no expense. You also have the right to be represented by a military lawyer of your own selection, and if the military lawyer that you request is reasonably available, then he or she would be appointed to represent you, also free of charge. Do you understand this?"

"Yes, Sir, I do."

"In addition, you have the right to be represented by a civilian lawyer. A civilian lawyer would have to be provided by you at no expense to the Government. That means that you would have to make arrangements to hire and arrange to pay that civilian lawyer yourself. Your civilian lawyer may represent you alone or along with your military counsel. Do you understand your right to be represented by civilian counsel?"

"Yes, Sir, I do," he paused. "But I don't have any money, Sir."

The judge looked momentarily flustered, not knowing what to say. That's what happens when you don't represent real people. "Ah…

well, that's okay." He stopped and then continued. "All right, you may be seated. Would military counsel please indicate by whom you have been detailed and state your qualifications?"

I stood. "Yes, Sir. My name is Commander Michael D. DeMarco, I have been qualified and certified under Article 27(b) and sworn under Article 42(a) of the *Uniform Code of Military Justice*. I am licensed before the United States Supreme Court, the Court of Military Appeals, and the State Bar of Virginia. I have not acted in any manner that might tend to disqualify me in this court-martial."

"And are you prepared at this point to place on the record your training and experience related to capital litigation? And how many cases you have tried?" said the judge.

"Yes, Sir, I am." Where should I begin? "Judge, I have been in the military for almost twenty years; I have tried well over three hundred jury trials, consisting of all major felonies, including rape and murder. I have represented the accused in ten capital cases."

"Thank you, Commander. You may all be seated." The judge paused until I was almost seated then said, "Commander DeMarco, is your client in the proper uniform, including all awards and decorations, to which he is entitled?" I stood back up. I thought I detected a slight smirk on his face.

"Yes, Sir, he is."

"And would you please enumerate what those are?"

"Yes, Sir. Intelligence Specialist Miller is entitled to wear, and is wearing, the Navy Achievement Medal, with gold star in lieu of second award, the Navy E Ribbon, with the second E meaning second award, the Navy Good Conduct Medal, the Navy National Defense Service Medal, the Iraqi Campaign Medal, the Global War on Terrorism Expeditionary Medal, the Global War on Terrorism Service Medal, Sea Service Deployment Ribbon, Bronze Star in lieu of second award, and the Navy/Marine Corps Overseas Deployment Ribbon with Bronze Star in lieu of second award." It was a pretty impressive array for someone who had not been in the military all that long.

"Thank you, Counsel. I have detailed myself to this General Court-Martial under my authority as the Chief Circuit Military

Judge of the Central Judicial Circuit, Navy/Marine Corps Trial Judiciary. I am certified and sworn as a Military Judge in accordance with Articles 26(b) and 11(c) and 42(a) of the *Uniform Code of Military Justice*. I am not aware of any matter that I believe would be a basis for challenge against me."

With that he stopped and looked over his glasses at me. "However, does either the prosecution or the defense wish to voir dire or challenge for cause the Military Judge?"

Commander Dempsey rose. "No, Sir." She quickly sat down as I slowly rose to my feet.

Captain Johnson and I stared at each other for quite some time. As tempting as it would have been to ask him some questions, I replied, "The Defense does not have any questions of His Honor and does not desire"—I smiled at him—"at this time, to challenge him for cause."

That took the smirk off his face. Irritably he continued, "Trial Counsel, please announce the general nature of the charges."

"The general nature of the charges in this case is a violation of the *Uniform Code of Military Justice*, Article 118, "Murder," supported by one specification, and Article 134, "Kidnapping," supported by three specifications. The charges were preferred by Lieutenant Dancy, JAG Corps, United States Navy, and forwarded with recommendations as to the disposition by a General Court-Martial. These charges were investigated by Commander Terry Milligan, JAG Corps, United States Navy, with a recommendation that they be referred as capital, with the Government being allowed to seek the death penalty."

"Thank you. Intelligence Specialist Miller, I'm going to ask you a few more questions regarding your rights." I guess the Judge was through playing his little games as he said, "You and your counsel may remain seated while I review your rights with you.

"You have the right to be tried by a court consisting of at least twelve officer members, that is, a court composed of commissioned officers, including warrant officers. Also, if you request, you may be tried by a court consisting of at least one-third enlisted members, but none of those enlisted members would come from your Command. You are also advised that no member of the court can be junior in rank to you. Because this case is referred with instructions to be tried as a capital case, that is, a case in which the imposition of the death penalty is an authorized punishment, you may not be tried by a Military Judge alone. Do you understand what I've said so far, Petty Officer?"

"Yes, Sir." I could see the sweat beginning to glisten off of Miller's upper lip.

"Now, in a trial by a court that consists of members, the members will vote by secret written ballot and two-thirds of the members must agree before you could be found guilty of any offense. If you are found guilty of any offense, then two-thirds of the members must also agree in their voting on a sentence. Three-fourths of the members must agree on any sentence that includes confinement for more than ten years. For the death penalty to be adjudged, all court members would have to agree on both the findings of guilt and the sentence. In this case, that means that the court members must have an unanimous vote of guilty on the charge and specification for which death is authorized, that is, the sole specification of Charge I, "Premeditated Murder," a violation of Article 118 of the *Uniform Code of Military Justice*. Do you understand that?"

"Yes, Sir."

The judge took a breath. "Additionally, Petty Officer Miller, to impose the death penalty the Court members must, first, unanimously find, beyond a reasonable doubt, that you are guilty of an offense for which death is an authorized punishment under the law;

"Second, unanimously find, beyond a reasonable doubt, evidence of at least one aggravating factor;

"Third, unanimously find that any extenuating or mitigating circumstances are substantially outweighed by any aggravating factors or evidence; and

"Fourth, unanimously vote to impose the death penalty.

"If anyone of those four factors is not unanimous, then the death penalty may not be adjudged. Do you understand this?"

"Yes, Sir."

"Do you understand the choices you have with respect to the composition of your court?" I'm not sure, after hearing all that, that Miller wanted the court to be his.

"Yes, Sir."

"By what type of court do you wish to be tried?"

Miller looked at me. I nodded. "A court composed of enlisted members, Sir."

"Very well. A court composed of members with enlisted representation. The accused will now be arraigned."

Commander Dempsey rose once again. Every time she did, her dress was hiked up over her thighs. That was going to be a distraction. "All parties to the trial have been furnished with a copy of the charges. Does the accused desire that they be read?"

I stood again, "Your Honor, the accused will waive the reading of the charges and specifications."

"Thank you. Accused and Counsel, please rise." We did as instructed. I could feel Miller shaking beside me. "Intelligence Specialist Joshua Miller, I now ask you, how do you plead?"

Miller turned slightly and looked at me; I looked back at him and nodded. It was his time to tell the court, the prosecutor, and the world that he didn't do it. That he didn't kill anyone. That this was all a mistake.

Miler looked toward the bench, then at Commander Dempsey, then back again at me. His eyes were wide. His breathing shallow. He opened his mouth but no words came out.

"Not guilty!" I shouted.

Miller fell back in his chair.

CHAPTER TWENTY-ONE

I DROVE THROUGH THE DOWNTOWN Tunnel, a half-mile four-lane roadway built under the Elizabeth River, connecting the cities of Norfolk and Portsmouth. Built in 1952 the tunnel handles more than three million vehicles a month. I hoped no damn fool caused an accident today. A fender bender in the tunnel could easily delay you for hours. I was already late.

Once I crossed into Portsmouth, I made a quick right turn onto Effingham Street, then a left onto Williamson Drive. This would lead me past the main hospital building to the parking garage.

Portsmouth Naval Hospital, built in 1830, is the Navy's oldest continuously operated hospital. Originally constructed on twenty acres on the historic site where Fort Nelson once stood, it now encompasses one hundred ten acres. The hospital was originally designed to accommodate three hundred patients. During World War I, that number rose to over one thousand four hundred. At its peak in World War II, it housed almost three thousand four hundred. Now the hospital was seventeen stories tall with more than five thousand healthcare professionals providing medical care to more than four hundred thousand active duty, retirees, and dependents annually in a million-plus-square-foot acute care facility.

The "Grande Dame" of Navy medicine had treated many of our nation's heroes since its founding. On March 8, 1862, during the naval battle of Hampton Roads, which pitted the Union's ironclad, the USS *Monitor*, against the Confederacy's CSS *Virginia* (formerly the USS *Merrimac*), the Commanding Officer of the *Monitor* was blinded and was treated here. Later, Commodore Franklin Buchannan, the first superintendent of the US Naval Academy and the skipper of the *Virginia*, was a fellow patient after being hit in the leg by a mini ball in battle. One hundred years later Rear Admiral Jeremiah Denton, a POW in the Vietnam War, came here upon his release from captivity. The list is longer than it should be.

I drove into the massive parking garage and found an empty spot on the fifth floor. I parked my black Datsun 280-ZX and walked down several flights of stairs until I found an exit that would lead me to the original hospital building, which now housed the doctors' offices. As soon as I stepped outside, I could feel the cool breeze blowing in from the river. Even though winter had passed, it was still chilly. I tightened my old Navy pea coat around me. I had purchased this jacket while out at sea because I liked to stand on the bridge at night and gaze up at the stars. At sea, they are crystal clear and luminous; there are few more wondrous sights. The coat, while bulky, allowed me to remain outside as long as I liked.

The old structure was built of granite and Virginia sandstone. The main entrance had ten massive columns with twenty steps, ninety-two feet wide. I paused for a moment to gather my thoughts. I was meeting a doctor, a potential expert witness, who had not yet been granted by the court. Technically, I was violating the lawyer's code of ethics, even if he was a friend—and former client.

I found the walkway that ran along the back of the building. It led me past a small cemetery, which, despite the construction through the decades, remained intact. The oldest marked grave was that of sailor who died in August 1838 after a fall from one of the yardarms of the Constitution. I kept walking.

He asked that we met under the magnolia trees across from the "Dungeon". The dungeon was located under the back stairs of the old building. Its back door and windows had bars across them, which led many to believe that it was here that the Navy used to house its prisoners. It was also surmised that this room was used to treat the mentally ill because many early health care practitioners believed that the moon affected their patient's behavior. In reality, the bars were probably used to keep thieves from stealing the materials stored inside. But it made for some interesting stories. It was an appropriate place for our meeting.

As I rounded the back of the building, I saw Lieutenant Commander Joe Tanahill lounging lazily on a bench under a forty-foot tall southern magnolia tree. The weather had caused it to shed many of its glossy oval-shaped leaves.

"Tanney" and I first met at Officer Indoctrination School. He was tall and lanky with a dark complexion, apparently of Eastern European descent although no one knew from where. Most things came easy to him. Tanney was popular with the college girls at Salve Regina, the local Catholic liberal arts college. Because he would only grudgingly cut his long hair a little at a time, he failed his first six inspections. I wondered why Tanney chose the military; maybe it was the free education or the uniform. Despite his lack of military bearing, he was one hell of a shrink.

Tanney and I had kept in touch over the years. A few years back I represented him at a "Show Cause" hearing for an "alleged" affair with a young enlisted nurse. The military frowns on "unduly familiar" relationships between the officer and enlisted ranks. His CO wanted Tanney kicked out of the Navy even though relationships between doctors and nurses occur all the time at the military hospitals. We convinced the Board that given his outstanding medical credentials, the short duration of the relationship, and that alcohol was involved, most of the time his conduct was not service discrediting. The Board members narrowly voted to keep him in, but he was going to have a hard time getting promoted.

"Your boy has issues," Tanney said as I approached.

"You think?" I replied. "Not even a hello for an old friend?" I sat down next to him.

"You know I'm not supposed to be doing this." He didn't appear concerned as he crossed his legs.

"When has that ever stopped you?" We had to meet outside his office as a JAG Officer meeting a Staff Corps Psychiatrist might raise suspicions.

"I get in trouble every time I come near you." He paused and smiled than dove right into the twenty-page report I had given him a few days ago. "I reviewed the 706 findings." Section 706 of *The Rules for Courts-Martial* provides that when an accused's mental capacity is at issue, the Convening Authority can order that he be examined by a panel of psychiatrists. It is routinely performed on all murder suspects. A summary of the findings gets sent to the Command; the defense counsel gets the full report.

"I also interviewed your guy—and I use that term loosely—for about three hours. It was tough getting him to open up. He had no clue as to why we—*I*—was talking to him and I didn't know what the hell to tell him."

"So what did you tell him?"

"Nothing."

"Guess he found that informative." I was anxious to find out Tanney's impressions of Miller since I had little else to go on at this point. "What did you think of Board's findings?"

"Well, your client has a host of issues, but dissociative identity disorder, narcissistic personality disorder, and impulsivity are the three you should be most concerned with."

"How did they come up with those diagnoses?"

"The Board did a personality functioning test as well as the regular battery of testing, the mini mental state exam, the Wechsler adult intelligence scale, a wide-range achievement test, a grooved pegboard trial making test, the Minnesota multiphasic personality inventory two, or MMPI-2, as it is commonly known, and the Rorschach ink blot test. They also did a mental status exam, which noted their behavioral observations."

Not certain of what the heck he was talking about, I asked, "So what do you think?"

Tanney put on his reading glasses and began looking at his notes. "The test performances, as well the behavioral observations made throughout the testing, indicate that the test results were a valid measure of Miller's current neuropsychological status. Miller's intellectual functioning falls in the superior range of intelligence with a full scale IQ of 130." He looked up over his readers and said to me.

"If you compare Miller's age and education to his peers, he is smarter than most."

"Okay, so he's a smart son of a bitch. How crazy is he?" Tanney just shook his head and continued.

"Miller's performance testing on Executive Functioning was broadly within the superior range. On a test of novel problem-solving, he solved all six categories; when compared to the same age and education level of his peers, he had fewer expected errors."

"Come on, Tanney, get to the good stuff." I hated all this pyscho mumbo-jumbo. But Tanney was not to be rushed. He was in his element. He flipped over a couple more pages.

"All right, let's talk about the psychological testing along with my interview. On the RISB, a projective test of personality adjustment, Miller completed all the items in a manner demonstrating his tendency to internalize and intellectualize the events in his life. In addition, his anger at his present circumstances and his dissatisfaction with his inability to achieve the goals he set for himself were evident in his responses to me.

"On the MMPI-2, he endorsed a number of items that are not normally noted by the majority of people taking this test, which highlighted his perception that he has had many unusual experiences in his life. His profile also indicated that, for the most part, he is likely to blame others for his inability to gain the sense of happiness he perceives in others around him. He is resentful and suspicious of others and broods about perceived slights for a considerable period of time. He's likely to react without thinking. He also has a problem with authority."

Tanney looked at me over his glasses. "You are aware, I suppose, doing what you do"—he paused and gave me a goofy grin—"and being pretty good at it, that individuals who demonstrate this combination of rumination and resentfulness are often prone to one day act out in an aggressive or violent manner." Well, no shit, I thought. I just stared at Tanney.

He gave me a condescending look and continued on without my response. "Interpersonal relationships appear to be a particular source of difficulty for Miller, primarily because of his suspicious and reclusive nature. His response pattern suggests he views his family as uncaring and critical and also reveals his belief that no one understands him or his way of doing things." Tanney stopped and looked at me. "Do you want me to continue?"

"Please do, this is riveting stuff," I said. He just smirked.

"On the MCMI-III, an objective measure of personality organization and psychological symptoms, Miller produced a valid profile that suggested he is likely to be distrustful and suspicious of others, leading him to be very independent and self-determined in an effort to protect himself. Individuals with a similar manner of responding are often viewed by others as egoistic or inconsiderate because of their need to prove themselves and their insistence that their rights should be respected above anyone else's. Anyone who does not respect these individuals is likely to be viewed with disdain and loathing. Miller's pattern of responding indicates he frequently becomes preoccupied with self-glorifying fantasies of success and heroism and has a tendency toward embellishment and taking liberties with the facts. In particular, he is apt to go to great lengths to justify or rationalize his behavior."

Tanney paused and took a sip from a water bottle he had sitting on the bench beside him. I could have used a strong cup of coffee. "I got him to eventually talk about people who have not supported or cared for him. He had feelings of futility and humiliation at his inability to gain what he desires. Miller doesn't appear to understand others very well and does not feel understood by them. These qualities make it difficult for him to engage in the give and take aspect of relationships, which in turn prevents him from forming warm or close relationships with others, particularly those of the opposite sex.

"On the RIBT, he does not appear to have a well-defined manner of coping with stress. His profile suggests he spends considerable time focused on his self-image, which is overly self-involved and filled with an inflated sense of personal worth. He demonstrated a strong concern with self, a sense of personal dissatisfaction, and uses narcissism and impulsivity defensively."

I thought Tanney was finished but he continued. "Furthermore, his profile suggests he is uncomfortable dealing with emotions. He is not able to understand his own and others' feelings. This is additionally complicated by a tendency to distort reality through the use of fantasy. He appears to exert stringent control over his feelings and this appears to be rather maladaptive as his limited coping and low tolerance for frustration is likely to overwhelm his tight emotional control. He is also likely to be less sensitive to the needs and interests of others causing him difficulty in sustaining relationships, which in turn leads to interpersonal dissatisfaction. Despite his social difficulties, Miller frequently seeks out close and enduring relationships, but his incompetence in relationships leaves him vulnerable to rejection. As such, he does not anticipate positive interactions with others and may be cautious about emotional ties. Consequently, he may become socially isolated due to his difficulty creating and sustaining meaningful interpersonal relationships."

"Okay, Tanney, sum it up for me, please. I do have other clients."

"You came to me, remember?" He sat back and looked up as if lecturing to a room full of interns. "I believe Miller's psychological assessment suggests someone who is an angry and pessimistic individual, who is suspicious and resentful of others and spends considerable time ruminating about perceived slights and personal inadequacies. There is evidence to suggest he may act out in a violent manner in an effort to avoid harm to himself or to harm others. His ability to cope with stress effectively is poor, underdeveloped, and inconsistent. While he tightly controls his emotions, this control is maladaptive and can easily be overwhelmed by his poor coping, which can lead to emotional outbursts. Miller's self-image is extremely important and he may go to great lengths to prove his worthiness."

"So is he crazy?"

Taney paused and again looked at me over his glasses. "As a bed bug."

CHAPTER TWENTY-TWO

THE BRIG WAS HOT. BOTH of us were sweating in the small room. We were into our second hour. The trial was starting in two days.

I stood, picked up the stack of telephone records, and dropped them on the table. I was frustrated. The prosecutors had subpoenaed Miller's cell phone records hoping to find a connection between him and Williams; there wasn't any. They handed them over to me, not realizing the significance of the number of calls or to whom they were made. Now I did.

Military defendants have more rights than their civilian counterparts. In the military there is full disclosure—the Government has to turn over everything they find unlike the civilian world where it is often trial by ambush.

When I received the telephone records, I went through them call by call. I quickly noticed there were an unusual number of calls made to a 252 area code—eastern North Carolina. They were made at all hours of the day and night. I called the number. No one answered the first few times. Then I blocked my number. A young girl finally answered. She sounded sweet. Before she could hang up, I told her I was a lawyer representing Joshua Miller who was charged with a crime and that she was a material witness. After some coaxing, I got her to talk to me. Her story was much different than the one Miller had been telling me over the last hour.

"Joshua, she wasn't real! It was a lie! All of it lies! The whole freakin' five thousand phone calls were lies! I talked to her." I was almost yelling at him.

He looked at me dejectedly, not wanting to believe what I was saying. His arms were crossed.

"And her name isn't even Samantha, it's Susan, Susan Jenkins."

Miller just shook his head. "I knew her as Samantha. Please call her that."

"Okay," I took a breath and sat back down. "Let's start from the beginning. So when did you first meet 'Samantha'?" I asked.

"We never met, Sir," he responded quietly in that Southwest Virginian drawl.

I pushed my chair back against the cinder block wall. "Petty Officer Miller, let me get this straight—you spent all this time and effort, and God knows what else you might have done, over someone you never met?" His strange gaze never left mine. I didn't directly ask him the question as I'm not sure I wanted to know the answer.

Then he said slowly, "I don't remember all of it."

I moved closer to him. "Joshua, I talked to Dr. Tanahill. Let me have you tested." Maybe I should have said "officially" tested.

"No, I'm not crazy." How many times had I heard that before? But what he was telling me made no sense.

"Joshua, there is such a thing as a psychotic break. It can be a defense under the law."

"I'm not crazy… I was… ah… just, well, you know…" His voice trailed off. He looked away.

I had represented sailors charged with every variation and degree of crime in my career—some were innocent, most were not. I found those who committed violent crimes were no worse than others; maybe their passions ran higher. Most of the time there was at least some explanation that I could work with, if not for an outright acquittal, then for a finding of guilt to a lesser included offense and thereby a lighter sentence. Victory in the criminal justice system comes in all different forms.

"Okay, let's start from the beginning. How did this, whatever you call it, 'relationship' start?" He looked up with that strange look, as if he heard my words but was processing thoughts in recesses of his brain that I would never reach.

"She called me."

"She called you? Did you know her? Did someone you know, know her?"

"No, Sir."

"Petty Officer Miller, you never met her, you didn't know her, but she's calling you?" I said somewhat confused.

"Sir, I had just checked into the barracks. You know the berthing where all the ISs stayed while in advanced training," he added needlessly. "The phone rang and when I picked it up, the girl on the other end asked for "Christina." He went silent.

I waited several seconds, then said, "And?"

"She sounded nice." I bet she did.

"So what happened?" I knew there was more to the story then he was telling me.

"Well, we began talking every day and night, she sent me pictures..." He hesitated. "We talked about things I never talked about with anyone before."

"But you never met her? Ever?"

"I tried but..." He was silent for a longer period this time. I didn't interrupt. Then he said almost in a whisper, "She said she was raped." He hunched over again with his head hanging down looking at the floor, hands clasped together.

I said as gently as I could, "Joshua, she told me she wasn't raped. She said she was at a party drinking with friends and it was you who kept asking her if she was raped. She said she kept telling you nothing happened but you kept bringing it up." He looked up at me and just shook his head sadly.

I had to know. "Joshua, what happened? Did you kill Corporal Williams?"

He kept shaking his head slowly side to side and finally said in a stronger voice than I expected, "I want to tell my story. I want to take the stand and tell my story. I was protecting her. She was raped."

I pushed my chair back and stood over him. "Joshua, if you do that, they will give you the death penalty." He looked up at me—there again that damn look. "Do you understand me?"

"But, Sir—"

"Damn it, Joshua! Haven't you been listening? There is no body! They can't even prove a murder was committed and you want to take the stand and admit it? They will kill you."

"But, Sir, isn't it my right to testify? You told me it was."

I was angry. "Joshua, you haven't said shit to me all these months and now a few days before the trial is to start you want to take the stand? We have no defense! It wasn't self-defense and 'Samantha' will say she wasn't raped. What do you want me to tell the jury for Christ's sake?"

"I need to explain things to them."

"Joshua, if you take the stand, Commander Dempsey will get to cross-examine you. She will twist every word you say. She will be relentless. If you can't remember something, she will make you out to be a liar." I paused. "And a cold-blooded killer. I can't allow that." I paused again. "I won't allow that."

"It don't matter. I want to take the stand," he insisted.

I exploded. "Damn it, Joshua, they have no evidence tying you directly to any crime. They have a weak eyewitness, a shitty video, a suspect telephone call, and a ring with no identifying marks! And did I mention no body! We can win this case if you just keep your mouth shut! Do you know what a jury will do to you if you testify? You are not taking the stand!"

"We haven't picked a jury yet."

I shot back. "Don't get technical with me. If you get on the stand under oath, both the Trial Counsel and the jury can ask you questions." There was silence. "What will you tell them? That you killed a man, a decorated war hero, a father-to-be, over a woman you never met and who was never raped?"

"I loved her."

"God damn it, Joshua, you never met her!"

"Doesn't make it less real."

I sat back down and took a deep breath. "Okay, maybe you can explain how you felt about Samantha and you were concerned about her being raped. But what evidence did you have that Williams was involved in a crime that even Samantha says never happened?" That look again. He didn't answer.

"Joshua, if you insist on taking the stand, let me at least get you a deal." I was almost pleading.

"I don't want a deal. I just want to tell my story."

I couldn't let that happen.

CHAPTER TWENTY-THREE

THE BAILIFF CALLED THE COURT to order at 12:59 p.m. It was June 15. The most important part of the trial was about to begin—picking the jury. Captain Johnson lumbered through the door that connected his office to the courtroom. Everyone stood. The judge sat down heavily and banged his gavel.

"Please be seated. Good afternoon, everyone. This General Court-Martial will now come to order in the case of *United States versus Intelligence Specialist Third Class Joshua Miller, United States Navy.*" Captain Johnson looked over at the jurors who were seated to his right. "Members of the court, please open the folder that has been provided to you and review the information in it. Ensure that your name appears on the convening order with the correct rank, rate, spelling of your last name, and branch of service. If a correction needs to be made, simply raise your hand." He paused and glanced over to the jury box. No one moved. Satisfied, he continued. "The members will now be sworn."

The Bailiff, a First Class Petty Officer who was temporarily assigned to the Navy Legal Service Office because he was on medical hold and had nothing better to do all day, shouted, "All rise." The members did as directed and were sworn in by the Assistant Trial Counsel Lieutenant Commander Mays.

The Military Judge, trying to sound regal, stated, "This General Court-Martial is assembled. Please be seated." This was beginning to feel like a Catholic mass with everyone standing up and sitting down. "Trial Counsel, is the Government ready to proceed?"

Commander Dempsey stood once again. "Yes, Sir. The Prosecution is ready to proceed with the trial in the case of *United States versus Intelligence Specialist Third Class Joshua Miller.*"

Captain Johnson continued, "Thank you. Members of the court, it is appropriate that I give you some preliminary instructions before we begin. It is my duty as Military Judge to ensure that this trial is conducted in a fair and orderly manner. I will rule upon objections and I will instruct you on the law that applies in this case. You are required to follow my instructions on the law. You may not consult any other source of the law pertaining to this case unless it's admitted into evidence. This rule applies throughout these proceedings, including in your closed-session deliberations and during periods of recess or overnight adjournments. Any questions that you have must be asked of me in open court.

"You will have to determine by legal and competent evidence whether this accused is guilty or not guilty as to each and every element of the crime charged beyond a reasonable doubt. If you find him guilty, your duty will be to determine what punishment, if any, should be imposed as a result of your findings. That duty is a grave responsibility requiring the exercise of wise discretion on your part. Your determination must be based upon all the evidence presented and the instructions I will give you as to the applicable law. Since you cannot properly reach your determination until all the evidence has been presented and you've been instructed, it is of vital importance that you keep an open mind until all the evidence and the instructions have been presented to you.

"With regard to sentencing, if any, you may not have any preconceived idea or formula as to either the type or the amount of punishment that should be adjudged. You must first hear the evidence in mitigation and extenuation as well as any evidence in aggravation, the law with regard to sentencing, and again, only when you are in your closed-session deliberations may you properly make a determination as to an appropriate sentence after considering all the alternative punishments that I will explain to you later.

"While you're in your closed-session deliberations, only members will be present. You must remain together and you may not allow any unauthorized intrusion into your deliberations. Each of you has an equal voice and vote with the other members in discussing and deciding the issues that are submitted to you. The senior member's vote counts as one, the same as the junior members. The senior member will act as your presiding officer during your closed-session deliberations and will speak for the panel in announcing the result of your findings.

"It is the duty of the Trial Counsel, Commander Dempsey and Lieutenant Commander Mays, to represent the Government in the prosecution of this case. It is the duty of the Defense Counsel, Commander DeMarco, to represent the accused.

"In a few minutes, I will pose some questions to you. Counsel will also be given the opportunity to ask you some questions. If you know of any matter that you believe might affect your impartiality to sit as a member during this case, then you must disclose that matter when you are asked to do so. Please bear in mind that any statement you make should be made in general terms so as not to disqualify the other members who might hear it. For example, if you've read a newspaper account of this incident, you should so state. However, you should not state what in particular that you read or any opinion or conclusion you may have arrived at as a result of having read that account. If you believe that what you might say would disqualify another member who hears it, then you should request to make the statement outside of their presence.

"Questions by counsel and by me are not intended to embarrass you, they are not an attack on your integrity, but they're merely asked in order to determine whether a basis for a challenge exists.

"Now there are two types of challenges. One is known as a challenge for cause, that's fairly self-explanatory. The other is known as a peremptory challenge—this gives counsel for both sides the opportunity to excuse one panel member for no reason at all. It's not an adverse reflection on you to be excused from the case. You may be questioned either individually or collectively, but in either event, you should indicate an individual response to any question that's asked. Unless I indicate otherwise, you are required to answer all questions.

"I anticipate the following order of events in this case: voir dire of the members followed by challenges and excusals, then opening statements by each counsel, presentation of the evidence by both sides, closing argument of counsel, and then instructions on the law that you must follow. Thereafter, you will deliberate and announce your verdict.

"I anticipate this case will last the duration of this week and may go into next week. There may be some extended sessions. The appearance and the demeanor of all parties to this trial should reflect the seriousness with which this trial is viewed. Careful attention to all that occurs during the trial is required of all parties. Are there any questions as to these preliminary matters? If so, please raise your hand." No one moved.

"Because of the prior publicity and the probability for more publicity in the news media, you are instructed not to listen to, look at, or read any accounts of the charges involving IS3 Miller.

"You may not consult any source, written or otherwise, on any matter involving this case. Should anyone attempt to discuss this case with you or talk to you about your involvement as a court member, then you must immediately forbid them from doing so and you must report that occurrence to me at the earliest opportunity.

"You're advised that as a member of the military, you are required to follow my instructions and not intentionally do anything contrary to the requirements of my instructions. Are there any questions?" Again, the members sat stone-faced.

"Good. I am now going to put some questions to you as a panel. I'll allow counsel for each side the opportunity to pose additional questions in a few minutes. If your response to my question is 'Yes,' you may do so by simply raising your hand and I'll record your response for the record. If you do not raise your hand, I'll indicate that it is a negative response. If you're asked a question individually, then you should respond verbally.

"Each of you completed a court-martial member questionnaire prior to today's session of the court. Does any member feel the need to correct any information that you provided in those questionnaires or to update the information?"

The jury panel remained silent. If someone shuffled a paper, you would hear it. "Let the record reflect a negative response from the members.

"Does any member know either counsel or the accused in this case?" One of the senior enlisted in the back row fidgeted. He looked familiar. "Let the record reflect a negative response from all.

"I'm going to read to you a long list of approximately twenty names of witnesses who may be called in this case. At the end I will ask if you know any of these people." The judge read through the list of names ranging from police officers, forensic experts, medical personnel, family members, friends, and military coworkers and supervisors. I began to wonder if we could get through this case in a week.

"Does anyone know any of these witnesses?" After a pause, he said, "Let the record reflect a negative response from the members."

The judge then moved into the legal precepts that make our criminal justice system the best in the world. "When you as a member decide whether to believe or disbelieve a witness, you should consider the witness's intelligence, their candor and manner of testifying, their relationship to either side of the case, whether the testimony is corroborated by other evidence, and any other factors from your own experience that would indicate to you whether or not that person is telling the truth.

"Do any of you have any personal prejudices or feeling that would prevent you from weighing the testimony of each witness in this case by the same standards as you would the testimony of all other witnesses?" The judge took a little longer this time, pausing as he looked at each juror. "Let the record reflect a negative response from the members.

"A person's status, such as an officer or a policeman, cannot be used as the sole basis to consider that person's testimony more believable than the testimony of any other witness. However, you may consider that status along with all the other factors when weighing the credibility of the person. Would any of you give the testimony of a law enforcement official, such as a county sheriff or Naval Criminal

Investigative Service agent, any higher credibility solely because of that person's occupation?" I specifically asked for this question at our pretrial conference as many of us are taught from a young age to believe that police officers tell the truth. I knew from experience that wasn't always the case. "That's a negative response from the members.

"Does any member know anything at all about this case?" Several hands went up. It was the first sign of life by the jurors in the last half hour. The judge seemed annoyed.

"We have several hands raised in the first row. We have Lieutenant Faber, Captain Hagan, and Commander Joyner. Captain Hagan, have you read something or has someone mentioned something to you?"

Captain Hagan was the most senior member of the panel. His questionnaire noted he was a Naval Academy grad, was a ship driver with twenty-eight years and was getting ready to retire. I needed to strike him for cause. Academy grads tend to favor the Government. And if he was getting ready to retire, he probably wouldn't care what happened to my client. "I read an article in the *Virginia Pilot* last week. I caught the first two sentences saying a sailor was charged with murder, so I stopped reading when I realized that it might be concerning this trial." No luck.

"Thank you. There was another other hand. Lieutenant Faber?"

"There was a brief article in the 'early bird' edition today from the *New York Times*." I liked him. Anyone who read the editorial page and the op-ed pieces of the *Times* had to be a liberal.

"Okay," said the judge. "We don't need to repeat what it said, but that's the source of your information?" Looking displeased that a naval officer would read such tripe.

"Yes, Sir." The lieutenant didn't look intimidated-definitely a keeper.

The judge was getting ready to move on when Commander Dempsey stood up. "Sir, I believe Commander Joyner also read something." She looked at me with that "just trying to be helpful" look.

"Oh, Commander Joyner, I'm sorry. Thank you. Have you read something or has someone mentioned something to you?"

Commander Joyner spoke with a Southern drawl. Maybe she would relate to my client. "Someone mentioned something to me at work. Nothing specific that I remember." She was safe for now, although senior officers trying to make rank worry me.

"Okay, thank you. Anybody else?" No one spoke. "During the court-martial, it may occur that the testimony of a witness or other evidence offered will cause you to recall something that you may have read or heard about this case that you presently do not recall. If that happens, then you must totally disregard any recollection or impression that you have about that matter just as if you'd never heard it. This applies throughout the court-martial. Is there any member who is unable to follow that instruction?"

We have many legal fictions in our justice system; I wondered how someone could disregard something that they already knew or something they had just recently heard just because the judge told them to do so. You can't "unring" the bell.

Now they were really confused. "Okay, that's a negative response." He moved on quickly as some of the jurors were getting glassy-eyed.

"Does any member have an immediate family member who is employed in law enforcement? Lieutenant Holcomb?"

The lieutenant was young and perky. "Yes, Sir. My husband is a master-at-arms. Oh, wait. Are you referring to civilian or military?"

The judge again looked annoyed. "Both."

"And my brother is a lieutenant with the Virginia Beach Sheriff's Department." I was going to miss her. The judge nodded and continued.

"It appears this case may have extended sessions during the day, as I indicated, and will last at least through this week. When you were assigned as a member of the court-martial, this assignment became your primary duty and takes precedence over all other duties. Having said that, do any of you have official duties or personal matters that you believe might affect your ability to sit as a member due to extended sessions of this court?" No one raised their hand, although I'm sure many of them would have liked to. "That's a negative response from the members."

Next came the question that interested me the most. "You may expect or desire the accused to testify. The accused has an absolute right not to testify. The fact that an accused may elect not to testify in his own behalf may not be considered adverse to him in any way. Is there any member who cannot follow this instruction?" I watched closely to see if I could detect anyone having an issue with that proposition. It was difficult to watch all twelve at one time. Was the Master Chief in the back row uncomfortable with that or was he just shifting in his seat? "Negative response.

"If the accused is found guilty, it will be your duty to determine an appropriate punishment. You must each give fair consideration to the entire range of permissible punishments in this case from the least severe, which would include a mandatory minimum sentence of life in prison with the possibility of parole after twenty years, to the most severe, which is the death penalty. Will each of you be able to give such consideration to the full range of punishments?"

No one moved or said a word; several shifted uncomfortably in their seats. The judge raised his voice. "Members, that is not a trick question." Slowly they all began to nod, a few remembered to raise their hand. "That's an affirmative response from all the members.

"Is there anything at all in your past education, training, or experience, or any other matter, that you feel you would not be able to set aside or would make it difficult or impossible for you to conduct your deliberations in a completely fair, impartial, and unbiased manner?" The judge was moving quickly now; he was getting tired. "Negative response from the members.

"Are any of you aware of anything whatsoever, whether I've touched on it or not, that you feel would have any effect on your ability to sit as a fair and impartial member in this case or that might in any way improperly influence your deliberations in this case?" Silence. The judge said, "Negative response.

"Do any of you feel that you have any religious or other prejudices that would prevent you from serving as a fair and impartial member of this court-martial?" Again silence. "Negative response." The judge leaned back satisfied with himself. "Does the Government desire to conduct voir dire of the members?"

Commander Dempsey rose, straightened her skirt, and walked up to the jury box, no notes in hand. She stared at each of the jurors. "Good afternoon. My name is Commander Nora Dempsey. I represent the United States in its case against the accused." I sat back and admired her as she worked.

"How many of you expect that when a sailor is standing before the CO at NJP he ought to say something for himself?" Where was she going with this? This was normally a line of questioning I would pursue. The members just looked at her; I don't think she cared if they answered. "Do all members understand that in a criminal trial, as the judge just mentioned, the accused has an absolute right to remain silent and say nothing at all?" They all raised their hands. "That's an affirmative response from all members.

"Does everyone understand that should the accused decide not to testify that you cannot hold that against him?" Again everyone raised their hand. "Affirmative response from all the members."

Smart. Dempsey was telling the jury she didn't care if my client testified, that nothing he could say would matter. Plus it protected the Government regarding any issue on appeal. Really smart.

"Members, there are two ways I can present evidence to you. One is called direct evidence—when someone witnesses something for example. The other is called circumstantial evidence. For example, when you wake up in the morning and see that the roadway is wet you can infer circumstantially that it rained last night. Very few crimes are committed in the light of day, so to speak. The law makes no distinction between the two forms of evidence. Does anyone have a problem convicting the accused if most, or even all, of the Government's evidence is circumstantial yet you feel we have proven our case?" No one seemed to have an issue with that. As I've said, military juries are smart. "That's a negative response by all.

"Members, do you understand that the Government doesn't have to prove that there was a motive for this crime?" Now the members appeared confused again. Isn't there always a motive? Nora continued. "We may never know what happened or why in this case?" That was smart because a body still hadn't been found. Hesitantly, twelve hands went up.

"There are only three possible punishments for murder in this court: confinement for life with the eligibility for parole after twenty years, confinement for life without the eligibility for parole, or"—she paused for dramatic effect—"death." She emphasized the word. "If selected as a court member, could you impose the death penalty if the circumstances warranted it?" More quickly than I would have liked, they all nodded and raised their hand. "Let the record reflect an affirmative response from all.

"Thank you, members. Judge, that's all I have." She sat down. Short, sweet, and to the point.

"Does the Defense desire to conduct voir dire of the panel?"

I stood and approached the podium that had been placed before the jury box. "Thank you, Judge. Good morning, members. My name is Commander Mike Demarco. I'm going to ask you a few additional questions. I'll try not to go over the same topics covered in the questions you've already been asked."

It was time to educate the jury and let them know who was in control of the courtroom. "This portion of the trial, as you've heard, is called voir dire. It means 'to speak the truth.' My questions are not designed to place you on the spot or to embarrass you in any way. What I'm trying—what we're all trying—to do is to determine if you have any strongly held views or life experiences that may make it difficult for you to sit as a member in this case. Please remember there are no right or wrong answers, only open and honest ones. And if I ask you a question and it's not clear to you what I'm asking, please let me know and I'd be glad to rephrase it.

"As you've already seen, I go last. This is because under our system of justice, the Government has the burden of proof. So the first question I have is, will you be able to wait until you hear all the evidence in this case before you make your decision as to what is the appropriate disposition?" They all seemed engaged, which was a good sign, and raised their hands. "Let the record reflect an affirmative response by all."

I had to be careful with the next question knowing what I just learned from my client. "Does anyone believe that just because we're at a General Court-Martial, IS3 Miller is guilty before hearing any of the evidence?" They all shook their head. "That's a negative response from all the members as well.

"As the Military Judge just informed you, the maximum sentence "*if*", and I emphasized the word *if*, you find Petty Officer Miller guilty is the death penalty. The minimum sentence is life imprisonment with the eligibility for parole after a certain period of time. Would anyone have difficulty with someone who was convicted of murder being eligible for parole one day?" Several on the panel again began to fidget in their seats. It was time for me to bail them out.

"Let me put it this way, and we may never get to the sentencing phase." Well, I guess that was true enough. Commander Dempsey could suddenly develop amnesia and forget how to try a case. "Would each of you agree to listen to all the evidence, particularly any in extenuation or mitigation or any motivating factors behind this event, before you decided on your verdict?" Commander Dempsey was now looking strangely at me. I had to be careful; I couldn't tip my hand, nor could I be dishonest. The panel liked this question much better. All raised their hands. "That's a positive response from all members.

"Will everyone take into consideration Petty Officer Miller's age, his background, his motivation, in other words, the entire defense's evidence before deciding on an appropriate verdict?" Now Nora was positively staring at me. I was walking a thin line. "That's a positive response by all members.

"If a witness testifies that he or she acted in certain way that you personally wouldn't have acted, would that automatically make you discredit that testimony or would you be able to listen to the circumstances behind why that person acted the way they did?" Several of the members desired clarification on that question.

"Okay, I'm sorry. I'll try to simplify that question. If somebody testifies that he acted a certain way and you personally wouldn't have acted in that way or might not even understand someone who acted that way, would that fact alone make you discredit that person's testimony?" I don't think that cleared it up but no one said anything. "That's a negative response by all members.

"Does anyone know someone who's had a romantic interest online?" I doubted anyone of this panel would, but you never know until you ask. Now everyone in the courtroom was looking at me. I didn't wait for a reaction from the jury and quickly moved on.

"I know we all come to this courtroom with personal opinions and personal feelings about how things should be, particularly within the criminal justice system. Will everyone be able to set aside those personal feelings and be able to follow the judge's instructions when he gives them to you at the end of the case?" They all quickly raised their hands. "That's a positive response by all members.

"Evidence will be presented in a variety of ways over the next several days. Some people will give live testimony. Some will be by sworn statement. A lot of evidence will be circumstantial. I will ask you to examine that evidence very carefully." I paused and looked over at Commander Dempsey. "As mentioned, Petty Officer Miller, under the rights afforded by the Constitution, doesn't even have to testify or can even make an unsworn statement, which is one of the ways authorized under the *Rules of Courts-Martial*. Would anyone have a problem if Petty Officer Miller didn't testify or gave an unsworn statement in lieu of live testimony?" I knew they were thinking: if he's innocent, wouldn't he want to testify? "That's a negative response from the members.

"One last question. There isn't a body in this case. One hasn't been found." The members began looking at each other, then to the judge, and then to Commander Dempsey. "Yup, that's right—no body. Will the members take that into consideration when you begin your deliberations?" I didn't wait for a response. I hurried back to my table and sat down. "Thank you, Judge, that's all the questions I have."

I had gotten off to a good start. It wouldn't last.

CHAPTER TWENTY-FOUR

WE HAD FINALLY SELECTED THE jury. It was late afternoon. You could see the dust particles rising through the rays of sunlight which peeked through the windows on either side of the judge's bench. All was still. I sat at counsel table with my hands clasped in my lap, staring straight ahead. I waited for the jury to reenter the courtroom. Opening statements were about to begin.

I could sense Miller beside me. He didn't move. There was a small railing behind us with an opening that separated the public from the trial arena, the place where the judge, jury, prosecutor, court reporter, and witness box were located. Behind the railing, seated closest to the jury, was the Williams family sitting quietly.

The parents were from the Midwest, sitting closely together holding each other's hand, their eyes downcast. His wife, young and pretty, was hugging their newborn child to her chest, a baby Lance Corporal Williams would never get to hold. They would eventually be witnesses.

The jurors entered slowly and took their assigned seats. You could hear their chairs creak as they sat. The silence continued.

After a few seconds, Captain Johnson nodded to Commander Dempsey who rose and walked confidently to the podium. She gave a slight smile to the judge. "May it please the court." Then looking over her left shoulder, she nodded to me. "Counsel." She paused and looked directly at the jurors. "Members of the jury." She came from around the podium and walked slowly toward the jury box, placing both hands on the railing when she reached it. Nora took her time as she looked each juror in the eye. She was in control.

"There is no body." She paused again for effect. "Does that matter?" Another pause, longer this time. "Not really." She stepped back placing her hands on her hips. "You see, Lance Corporal Williams was an outstanding Marine. An outstanding person." She walked over and stood in front of the family. "An outstanding son, husband, and father-to-be. He wouldn't have left his post. He wouldn't have walked away from his responsibilities, from his duty. Something happened to him." She turned and pointed toward my client. "And that something was IS3 Miller." She held out her arm longer than I thought necessary, but this was Nora's time.

"So this will not be a trial about 'who done it' or a 'murder mystery.' The one thing you will know at the end of the Government's case is who did it. Of that I will assure you." Nora began to pace back and forth in front of the jury box.

"Now I'll be honest with you. I'll admit right up front that there will be some circumstantial evidence in this case. But I'm going to ask you, and I believe the Military Judge will instruct you, to use your common sense when reviewing that evidence. If you do, you will find that it is the accused, Intelligence Specialist Joshua Miller, who is the murderer. Of this, there will be no doubt.

"Why do I say this? It's simple. Just connect the dots. Here are the undisputed facts," she said as she stopped walking and turned once again to face the jury. She raised the index finger of her left hand.

"Shortly, before Christmas break, during exam week, a person alleging to be an NCIS agent went to Lance Corporal Williams barracks asking to see him. We don't know why or what was said. We later learn that Williams thought someone had accused him of rape. However, a check with the local NCIS office shows that there was no active rape investigation ongoing, no agent assigned to interview Lance Corporal Williams, and no crime whatsoever in which Williams was involved. We will call to the witness stand the barracks petty officer who was on duty that evening who will tell you that the alleged agent bore a remarkable resemblance to the accused."

Nora raised the second finger. "Next, we will introduce into evidence telephone records showing a call was made from outside barracks 508, the barracks where Petty Officer Miller lived, to Williams's room in the early morning hours of New Year's Day. Again, we don't know why or what was said."

Her third finger went up. "Then you will see a surveillance video of the parking lot outside of Corporal Williams barracks from that night which shows a vehicle with a license plate bearing the letter B and the number 1, letters and numbers that match the license plate of the accused vehicle, leaving the parking lot with Lance Corporal Williams in it."

Dempsey paused. "Members, Defense Counsel may try to make you believe that this is a difficult case, a circumstantial case, that these events are all coincidences. He may try to offer you plausible explanations for the evidence. But I know you will find that there is simply no logical explanation that anyone else was involved. Miller is the murderer."

She began pacing again. "Now why did this terrible crime occur? Unfortunately, I can offer you no good reason, absolutely none. If you are looking for any logic in this case, you are not going to find it. But remember, the Government doesn't have to prove motive. Jonathan Williams may have simply been in the wrong place at the wrong time. Maybe there was some beef between the two. Maybe not. Who knows? We don't know what chain of events brought the accused and Jonathan together. But something did and now Jonathan Williams is dead.

"Members, at the conclusion of evidence, after you find the accused guilty, we will proceed into the sentencing phase. You already know that there are only three options in regards to punishment. The Government is going to ask that you award Miller the punishment that the facts of this case demand.

"The murder of another human being is the most heinous crime in our ordered society. What should the punishment be for someone who kills another who is so totally innocent of any wrongdoing? During your deliberations, ask yourself that question. Ask yourself what is fair and what is just and you will know the answer." She again paused. "You will know."

The courtroom was deathly silent as she walked slowly back to her counsel table where she stood for a moment, looking at the jurors before she sat down.

The Military Judge looked over at me and perfunctorily asked, "Defense Counsel, do you have an opening statement?"

I stood and looked at the jury, then at the judge and finally to Commander Dempsey, who sat patiently waiting to hear what I would say. Then I did something I had never done before in my legal career.

"Judge, I would like to reserve my opening statement."

CHAPTER TWENTY-FIVE

I REACHED DOWN AND SNAGGED my briefcase as I rushed past Miller, who sat looking after me, confused. As I ran out the back of the courtroom door, I barely heard the judge declare a recess until the next day.

Once in the hallway, I pushed past several of the court personnel who were loitering there. As I hurried down the passageway, I sensed Commander Dempsey close behind me. I was almost at the elevators when I heard her yell, "Mike! What are you doing?" I kept going. "You heard me! Michael! Wait!" Everyone had stopped what they were doing and were now staring at us.

I slowed and then turned to face her. She came within inches of me glaring up into my face. Her words came quickly. "Michael, you can't do this! You can't waive your opening. It's just not done. Certainly not in a capital murder case." Her eyes were wide. She was pleading with me. What could I say to her?

"Nora, you don't know," I responded weakly, trying to back away. She wouldn't let me. People began to move back into their offices, uncomfortable witnessing a confrontation between two senior officers in a public hallway.

"I don't know what? Tell me." Her voice remained loud. I wouldn't have been surprised if she punched me. I looked her in the eyes but remained silent, a dozen thoughts swirling around in my head. "Michael, you have given the jury nothing. Nothing! They don't even know what your side of the story is. What are they going to think?" I knew damn well what they were going to think. That this bastard is guilty and the Government has all the evidence needed to convict him, circumstantial or not. Once people make up their minds, it's hard to change their opinion. Studies show that 70 percent of jurors have decided if the accused is guilty or not after opening statements—before they hear any evidence!

After a few seconds, I said quietly, "Nora, I can't. I can't talk about it. I have to think. I'll see you tomorrow… and thanks." I turned and continued down the hall and into the elevator. Dempsey followed me.

Once inside I pushed the button for the second floor. I leaned against the back wall, hands stuffed in my pockets, and looked up at the ceiling. Nora stood in front of the closed doors, looking at me with an inquisitive look on her face. Neither of us spoke.

The door opened and I brushed past her. She turned and followed me out. It was unusual for a senior prosecutor to be seen on the second deck. I was in no mood to point out this breach of etiquette. Besides, she was just being a friend.

I started to turn left to go to my office but stopped and looked back toward Nora. I said, "I appreciate your concern. I really do. It's just… well, I gotta sort some stuff out." Nora only nodded her hands on her hips.

She continued to stare after me as I hurried away.

CHAPTER TWENTY-SIX

NORA TURNED RIGHT AND INSTEAD of getting back in the elevator took the stairs down to her office on the first floor. She walked past her doorway and kept on going. She had to get out of the building. It was too confining. Nora exited the back door at the end of the hallway and into the parking lot that was reserved for judges and senior officers. She jumped into her black BMW Z3 Roadster, which she had parked next to the building in a no parking area.

As Dempsey settled into the driver's seat, she noticed both hands were tightly gripping the steering wheel. She paused and let out a deep breath. She looked around the interior of the car. After a few seconds, she found the button that lowered the convertible top. She relaxed as it was lowered. Nora knew she had to have this car after seeing it in the James Bond movie *Golden Eye*. She was a big Bond fan. Nora put the car in gear and quickly sped out of the parking lot. She drove the short distance to the guard shack and then out the front gate. She needed to get to the interstate, step on the throttle, and feel the wind in her hair.

"What was he thinking?" she wondered. And why did she care? She liked DeMarco. They went back a long way. And he was a damn good lawyer. What was going on in his head?

It was the beginning of summer and the early evening air felt good on her face. The sun was starting to set. It would be too soon before the tourists begun to arrive and she would be heading back to DC with all the congestion and politics.

Nora Dempsey was born to be a prosecutor. When she was eight years old, her family moved to Fayetteville, North Carolina, a city of less than one hundred thousand, located in the Sand Hill region of the state on the Cape Fear River. Her dad, a Navy doctor, was transferred to Womack Army Medical Center, home of the Eighty-Second Airborne, the "All-Americans," to treat soldiers with PTSD. Their motto "All the Way" suited her. She would often accompany her father on his rounds and to many of the command functions. She learned how true warriors handled themselves.

Dempsey was tough. When she played her older brothers in basketball, she never asked, or gave, any quarter. Calling fouls was for sissies. If Nora got knocked down, she immediately got up. And heaven help the next brother that tried to drive the lane. If she was bleeding, she wiped the blood off on her sleeve. In high school, Dempsey competed in every sport that was available to her, earning all-state honors in soccer, basketball, and softball. Even though girls weren't allowed to wrestle the boys, coach wanted her on the team; the school board said a girl might get hurt. Little did they know.

Nora was recruited by several major colleges. She wanted to play soccer for the University of North Carolina at Chapel Hill. Carolina had won several National Championships in women's soccer. While eating in the cafeteria during her recruiting visit, she unexpectedly met the lacrosse coach. Up to that point, the Tar Heels had accomplished very little in the sport. The coach shared with Nora her vision to one day challenge the traditional powerhouses in the Ivy League and Big East. The prospect of doing something no one else had yet done appealed to Dempsey, so even though she had never played lacrosse, she signed a letter of intent right then and there. Just another way to prove herself. Dempsey quickly became dangerous with a stick in her hand, ending her career as a four-year starter being named a member of the women's national team her junior and senior year.

After graduation it was on to law school, where she excelled as expected, and then into the military to serve her country like everyone else in her family.

Dempsey valued a worthy opponent. Competition brought out the best in her. Her world was simple; it was either black or white. You were either right or you were wrong. You did your job or you didn't. No excuses. Oftentimes she found herself giving lip service to the ideals of the prosecutor's office—that they were there to see that "justice" was served, that they represented the "conscience of the community." Nora wanted to win—just like most lawyers. That's what she liked about the courtroom. It was a sports competition in a suit and tie, or in this case, a uniform. And at the end of the day, you knew the score—who won or who lost. Dempsey was always testing herself against others and rarely came up short.

This temporary assignment suited her. When Nora learned that DeMarco was on the case and that he was giving the younger attorneys a hard time, she quickly volunteered. She met DeMarco while in Newport and they became fast friends. There were thoughts of a romantic interest, but there was no time. They had some fun together, but each was more interested in advancing their own career.

Nora was working in the appellate court division in Washington, DC, and only took this assignment because of the heightened visibility. Nora Dempsey fully intended to be the Judge Advocate General of the Navy, a two-star admiral, one day. But this was a capital murder case and even a rookie defense counsel defending a simple assault case didn't waive his opening statement, even if his client was guilty.

Dempsey didn't want to win this trial by default. She had heard rumors that DeMarco was getting out of the military, but she couldn't imagine him just mailing it in. Michael was just too good an attorney. Nora had come to know many lawyers who didn't want to put in the time and make the sacrifices that it took to be a good trial lawyer. If you had a big case, you thought about it all the time. It consumed you. But DeMarco was probably the best trial lawyer the Navy had. He didn't mind the work.

Should she talk to him in private? Was that even ethical? Not that it would stop her. Nora did what she thought was right, damn the consequences. And this just wasn't right.

What was going on in his head? Nora stepped on the accelerator. The miles slipped on by. Finally, she decided she couldn't worry about DeMarco any longer. The evidentiary part of the trial started tomorrow. She had to be ready.

Nora kept driving.

CHAPTER TWENTY-SEVEN

"PETTY OFFICER SMITH, YOU TOLD Commander Dempsey on direct that you were working the front desk of the marine barracks the evening on December 21, correct?" It was Thursday morning. Nora had started off with her "eyewitness." She wanted to establish right up front that it was Miller who had committed this horrendous crime. I had to cast some doubt in the jury's mind.

"Correct, yes, Sir."

"And what time did you say you reported for duty?" I moved closer to him.

"At 1600 hours, Sir. It's an eight-hour shift." When witnesses were nervous, they volunteered information I hadn't asked for. Once they started anticipating my questions, I had them.

"And your final exam was the next day at 0800, is that correct?"

"Yes, Sir."

"I believe you said it was in propulsion systems?"

"Yes, Sir."

"That's a pretty complicated subject, isn't it, Petty Officer? You are dealing with the power requirements of a ship, the rate of revolutions of the screw, the ship's hull form, displacement, block coefficient, propeller design, flow conditions—topics such as those, correct?"

He just started at me wondering how a lawyer would know the intricate workings of a ship. He slowly answered, "Ah... yes, Sir." I needed him to know I was in control; the best way to do that was to show him I had done my homework.

"So when you got off work at midnight, you probably still had several more hours of studying to do, did you not?"

He proudly answered, "I think I pulled an all-nighter, Sir."

I smiled, thinking back to all those late nights in law school. "I remember those days. Every minute you get to study is important, isn't it?"

"Yes, Sir. You got it." He nodded.

"Because you needed to make a good grade in that class to get your Surface Warfare pin, correct?" He smiled and straightened his shoulders a little. I could see he had done well as he was wearing the Enlisted Surface Warfare Specialist insignia with its silver cutlasses behind the hull of a ship over his breast pocket. Historically, cutlasses were traditionally the sidearm of enlisted men; swords were for officers. An enlisted man who wore the ESWS pin had put in a lot of hours and should be proud.

"Yes, Sir."

"Congratulations." It didn't hurt to make a friend of the witnesses whenever you could. "And I imagine you had been studying for days and hadn't gotten much sleep?"

"Not much, Sir." He was feeling comfortable, so I decided to get to the point.

"Petty Officer, you testified that a few minutes after you came on duty, a person in suit came into the barracks?"

"Yes, Sir."

"And he identified himself as an NCIS agent?"

"Correct, Sir."

"But he never showed you a badge or any other type of identification?"

The petty officer looked embarrassed. "No, Sir." He knew he had screwed up and hadn't followed procedures. It was apparent he was more concerned with his test the next day.

I decided to let him off the hook and get him back on my side again before the really important questions were asked. "Well, everything was quiet in the barracks, it was exam week, everyone was studying, so there was no reason to think anything unusual was going to happen, was there?"

"Yes, Sir, absolutely. Everything was very quiet, Sir." He was thankful for the lifeline.

"So, Petty Officer Smith, isn't it true that you really didn't get a good look at the person claiming to be the NCIS agent?"

He didn't hesitate. "Yes, Sir. I guess that's true."

"You can't even be sure what color suit he had on, can you?"

"No, Sir."

"Can't be sure how tall he was, the color of his hair, really any specifics about the person at all, can you?"

"I guess not. No, Sir."

"Would it be fair to say, Petty Officer, that the entire encounter with this person took less than fifteen seconds when your attention was really directed elsewhere?"

He paused. "Yes, Sir. I guess that's fair to say."

"So you can't say beyond a reasonable doubt that the person you saw was IS3 Joshua Miller, can you?"

Again, he hesitated. "No, Sir."

"Even if your life depended on it?" Miller's did. There was silence in the courtroom. The witness just shook his head.

"No further questions." I looked at the jury then turned and walked back to my table.

I wondered if they would all be that easy.

CHAPTER TWENTY-EIGHT

COMMANDER DEMPSEY APPROACHED SPECIAL AGENT Hansen once again. He tried not to stare at her legs as she approached. Hansen had been on the witness stand for almost an hour. It was almost time for lunch.

"May the record reflect I am handing Special Agent Hansen what has previously been marked as 'Prosecution Exhibit Number Four for Identification.' Agent Hansen, do you recognize this?"

"Yes, Ma'am. It's the surveillance video taken from the parking lot in front of the marines BEQ."

"And what is the time period of that video?"

"The evening of Friday, December 31, through the early morning hours of Saturday, January 1."

"Do all parking lots on the Naval Station utilize surveillance video?"

"Yes, Ma'am. We began about four years ago. There was a rash of break-ins with the student vehicles, so the Captain ordered cameras installed."

"Were you the agent responsible for obtaining this video?"

"Yes, Ma'am."

"Has it been in your custody the entire time?"

"Yes, Ma'am. I have the chain custody document if you'd like to see it." She looked over at me; I shook my head. Hansen continued, "After I pulled it from the camera, I went directly to the lab. I was also the agent responsible for analyzing the video."

"Captain, if it pleases the court, pursuant to our pretrial motion, we would like to show a segment of this video to the members."

"Any objection, Commander?"

I rose. "No objection, Your Honor." We had already argued over the tapes admissibility and I had lost. So if you have nothing to give, give it graciously, I thought.

Commander Dempsey stepped to the side. The video began to play on the big screen, which had been erected in front of the jury. Several members leaned forward to get a better look. I got up from my counsel table and walked to the wall at the back of the jury box so I could see exactly what the jury was seeing.

"Now, Special Agent Hansen, could you take us through the video, focusing particularly on the time period 0320 through 0345?"

"Yes, Ma'am. As you can see—"

Dempsey stopped him. "Excuse me, Special Agent Hansen, can you tell us why the quality of the video is not that good and why there is no date shown?" It was smart of Nora to point out the weaknesses in her evidence before I had the chance to do so.

"Yes, Ma'am. The video stream runs in a continuous loop every seventy-two hours. If there is nothing to review, it gets taped over. Since we didn't get a report of a missing marine until mid-January, the loop had run through approximately seven times. We had to go back and remove several layers of video imagery and try to pull the old images off. I estimated the date given a fixed starting point of the date I obtained the video and worked backward. Because I had to remove several layers, the quality is not as good as we'd like it to be."

"Thank you, Special Agent, you can continue."

"Yes, Ma'am. As you see there's a vehicle, it appears to be a pickup, but I'm not really sure, leaving the outer boundaries of the parking lot at approximately 0332."

Dempsey looked at him sternly. They had talked about his uncertainty as to the type of vehicle during his trial prep. Dempsey didn't like uncertainties in her case. "Were you able to identify the license plate on the vehicle?"

"Yes, Ma'am. As you can see from the next frame"—Hansen paused the video and enhanced the picture—"which is blown up approximately tenfold, you can make out the letters B and the number 1." Before he could help himself, he continued, "Even though it's kinda grainy."

Dempsey certainly didn't like her witnesses to ad-lib. She gave him another stare before continuing. "And did you run all the license plates for vehicles of the recruits in the Training Command through the DMV data base to determine if any vehicle had a similar combination in their plates?"

"Yes, Ma'am, I did. Approximately ten vehicles showed up with that combination in their license plate."

"Were you able to match the appearance of the vehicle you saw in the video with any of the ten vehicles whose license plate had that combination of number and letter?"

"Yes, Ma'am, I was."

"Did you then pull the registration information for that vehicle and match it to any specific student?"

"Yes, Ma'am, I did."

Special Agent Hansen hesitated for a moment; he knew that Commander Dempsey was almost finished with her direct, which meant I would get a chance to cross-examine him. He'd been there before.

"And…"

"Well, Ma'am, to the best of my ability, I narrowed it down to Petty Office Joshua Miller."

Dempsey stood in front of him with her hands on her hips. Hansen didn't think she was pleased. "Thank you, Special Agent. Please answer any questions Commander DeMarco may have of you."

I stood and approached the well of the courtroom. "Good morning, Special Agent Hansen." I smiled at him.

"Good morning, Sir." Hansen smiled back.

"You did all this work, I think you used the term 'to the best of my ability.' Is that the term you used?"

"Ah, I believe so, yes, Sir."

"And you would agree with me that no one is infallible, are they, Special Agent Hansen?"

"I would have to agree with that, Sir."

"Certainly not me… and not you either, I suppose?"

"Objection!" Dempsey was on her feet.

"I'll withdraw the question, Your Honor." Having made my point, I moved on. "Now, would you agree with me, Agent Hansen, that the quality of this surveillance video is not very good?"

"Yes, Sir, it is not as clear as I'd like it."

"And you *estimated*," I emphasized the word, "the date on the video, is that correct?"

"Well, Sir, that's a good estimate based on—"

I cut him off. "Special Agent Hansen, please just answer my question. The date is an estimate, is it not?"

"Yes."

"Thank you. And would you also agree with me that the year, make, and model of the vehicle shown are uncertain?"

He looked over at Dempsey. "That's true, Sir."

"So you cannot say with any *certainty*," again I emphasized the word, "whether it's a Chevrolet, Ford, Dodge, or whatever?"

Hansen again glanced over at Dempsey. "Yes, Sir, that is correct."

"And I believe on direct you were not even certain it was a pickup truck were you?" Hansen couldn't look at Dempsey again but rather stared straight ahead.

"Ah… that's correct, Sir."

"And, Special Agent Hansen, isn't it true that there are over five hundred vehicles in the recruit training barrack parking lots at any one time?"

"Yes, Sir, that's a pretty good," he paused and gave me a slight grin, "estimate."

I had to appreciate his quick wit. I continued, "And a license plate usually has seven numbers or letters, correct?"

"Yes, Sir, that's correct."

"And you were able to identify only two on this license plate, is that correct, Agent Hansen?"

"Only two, Sir."

"So you were able to identify less than 30 percent of the characteristics on that plate?"

"I guess that's correct, yes, Sir."

"Special Agent Hansen, let me ask you this. If there are twenty-six letters in the alphabet and ten prime numbers used by the DMV, there are thirty-six distinct possibilities for each of the seven characters used on a license plate. Correct?

"Yes, Sir," Hansen answered warily.

"Assuming the same character can appear multiple times, what would be the total number of combinations you could have on a license plate?"

Hansen had to smile. He knew he would get at least one question he couldn't answer. He sat back in his chair. "Sir, I imagine the possibilities would be endless."

"Yes, I imagine they would be." I nodded and started to walk back to my table. I paused and turned back toward him. "Actually, Special Agent Hansen, it would be over seventy-eight billion."

Nora shot out of her chair. "Objection!" Hansen just shook his head.

The judge angrily replied, "Sustained."

I moved on to a different topic. "Special Agent Hansen, you also testified that you reviewed the telephone records from Corporal Williams's room correct?"

"Yes, Sir."

"And a telephone call was made to him on the night of his disappearance a little after 0300 from a telephone stand located outside of Barracks 508, correct?"

"Yes, Sir, that's what the records showed."

"And would you agree with me that there are also an endless number of possibilities regarding who could have made that telephone call?"

Hansen just looked at me without answering, knowing he had, once again, been boxed into a corner.

I moved back to the video. "Agent Hansen, let's take a look at that video again." I hurried over to the screen and pressed the play button. "Doesn't it appear to you that Lance Corporal Williams is voluntarily getting into that vehicle with whoever is driving? He doesn't appear to be forced or coerced, does he?"

"Ah... no, Sir."

"And we don't know where the two of them were going, do we? Could be hunting, to a friend's house, to a party?"

Dempsey again jumped to her feet. "Objection! That calls for speculation."

"Yes, it does," I agreed with her while looking at the jury.

"Sustained," bellowed Captain Johnson for the second time.

I paused, then turned from the witness stand and began walking toward my counsel table. Hansen thought he was finished with his testimony when I suddenly stopped and turned back toward him one last time.

"Special Agent Hansen, you found a thin silver ring in a desk drawer in Petty Officer Miller's room, didn't you?" Hansen stared at me, stunned. "But you didn't testify about that, did you?" Before he could answer, I quickly sat down.

"Thank you, no further questions."

The afternoon session was going to get interesting.

CHAPTER TWENTY-NINE

I was hoping to out maneuver Dempsey. Corporal Williams's wife was on the witness list, but I knew Nora didn't want to call her. She had been through enough. Now I had forced her hand. It was a calculated risk.

Even though the ring was the only tangible evidence linking Williams and Miller together, it was tenuous at best—like all the Government's evidence so far. Dempsey hadn't even mentioned it; now she had no choice. If she didn't call the wife to testify about the ring, the jury would wonder why now that they knew about it. What was she hiding? If she did, I hoped my cross-examination would dramatically point out another, and perhaps final, weakness in the Government's case. Jury's don't like it when you over reach.

Jessica Williams was only twenty years old, but she looked younger. Her dark hair was pulled straight back. Dempsey didn't have her on the stand long. She leaned forward intently as I rose.

"Mrs. Williams, I understand how difficult this is for you." I couldn't concede that her husband was dead, yet I needed to show some compassion for this young mother who had suffered through so much. She just nodded.

"Mrs. Williams, Commander Dempsey showed you a ring that you identified as the one your husband wore, correct?"

Again, she just nodded.

"And is it your understanding that this ring was found in an empty desk drawer in my client barracks room?"

"Yes," she answered quietly.

"Did you know that Petty Officer Miller had only been a resident in that room for a few weeks?"

She hesitated. "I'm not sure."

"Do you realize that many people can live or visit that room in a year's time?" She just shrugged, clearly uncomfortable with my questions. Who could blame her?

I moved closer and asked her gently, "So, Mrs. Williams, would you agree with me that there is no way to know for sure how long that ring had been in that desk drawer or even who put it there?"

It was a risky question. She could answer that she didn't agree with me, that the ring had been in the drawer only as long as her husband had been missing and that it was Miller who put it there; I didn't think she would react that quickly given the stress she was under. However, before I had a chance to be concerned, Commander Dempsey rose, trying to protect her witness. "Objection to the compound question, Your Honor."

"I'll move on, Judge." I had made my point and was glad I didn't have to find out how she would answer.

"Mrs. Williams, there were no identifying marks on the ring, such as initials or wording of any kind were there?"

In a small voice, she answered simply, "No, Sir," seeming to shrink within herself.

"And, Mrs. Williams, you testified that you and your husband bought a ring at a kiosk at Lynnhaven Mall shortly before he deployed?"

She straightened up and, with some defiance this time, answered, "Yes, Sir, as I said we were going to save up our money while he was in Afghanistan, and when he returned, we were going to buy real matching wedding bands." I wanted to cut her off and ask her to just answer my question, but I couldn't do that without looking like a real bastard.

"Yes, Ma'am, I understand. But wouldn't it be true that if you and your husband bought a ring at a mall kiosk that hundreds, or perhaps even thousands, of others might have bought a similar ring?"

"But I know that's his ring, it's the size he wore," she pleaded.

"Yes, Ma'am. But out of all those people who might have bought a ring at that kiosk, or a similar kiosk in any mall in this country, a great number would also wear a size 11 ring, wouldn't they?" She was looking around the courtroom for help, not knowing how to answer. I didn't want to inflict any more pain on this helpless woman.

"Thank you, Ma'am. I have no further questions."

Some days I really didn't like my job.

CHAPTER THIRTY

THE JURY WAS WAITING IN the deliberation room. It was late Friday morning. Dempsey had gotten through her other witnesses, class-mates who were with Williams before his disappearance, local police officers who had checked the local hospitals and jails, custodians of DMV and other records. Dempsey had tied up all the loose ends she could and the Government had rested its case.

A motion for a finding of not guilty is made by the Defense after the Prosecution has finished presenting its evidence. You are asking the judge to dismiss the Government's case because they failed to prove one or more of the essential elements of the crimes charged. If you are right, the judge is required to dismiss the charges.

It sounds better than it is. In real life, the motion is rarely, if ever, granted—particularly in major felony cases. Nowadays, most young defense counsels don't even bother making the motion. If they do, it's a mere formality. Personally, I think it's seldom granted because most judges were former prosecutors and don't want to embarrass any member of the club. But maybe I'm jaded. It might also be that prosecutors are so anal they are too afraid not to dot every *i* and cross every *t*.

Practically, there is usually some evidence which allows the case to go forward. I can count on the fingers of one hand how many times I've actually had the motion granted. And in a major felony case, not to mention a capital murder, should a judge grant such a motion there would be hell to pay all around. Well, except for the defense counsel and his client! For a prosecutor it's the most anxious time of the trial.

"Does the Defense have any motions to make?" Captain Johnson said in a bored voice, not really expecting me to ask for, or if past history was any indication, was I anticipating him to grant, my motion to dismiss the Government's case. But this time was different; this time I didn't think he could ignore me. Although part of me wished he would.

I had poked a bunch of holes in the Government's case. There was doubt. Plenty of it, I thought. But was it enough? And what was I going to do with Joshua if the case went forward? He desperately wanted to tell his story. How would I feel if he went free? How would I feel if he didn't? I glanced over at him before I stood. He sat there with a blank expression on his face.

"Your Honor, under Rule 917 of *The Rules for Courts-Martial*, the Defense respectfully requests that the Military Judge grant a motion for a finding of not guilty regarding all charges and their supporting specifications." God, of all times for Judge Johnson to summarily disregard me, now was the time.

Captain Johnson wore a pained expression. Even a lawyer with his limited legal abilities knew where I was headed. He blew out both his cheeks. "Counsel, do you wish to be heard on the motion?" Well, not really!

"Captain, the Government's case, as you are well aware from the beginning, is totally circumstantial." I couldn't help myself. "First, and I guess this is fairly obvious, there is no body. There is a questionable disappearance but no body. For any number of reasons, Lance Corporal Williams got into a vehicle with someone on New Year's Day. The video is clear"—or maybe not so, I wanted to add—"that he wasn't forced—he just left. Maybe he was fed up with the Marine Corps, maybe he was suffering from the effects of PTSD, maybe he was going on an excursion, and maybe he just didn't want to face the responsibilities of fatherhood." It pained me to say that. "We just don't know."

I took a breath and continued. "And there is no credible physical evidence linking my client to Corporal Williams. There is only a ring, a ring like a thousand others, with no identifying marks, found in a desk drawer in a room that had several occupants and an untold number of visitors throughout the year.

"Further, there is no evidence that my client and Lance Corporal Williams even knew each other, no eyewitness identification linking the two. The barracks petty officer readily admits, and I quote, 'if his life depended on it,' that he could not identify the person who came to see Corporal Williams in late December.

"Apparently, there was a telephone call in the early morning hours on New Year's Day from outside the barracks where the new recruits reside. A telephone booth that is accessible to thousands of sailors." I was taking a little liberty with the evidence, but I was getting worked up. "We know young sailors and marines come and go at all hours of the day and night for a variety of reasons.

"The only connection, and its tenuous at best, that the Government has linking my client to this crime is a grainy parking lot surveillance video showing a vehicle leaving the parking lot of Corporal Williams's barracks, we think, in the early morning hours of his disappearance. However, as I pointed out on cross-examination of the NCIS agent, there is no date stamp on the surveillance video. And perhaps most importantly, we can't determine with any certainty the year, make, or model of the vehicle Lance Corporal Williams got into or if that vehicle was even involved in his disappearance. The only connection this vehicle has to my client is two digits on the license plate bearing the letter B and the number 1, the two most common characteristics on license plates in this country." I noticed Judge Johnson nodding in agreement and started getting a sick feeling in the pit of my stomach. I was doing what I was trained to do but wasn't feeling very good about it.

I could go on no further, so I abruptly sat down. "Thank you," was all I could muster. Miller just looked at me—he didn't appear too happy either.

I glance over at Nora, who was sitting at her counsel table with her legs crossed and her hands folded nicely in her lap. She looked as though she didn't have a care in the world. It seemed an eternity before she rose. She walked comfortably and confidentially to the podium. I turned in my chair to look at her as she began to speak. Come on girl. Show me what you got.

"Your Honor, I do not dispute much of what my learned colleague says"—that was tongue in cheek, I thought, but it made me crack a smile—"but I will remind the court that they must, for the purposes of this motion, review the evidence in the light most favorable to the nonmoving party, the Government." That a girl—remind the fat ass of the law.

"It is not up to the Government to prove motive. There may or may not be a connection between the two service members in this case. However, as the court is well aware, some murders are random acts of violence.

"Mrs. Williams did identify the ring as being that of her husband's and it was found within the defendant's possession and control by virtue of it being in his barracks room.

"There is a marked similarity between the defendant's"—that's right, don't humanize Miller—"vehicle and the one shown on the video. The defense did cross-examine the agent as to the commonality and the number of possible variations of license plate numbers, but that goes to the weight of the evidence and not to its admissibility. The fact remains that there is a certain percentage of probability that the license plate number shown on the video match's the one on the defendant's vehicle." We don't deal in probabilities in criminal law, but I let that slide.

"Finally, the phone call being made in the vicinity of where the defendant resides and has access to is again a matter for the jury in deciding how much weight to give that evidence.

"We believe the jury will not be swayed by the fact that our case is largely circumstantial. Most crimes have no eyewitnesses or direct evidence. There is a jury instruction, as Your Honor well knows, right on point regarding direct or circumstantial evidence—either can be used to prove any fact in controversy."

She confidentially concluded, "Your Honor, this case needs to go to the jury for their decision." She sat down.

Captain Johnson looked at us both for a few seconds. "I will take this matter under advisement and let you know of my decision as soon as possible." He then quickly got up and hurried out of the courtroom.

Dempsey turned and smiled sweetly at me. Damn, I love that girl!

CHAPTER THIRTY-ONE

JOSHUA HATED THE SOUNDS AND the smell. He had a single stainless steel toilet. It was a dull gray from not being cleaned properly. You could smell the sewage below. The small sink was not much better. Orange-tinted water dripped from the faucet and smelled like sulfur. His bed frame was ancient metal. It was discolored from years of use and neglect; the mattress so thin you could feel the supports below. The bedding was old and frayed at the edges. The thin sheets were washed once a week—the threadbare blanket hadn't been washed in months. The prisoners smelled of sweat, even in the winter months, and fear. The guards wore too much cologne. Joshua longed for the fresh smells of the outdoors back home—pine trees, smoke from a fire pit, dew on the grass.

The guards had returned him to his cell to await the judge's decision. The heavy iron door to his cell slammed shut. He jumped. After all these months in the brig, he still wasn't used to the sound. He heard the squeak of the guard's rubber sole boots as he walked the few paces to the heavier main door, which divided his wing from the next. The buzzer went off as it closed electronically. When the guard left the area, the noise from the other inmates intensified. Some yelled at the guards, some at each other. A few sang to themselves. He could hear the sound of sobbing from a few cells away. Joshua didn't know how much more he could take.

He sat down on his bed. The Government had rested its case. His lawyer told him if the judge denied their motion, then it was their turn to present evidence. DeMarco was trying to tell him what to do. And that stupid shrink was asking him all these questions. Why was everyone trying to get inside his head? Did they think he didn't know what he was doing? His lawyer said he didn't want him to testify. Did they think he was crazy? He did what he had to do, didn't he? Maybe he wasn't the hero he wanted to be, but he tried. He would tell the jury that. He thought someone needed him. But maybe Samantha was like all the others. Was she even real? He liked the way he felt when they talked. All those hours spent talking. And now look where he was.

Joshua was scared. But he couldn't admit that to anyone. Not even to himself. Whatever happened to him in here, he had to be prepared. He had to be strong. He was strong. He didn't need anyone. Did he? All these thoughts were running around inside his head. Maybe he was crazy. Maybe he should let DeMarco have him tested.

Joshua sat back against the cool cinderblock wall. He remembered back to when he was a young boy—his parents' wedding. His dad. Not his biological father but the man who raised him, his real dad. He had sat in the front row. It was the first time he wore a tie, a clip-on. He wore a white shirt and black pants, no jacket. He could still remember the minister's words:

> We are gathered here today to join Anne and James in a life of mutual commitment. It is fitting and appropriate that you, their family and friends, are here to witness and to participate in their union. For the ideals, the understanding, and the mutual respect, which they bring to their life together had their roots in the love, friendship, and guidance you have given them. The union of two people makes us aware of the changes wrought by time. But this new relationship will continue to draw much of its beauty and meaning from the intimate associations of their past.

At that moment, to Joshua, there was no past only the future. He rose from the front pew and handed the minster the thin silver rings he had in his front pocket. He had been holding them for hours.

The aging minister continued, "A ring is a fitting symbol for a wedding promise. It is a circle with no beginning and no end. Love without end is what we hope to achieve in marriage. These rings mark the beginning of a journey filled with wonder, surprise, tears, laughter, celebration, joy, and grief."

Joshua had always remembered those rings. How they felt. So round and perfect. They gave him comfort. They meant a new beginning, commitment, love, happiness.

He closed his eyes. Suddenly, he saw Williams's face appear. He leaned forward startled. Joshua grabbed his head with both hands and began rocking back and forth, the thoughts of Williams racing through his mind. He didn't deserve to die, did he? Was he even involved? All those phone calls. All the craziness. Joshua didn't even know what was real anymore. And Williams was expecting a son. He was going to be a dad—the greatest person in a young boy's world. He started to sweat. He drew his knees to his chest and hugged himself.

Joshua missed his dad. All the fun things they used to do together, and all the things they never would get to do. He used to sit on his dad's lap as he smoked his pipe. Joshua felt safe there. Without your dad, there was no one to talk to as you got older. Your mom loved you, but she didn't know what it was like to be a man. She couldn't tell you what to do or how to act or feel. It was all emotions with women.

Now Williams's son would never know that love and would never have that guidance and it was all his fault. Or that woman's. How could he have been so stupid? Love. What did that mean? How did he let himself get involved in this?

His lawyer said that without a body the Government couldn't prove that a murder had been committed, that the Government's case was all circumstantial. That it was weak. That he didn't need to testify. That he had a good chance of being acquitted.

153

The judge was thinking about all this right now DeMarco told him. All he had to do was sit here in this damn cell and be quiet about what he did and why he did it. His lawyer said if he remained silent, he had a good chance of being set free. A good chance of getting out of this hellhole and going back to the country, back to his old life where he could roam the countryside, free from everyone bothering him. His lawyer said he wasn't going to let him testify. But that was his decision, wasn't it? God, he hated this place.

Joshua stood up. The defense case would start on Monday. If he didn't take the stand, Williams's son would never know what happened to his dad. He would always wonder. Always have that doubt. He would never be able to go to a place and talk to him or say a prayer. That wasn't right. A little boy didn't deserve that. No little boy deserved that. Little boys needed their father.

Joshua got up from his cot and walked the few steps to his cell door. "Guard," he yelled! "Guard, I need to make a phone call."

CHAPTER THIRTY-TWO

It was Friday afternoon. Hansen had just returned from the late lunch he took after court let out. It was hotter than hell this June! There was no breeze coming off the water. He had sweated through his undershirt and his white dress shirt had lost its crease. He took off his sport coat and started to hang it behind his office door when the telephone rang.

"Special Agent Hansen," he said as he sat down at his desk. A muffled voice began speaking. The caller didn't identify himself. The words came quickly. Hansen didn't understand them at first, then a chill ran down his spine as it became clear what he was being told. The caller abruptly hung up.

Hansen jumped from his chair and immediately began making calls from his cell phone. He grabbed his coat with one hand as he ran out the door and down the hallway. He brushed by two other agents as he flew out the front door nearly knocking them over. Hansen jumped into the Crown Victoria, which was parked in the reserved spot near the front entrance. He was trying to sort out all the things he needed to do as he sped off toward the Outer Banks.

Hansen maneuvered the big car onto the interstate and accelerated to eighty miles per hour. Hansen hated the traffic this time of year. Everyone seemed to be headed toward the beach. With one hand on the steering wheel and the other on his phone, he weaved in and out of the growing number of cars.

After only a few miles, Hansen noticed a backup ahead. He knew a short cut so he exited off the highway onto a rural two-lane road. Within minutes, this country road was also bumper to bumper. He was going to have plenty of time to think about what needed to be done. But now he might have the final piece of the puzzle.

As the traffic crept along, Hansen began going over the investigation in his mind. He knew Commander Dempsey wasn't happy with his testimony in court. But he was sworn to tell the truth. The evidence was what it was. He couldn't make it up. He did the best he could with that crappy surveillance video. He had manipulated it until you could tell it was Williams who walked out of the marine barracks a little after 3:00 a.m. on January 1. You could see a vehicle, he still wasn't sure if it was a pickup truck or not, leaving the scene. Given the distance and the weather conditions, he was still able to make out the letter B and the number 1 on the license plate. His interviews with Williams's buddies revealed that Williams told them that a purported NCIS agent showed up at his barracks and accused him of being involved in a rape case. Williams told the agent that he must have the wrong person. A check of all ongoing investigations with the local NCIS offices didn't list Williams as a potential suspect in any crime. Hansen's research of the telephone records showed that a call was made to Williams's room the night of his disappearance from a telephone stand outside of Barracks 508. Then they found the ring. What more could he have done?

But all of that was circumstantial. Any good lawyer could poke holes in that. And DeMarco was better than good. And he was poking a lot of holes. Hansen was worried that the judge could come back with a decision dismissing the case. They needed a body.

The traffic had finally cleared. Hansen picked up speed. He replayed in his mind the words the anonymous telephone caller had told him. He said the body of Lance Corporal Williams could be found in Currituck County, North Carolina. The caller gave the location and then hung up. Why would someone call six months after Williams's disappearance? Why didn't he identify himself? Was he a Good Samaritan that didn't want to get involved? Plenty of people like that.

The caller told Hansen to make the first left turn onto an unmarked dirt road after the small rest stop off of Highway 158. The road was approximately two and one half miles south of the Coinjock Bridge, which spanned the Intracoastal Waterway. As Hansen crossed the bridge, he began watching his odometer. After a few minutes, Hansen spotted the rest stop in the distance. As he passed it, he suddenly saw the road up ahead. If you weren't looking for it, you would probably drive right by.

Hansen was the last to arrive. As he slowed to turn onto the narrow road, he noticed the vehicles of the various agencies his telephone calls had put in motion. There were two Currituck County sheriff vehicles, a North Carolina State Bureau of Investigation car, and a van from the City of Norfolk's Major Case Response Team; the MCRT would conduct the death scene examination and, hopefully, help identify the remains of the body. Four other members of the NCIS field office had turned in behind him.

After Hansen found a spot to park, he got out and quickly walked up to the other agents. Even though he technically wasn't the lead agent, he knew more about the case than anyone else. He had tried to brief everyone on the drive down, but the cell phone reception wasn't good. Sargent Mineo from the Currituck County sheriff's department was the first to meet him.

"We've already made contact with the property owner and he gave us consent to conduct a search of the property."

"Thank you, Sheriff," Hansen replied.

One of the SBI agents in the group sidled up to him and asked about the ongoing trial. Hansen, knowing that time was of the essence and wanting to get to the group that was gathered around what was apparently the burial site, replied curtly as he started walking, "The investigation started in January after the disappearance of a Lance Corporal Williams. Much of the evidence is circumstantial. A blurry parking lot video, a shaky eyewitness ID, and some phone records." He didn't mention the ring. "The primary suspect is a Petty Officer Miller, who is currently on trial charged with murder, kidnapping, and impersonating an NCIS agent."

157

"You didn't have a body?" the agent asked incredulously. Hansen just shook his head and kept on walking through the burned brown scrub grass. "You Navy guys have big balls!" Hansen smiled. That or dumb luck, he thought.

Approximately one hundred yards from where Hansen parked was a group gathered around a dark burned out area on the ground. It was evident the dirt had been disturbed. As he approached, Hansen overheard a female dressed in a lab coat say she believed the soil sample she had just gathered contained blood. Clumps of dirt were all around the perimeter.

Adjacent to the burned area there was a flurry of activity. Hansen noticed two agents making plaster impressions of partial automobile tire marks. Several officers were kneeling down in a semicircle, each taking a portion of an area that was marked off by string, and were scraping away dirt and debris. It was going to take several hours of painstaking work. But these were professionals. As the evening hours were fast approaching, two technicians hurried to the van to get a set of illumination lights.

The head of the Norfolk MCRT approached Hansen. "Agent Hansen, there's not much you can do here tonight. If the body has been in the ground for six months, it'll be pretty decayed. Once we dig up any remains, we'll transport them to the Medical Examiner's office in Greenville and see what we can come up with."

Hansen said, "If this is who I think it is, I have his medical and dental records back at my office. I can fax them over as soon as I get back."

"That would be a big help," the officer replied as he continued writing in his evidence log.

Hansen continued, "Sir, I don't want to rush you, but we're right in the middle of a trial. In fact, the judge is considering a motion to dismiss as we speak. Anything you find may be of critical importance."

The officer looked at Hansen as if he was crazy. He blew out his cheeks before pausing and saying, "Well, I'll do my best to put a rush on it. If you can get me those medical and dental records, maybe the

ME can get you some preliminary results by Sunday night. But no promises."

"I understand. I really appreciate it. Here's my card with my fax number. I'll call the Trial Counsel tonight and let her know to stand by. Thank you, Sir." Hansen turned and hurried back to his car. He got in, put the car in drive, and hurried back down the road.

The sun was setting as Hansen crossed over the Virginia border. Traffic wasn't as congested on the ride north. He waited to call Commander Dempsey and update her until the reception was better. He didn't want the call to drop in midsentence.

The conversation with Dempsey was short. Her instructions were clear. Hansen was to call her immediately if he received any information from the medical examiner, no matter what time.

On Sunday evening, Hansen returned to his office. On the fax machine were several pages of papers sticking out. The bold letters at the top indicated the correspondence was from the medical examiner's office. He pulled them from the machine and read:

> The following are the preliminary results of the investigation and subsequent recovery of the unknown remains of a body found in Currituck County on Friday evening. A search of the area resulted in the recovery of numerous items of evidentiary value to include bloodstain evidence, clothing fibers, and tire impressions. Additionally, medical and dental records of Lance Corporal Jonathan Williams were forwarded for comparison purposes with the corpse found.
>
> The body was transported to the East Carolina University School of Medicine in Greenville, NC. An autopsy was conducted by Dr. R. McDermitt, Regional Forensic Pathologist, NC Office of the Chief Medical Examiner.
>
> Even though the body was badly decomposed, two major wounds were noted to the neck. The left side of the neck exhibited a single

stab wound; the right side showed a laceration extending from the midline to behind the right ear. Dr. McDermitt's findings indicate the cause of death was the severe wounds to the neck. The manner of death was homicide. The final homicide report is pending results of the toxicology report.

Further, dental records were forwarded to Dr. D. Wilson, Capt., USN, a Forensic Odontologist at the Navy Medical Center Portsmouth, VA. Dr. Wilson traveled to Greenville, NC, on Saturday to provide identification of the remains. Upon examination of LCPL Williams's antemortem dental records the panoramic and bitewing x-rays and numerous other digital x-rays and dentition of the remains, as well as charting of both ante-mortem and postmortem dentition, Dr. Wilson was able to provide verbal confirmation of the positive identification of the body as being that of Lance Corporal Jonathan Williams.

Hansen took the papers, sat down at his desk, and picked up the telephone.

CHAPTER THIRTY-THREE

IT WAS EARLY MONDAY MORNING. I was sitting at my desk, putting the final touches on my opening statement. I thought better in the morning, particularly after my second cup of coffee. I drank my coffee black, a habit I picked up while out at sea. It was stronger and would get me going quicker—at least that's what the Chiefs told me. I didn't think Captain Johnson was going to grant my motion so I wanted to be ready. The telephone rang.

"Michael, its Nora." I briefly wondered why she was calling me so early. She didn't sound good.

"What's the matter? Are you okay?" I asked.

"Michael, they found the body." She didn't need to say anything more. I remained silent. I was stunned, but then again, maybe not. "Hansen received an anonymous phone call Friday afternoon. NCIS, SBI, MCRT, and the local LEOs dug up the body late that night. The ME and the labs have been working all weekend. It's Williams."

"You sure?"

"One hundred percent."

A thousand thoughts began to race through my mind. How the heck did they find the body after all these months? How could they be so sure it was Williams? What was I going to tell the jury? What was I going to tell my client? Then it hit me. It was Miller. It had to be him. He had to have told them. But how? He's in the brig. Nora said they received an anonymous call. Prisoners are allowed to make phone calls. But why? I told Miller without a body he had a good chance at an acquittal. The Government's evidence was all circumstantial. He wouldn't even have to testify. Was that it? Did Miller want to tell his story? Did he need to tell his story? Did that SOB want to get convicted?

"Michael, I guess you need some time to talk to your client." It was a statement, not a question.

"Ah, yes, Nora. Thank you. I'd appreciate that," was all I managed to say.

"Okay. I'll send you over the reports. I'm also going to notify the court that I will need to reopen my case." She almost sounded apologetic.

"I understand." I needed a favor. "Nora, can you give me a few hours? I'm going to the brig right now and talk to Miller. I don't know where that will leave us. Could you ask the judge if he could give me until tomorrow morning? We can schedule an 802 conference and I'll update everyone then."

"Sure. No problem." Then she hesitated. "You going to be okay? I know it's a shock, but you know how these cases go."

I managed a smile. "Thanks, Nora. Just got to figure out what Miller wants to do from here. No worries." And for the second time in the last few days, I added. "I appreciate your concern. Just need to sort it all out."

She didn't know what else to say. I knew her well enough to know that what she had done was as far as she could go. Nora still wanted to win. For me it wasn't that simple.

Son of a bitch!

162

CHAPTER THIRTY-FOUR

I DROVE EAST ON SHORE Drive and turned right onto Great Neck Road. After a half mile, I turned left into the middle school parking lot. It was empty. School had just let out for the summer.

I parked my car and walked over to the bleachers lining the football field. I sat down. It was midafternoon. The sky was cloudless. The sun beat down on the metal bleachers. I could feel the heat through my pants. I love the smell of the salt air while out at sea but nothing beats the smell of cut grass.

In my younger days, while preparing for the Physical Readiness Test, I'd come to this school and run the track. Push-ups, sit-ups, and a mile-and-a-half run. Not too difficult. When school was in session, I enjoyed watching the young kids play. They were so alive, no worries, their futures unlimited.

I grew up during the time when the Kennedy brothers were inspiring Americans. One of my favorite quotes was from Robert F. Kennedy's "Day of Affirmation" address to South African students:

> It is from numberless diverse acts of courage and belief that human history is shaped. Each time a man stands up for an ideal, or strikes out against injustice he sends forth a tiny ripple of hope, and crossing each other from a million different centers of energy and daring, those rip-

ples build a current which can sweep down the mightiest walls.

I had just returned from seeing Miller in the brig. I had to get away to think. I couldn't go back to the office. For the moment, I didn't want anything to remind me of the military. What events, divinely inspired or otherwise, had brought these individuals together? A young sailor from a small town in Southwest Virginia who knew nothing of the ways of the world; a marine, an expectant father from Iowa, recently returned unscathed from two tours of duty in a war zone; and a young lady from the Outer Banks, North Carolina, who apparently fantasied about being someone she could never be. And lawyers who were once classmates, and maybe more, so long ago. All our lives changed so dramatically by a chance telephone call.

I sat back and leaned my elbows on the row behind me. The heat caused me to flinch, reminding me that I was wearing short sleeves. Now what do I do? I had never had a case like this one. I basically led the jury to believe that my client was innocent, that the Government didn't have enough evidence to convict him—certainly not enough to give him the death penalty. Now my client decides he wants to tell his story, an incredible story at that. And now Commander Dempsey has a body.

So what was important? What ideals did I believe in? What injustice was I fighting against? If Miller had just listened to me. If he had just remained quiet, we could have won. Was that what was important? Winning? My individual won lost record? What about justice? What about the victim's family? Could I keep telling myself that I was just doing my job, that I was only a cog in the criminal justice system? That if I was better than the prosecutor, then so much the better for my client.

Could I have ethically kept Miller off the stand if he insisted on testifying? Sure, I had done it many times. I told my clients that it was their choice, but that I was the expert, that they should listen to me. And they usually did.

I must be losing my edge. Did I even know what was important anymore? Was it me, my career, my client, or the system that mattered most? Was it that I just liked to embarrass the command? Did I have a problem with authority? I smiled at that thought. The judge? Commander Dempsey? Did I even want to do this anymore? The sun beat down on my forehead.

All these thoughts and questions were running through my head. For the first time I started to question my own integrity. Would I have insisted that Miller not testify because I knew that increased my odds of winning? Would I have then been complicit in letting a guilty man—a murderer—go free? What about the Williams family? Didn't they deserve justice? Closure? What was ethical? What was right?

How was I going to look myself in the mirror?

The sweat was soaking through my uniform. I took a deep breath and slowly exhaled. I got up and walked back to my car. I got in the driver's seat and turned on the air conditioner. I just sat there. I had never questioned myself so much.

After a few minutes, I knew what I had to do. Miller was still my client. I was still his lawyer. He still needed my help. Maybe now more than ever. I put the car in drive, pulled out of the parking lot, and drove back to the base.

There was still a lot of work to be done.

CHAPTER THIRTY-FIVE

It was 8:00 a.m., Tuesday. Nora and I sat in front of Captain Johnson's massive desk. I looked around at his "I love me" wall, various plaques from different Commands thanking him for his "Outstanding Service to the Fleet."

I had just made my request. The judge's face was beet red; he was ready to explode. I couldn't remember if I still knew CPR.

"Commander DeMarco, I thought we discussed this?"

"Yes, Your Honor... well, not exactly." I was trying hard to remember my military courtesies.

"Commander, when you took this case, you said you were ready to proceed." He leaned forward, pointing his meaty index finger at me.

"Captain, with all due respect, at that time I was."

"And now you want a continuance?"

"I think the circumstances demand it." I was trying not to get testy.

"Commander DeMarco, you came into this court and pled your client not guilty. I'll have the court reporter review the transcript if you'd like. I believe you even said, and I quote, 'with the Government's case being what it is, I wouldn't need any extra time.' And now you're coming to me after the prosecution has concluded their case asking for a continuance?"

"Captain, my client's situation has drastically changed."

"Commander, when I was trying cases, I would interview my client well in advance of trial to find out what his testimony was going to be." Strange, I don't remember him trying cases, but I didn't think now was the time to bring that up.

"Captain, again, with all due respect, my client wouldn't talk with me and that was something that I could not, as you might well understand, share with the court or Trial Counsel."

"Commander, this is highly unusual." He was really agitated. I can't say I wasn't enjoying that.

"Yes, Captain, it is." We did agree on some things.

"And now your client wants to plead guilty? Is he going to take the stand?"

"Captain, we haven't made that decision yet." He was really pushing it. He didn't need to know that at this point. I remained calm.

"Are you and Trial Counsel going to enter into a stipulation of fact?"

I looked over at Commander Dempsey. She was sitting there serenely with her legs crossed and hands folded in her lap. I appreciated her remaining quiet throughout this entire ordeal.

"Captain, I think that Commander Dempsey and I can work something out." She nodded.

"Will there be a plea agreement?" Nora and I again looked over at each other but remained silent. I shook my head. The judge looked at us as if we were rookies trying our first case.

"Commander, again I must say I find this highly, highly irregular. During your voir dire of the jury your entire theme, at least from my perspective, was that the Government didn't have enough evidence to prove your client guilty. Then you waived your opening statement. Next you made the Government put on their witnesses and now you want to change your plea. And all of this without any type of plea agreement." I couldn't disagree with his synopsis of this unusual case.

"Captain, having the Government put on their witnesses is something they would have had to do in any event. The burden of proof is on them. I have no obligation to make the Government's job easier."

He sat back in his chair and stared at me. Maybe I shouldn't be lecturing the judge on the law, but the last few days had been rather taxing.

167

"So now you want me to instruct the jury that in the middle of the trial your client has suddenly changed his mind?" He paused. "Commander, have you thought how that might look?"

I wanted to tell him that's all I've been thinking about but remained silent. "Yes, Sir," was the only response I could muster.

He placed his fingers together as if making a steeple. He bowed his head for a few minutes. When he looked up, he said, "Commander, I will give you one day to work out a confession and stipulation of fact with Trial Counsel. We'll go back on the record and tell the court members that due to unforeseen circumstances, we are going to delay the trial until Thursday. Your motion for a longer continuance is denied.

"Here is my schedule." He glared at me. "The instructions to the court members and the guilty plea will start Thursday morning. We will hear sentencing arguments and the Government's case in aggravation after that. I suggest you gather up whatever witnesses you need to put on your case in extenuation and mitigation on Friday and Saturday if necessary." He continued to glare at me. He finally took a breath and said, "We are going to finish this trial. Are we clear?"

"Yes, Sir," Nora and I said in unison.

So I had two days to subpoena witnesses, prepare them, get them to court, and try to save my client's life.

Things could be worse.

I'm just not sure how.

CHAPTER THIRTY-SIX

JOSHUA SAT IN HIS CELL and began writing:

I know my behavior is going to sound crazy because I never actually met Samantha Stevens, my girlfriend. Her actions at times didn't make sense to me, but what she told me and her emotional reactions seemed genuine. I loved her.

It first started in November when she called my barracks room accidentally. She dialed a wrong number, she said. After hanging up, she called back several times. I wanted to talk to her because she sounded cute. We talked several hours that first night. We talked and texted each other every day and night thereafter. This led to sex talk and her sending me naked pictures. I tried several times to meet her in person but never did. I went to great lengths to locate her, but she would never tell me exactly where she lived. We would agree to meet, but she made last-minute excuses and didn't show up. One time she even said she was in a car wreck. I asked her several times whether she was leading me on, but she said she wasn't. I believed we had a loving relationship despite her strange conduct.

In early December, Samantha told me that she had been raped. We had been arguing and I wanted to break up with her. She described her assailants as marines. She later told me they had broken into her house and killed one of her pets. I told her several times to call the police, but she wouldn't. She later told me that she had reported the rape, but the police told her that it was too late to prosecute.

I told a classmate of mine who was a police officer about the rape. He said there was little I would be able to do without Samantha taking some action. He also asked me in a joking way if I was planning to kill the guy. When he couldn't help me find Sam, I drove to North Carolina, where she said she lived. I even went by the sheriff's office. After telling him what was going on, the sergeant thought she was messing with my head and was a dancer or something. I got a county map and spent countless hours driving around trying to locate her.

Sam told me that her attackers attended the same school on base that I did. So I started to look for people who fit their description. One day I encountered Lance Corporal Williams in the cafeteria. He fit the description pretty well and he gave me a funny look. I asked Samantha if one of the marines' name was Williams. She initially denied it but then said that Williams was there when she was raped and helped hold her down. I didn't doubt her, especially after she gave an accurate physical description of Williams.

In our later conversations, she told me to stop my efforts to get more information about the rape. At the same time, she frequently added additional information, such as the breaking into her house.

Before I went home on Christmas leave, I was determined to get more information about Williams because I didn't want anything to happen to Samantha. I went to the marine barracks and asked for him. I thought if I confronted Williams directly, it might go bad. I also thought that Williams might recognize me as a student and lie about his involvement with the rape. After giving the matter a lot of thought, I bought a secondhand suit and posed as an NCIS agent. I hoped to scare Williams into telling the truth. There was a senior barracks petty officer that evening and he gave me Williams's room number. I talked with Williams and he denied everything. I got nervous and hurried off. When I got back to my room, my mind was going one hundred miles an hour. I thought that I had put myself and Samantha at risk if Williams was involved.

I went home for Christmas and thought about it a lot. Sam was supposed to show up but never did. Since she didn't, I had a lot of time on my hands. My primary concern was finding out who raped Samantha.

I went back to Williams's barracks on the night of New Year's Eve. I brought my 9 mm pistol, a police baton and a knife for personal protection. I also had a pair of handcuffs that I received as part of a private eye course I had taken. I thought Williams might attack me if I confronted him about the rape. I was not thinking about killing Williams but wanted to be able to put him under 'citizen's arrest.'

I called the barracks and was put through to Williams's room. I think it was a little after 3:00 a.m. I chose that time to reduce the likelihood that witnesses would see me talking to Williams. When he picked up the telephone, I identified myself as the NCIS agent that talked to him before. I told Williams that we needed to talk about the girl who was raped. When Williams got in my car, he again denied it but seemed nervous.

During that conversation, I was beginning to feel a little stupid because Williams seemed innocent. But again, he could have been hiding something. I also thought that Williams was extremely gullible for giving me any information because I had never shown him any official identification or a badge. I told myself that I was making a serious mistake because Williams might be innocent. But if I didn't go through with my plan, I would never be able to help Samantha or look her in the face when we did meet if I didn't do my best.

I told Williams that I had to take him to North Carolina. I laid it on thick. I said he didn't have to come with me unless he wanted to prove his innocence. Williams voluntarily got into my truck. At some point, I feigned receiving a phone call. I told Williams that the call was from the office and that I had to handcuff him. Williams readily complied. I went ahead and handcuffed him, thinking that it would force Williams to confess. I didn't think of the consequences if he didn't confess.

After I cuffed Williams, we got back in the car. While driving, Williams stuck to his original story that he was not involved. He told me information about himself. I found out he was married. He told me that he detested the idea of rape and could not even watch stories about rape on television. He further told me that he loved the Marine Corps and was faithful to his wife.

We drove for almost two hours. I planned to go to a communication tower I had previously seen near Kitty Hawk, North Carolina, while I was looking for Samantha. When we got to the tower, I asked him if he had to use the bathroom. Williams said he did. At that point, he had been sitting with his hands cuffed behind his back for a while. When I got him out of the car, I threw him to the ground

On the ride down to North Carolina, I felt a lot of anxiety. However, as soon as I saw Williams lying on the ground, I felt cold and strangely no emotion except for my feelings for Samantha. I bent down and put my knee into Williams back. I pulled my gun and put it to Williams head. I told Williams that I was not really an NCIS agent. Williams continued to deny any involvement in the rape. He told me about an unborn son. I started to feel really bad. I put my gun away. At that point, I wasn't sure that Williams was involved in the rape.

I wanted to let Williams go but was afraid he would attack me if I did. I was having all these emotions about Williams, Samantha, and my own safety if I released him.

I think I then made myself believe that Williams was involved in the rape. I felt great remorse over what was happening. I felt I had ruined any chance at finding out the truth about the rape and that the only way out was to kill Williams. I debated ways to kill him and decided that my knife would be the quickest and quietest way to do it. I drew my knife and again wondered whether I should release Williams.

I did not release him. Instead, I pulled up on Williams's chin to expose his throat. I then used my knife to make an incision starting at about the midline of his throat going back to his right ear. He bled a lot from his neck. I heard him say that he could not breathe. I made another incision that started farther to the left side of his neck. I felt like the biggest piece of shit in the world because Williams was suffering. I remember saying, "Just die, damn it!" It was so sad to watch Williams die.

At the same time, I told myself that it was stupid to have sympathy for the enemy and wondering how I could have jeopardized my own life by killing Williams. I thought about the normal Joshua versus my vigilante side and thought that, in some ways, I was justified by my actions. That maybe I was a hero. I saw that he was wearing a silver wedding ring. It reminded me of many things, especially my dad. I took it with me.

I started to worry about getting caught. I was afraid that someone would come up to the tower. I was pleading for the robot function that I had experienced in the past when I was under stress would come back. I tried to will myself into the unemotional state I was in before the killing. I started panicking but got myself to start thinking. I tried to drag Williams into the woods, which was approximately one-tenth of a mile away. I pulled Williams by the hinge of the handcuffs. I wondered how he actually died and thought that I would feel worse if Williams suffocated as opposed to bleeding to death.

I decided that I needed to bury Williams's body so that it would not be found. I removed the handcuffs and Williams's clothing so that that material would not be discovered as evidence. After I removed the clothing, I stood over Williams's body and said a prayer. Then I vomited. I decided that I needed to get out of the area. I thought that the smell of the body might attract attention, so I decided to burn it, which would also cauterize the wound and reduce the likelihood of the body being discovered. I got some gasoline from my truck, poured it over the area of the body that was bleeding, and lit it on fire.

I didn't want Williams's body to burn for too long, as I had already disgraced him enough. After about thirty seconds, I put out the flame with my coat. I then apologized to Williams's body, made the sign of the cross, and said a prayer to Williams's God in the wish that Williams would go to heaven. I also told Williams that I would come back that night to bury him.

I then left the scene and returned to base. I disposed of Williams's clothing in four different Dumpsters. I thought about turning myself in to the police but rejected that idea as it would prevent me from getting to the bottom of Samantha's rape. I went to McDonald's to wash my hands. I felt hungry, so I ordered a cheeseburger meal but was not able to finish it.

I then went through Williams's belongings. I checked the messages on his cell phone. There was a text message from his wife. It said, "I love you—happy New Year." I threw the phone in a lake. I grew worried because it did not sink right away.

I then went back to my room. I took a long, soothing shower to wash away the grime for what I had done. I washed the handcuffs and the knife and drank a protein drink. After that, I felt exhausted but couldn't sleep. I pondered what I should do and decided to stay on the same path.

In the afternoon, I bought a shovel. I had a short conversation with Samantha. In the evening, I drove back down to North Carolina to bury the body. It seemed as if the ride took forever. While I was burying the body, I cried and spoke to Williams, apologizing again for my actions. I didn't bury the body deep because I didn't want to stay there long enough to dig a deep hole.

The next day I went to school. I didn't have any difficulty in class. It was good to focus on my schoolwork. After class I decided I had to see Samantha in person and soon. As I was driving to North Carolina, Samantha called. I told her where I was and she said not to go to North Carolina, that she wouldn't see me. At that point, I was more convinced than ever that Samantha had been lying to me.

What had I done? After that every hour now it's becoming worse. It's all I can think about. My head is exploding. The nightmares won't stop. I can't keep it inside me anymore.

I'm sorry.

CHAPTER THIRTY-SEVEN

A FOCUS GROUP IS A tool civil lawyers regularly use. The purpose is to simulate what the real trial will be like. Both plaintiff and defense put on abbreviated cases; you then ask the participants their views on the evidence and get their perceptions, opinions, beliefs, and attitudes regarding the issues. It can cost thousands of dollars finding a place to host the event and paying people to come spend several hours listening to you.

Given this, it is rarely used in criminal cases. Most criminal clients can barely afford to pay their lawyers, something I've never had to worry about in the military. I get a regular paycheck every two weeks whether I represent one client or one hundred. Lately, I've wondered what it would be like to get paid by the results you achieve. Maybe I'd find out soon.

We got together Wednesday evening after work. We received permission to use a vacant classroom. I asked some of the younger defense counsel for their help in organizing and presenting the mock trial. We planned to be there for as long as it took. The sentencing phase of the trial started in the morning. It was no longer about me or even Miller. It was about the jurors.

My issue was simple. I needed to know whether a jury could put to death a young sailor who killed an innocent Marine over a girl he "loved" but never met. I had to know what to say to them in order to save this young man's life.

The Armed Services have only twenty-five convicts on death row. The last time the military executed someone was during President Kennedy's administration. The appeals process can take decades. The makeup of the condemned was remarkably similar; most were either Marines or Army—those who were used to killing up close and personal. There were only three Air Force and two Navy service members on death row. They were from ratings that involved weapons or explosives: machine gunners, infantryman, ordnance disposal—not intelligence specialists.

I watched as they filed into the large conference room, eleven men and five women, all in civilian clothing, giving away their military status only by their erect bearing and haircuts. We decided to use active-duty military members as mock jurors to determine how likely the death penalty was among those who were used to being around death. Coffee and sandwiches were available for anyone who might have missed dinner or got hungry later. As they entered, we encouraged them to eat; they might not be able to later when the autopsy photographs were shown.

Military jurors tend to be smarter than civilian jurors; all officers have college degrees, as do many of the enlisted. They are used to working with people from all walks of life under difficult circumstances. They tend to be deliberate and fair in determining guilt or innocence. They spend a lot of time examining the facts. But when it comes to sentencing and meting out punishment, they are much harsher than their civilian counterparts.

The group ranged in rank from E-7s (Chiefs) to O-6s (Captains). There were a variety of designators or job descriptions among them. We had pilots, computer geeks, supply personnel, ship drivers, and gunners. Each was a friend in some form or fashion, although not a close friend. Each agreed to come spend five or six hours after a long day's work helping us to decide how best to present this difficult case.

As the moderator for the evening's event, I stood and walked to the podium. I asked them all to be seated. One of the more experienced defense counsels was going to play the role of Commander Dempsey; one of the newer ones was playing me. I cleared my throat and began my opening remarks.

"Petty Officer Miller has pled guilty to the murder of a marine. We are now in the sentencing phase of the trial. One of the authorized punishments is the death penalty.

"Each side, the Government and the Defense, will have one hour to present their case. Lieutenant Cynthia Julius will present the prosecution's case followed by a fifteen-minute break. Lieutenant Jeff Verdi will then present the defense's side similarly followed by a fifteen-minute break.

"I ask that you pay particular attention to Petty Officer Miller's confession. It is undecided if IS3 Miller will testify at the trial. There is a stipulation of fact, which has been entered into with the Government, which will be read to you.

"Each side will have a maximum of ten minutes for their opening statement followed by forty minutes of witness testimony, which they will read to you, or to present other evidence, such as photographs, which they will show you. Assume that what you hear or see is exactly what the witness will testify to on the witness stand or what will be presented as evidence in court.

"The prosecution and the defense will then have a maximum of ten minutes to give a closing argument. After hearing both sides, the panel will have one hour to discuss, as a group, your thoughts and to come up with an appropriate sentence. You will have three choices: the death penalty or life imprisonment with or without the possibility of parole. We will then spend one to two hours discussing your opinions. Are there any questions?"

There being none, Lieutenant Julius approached the podium. While not as attractive as Commander Dempsey, she was not far behind. As I listened to her opening statement, I tried to envision what the real jury would hear and the passion in which Dempsey would deliver it.

The jury would not get to know Miller as I did. Not that I knew him well. Lieutenant Julius's version of the events made Miller appear to be a cold-blooded killer. It didn't get any better after the synopsis of her witnesses' testimony. She highlighted the testimony of the Medical Examiner (when she showed the autopsy photographs the panel was visibly shaken), Lance Corporal Williams's fellow Marines, and finally his wife.

When it was Lieutenant Verdi's turn, there was not much he could do to minimize the damage. He talked about the Miller family, his friends, and the hardship he was going to face spending the rest of his life in Leavenworth. He spent a majority of the time talking about "Samantha" and how her actions influenced a young naive sailor. Would a jury buy that? Would that be enough of an excuse to spare the young man's life?

When the evidence was concluded, I noticed the panel members were stunned. They hadn't realized what they had signed up for. After closing arguments from each side, I again approached the podium and read the following jury instructions to them.

"There are several matters which you should consider in determining an appropriate sentence. You should bear in mind that our society recognizes five principles for the sentence of those who violate the law. They are rehabilitation of the wrongdoer, punishment of the wrongdoer, protection of society from the wrongdoer, preservation of good order and discipline in the military, and deterrence of the wrongdoer and those who know of his crimes and his sentence from committing the same or similar offenses. The weight to be given any or all of these reasons, along with all other sentencing matters in this case, rests solely within your discretion.

"You will vote on the appropriate punishment in this case. Specifically, you will decide if that punishment will be either life with the possibility of parole, life without the possibility of parole, or death. Each person is entitled to one vote. You will vote after a full and free discussion of the matters presented.

"In order to vote for death, you must believe that the aggravating evidence, to include the two aggravating factors that have been shown, kidnapping and obstruction of justice, substantially outweigh the evidence in mitigation.

"After your deliberations or after one hour, whichever comes first, you will submit your vote in secret written ballot. The senior member will collect and tally the votes and will announce the verdict.

"You will begin your vote with the least severe sentence, that of life with the possibility of parole. If you reach a vote of at least twelve members, that is your sentence. If you do not, then you will vote for life without the possibility of parole. Again, if you reach a vote of at least twelve members, that is your sentence. If not, you may continue to discuss or you may vote for death. If you vote for death, unless all members vote for death, your verdict is life without the possibility of parole. If even one person votes for life, then the verdict is life without the possibility of parole. Any questions?"

The panel looked at me solemnly but said nothing. We left the room so they could deliberate. Within minutes, we heard shouting and arguments coming through the thin walls. There were heated exchanges. At the fifty-five-minute mark there was a knock on the door. They were ready to discuss their findings.

We walked back into the room; all sixteen were looking down at the floor, wearing somber expressions. The senior Captain held a piece of paper in his hand. He looked up and silently handed it to me.

I read the slightly crumped blue-lined white sheet of notebook paper. The vote was fourteen to two for the death penalty.

Not good.

CHAPTER THIRTY-EIGHT

THE JUDGE ENTERED THE COURTROOM precisely at 9:00 a.m., Thursday, June 23. Everyone rose. It had been over a week since the trial first began.

Captain Johnson got right to it. "I understand that the accused has decided to change his pleas. Do we have anything to discuss prior to him doing so?"

"Not from the Government, Sir," said Commander Dempsey.

"Anything from the Defense?"

I waited for a moment just to bust his balls. "No, Sir." I could feel Miller shaking slightly as he stood beside me.

Johnson looked at me with an aggravated look while he spoke to my client. "Intelligence Specialist Third Class Joshua Miller, United States Navy, I now ask you, how do you plead? However, before receiving your pleas, I advise you, once again, that any motion to dismiss any charge or to seek any other relief should be made at this time. Commander Demarco, are there any further motions?"

"No further motions, Sir." Just for once, I wish he would go off script.

"Very well. How does the accused plead?"

"Sir, Petty Officer Miller has authorized me to enter the following pleas on his behalf: To all charges and specifications..." I hesitated. "Guilty." The words stuck in my throat.

"Petty Officer Miller, has your counsel correctly entered the pleas on your behalf?"

"Yes, Sir, he has," said Miller in a low voice.

The judge continued. "You may all be seated. Petty Officer Miller, I'll only accept your pleas of guilty if you understand their meaning and effect. So I'm now going to discuss those pleas with you. Please keep a copy of the charge sheet there in front of you so you can refer to it readily. If at any time you become confused, you may stop me and I'll allow you time to consult with your counsel. Do you understand that?"

"Yes, Sir."

"A plea of guilty is the strongest form of proof known to the law. Based on your pleas of guilty alone, without receiving any further evidence, this court can find you guilty of the offenses to which you are pleading guilty. However, your pleas of guilty will not be accepted unless you understand that, by pleading guilty, you admit each and every element of the offenses to which you are pleading guilty and that you're pleading guilty because you really are guilty. If you don't believe that you're guilty, then you should not plead guilty for any reason. Do you understand that?"

"Yes, Sir." For the first time Miller glanced over his shoulder and saw everyone in the gallery staring at him—those from the local press, military personnel from the NLSO, and members from both his and Williams's family.

"Even if you believe you are guilty, you still have a legal and moral right to enter a plea of not guilty and to require the Government to prove its case against you, if it can, by legal and competent evidence beyond a reasonable doubt. If you were to plead not guilty, then you would be presumed under the law to be innocent and only by introducing evidence and proving your guilt beyond a reasonable doubt could the Government overcome this presumption of innocence. Do you understand this?"

"Yes, Sir," Miller said, his voice barely audible.

"By pleading guilty, you're giving up certain important rights. They are, first, the right against self-incrimination, that is, the right to say nothing at all about these offenses. Second, the right to a trial of the facts by a court-martial, that is, the right to have this court-martial decide whether or not you are guilty, based on the evidence presented by the prosecution and, if you so choose, by the defense. And third, the right to confront the witnesses against you and to call witnesses on your own behalf. Do you understand this?"

"Yes, Sir," Miller said, looking down.

"You are also advised that if you plead guilty, there will not be a trial of any kind as to the offenses to which you're pleading guilty. Do you understand that?"

Miller nodded.

"Have you discussed these matters with your counsel?" I wanted to jump up and say, "Boy, have we ever!"

"Yes, Sir."

"Do you agree to give up these important rights with respect to the offenses to which you've pled guilty and to answer my questions?"

"Yes, Sir."

"Commander DeMarco, what advice have you given the accused as to the maximum punishment for the offenses to which he's pleading guilty?"

I stood. "Sir, I have advised Petty Officer Miller, the maximum punishment is forfeiture of all pay and allowances, reduction in rank to E-l, discharge from the military service with a dishonorable discharge." I paused. "Oh, and to die by lethal injection." The judge and I stared at each other for a moment. How the hell else did he want me to say it? Everyone in the courtroom was deadly silent as they watched us. Without taking his eyes from me, he said, "Does the Government concur?"

Commander Dempsey said softly, "Yes, Sir, we do." I sat down.

"Petty Officer Miller, the maximum sentence that can be adjudged for the offenses to which you've entered a plea of guilty is total forfeiture of all pay and allowances, reduction in pay grade to E-1, discharge from the naval service with a dishonorable discharge and to be sentenced to death. Do you understand that?"

Joshua hesitated. "Yes, Sir."

"Have you had enough time to prepare your case with your counsel?" I'm glad he didn't ask me that question.

"Yes, Sir."

"And do you believe that his advice is in your best interest?"

"Yes, Sir, I do." Well, that's good to know since he didn't take it.

"Are you pleading guilty voluntarily? That is, this is of your own free will?"

"Yes, Sir."

"Has anybody forced or coerced you into entering a plea of guilty?"

"No, Sir."

"In a moment I'm going to have you placed under oath so that we can discuss the circumstances of these offenses. If what you say is not true, your statements may later be used against you in a prosecution for false statement or for perjury. Do you understand that?"

"Yes, Sir."

"In addition, the Government may later ask that your answers be used against you in the sentencing portion of the trial. Do you understand that as well?"

"Yes, Sir, I do."

"Very well. Please stand, face the Trial Counsel, and raise your right hand. Commander Dempsey, would you please administer the oath?" She did as directed.

"Is there a stipulation concerning the pleas?" With a stipulation of fact, both parties agree to what happened in the underlying crime without the need to put on evidence. Whenever I have a particularly egregious case, I gladly entered into one in order to avoid having the prosecution call witnesses and have the jury hear all the gory details. I wasn't sure this one would accomplish that.

"Yes, Sir, there is. May I approach?" All eyes followed Commander Dempsey as she glided toward the court reporter and handed her the document. Captain Johnson rarely accepted documents directly from counsel. I'm sure there is some judicial edict for not doing so; personally, I believed he didn't want to catch any germs from us mere mortals. "I am handing the court reporter what has previously been marked as 'Prosecution Exhibit Twelve for Identification, the Stipulation of Fact.' I ask that this exhibit be admitted into evidence and that the words for identification be deleted.

"Petty Officer Miller, I have what's been marked Prosecution Exhibit Twelve for Identification. It contains ten pages and is entitled

'Stipulation of Fact.' Do you have a copy there at the counsel table you can refer to?"

"Yes, Sir."

"Is that your signature on page 9?"

Joshua took minute to examine the document. "Yes, Sir."

"And prior to signing this document, did you read it over completely and discuss it with your counsel?"

"Yes, Sir."

"Did you understand everything that's in the stipulation?"

Again, he just nodded.

"And is everything in the stipulation the truth?"

"Yes, Sir, it is."

"Does counsel for both sides agree to the stipulation and also that those are your signatures on page 9?"

"Yes, Sir," we said in unison.

"Thank you. Petty Officer Miller, at this point, we're going to discuss the stipulation of fact to ensure that you understand it and agree to its uses. A stipulation of fact is an agreement between the Trial Counsel, the Defense Counsel, and yourself that the contents of the stipulation are true, and if they're entered into evidence, they will become the uncontradicted facts in your case. Do you understand that?"

"Yes, Sir," he said in a stronger voice than he had used all morning.

"You have the right not to enter into the stipulation and the stipulation will not be accepted by me without your consent. Do you understand that as well?"

"Yes, Sir."

"Has anybody forced, threatened, or coerced you in any way to sign this stipulation of fact?"

"No, Sir," he continued to use a stronger voice, which surprised me.

"Now, if I admit the stipulation, it's going to be used in two ways. First, it will be used to determine if you are, in fact, guilty, and second, it will be used during the sentencing hearing. Do you understand that?"

"Yes, Sir."

"And when it is used for the sentencing hearing, the Trial Counsel will read it to the court and they will have it with them when they decide upon your sentence. Do you understand that?"

"Yes, Sir." Again he looked over his shoulder to those in the courtroom. It was eerily silent for so many people.

"Do you agree to both of those uses?"

"I do."

"Thank you. Petty Officer Miller, once again, a stipulation of fact is uncontradicted and ordinarily may not be contradicted during the course of these proceedings. So if there is anything you want to add or correct, we need to do it now."

"No, Sir, I'm good with it."

"Okay. Let's go through it."

I leaned forward and bowed my head. I didn't want to hear the story again.

CHAPTER THIRTY-NINE

NORA STOOD INCHES FROM THE jury box. "It is New Year's Eve off a small dirt road in Grandy, North Carolina. It's a wintry night. The ground is hard and cold. Lance Corporal Jonathan Williams felt it.

"His face was in the dirt, his hands handcuffed behind his back, a knee in his spine. Out of the corner of his eye, he sees a Glock pistol and wonders in his panic why he is here. He was never this afraid in Afghanistan where he met his enemy face to face. He knew why he was there, unlike this night.

"Scared and alone, this 6'4" marine never had the opportunity to fight back. A hand lifted up his chin and Williams felt the cold blade of a knife pierce the skin at the center of his neck and move to his right ear, cutting through his windpipe and jugular vein. But that was not the end of it. The blade was pulled out and again plunged into his neck near his left ear and moved toward the center of his throat. Jonathan couldn't breathe. And there he lay, handcuffed on the cold dirty ground with blood rushing out of his neck and breathing his last breath. We can only imagine his last thoughts." Dempsey paused for what seemed an eternity, every member of the jury staring at her. "And then Jonathan Williams died." Another long pause. "Needlessly."

She walked a few feet to her right and continued. "The defendant then dragged Jonathan's lifeless body deep into the nearby woods and dumped him into a depression facedown. He cut off his clothes and stole his jewelry, his wedding ring. He poured gasoline on the

186

body from head to toe. Then he lit the gasoline with a match and watched the body burn. He put Jonathan's clothes in trash bags and scattered them in Dumpsters throughout Hampton Roads. Finally, he threw Jonathan's mobile phone in a lake but not before reading a private text message from Mrs. Williams, his wife. It said, 'I love you—happy New Year,' a message Jonathan never got to see.

"Members, you may be sitting here wondering why Lance Corporal Jonathan Williams died that night—that there must be some good reason for this tragedy. Every important event in life happens because of a reason, doesn't it?" She shrugged with the palms of both hands facing upward. "Well, at the moment Jonathan died, he didn't know much more that you do right now as to why he was facedown in the dirt off a small road in North Carolina with a knife in his neck." A pause. "And that is tragic.

"I suspect that Commander DeMarco is going to try to justify his client's actions by telling you some fascinating 'love' story." She almost spat out the word. "Yes, that's right. A love story that's founded in deception and lies and ends in the death of an innocent man. Listen if you'd like. It won't matter and it won't justify the defendant's actions.

"Allow me to tell you about a real love sorry. A story of a hero. I'm going to tell you about Jonathan Williams, because he is the real reason that we are here. He is the victim. Let me repeat that. Jonathan is the victim. Don't forget that because the defense is going to spend the next few days trying to point fingers everywhere else but at his client." She turned to point at Miller. "But he is the one responsible. He is the murderer.

"Jonathan Williams was a marine. He was passionate about the Marine Corps. He wanted to join the Corps since his freshman year in high school. He initially began his career as a mechanic because he loved working on cars. At the time of his murder, he was attending class at the Navy and Marine Intelligence Training Center. He loved the Marine Corps so much he recently reenlisted, even though he was beginning a new family.

"Jonathan was a war hero. After two six-month tours in Afghanistan, he was going back for a third. He earned a Combat

Action Ribbon. Listen as his platoon mates take the stand and describe him. IS3 Miller took that marine away from the Corps." Dempsey turned and again pointed at Miller. "That murderer took Jonathan away from all he loved and from all who loved him.

"Jonathan Williams was a friend. His friends called him 'Johnny.' He loved softball. He was one of those guys that always had a smile on his face. He was always in a good mood, no matter what was going on in his life. We all know someone like that. Jonathan was a guy who would drop everything to help out a friend no matter what the cost. And that murderer seated there"—Dempsey pointed at my client a third time—"took away that friend.

"Jonathan was a son. He was born to Brad and Terri Williams and grew up in the Midwest. He was their only son. When Jonathan was young, his mom had cancer. You will hear how six-year-old Johnny held the bucket when his mom was vomiting due to chemotherapy. And because of that murderer, they will never see him again except in their memories. That murderer took away their only son.

"Jonathan Williams was a loving husband and best friend. You will hear from his bride, and I say bride because Johnny and Jessica had only been married for six months at the time of his murder— six months." Dempsey stood in front of the jury, shaking her head. The jury was hanging on her every word. "They were married without family present and planned to have a formal ceremony when Jonathan returned from his third tour to Afghanistan. You will hear how they met and how the accused's actions have devastated her. That murderer took away her soul mate.

"And finally, members, you are going to learn that Jonathan was a father. He was a father of an unborn child. Jessica was three months pregnant at the time of the murder, and Jonathan never got to see his son—the only child he would ever have." Dempsey's words were sucking the air out of the courtroom. It was hard to breathe.

"Now, members, at the conclusion of the sentencing phase the Military Judge will instruct you as to the authorized punishments. You already know that there are only three choices. And as I asked you at the beginning of this case, I will ask you again now, but this time even more strenuously. The Government is going to ask you to give the defendant the punishment society demands—not the punishment he wants.

"Because it was Miller," she spat out his name, "that kidnapped Jonathan, it was Miller that drove him down that dirt road in North Carolina, it was Miller that threatened him with a pistol, and it was Miller that put that knife in his neck, knowing that he was a father-to-be, a son, a husband who was totally innocent of any wrongdoing. And then, not satisfied that Jonathan was dying fast enough, he put that knife in his neck a second time. And the last words on this earth that Jonathan heard were not the sweet words of his wife saying 'I love you' but those from the mouth of his murderer: 'Just die, damn it!'"

She stared into each juror's eyes. "Give him the same sentence he gave Lance Corporal Jonathan Williams.

"Give him death."

CHAPTER FORTY

No one moved. The only sound you could hear was Commander Dempsey's chair as she sat down at her counsel table. I stared straight ahead afraid to look at the jury. "Does the Defense desire to make an opening statement?" said the judge quietly.

"Yes, Your Honor, we do." He nodded slightly at me. For the first time in many years, I thought I saw empathy in his eyes. I needed to take some of the emotion out of the courtroom.

"Thank you, Sir." I walked up to the jury and stopped within a few feet. "Members, what you've heard, and what you will hear over the next few days, is a tale of three young lives that became unexpectedly and tragically intertwined. It was a tragedy for Jonathan Williams, a tragedy for Joshua Miller, and a tragedy for a young lady that you will get to know, to some extent, by the name of Samantha.

"At the outset, I acknowledge that none of us can fully understand what the Williams family is going through. I will try to handle their feelings with the dignity and respect that their situation demands." I glanced over at Miller. He was looking down with his hands clasped in his lap. "But for you to do your job, I will need to focus on what was going on in those young lives during the time of these unfortunate events. Not as an excuse and not as a justification but as a way to get to the truth. Because there have been far too many lies in this case." The Captain in the first row looked at me strangely when I said this.

"Like most tragedies in this world, there is a reason why it occurred. And by examining that reason, hopefully, you will make the right decision. The fair and just decision. So before you do, we will need to examine Joshua Miller's circumstances in its entirety.

"Trial Counsel has just talked about that night, you will undoubtedly hear more about that. But I am going to ask you to look beyond that—to put the entire chain of events into context as you examine what happened and why.

"I will also ask that you remember two things. The first, Joshua has now made a full confession. Without his cooperation, Corporal Williams's body would not have been found, and I submit, his death would remain a mystery. His family would have no closure." I thought about apologizing to them for my part in his silence but knew they would figure it out. "The second, Joshua has now pled guilty at this court-martial without asking anything from the Government." That wasn't my fault! "I submit that while Joshua can't change what happened he would do anything in his power if he relive those last few months. Simply put, he has taken responsibility for his actions." I was expecting Nora to object, but she remained silent, giving me, at least, a fighting chance.

"So at the very least, Joshua will serve life in prison. He does not need to be put to death." I said it again, almost to myself. "He does not need to be put to death." I paused, then continued, "Joshua will live a large portion of his life in Leavenworth, one of the harshest prison environments in our criminal justice system. And if the experts deem it appropriate, and he works hard enough, he *might*, and I emphasize the word *might*, be eligible for parole after twenty years. That is what I'm going to ask you to consider at the end of the evidence." A small trickle of sweat was inching its way down my back. The T-shirt under my uniform was already damp.

I continued. "Suffice it to say, there will be no winners in this case." Except for Commander Dempsey, I thought for a moment. "Joshua will suffer a substantially harsh punishment and whatever you decide, unfortunately, there is nothing we can do to change what happened to Corporal Williams. As for Samantha, well…" I let that thought hang in the air as I walked to the other end of the jury box.

"As we go through the evidence, what I'm going to ask you to do is to focus on three distinct and lengthy periods of time. Commander Dempsey is asking you to focus on three or four hours. We both agree that a monstrous act was committed. But you will have to decide if Joshua Miller is a monstrous person. Three time periods, no period more important than the other." I paused.

"The first time period is from Joshua's birth to November of last year. You will learn that Joshua, at a young age, was greatly troubled by the death of his dad. And there again, not as an excuse but as an explanation, I'd ask that you examine some of the events in his life that followed that loss. Joshua dropped out of school, worked at his family video store, did odd jobs, and generally just drifted." I didn't want the jurors to think I was going to give them some societal excuses for this tragedy, but I had to throw in as much as I could and hope something would strike home with one of them. "You will hear testimony from his mother, his brother, and his friends that Joshua was a good person. They were all shocked when they learned about these tragic events. You will learn that Joshua was kindhearted, not violent. That he's not a monstrous person.

"Joshua then decided he wanted to serve his country and make something of himself." Miller never told me that, but it was a good assumption. "He joined the Navy and served onboard the USS *Coral Sea* for three years. You will be able to read statements from people onboard his ship that served alongside him. As you know, when you serve with others while out at sea for months at a time, those people get to know you the best. Carefully review those statements and you will see what type person Joshua actually is.

"I will ask you to balance the morning hours of January 1 against those twenty prior years of his life as told by the people that knew Joshua Miller best.

"The second period of time Commander Dempsey has already alluded to. It's the seventy-seven days before this tragic event. There again, not by way of an excuse but by way of an explanation of what was going on in this young man's life. Joshua had just arrived at Dam Neck. He was in his barracks room when he received an unexpected telephone call from a young lady who was looking for a friend. She hung up but called back several times. Finally, Miller and she ended up talking for many hours that night. And over the course of the next few weeks, they developed this torrid telephone relationship. I'll admit, you'll probably find it quite unusual. I don't expect you to understand it, but it happened.

"This young lady called herself "Samantha." She described herself to Joshua as being blonde, five feet tall, and weighing one hundred pounds. Why is that significant? Joshua's mom will testify she had a psychic reading at her house and was told Joshua would meet and fall in love with a blonde girl. Samantha went on to say she was from Texas and that her family was rich. That she owned three houses in the Outer Banks and was an Old Dominion University student majoring in art history. Joshua, as naive and gullible as he was, believed that this was the woman of his dreams.

"We will admit into evidence telephone records between the two, which show the number of calls and text messages made during those seventy-seven days. They made over 5,000 telephone calls to each other and, you will learn, Samantha was also calling other sailors. There were also 487 text messages and 47 pictures sent. You will see some of the pictures as she portrayed herself to be. Joshua and Samantha talked almost 9,127 minutes. One day they made 133 telephone calls to each other. It was a crazy relationship.

"Joshua will tell you"—and I still wasn't sure that I was going to let him testify—"that he fell in love. That he found his soul mate. Joshua and Samantha tried to meet several times over the next month. You will hear testimony that every time Joshua tried to meet Samantha, he was at the wrong place, it was the wrong time, there was a car wreck. There was always a crisis. Samantha never showed up. Finally, after a month of this Joshua said, 'That's enough. I don't believe you really exist.' And they had a big fight.

"You will learn from the telephone records that Samantha"—I should have started calling her by her real name, Susan, but that's not how I came to know her—"called Joshua the evening of December 3, and they argued. Joshua told her he wanted to end the relationship. You will learn that Samantha was upset, that she was not her normal self, that she had been drinking. Samantha then claimed she had been raped by three marines. She said she couldn't tell Joshua who they were because they went to school with him. We now know that there was never a rape. That it was just another ploy by Susan"—finally, I had said her name—"Susan Jenkins that's her real name, to keep Joshua's attention and to keep stringing him along.

"However, Joshua truly believed a rape had occurred. He urged 'Samantha' to call the police. You will hear testimony from Petty Officer Holmes, a classmate and former police officer and Sergeant Mineo, from the Currituck Country Sherriff's Department of the efforts Joshua took to find and to help her. Everyone told Joshua he was crazy, that a crime hadn't occurred, but he sincerely believed that it had.

"When Joshua couldn't get 'Samantha' to report the rape to the authorities he decided to conduct his own investigation. 'Samantha' then began telling him that the marines were harassing her, that they were breaking into her house, killing her pets. Joshua became so concerned, he bought her a pistol.

"Then in mid-December a fateful event occurred. Joshua was eating lunch at the base cafeteria when he believed a marine was staring at him and giving him a 'funny look.' That marine was Jonathan Williams. He called 'Samantha,' or Susan, and asked if Williams was one of the marines that was involved. She denied he was but later changed her story to say he was one of the marines that held her down. It was a lie but now Joshua had a suspect.

"Joshua went to Jonathan's barracks to confront him. When questioned about the rape, Corporal Williams denied any involvement. Joshua didn't know what to do. He became conflicted about the truth. Finally, on New Year's Eve, Joshua decided he had to find out what was actually going on.

"I won't try to explain, and there's no psychiatric evidence to explain, why the events of that night got out of hand. The innate desire for self-preservation took over, and well… certainly it's a tragedy that no one can rationally explain." I stopped speaking for a few seconds trying to collect my thoughts. Finally, I continued. "And it's all compounded by the fact that everything that 'Samantha,' the woman that he loved, said was a lie. Look at the number of telephone calls, pictures, and texts and imagine how that might affect what was going on in a young man's head. It's a crucial piece of the puzzle."

I walked to the other end of the jury box. "The last period of time starts from today—from the time Joshua made his confession through the end of his expected life age, seventy-two. Fifty years. That's why we are here. Sadly, there is nothing anyone can do to bring Jonathan Williams back. We now have to deal with the one who is before you: Joshua Miller.

"The Military Judge will instruct you that there are five principles of sentencing: the protection of society, punishment of the wrongdoer, the rehabilitation of the wrongdoer, the preservation of good order and discipline, and deterrence of others. You will be asked to balance all those factors in determining an appropriate sentence.

"The law has determined that someone who is given a life sentence can be eligible for parole after serving a minimum of twenty years—that's the starting point. So we all agree, Joshua included, that he will serve at least twenty years at Leavenworth, as I said, one of the harshest prison environments around.

"We will present a stipulation of testimony for your consideration from the Executive Director of the Disciplinary Barracks at Leavenworth, Kansas. He will tell you about the process and the programs offered, which are all voluntary. A prisoner doesn't have to participate. Their board will evaluate a prisoner's risk factors and make risk assessments. A prisoner can get counseling if he chooses to do so.

"We will also present evidence from Colonel Butler, a retired Marine Corps Colonel, who was the past President of Navy Clemency and Parole Board. He will tell you that parole is a privilege, not a right. He will explain the criteria for somebody to be eligible for parole and how difficult it is."

I paused. "Members, I know that you have a weighty decision before you. Awarding the death penalty or even life imprisonment to a young sailor is an amazingly difficult task. I understand that you don't have a crystal ball. I know you realize from your own life experiences that people can change in twenty years. I ask you to allow Joshua that opportunity. Make Joshua work. Make him get up every day with a purpose. Make him, in some small way, repay society for what he has done.

"Again, I submit the death penalty is too harsh a penalty. We live in a society where an eye for an eye is no longer appropriate. And if you give Joshua life imprisonment without the possibility of parole, then all he does is sit around and watch TV every day. Think about that. Make Joshua work every day, make him pay for the decisions he has made." I looked each one in the eye as Commander Dempsey had done. I could think of nothing further to say.

"Thank you."

I sat down exhausted. And it was only lunchtime.

CHAPTER FORTY-ONE

THE COURT-MARTIAL WAS CALLED BACK to order at 1300. Captain Johnson entered the courtroom and took his seat. "The court will come to order. All parties who were present when the court recessed are once again present. Everyone, please be seated."

The Government called as its first sentencing witness, Dr. R. M. McDermitt, the medical examiner. Dr. McDermitt slowly approached the witness stand. He wore a tweed jacket with elbow patches, his hair slightly disheveled; he looked every bit the professor he was at East Carolina University Medical School in Greenville, North Carolina. Commander Dempsey stood.

"Dr. McDermitt, please face me, raise your right hand, and place your left hand on the Bible," she ordered. "Do you swear that the evidence that you are about to give in this hearing is the truth, the whole truth, and nothing but the truth?"

"I do."

Lieutenant Commander Mays, Dempsey's underling, took over the questioning, and began going through the good doctor's extensive resume. I cut him off.

"Your Honor, the Defense will stipulate to the doctor's expertise as a medical examiner," I said, partially rising from my chair.

"Thank you, Counsel," responded the Military Judge, not really thanking me at all. He looked over at the Assistant Trial Counsel, who looked relieved not to have to go through the ME's experience over the last forty years.

"Dr. McDermitt, can you please tell us about your involvement in this case?" Mays asked stiffly.

"I performed the autopsy of Lance Corporal Williams. I also signed off the death investigation, as well as the death certificate." The jurors began to squirm uncomfortably in their seats, not eager to hear the gruesome details particularly after lunch.

"Doctor, I want to show you several exhibits."

"Your Honor, again the Defense will stipulate to the Government's exhibits as being true and accurate depictions of the work performed by Dr. McDermitt." A nod from the judge. Maybe he would be able to get home for a late dinner after all.

"Doctor, what was the cause and manner of death of Corporal Williams?" Mays said as he handed a stack of exhibits to the witness.

The doctor leaned forward. He looked down over his bifocals and examined the color photographs he was holding in his wrinkled hands. "I determined the cause of death was an incision to the neck. The manner was defined by the type of wound. I determined that it was a homicide."

"Your Honor, I'd like to publish these ten photographs of the deceased to the jury."

I rose once again. "Judge, is that really necessary?"

"Counsel, two or three pictures will be enough to illustrate your point," said the judge, nodding to the bailiff. I toyed with my pen while he took the pictures to the jury, who passed them around. I had just received them that morning without submitting a discovery request. Usually it takes the Government weeks to provide the evidence they have. The longer it takes to get, the less time you have to prepare. Given the circumstances, I got these pictures rather quickly. Nora even sent a few extra 8×10 glossies. They were gruesome in every detail. Williams's neck had been sliced from ear to ear. The gaping wound seemed a foot wide.

"Doctor, one last question." He paused for dramatic effect, the asshole. "How long did it take Corporal Williams to die?"

"Objection!" For the fourth time that morning, I rose out of my chair. "How in the world would the doctor know that?"

Before Commander Mays could respond, the Military Judge said, "Counsel, I don't need to remind you that the doctor is testifying today as an expert who has performed thousands of autopsies."

"Your Honor, I am not arguing with the witnesses expertise. However, I think the judge would agree with me that in this courtroom we don't deal in speculation. Is the witness ready to testify with any specificity how long it takes someone to expire?" That word was much nicer than *die*, I thought.

"Your objection is overruled."

I sat down heavily. The doctor continued, not seeming to care one way or the other. "Because it was a venous wound, I determined the time from the infliction of wound until death was five minutes, possibly longer. They don't bleed as fast as an arterial wound would."

"No further questions." The young barrister went back to his table, seeming quite satisfied with himself.

I stood and walked toward the doctor. What questions could I possibly ask to minimize that testimony? I had to think fast.

"Doctor, the body contains approximately six liters of blood does it not?"

"Yes, that is correct more or less."

"And about 20 percent of that volume is sent to the brain?"

"Also correct."

"And the jugular vein is a major return conduit from the brain, isn't it?"

"Yes." The doctor sat up in his chair. He appeared interested in where this line of questioning was going.

"So a loss of 20 percent of blood volume would certainly induce shock, would it not?"

"Yes. That's quite right." He was nodding.

"And stress also increases ones susceptibility to shock, does it not?"

"Indeed it does. Yes."

"So isn't it true, Doctor, that a person in the circumstances you just described, along with the combination of stress and shock, would experience a quick loss of consciousness?

"Yes. Yes. That's true," he answered, again agreeing with me.

"And that person, although technically alive, would feel no conscious pain would he?"

The doctor sat back in the witness chair. He took off his glasses. He paused and then answered. "Yes, I guess that is true."

"Thank you, sir. No further questions."

Sometimes you take what you can get. I quickly sat down.

CHAPTER FORTY-TWO

HE WALKED TO THE WITNESS stand back ramrod straight. His haircut was high and tight, pants with a sharp crease, shoes shined to a high gloss. No one looks better than a marine in dress uniform.

"Please state your full name, spelling your last."

"Richard H. Carlson, last name spelled C-A-R-L-S-O-N."

"Thank you. Are you currently on active duty in the United States Marine Corps?" Dempsey asked.

"Yes, Ma'am, I am."

"What is your rank?"

"E-5, Sergeant."

"How did you know Corporal Williams, Sergeant?"

Carlson inhaled deeply. "We were both students at Dam Neck, Ma'am."

"When did you first meet him?"

"It was a couple of days after we got to the school. We were just hanging out. I walked up to him and we started talking, asking each other where we were from, what MOS we did because we were both lateral movers. And we started talking about family and how we got to this point in our careers, where we've been, stuff like that."

"You mention that you met him at the MOS school. Is that the NMITC?"

"Yes, Ma'am."

"What type school is that?"

"It's an intelligence school, Ma'am."

"And what were you learning to do?"

"To be an OT-31, that is a basic intelligence analyst, Ma'am."

"And you're moving in from another field?"

"Yes, Ma'am. I was prior 03-11, Infantry." I knew Commander Dempsey had studied up on the Marine Corps military occupational specialties, or MOS, codes. Marines separate all jobs into occupational fields numbered 01 to 99 and include general categories such as intelligence, logistics, infantry, ordnance, etc. She probably could cite them all from memory. Nora prepared well, even for character witnesses.

"How does a marine get selected for the intelligence field?"

"Ma'am, you have to be recommended and have good GT—ah, general technical, scores. It's pretty competitive, so to be selected is pretty much an honor."

"What did you and Corporal Williams do during your free time?"

"We were both family men, married, so a lot of our time was spent just hanging out around the base, in our rooms. Or we'd go bowling. We went down to the beach a couple of times but pretty much just hung out with each other."

"Did you two become close?" Dempsey asked softly.

"Very close." Sergeant Carlson's voice began to crack slightly.

"Can you describe your relationship for the members?"

Carlson hesitated. "I considered Jonathan like my own flesh and blood. I only knew him for three months, but he was probably the best friend I ever had, and I consider him... like a brother." He was trying to compose himself. A battle-tested marine wasn't supposed to cry.

"How did Corporal Williams get along with the other marines in the class?"

Carlson answered in a stronger voice. "Very well, Ma'am. Everybody looked up to him. He was a natural-born leader; he had a lot of charisma. Everybody came to him with their problems. If he saw that a marine was having a problem, he'd reach out to him. You know, just an all-around great guy."

"When will your class graduate from NMITC?"

"The end of July, Ma'am."

"When did you find out that your classmate and best friend was missing?"

"We have this exercise we do at the end of each class to test our skills. Our Staff Sergeant brought us all in. They were holding us after hours. Master Sergeant Burton, our class coordinator, came in and told us that Jonathan was missing. We all knew something was wrong. He just wouldn't have taken off without a reason. We wondered all these months what had happened to him. Then two nights ago, they told us they had found a marine in the woods of North Carolina and they were pretty sure it was Corporal Williams." Carlson was getting choked up again.

"Describe the reactions of the marines in the class when that announcement was made."

"It was shock and sadness, Ma'am. Everybody turned to the NCOs, his friends especially, to see how we were taking it. I didn't want to get upset in front of the marines there. So I just basically told everybody to leave me alone. And me and the other NCOs found an empty classroom and we went and cried together and just started kind of reminiscing about Jonathan."

"Did the school do anything to honor Corporal Williams?"

"We held a memorial service last night at our chapel. A lot of people attended, a lot of people not from our school. The church was overflowing. There was a big turnout."

"Did you and Corporal Williams make any future plans together?"

"Yes, Ma'am. He wanted to get transferred to my unit so that we could go to Afghanistan together. I knew our friendship would be a lifelong friendship. We were going to hang out on the weekends, have barbecues, hang with the family, you know, do what best friends do."

"What impact did Corporal Williams's death have on you, Sergeant?"

Carlson could no longer hold back the tears. "You know, everyone here has had friends that have died in Afghanistan or Iraq. And that's okay because that is a good death to die in battle. You don't cry for those guys." He hesitated while he wiped away a tear. "But the manner that Corporal Williams died, it kind of pisses me off. I mean, I loved the guy like a brother. I loved his family. I loved his wife and her family. And it makes me angry that we were brought together under these circumstances instead of different circumstances. It makes me mad because, like I said, we were supposed to be lifelong friends, and I'm never going to get that chance. There are going to be no barbecues. Our kids are going to hang out together, but it isn't going to be the same. This tragedy will always be there. When we're together, we always going to know the reason behind why we're hanging out, because of the death of my friend." He paused again and stared hard at Miller. "That's how it's impacted me." For a moment, I thought he might jump from the witness stand and come after my client.

"What will you remember most about your friend?"

"Jonathan would give his right arm to you if you needed it. He was always there for you. Even though I outranked him, I considered him my mentor. And I was older than him, but I considered him my older brother. He was such a natural leader, and he drew people to him because he was such a great guy."

"Thank you, Sergeant Carlson, no further questions."

I rose. "No questions, Sir." I wanted Carlson off the stand as quickly as possible. He glared at Miller as he exited the courtroom.

Commander Dempsey then said, "Sir, the Government would like to request a short break at this time."

From our pretrial conference that morning before court the judge knew the order in which the witnesses were going to be called that day. "Very well," he said. "The court is going to be in recess for fifteen minutes. Members, consistent with my previous instruction to you during the recess, please do not begin to discuss the case among yourselves or with anyone else or consult any source outside the courtroom regarding the issues. The members may depart at this time."

I watched them leave. I took a deep breath. I knew the last witness of the day was going to be the most difficult.

CHAPTER FORTY-THREE

A TRIAL IS ALL ABOUT persuasion. When presenting evidence I tell my young attorneys to remember the theory of primacy and recency. Jurors tend to believe what they hear first and remember what they hear last. Apparently, Nora was also a fan.

"Your Honor, we call as our last witness, Mrs. Williams."

Jessica Williams stood up from her front row seat where she sat next to Williams's parents. She had been in court every day, listening quietly. Today she wore a pale green dress that fell right above her knees. A gold cross on a thin chain hung around her neck. There were dark circles under her eyes. She once again walked slowly toward the witnesses stand. Hopefully, she would soon have some closure from this nightmare.

Nora began in a low comforting voice. "Mrs. Williams, please introduce yourself once again to the court."

"My name is Jessica Williams." The silence in the courtroom was deafening. All eyes were upon her. All felt her pain.

Commander Dempsey pointed toward the two-by-three foot portrait of Lance Corporal Jonathan Williams in his dress uniform that she had set up in the courtroom. I had tried to object to this outside the presence of the jury but the judge shut me down. "I'm sure we would all rather have Corporal Williams present," he admonished me. Not much I could say to that. It was another smart move by Nora. Let the jury feel the raw emotions of the living.

"Please tell the members of the jury who the man in that picture is."

She hesitated and then whispered, "That's my husband."

"Ma'am, how did you meet your husband?"

Mrs. Williams grabbed a Kleenex from the box of tissues that Commander Dempsey had thoughtfully left near the witness stand during the break. She patted the tears from her eyes. "Through a friend. My friend was married to his friend, and they were both stationed in Afghanistan. Out of the blue Jonathan called me on my birthday and wished me a happy birthday. When he came back to the States, our friends had a barbecue party at their house, and we met for the first time."

Nora smiled reassuringly at her. "What were your first impressions?"

"Jonathan was very funny, very honest, and easygoing."

"After you got to know him better, tell us what your husband was like?" Nora was drawing the jury in. I noticed many of them leaning forward so they could listen better.

"Jonathan loved the Marine Corps. He always talked about the marines. He cared a lot about people. He would go out of his way to help people. He would do anything for anybody. He was such a loving, kindhearted man."

"When were you and your husband married?"

"August 15 of that year," she said softly, dabbing at her eyes.

"Can you describe to the members a little bit about the circumstances?"

"He proposed on August 1. We were debating whether we were going to get married right away at the courthouse or save some money until he came back from Afghanistan so we could have a real wedding back home. We were so in love, we decided to get married two weeks later in a small courthouse nearby."

"Did you want to have a formal reception?"

"Jonathan was going to go to school here in Virginia. As soon as he finished, he would only have two weeks in the States, and then he would be going to Afghanistan for a year. So we decided we could save up some money while he was overseas, and when he came back from Afghanistan, we would have a big wedding and a reception back home for both families. And of course, buy real wedding bands." She looked away as the tears began welling in her eyes.

"What did you and your husband like to do together?"

"Go for long drives, rent movies, hang out in the apartment, go shopping, just about anything as long as we were together." The tears started to flow faster. Commander Dempsey appeared beside her with another box of Kleenex and then just as quietly moved away. No one seemed to notice.

"Mrs. Williams, do you have any children?"

She could only nod. She started rocking slightly back and forth in the witness chair.

"How many?"

She stopped and hunched forward as she said in a barely audible voice, "One."

"When did you find out you were pregnant?"

She whispered, "About a week after Jonathan left for school."

"Mrs. Williams, do you need a moment?" The witness shook her head and straightened up. Commander Dempsey continued. "How did your husband feel about becoming a father?"

"He was very excited. I was scared at first that he would be upset because he was in the military and was always deploying. I called him one day and I was crying. He asked me what was wrong. I told him I was pregnant. He just laughed and said, 'Don't be sad, be happy because this is the happiest moment of our lives.'"

"When was your son born?"

"May 17."

"What did you name your son?"

"Bradley Paul Williams."

"Who is he named after?" Dempsey asked.

"After our fathers."

"Can you please describe to the members how you felt the day your son was born?"

Even though she tried to remain composed, Mrs. Williams could not stop the tears this time. She tried to speak several times but the words just caught in her throat. We all waited patiently for her to answer. Finally she said slowly, "It was exciting, but it was also

207

very lonely because I knew how much my husband wanted to be there. Jonathan wanted to be there to hold our son. He was looking forward to being a father, that's all he wanted to be."

"Did you and Jonathan want to have more children?" It was the first time Commander Dempsey had used his given name. The question was objectionable but I knew better than to say anything now.

"Yes, we wanted three kids."

"Did the two of you talk about your future plans together?"

"We did. After Jonathan got out of the Marine Corps, he was going to go to a technical school to become a mechanic. Then he wanted to open his own shop, and we were going to have three kids and raise our children and grow old together."

Commander Dempsey paused for a few seconds. It seemed an eternity. "Now in honor of your husband, you put together a slide-show presentation, is that correct?"

She could only nod.

"Judge, this is 'Prosecution Exhibit Ten' for the record. We'll play it in a minute. Mrs. Williams, would you please describe to the jurors what you did to put that video together?"

She straightened up, pushed her shoulders back, and looked at my client. "I gathered up some pictures from his mom and dad and from friends and family, and of course from myself, from the day he was born until the birth of our son."

"When was the last time you saw your husband, Mrs. Williams?"

"December 30, when I dropped him off at the airport. I was crying. It was really early in the morning and I didn't want him to leave. We almost didn't make it to the airport on time. I had been crying the whole time. And I know he didn't want to leave me, but it was his duty. When we got out of the car, he looked at me and held me tight and said, 'Baby, don't cry because I'll be back in a few months, it will go by fast and you'll see me in no time.'"

"Was that last Christmas special for the two of you?"

"It was. When I was pregnant, I had really bad morning sickness. Jonathan told me I should just quit my job and stay home. He ate ramen noodle soup for two months so he could save his money and give me the best Christmas ever, and he did. We didn't know it was going to be our first and last Christmas together." Now some of the jurors were getting misty-eyed.

"When was the last time you spoke to your husband?"

"The late evening hours of New Year's Eve."

"What did you say to each other?"

"We wished each other happy New Year. We talked for over an hour. We talked about our future. He had to go to bed early because he had to be on duty the next day and needed to get some rest. The last thing he said to me was, 'Remember that I love you very, very, very much, and give my son a kiss for me.'"

"How did you find out that your husband was missing?"

"A few days later, one of the instructors from the school called me around nine o'clock in the morning and asked me if I knew where my husband was. I told him that he should be in class. He said he hadn't showed up for school the last few days. I said that there must be something wrong if he didn't show up, because the last time I talked to him he was really excited about his classes."

"What thoughts went through your mind when you found out he was missing?"

"That something must be wrong. I knew my husband would never go AWOL. He was a very hard-core Marine, very dedicated. He was one of those people that would show up ten minutes before the time that he was supposed to be there, and there was no way he would just not show up. He was not like that."

"So what did you do?"

"The first thing I did was call his parents and told them he was missing. I asked if they had heard from Jonathan and they said no."

"Where were you when you found out that his body had been found?"

"At the hotel where I'm staying."

"How did you find out about his death?"

"I had some friends that were supposed to come over and take me to court. One of my friends knocked on the door. When I opened it, there were two marines in uniform standing in front of the door, and my friend was standing right behind them. Right then I knew that my husband's body had been found."

"Was anything said?"

"I started crying. They didn't have to say anything. I just knew. I fell on my knees and said a prayer finally knowing that he was gone forever." Then she said, almost as if to herself, "He was supposed to come back in a few months."

"How has the death of your husband impacted you?"

She took several seconds before she answered. "I lost a big part of me. When I found out he was missing, I was pregnant. I couldn't see myself without my husband. I just wanted to die. I had so many thoughts, it was so bad. I had a dream that I found a gun and pointed it at my head and I just took my life. I thought that would be the best way because that way my son and I could be with my husband. We could be together forever. I had no reason to live anymore."

"What kept you from taking your own life?"

"Looking at my son's face. I knew Jonathan wouldn't want me to do that. He told me more than once that he was so glad that he married me. That even when he was on deployments, he could totally trust me with our son and not have any worries."

"Did the loss of your husband affect you in any other way?"

Again she hesitated. She was looking down at the hands folded in her lap. "I don't know. I feel like I've been very antisocial since he's been gone. I hate everybody. I don't want to talk to anybody. I don't trust anybody. My husband made me a better person, and honestly, this whole thing has made me see the ugly side of life." She paused. "I can't think about the future. I don't know how I'm going to raise my son. I don't know what I'm going to tell my son when he grows up. When he starts going to school and says, 'Mommy, I see everyone with their dads. I don't have a daddy,' I don't know what I'm going to tell him then. Some bad guy came and just took his life away? I don't know. That's all I can think about."

"What will you remember most about your husband?" Nora asked.

"His smile. The way he'd go out of his way to make people laugh, because he hated seeing people sad. Jonathan always had a smile on his face, no matter what."

"Does anything remind you of him?"

"Just seeing my son, the way he sleeps and the way he laughs. The way he smiles, it's just like Jonathan."

"How does your future feel without your husband beside you?"

"I don't see a future right now. All I can do is raise my son as best as I can. One day at a time. I will try my best not to disappoint my husband."

"Thank you, Mrs. Williams. I have no further questions. Judge may we now play the video?"

"Before we do that, Commander DeMarco, any cross?"

I just shook my head. The judge nodded to the bailiff. The lights dimmed and the video began to play.

Tough way to end the day.

CHAPTER FORTY-FOUR

It was Friday morning. The Government had rested its case. Now it was my turn. I needed to direct the jury's attention back to Miller's story. No better way than to start with the reason we were here.

She entered through the back doors of courtroom number 1, the largest courtroom in the NLSO. She could barely fit through the narrow center aisle with the spectator benches on either side. I had issued a subpoena to her at the motel in the Outer Banks, where she worked as a night clerk. There was quite a contrast between this witness and the last.

Joshua stared straight ahead, having never seen "Samantha" in person and not wanting to see her now. It took an eternity for her to reach the well of the court, sliding sideways through the swinging gate that separated the courtroom participants from the spectators and into the witness box where she sat down heavily.

I had also subpoenaed her telephone records. She had made over 5,000 phone calls, sent 487 text messages and 47 pictures in the 77 days from November 1 to January 17—an average of 72 a day! And not all of them were to my client. Apparently, not much work was getting done at the motel!

"Trial Counsel, please swear in the witness," said Captain Johnson.

"Ma'am, would you please stand, raise your left hand, placing your right hand on the Bible, and repeat after me?"

"Samantha's" face was flushed. The effort to stand up from the witness chair required more work than she was used to. At 5'4" tall, she weighed over 350 pounds. She wore a brown paisley smock covering Lycra stretch pants. Her ankles were swollen and wedged into flat shoes. Dempsey's instructions seemed to confuse her.

"Do you swear that the evidence you are about to give is the truth, the whole truth, and nothing but the truth?"

There was a hesitation. "Ah... I do." Then she turned to the judge and asked sweetly, "Do I need a lawyer?" The eastern North Carolina drawl was unmistakable. An odd English lilt. Many of the people living in the Outer Banks traced their descendants back to the time of the Pilgrims. The Lost Colony, a tale of 117 men, women, and children who established the first permanent settlement in the Americas and then mysteriously vanished, is still one of the area's favorite attractions. The voice didn't match the body. For a moment, I closed my eyes. Could I envision a sailor on the other end of a telephone falling in love with it? Killing over it? The judge interrupted my thoughts.

"Ms. Jenkins, you are not being charged with a crime. The Navy has no jurisdiction over you. You are being called to this courtroom as a witness to give evidence in the case of *United States versus IS3 Miller*. However, if you feel uncomfortable, I will allow you time to consult with an attorney of your own choosing." Good ole Captain Johnson trying to accommodate everyone.

"Thank you... No, I'm okay." Something about her was childlike; you wanted to protect her despite her size. She gave off an aura of vulnerability.

"Ma'am, would you please state your full name and home address for the record?"

"My name is Susan Jenkins... I'd prefer not to give you my address." That stopped everyone for a second. In the military, everyone followed orders and answered the question they were asked, especially when it was asked by an officer.

It took a moment for the judge to recover. "Ms. Jenkins, why don't you want to give us your home address?"

"I don't want him to know where I live," she said, glancing momentarily at Joshua, who was still intently staring straight ahead.

"Ms. Jenkins, Petty Officer Miller is in custody." Jenkins looked down and shook her head back and forth.

Somewhat exasperated, the judge said, "Very well. Would you at least tell us the county and state you live in?" Jeez, this was a material witness in a murder case!

After a moment she said, "Currituck County, North Carolina."

"Defense Counsel, your witness."

Finally, after weeks of thinking about her, I was ready. I rose quickly and walked to within three feet of the witness chair.

"Ms. Jenkins, isn't it true you didn't want to talk with me before your appearance here today?"

"They said I didn't have to." She glanced over at Lieutenant Commander Mays.

"Who said that?" I paused but quickly continued. "No matter, you have to talk to me now." The Assistant Trial Counsel stood to object. I motioned for him to sit down. "Captain Johnson, may I have permission to declare Ms. Jenkins a hostile witness." This would allow me to ask her leading questions and hopefully show the jury why we were really here.

"Counsel, is that really necessary?"

I had a material witness on the stand that deceived my client enough that he killed someone. Maybe I should just say "Please" and "Thank you."

"Yes, Sir, it is."

The Military Judge blew out his cheeks as if pained by my request; he finally acquiesced. "Very well."

I moved closer to her. "Miss Jenkins, how do you know Joshua Miller?"

"I talked to him on the phone for a few months."

"When did that phone relationship start?"

"November last year, I think."

"He wasn't the only sailor that you were talking to on the phone, was he?"

She paused and then answered quickly, "No, Sir."

"Please tell the court the names of some of the other sailors that you were talking to on the phone." I knew she couldn't remember them all.

"I can't recall them all."

"Come on now, you can't give us any names?" I asked incredulously.

"Brian Adams, that's the only one I can remember." Bingo! She had called him almost as much as Miller. He was on my witness list.

"So you would just sit around and make random telephone calls to sailors?" I said raising my eyebrows.

"Yes, Sir."

"Now why would you do that?"

"Just to talk to them, I reckon."

"How long have you been doing that, Miss Jenkins?"

"Since I was a teenager."

I walked back to my table and grabbed a stack of papers. "May I approach the witness?" Captain Johnson nodded. "Miss Jenkins, I'm going to hand you what has been marked as 'Defense Exhibit U,' it's a copy of your cell phone records for the months of November through January. Would you look at those, please?" She nodded.

"Do you recall Joshua's cell phone number?" She hesitated. She had to remember it as many times as she called. I interjected. "Does the number 7-5-7-5-5-5-7-4-8-9, sound familiar to you?"

"Yes, that's his number."

"Okay. And do you recall the telephone number of the training barracks over at Dam Neck?"

"7-5-7-5-5-5-2-6-0-0."

"Okay. Let's try one more. How about 5-5-5-8-8-8-3?" Again she hesitated. I moved closer to her. "Would that be Airman Adams's cell phone number?" I wasn't playing around. I had to let her know that.

"Yes."

"And how about your Internet address, what was the name you used for that?"

"I don't... it was... I don't remember what it was." She looked exasperated and was starting to get slightly annoyed, a side of her we hadn't seen yet.

"It was 'Sexy Sammy,' isn't that true?"

"Yes." The jury was beginning to sense just what type of person she really was.

"And Sammy is short for Samantha, right?"

"I guess." She shrugged.

"Now, let's look at those phone records again if we can." She had laid them on the side of the witness box and now looked down at them as though something on them was contagious. "It's hard to imagine but there are over five thousand phone calls made during the time period, November 1 through January 17, isn't there?"

She didn't answer as she stared silently down at the stack of records.

"Ms. Jenkins! That's accurate isn't it?"

She looked up and silently stared at me. I waited for a reply. Finally, in a voice barely above a whisper, she said, "I guess so."

"Let's take a closer look at some of those records if we can. The first date is November 1 and it's four pages of approximately 147 telephone calls. Would you look at those first four pages, please?"

She looked over and examined the exhibit although she still wouldn't touch it. It didn't matter; the jury would soon get my point.

"We've already established that 5-5-5-8-8-8-3 was Airman Adams's telephone phone number correct?"

"Uh-huh."

"And you made eleven calls to Airman Adams on November 1, isn't that correct?

"Yes, Sir."

"If you would, Ms. Jenkins, please go midway down on the first page, there's a 4-3-3 number. Would that be a number to one of the military installations?"

"Oh, yes. Yes, Sir."

"Whose number is that?"

"That's Brian's shop number."

"So you were also calling Airman Adams at work?"

"That was his work number."

"Now please turn to the second page." She finally reached over and touched the paperwork turning the pages but only with two fingers, "It appears the first time that you called the barracks number, the 5-5-5-2-6-0-0, was at 5:09 p.m. Is that correct?"

"Uh-huh, I guess."

"Would that be the first time you talked to Joshua—I mean, Petty Officer Miller?"

"I believe so."

"So it looks like you talked to him the first time at 5:09 p.m. and called back again at 5:12 p.m. Is that correct?"

"Yes, Sir."

"Then you called back twice more at 5:24 p.m. and 5:35 p.m.?"

"Yes. Yes, Sir. That's what these records say."

"Now toward the bottom of that page there are several calls to a 4-4-4 numbers. Is that also a military installation number?"

"Yes, Sir."

"And who were you calling there?"

"I don't know. I don't know, I'm not sure," she said as she was getting flustered.

"So there were other military members you were calling?"

"Could have been."

"If you would, go to the entry made at 7:57 p.m. that evening, the 5-5-5-7-4-8-9 number. Is that Petty Officer Miller's cell phone number?" She picked up the entire stack of records now.

"Yes, Sir."

"And you made four calls to that number until 8:00 p.m., is that correct?"

"I guess."

"And then at 8:00 p.m. you made three more calls to his barracks room number, correct?

"But they weren't but a minute long."

"I'm just asking you if you made those calls."

"Yes. I did."

"And then it looks like you switched back and made four more calls to his cell phone number?"

"Yes."

"Then two more calls to his barracks at 8:23 p.m. and 8:25 p.m.?"

"Yes, Sir."

"And then again at 9:13 p.m. you called his cell phone number?"

"Yes, Sir."

"So from 7:57 p.m. until 9:13 p.m., about one hour and fifteen minutes, you made fourteen calls trying to track him down?" She didn't answer. "And that was the first night you two talked?" Again, no answer.

"And then at 9:24 p.m. you made a call to his room and you two talked for seventy-seven minutes?"

"Yes."

"Miss Jenkins, when you made 147 phone calls that day. Would that be an unusual number of phone calls for you to make in one day?"

"Well, I was trying to get a hold of him and the numbers—I guess he was at dinner or something or at the gym or wherever he was."

"But this was the first time you met—I'm sorry, the first time you *talked* to Petty Officer Miller?"

"But he asked me to call him."

"That's not my question, Ma'am." I paused. "Hold on. Let's go back a second. Isn't it true that, until you walked into this courtroom today, you have never even laid eyes on Petty Officer Miller?"

"Yes, Sir. I mean… No, no, I haven't." Her face was turning red now.

"So let's go back to my question. Ms. Jenkins, was that an unusual number of phone calls for you to make in one day?"

"I don't know."

I kept pressing. "Well, Ms. Jenkins, on November 4, three days later you made 142 calls, sent 19 text messages and 10 pictures, isn't that true?"

She didn't respond. I made my point so I moved on. There was a lot of ground to cover.

"And am I correct when I say you were the one who first contacted Petty Officer Miller?"

"Yes."

"And that was just a random call?"

"Yes, Sir."

"And you told him you were looking for a 'Christina' at that time?"

"Yes, Sir."

"Why were you looking for 'Christina' at the barracks?"

"I don't know."

"This was just a ruse to talk to somebody, wasn't it?"

"I guess."

"What did you tell Petty Officer Miller your name was?"

"Samantha Stevens."

"And when you called other sailors, what name would you use?"

"Made up names. I would just make up any random name."

"Why would you do that?"

"Because I didn't want them to know my real name."

I moved over to the jury box so when she answered me, she would be now be looking at them. "Over the next several months, how often would you talk to Petty Officer Miller?"

"Every day."

"And what time during the day or night were those phone calls?"

"I would sometimes wake him up in the morning or we'd talk during the day or after his class until probably about midnight or 1:00 a.m."

"What would you talk about?"

"Everything."

"Can you give us some examples?"

"About what's going on, like, he would talk about work—well, not really. He wouldn't go into details about what he was doing, but we talked about cars, talked about family, stuff like that."

"Did you feel that you two had a lot in common?"

She hesitated and looked down again. Then quietly she answered, "Maybe."

"May I approach the witness again, Judge?"

"You may." Captain Johnson was actually looking interested.

"May the record reflect that I'm now handing Ms. Jenkins ten pictures that have previously been marked as 'Defense Exhibit Sierra.' Would you look at those pictures, please Ms. Jenkins?" As with the phone records, she wouldn't touch them. "Are these some of the pictures that you sent to Petty Officer Miller?" Most probably came from fashion or soft porn magazines. They obviously weren't her.

"Yes."

"Tell me how you described yourself to Petty Officer Miller?"

"That I was pretty and I was—I guess what he liked. I described it, you know..." Her face turned even redder and her voice trailed off.

"So I guess you're not five feet tall with long blond hair?" I couldn't bring myself to mention the obvious, that she didn't weigh 100 pounds either.

Again she was silent.

"Did you tell him that you went to Old Dominion University?"

"Yes, Sir."

"And that you were an art history major?"

"Yes. I told him all that because I didn't want him to know who I was."

"Why not, Ms. Jenkins?" A good trial lawyer never asks a question that he doesn't already know the answer, but I was sure I could handle any response she made.

"Because I didn't really know him. Yes, I was talking to him, but in the same sense, I just didn't want him to find out who I was. I didn't plan on talking to him forever."

"Did you tell him your family was from Texas?"

"I do have family from Texas."

"Did you tell him that your family was very well-off, in fact that they were rich?"

"Uh-huh."

"Is that a yes, Ms. Jenkins?" She only nodded.

"Would you tell these same types of stories to the other sailors you were talking to?"

"Sometimes."

"Did you send him, besides those pictures"—I pointed to the ten—"did you send him pictures of a girl naked?"

She hesitated. "Yes. Well, not all the way naked, but yes. I would make sure the face was blocked."

"Did you have phone sex with him?"

She nodded, her face reddening more.

"And you did that with other sailors as well, didn't you?"

"Uh-huh." I didn't ask her to clarify this time.

"Nothing you told Petty Officer Miller was the truth was it?"

She stared at me. Her silence was answer enough.

"He tried to meet you several times, didn't he?"

"Yes, he was persistent. He wanted to meet, he wanted to see me."

"Did you find that to be unusual?"

"No, but I didn't want to meet him, so I would make up excuses."

"What type of excuses would you make up?"

"That my phone wasn't working or I was at school. That he was at the wrong place or it was the wrong time. One time I said I was in a car accident."

"Would he show up at places and wait around for you?"

"Well, that's what he said he did, yes."

"Did he ask you to fly to Virginia to meet his family during the Christmas holidays?"

"Yes."

"Did he send you a plane ticket to use?"

She just looked down and didn't answer immediately. "I lied and told him I was coming in. I didn't show up at the airport."

In a voice stronger than I meant to use, I said, "He waited thirteen hours for you in the cold and snow at the airport." It wasn't a question. Nora didn't object. I continued. "He called you while he was at the airport, didn't he?"

"Yes, but I had my phone off."

"When you finally talked to him about, why you didn't show up? What did he say to you?"

She hesitated and then said, "He said it was okay, he just wanted to know where I was and if I was safe."

"And what was your response?"

"I lied and told him I was there and I didn't see him, and so I left."

"Now a moment ago you mentioned you told him you were in a car accident?"

"Yes."

"And let me guess—that wasn't true was it?"

This time Commander Dempsey rose with a half-hearted "Objection. Argumentative." The judge just shook his head and motioned for me to continue.

"Well, it was an excuse so he would stop calling. Because he would call and call to get a hold of me and my phone would ring and I would have to tell him that so he would leave me alone."

I looked at her incredulously. "Excuse me, Ms. Jenkins, but let's look at the telephone records again. You've made thousands of calls to him over this period of time. How is that trying to stop him from calling?"

She was getting mad again. "If you would get his phone records, you would see how many times he tried to call me."

"Well, we're in luck. I have them." I turned and went to my counsel table and retrieved the stack sitting on the corner. I walked back to the witness stand and handed the stack to her. She wouldn't take them. "Ms. Jenkins, let's not argue. Let's examine the evidence. If we count all the calls made, you've called Joshua three times as much as he's called you." I still had my arm outstretched with the records. She made no move to take them. "I have a synopsis on the front of these records, and if you want to disagree with me, please do. I've noted the calls where you two were talking thirty, forty, fifty, sixty, seventy times a day. There was one instance when it was over one hundred times. So let me ask you again, Ms. Jenkins, is that indicative of somebody that's trying to stop a relationship?"

She raised her voice and leaned forward. "I didn't stop because he told me he wasn't going to stop until he saw me."

I moved closer to her. "Did he say he loved you?"

"Yes."

"Did you say that you loved him?"

"Yes," she almost shouted.

I stepped back, paused, and said calmly. "So, Ms. Jenkins, do you think it was unusual for him to want to meet you?"

She said almost as if to herself, "I figured he would just leave me alone eventually."

I walked back over to the jury box and said, "So you were just leading him on?"

She was silent for a moment and then whispered, "Yes."

I walked back toward the witness stand and said firmly, "If you would, let's look at the telephone records again. I put a yellow sticky on the date December 3. Did you and Joshua have an argument on December 3?"

"I'm not sure."

"Do you remember—well, let me get right to the point, did you ever tell him that you were raped?"

"No, I never said it exactly like that. I never said, 'I was raped.' I never said that exactly."

I put my hands on my hips and said, "Well, how exactly did you say it... exactly?" I thought that would draw an objection but everyone was waiting for her response.

"I just agreed with him because he thought I was out. I was at a party. He just assumed some things."

"Ms. Jenkins, from the phone records of that night you called either his phone or his room fifty-four times beginning at 12:06 a.m. and continuing until 11:00 a.m. the next day. You called him fifty-four times, correct?"

She was silent again and looked away.

"Look at the records," I commanded. "On December 3 you called his cell phone at 12:06, 12:21, 12:32, 12:42, 12:43, 12:46; his room at 12:49, 12:50, 12:51, 12:53, 1:09, 2:01, 2:05, 2:06, his cell again at, 2:15, 2:16, 2:17, 2:21, 2:22, 2:23, 2:24, 2:25, 2:26, 2:27, 2:29, 2:40, 2:41, 2:42—"

"Can I explain?" she interrupted.

"Please do."

"Those calls, well, I was drunk at that time. I was out and about and I was hanging out with my friends when he was calling me before then. I don't really recall talking to him. We didn't get into any deep conversations until the next day."

"So why were you calling him so much that evening?"

"Because my phone reception—I don't know what was said and what he heard. I was with my friends at the bar and I don't know what he heard and I felt like I didn't... I don't know."

"Ms. Jenkins, let's talk about this allegation and what you said to Petty Officer Miller. What do you recall? You say you didn't tell him you were raped. Tell me then, what did you say?"

"I was drunk. I was hanging out with friends. I don't know if he heard us. I don't know how he got the whole rape thing. You know..." She paused. "I just didn't want him to know that I was sleeping with somebody else."

I stepped back. "Oh! So you were sleeping with someone! Who were you sleeping with?"

Commander Dempsey rose. "Objection! Relevance."

"Overruled." I knew Capitan Johnson would want to hear the good stuff.

"I don't remember his name, sorry. There was a whole bunch of people at the house."

"I'm trying to, well, let me just move on." I was getting frustrated with her lies but had to remain calm. "Let me ask you this. Did you ever get a call from a Sergeant Mineo from the Currituck County Sheriff's Department?"

"I don't remember."

"Do you remember talking to a sheriff?"

"The only time I got a call from a sheriff, I called him back from my work number. And I don't know what day that was. I was at work when that happened."

"Ms. Jenkins, is there any doubt in your mind that Joshua thought you were raped?"

"Well... I don't know. He was going to the cops. He told me he was driving down looking for where I lived and stuff. He bought me a gun."

"Didn't he tell you that you needed to go to the police about this rape?"

"I told him to just leave it alone because I didn't want him to know that…" At that point she let out a big sigh. "I just wanted him to leave it alone. It wasn't his business, what happened that night was my business. And he—"

I interrupted. "So why didn't you just say you weren't raped? Why keep lying?"

She paused again. "I don't know."

"Did you ever give him a description of the individuals that were involved in this alleged rape?"

"Yes. He thought I was in Virginia, so I told him I was hanging with military people."

"And you said they were marines, correct?"

"I said military people. I don't know if I said marines, I might have, but I'm not sure."

"And you knew that Petty Officer Miller went to school with marines, correct?"

"Yes, he told me that."

"Did you also, in the description you provided to him, say that they were tall, muscular, with short hair?"

"Probably."

"And then, shortly thereafter, Petty Officer Miller told you that he saw a marine fitting that general description that looked at him 'kinda funny' in the cafeteria one day, didn't he?"

"I vaguely remember him saying he was eating and there was this guy giving him a funny look named Williamson."

"And he gave you that name?"

"He said 'Williamson'—I don't know if he said 'Williams' or 'Williamson,' I'm not sure."

"And you told him that Williamson or Williams was involved, didn't you?"

"Williams? Williamson? I don't know no Williams."

Exasperated, I said, "I know you don't, but you said that's who was involved in this incident, didn't you?"

"I told him to leave it alone. I kept persisting, just leave it alone."

"Did you tell Petty Officer Miller that the marines were breaking into your home and had killed your bird?

"I had a bird that died. Yes, I did say that to him. But I didn't say, 'It was those guys.' I never said anything like 'It was those guys.' He just assumed it."

"And when he made, as you call them, these assumptions, you didn't try to correct him, did you?"

"I told him to leave it alone, it's none of his business, just leave it alone. And he's like 'Well, I'm worried about you' and stuff like that."

I moved to within inches of her as I said, "So, Ms. Jenkins, this is a man who you were calling constantly day and night and who was constantly calling you. A man who told you he loved you and who you told you loved him. A man who you led to believe that you were rich and beautiful, who you sent naked pictures to and had phone sex with. A man who bought plane tickets during the holidays so you could meet his family. A man whom you lead to believe that you were raped." I paused to gather my breath. "And never once, never once, did you try to tell him that this was all a lie?"

I didn't give her time to answer. I said with disdain, "No further questions." I turned and walked back to my seat angry that someone could perpetrate such a fraud on another with no consequences.

The courtroom was silent. Slowly the judge turned from staring at the witness and looked to the Trial Counsel. "Cross-examination, Commander Dempsey?" Nora hesitated. She hadn't had an opportunity to interview Jenkins, but she knew instinctively where to begin.

"Ms. Jenkins, am I correct in assuming you have low self-esteem?"

The witness nodded. "Yes, Ma'am."

"And you started talking with Miller because you were lonely?"

"Yes, Ma'am."

"And eventually he was trying to get too close to you?"

"Yes."

"And you made up this story about the car accident because you wanted to break things off with him, is that correct?"

She nodded again. "I thought he would figure it out. That he would put two and two together and say, 'She's lying to me, I'll leave her alone.' You know? Because I knew that's what they all…" She paused and wiped a tear that had begun to form in the corner of her eye. "They all just leave me alone eventually."

"When you called him on the phone, did he actually pick up every time?"

"No, Ma'am."

"So if your message goes to voice mail, does that register on your telephone records as a call?" I thought of objecting as I knew Jenkins had no clue as to the intricacies of telephone records—or maybe she did.

"Yes, every call that's made whether it's answered or not registers as a call, that's what happens." She seemed quite satisfied with herself with that answer.

"Now, the event in early December, what happened at that party?"

"I was at a bar first and then we went to a party. There was a whole bunch of yelling and people fighting. I was really, really drunk at that party."

"And you had sex with another person?"

"Yes."

"And the next day you wanted to let Miller down easy and let him know that you didn't want to talk with him anymore, is that correct?" I didn't think that's what she said but let it pass, hoping the jury would figure it out.

"Yes."

"And when you told him that you had had sex with another person he thought that you had been taken advantage of, correct?"

"Well, he was saying that before I told him much of anything."

"And he didn't believe you, correct?" Commander Dempsey's version of the events was getting interesting and Jenkins was just following along.

"Nope. No, Ma'am."

"When you told him you were not taken advantage of, he didn't believe you, did he?"

"Your Honor, I have to object at this point. Commander Dempsey is putting her own spin on the witness's testimony."

Jenkins, sensing that she needed to get her story back in line, blurted out, "Well, no, because then I just—he kept saying it over and over and I just went along with it. I just told him 'Whatever, just leave it alone.' I just changed the subject and just stopped talking about it." Since the witness answered, the judge shrugged and allowed Commander Dempsey to continue.

"And he thought the perpetrator lived in Virginia Beach?"

"Yes. Because I told him we were hanging out at a military bar."

"And sometime later, he told you there was a guy that had been staring at him at the cafeteria?"

"This was probably later on in December."

"And did he tell you what that individual's name was that had been staring at him?"

"Yes. I believe he said 'Jonathan Williams.' I'm pretty sure he said the name."

"Now, Ms. Jenkins, at some point, did he started scaring you?" How in the world did Nora sense this? Women's intuition?

I objected. "How is that relevant, Judge?"

Johnson grinned slightly. "Counsel, your client has pled guilty to murder. Overruled."

Jenkins continued. "Yes, Ma'am. Apparently, he was pulling up my phone records. I guess you can pay someone to do that, because I had people calling me and telling me, 'Well, there's this strange person calling me asking who Samantha is?' When I asked him he told me, he paid like sixty-nine dollars to pull it up off the Internet. He read off the numbers to me, from the phone record."

"Did that concern you?"

"Yes, because my telephone records have my address on it. He also told me he didn't want to find out that I was some fat girl."

Dempsey feigned indignation. "He used those words? Fat girl?" Jenkins just nodded.

"Ms. Jenkins, one final question." Dempsey walked closer to her. "You never asked the accused to kill anyone, did you?"

"No, Ma'am." Nora looked knowingly at the jury then sat down.

The courtroom was still. The Military Judge looked over to me and asked. "Any redirect?"

I couldn't let Nora's last question be the one the jury was left with. "Yes, Judge, just a few." I approached the witness once again.

"Ms. Jenkins, you've told other sailors that you've been sexually assaulted, haven't you?"

"Well, not really."

"You didn't tell Airman Adams that you were sexually assaulted?"

"I told him I could have been when I got robbed at my motel. Two guys robbed me and I told him I could have been."

"Was that when Airman Adams was trying to break off his relationship with you?"

"I don't remember."

"Ms. Jenkins, isn't it true that anytime someone tries to break up with you, you claim that you were sexually assaulted?"

"No."

"Well, you have to admit you're not a very truthful person, are you?"

She sat back in her chair as far as she could go. She glared at me. "What do you mean? I have been really emotional—I just don't remember a lot of things so much has gone on."

"Well, you haven't told the truth to Petty Officer Miller, have you?"

No answer.

"And you lied to Airman Adams?"

"I guess."

"And you lied to everyone that you've talked to online?"

"Not all the time."

"You said that you wanted to let Petty Officer Miller down easy on December 3 because you had slept with another guy, is that correct?"

"Yes, Sir."

"Please look at those phone records once again if you will." Again she refused to touch them. My anger started to rise. "You called him forty-four times the next day, December 4. You called him eighteen times on the fifth and sent three text messages. You called him thirteen times on the sixth. Sixteen times the day after that, plus sent six text messages. Fourteen times the next day along with fourteen text messages. A whopping ninety-eight times on Friday, the ninth, along with nine text messages. Twenty-nine times on the eleventh along with five text messages, and eight times on the twelfth. Ms. Jenkins, you called him five hundred nine times in the month of December alone and you're telling this court you were trying to let him down easy?"

Again, she was silent. I let that silence hang in the air for a very long time. Finally, in a low strong voice that I hoped could be heard throughout the courtroom, I asked her again for the final time, "Why didn't you just tell him the truth?"

She looked at me for a few seconds before answering. "Because I was scared."

"What were you scared of? The truth?"

"I guess of someone getting close to me."

"Ms. Jenkins, he was in love with you."

"No, he wasn't. He was in love with a lie."

"A lie that you started and allowed to grow."

We looked at each other for a long time. My anger started to melt away. I was starting to feel some pity for this person who had more issues than someone of her young age deserved.

She began to cry. The realization of what she had been doing to these poor sailors all these years was finally starting to sink in.

I had done what I needed to do.

"No further questions."

CHAPTER FORTY-FIVE

HE WALKED INTO THE COURTROOM, looking horribly out of place. His name fit him perfectly; his uniform, not so well. Airman Brian Winstead Charles Adams III, Aviation Electrician Mate, Third Class, was my next witness. He looked like someone who would have two middle names. Adams adjusted his glasses as he took the witness stand. His hair was slicked down. I imagined he had a slide rule hidden somewhere in his uniform.

The Assistant Trial Counsel swore him in. "Airman Adams, can you please state your name, spelling your last?"

"Brian Adams the Third, last name is spelled A-D-A-M-S."

"And what is your current duty station?"

"VF-81 Oceana, Virginia." A fighter squadron.

"Thank you, Airman Adams. Your witness," Mays said to me as he returned to his seat next to Commander Dempsey.

I continued to sit at my counsel table for a moment. I wasn't entirely certain what Adams might say. From interviewing him a few days ago, I knew he was book-smart but had little common sense. I had to be careful. "Good afternoon, Airman Adams."

He pushed the glasses back up to the bridge of his nose before he answered. "Afternoon."

"You work at the Oceana Jet Base, but where do you live?"

"I live out in Pungo, in Virginia Beach." So he was a country boy.

"Have you ever lived in the barracks on Dam Neck base?"

"No."

"Okay. Do you have a cell phone?"

"Yes." It was going to be a long afternoon.

"And within the last year what was your cell phone number… if you recall?"

He thought for a long moment. "Within the last year, I don't recall. The number I have now is fairly recent." He cracked a small smile.

It was time to lead the witness a little. "I have a 555-8883 and a 555-9883. Do those numbers sound familiar to you?"

"Yes, they do."

"Were those your cell phone numbers?"

"One of them was," he said proudly. Another faint smile.

I smiled back at him. "Well then, tell us what the other number was."

I think he was beginning to enjoy himself. "The other one that was one that Susan had taken out in my name." He paused; I waited to see if he would finish. "I believe the 9883 was that one."

Now we were getting somewhere. "Did you give her permission to do that?"

"No, I did not," he said indignantly.

"The Susan you're referring to is Susan Jenkins?"

He shook his head vigorously up and down.

"Okay. Let's talk about the young Miss Jenkins. How was it that you first came to know Miss Jenkins?"

"I was working TAD—that's temporary additional duty—in the gedunk where I was stationed in our squadron. And she just, I guess, she just randomly called that number. She talked to my coworker and then she got pushed over to me. I just started talking to her. The guys thought it was kinda funny."

"So you had a telephone relationship with her?" I didn't want to confuse him.

"Yes. It was basically a telephone relationship. I worked night check, so in the middle of the night, I would pretty much just sit and talk with her. We had nothing else to do." And that appeared to make perfect sense to him.

"When was the first time you talked to her, what month? Do you remember?"

"I think the fall of last year."

"Like maybe September?"

"Yeah, I think that's right." Again, that goofy smile. I liked Airman Adams.

"And how long did that phone relationship last?"

"Until about late December, or maybe it was late January."

"Airman Adams, what name was Ms. Jenkins using during that period of time?"

"Callie Smith."

"When did you first learn that that was not her real name?"

He frowned. "Not until NCIS called me in and then she kind of confessed it."

"How did she describe herself to you?"

He smiled, leaned back, and looked wistfully out the courtroom window. I would have loved to know what he was really thinking. "Thin, blonde, five feet tall. She showed me random pictures but…" His voice trailed off, and his face flushed.

"Your Honor, may I approach the witness?" He nodded. "Let the record reflect that I'm handing Airman Adams what has previously been marked as 'Defense Exhibit Sierra.' Airman, would you look at those pictures please?"

He spent awhile examining each of the ten pictures I handed him. I didn't want to interrupt but had to ask the next question.

"Are those the pictures Callie sent to you?"

He looked up slowly and stared at me. Subconsciously he pulled the pictures close to his chest and simply nodded. Without being asked, he said quietly, "A couple that were, you know like, not full body—where you couldn't see her face or nothing like that."

"What did she tell you about herself?"

"That she worked at a motel, which she said her mom owned, in North Carolina."

"Did she mention whether her family owned other properties?"

"She told me that they owned several motels and were pretty well-off."

"Did she tell you what her educational background was?"

"She said she was going to college at William and Mary. All she mentioned was that it was like a general type of program."

"Did you ever try to meet her?"

"A couple of times, yes."

"What happened?"

"Nothing would really happen. I mean, it would be a phone call, all right, you know, 'I'm coming to see you,' blah, blah, blah. And then she would never show up. We never actually met."

"I thought that you did meet her eventually?"

"Oh well... I thought you meant..." He appeared confused then continued. "Yes. The first time we did meet was in, I guess it was late January, right before I stopped talking to her. I kind of put a face to the—who I'd been talking to for the last few months."

"Airman Adams, let me ask you this before we move on. Did you consider her your girlfriend at this point?"

"Well, I thought it was a little strange since we hadn't actually seen each other face to face, but yeah, I guess. She considered me her boyfriend. On multiple times she would say she loved me and things like that."

"Did you tell her you loved her?"

"Not more than a couple of times, but yes."

"So this relationship was kind of unusual for you?"

"Very unusual. Most of the relationship didn't make much sense to me. It was kind of a weird thing because it was a different story every day. You know, you never knew what was going to happen with her or what she was going to call and say was going on or—it was always something different and none of it ever really made sense. But those pictures..."

"Did you ever try to meet her family or have her meet your family?"

"Not really. She said she wanted to go home with me for Thanksgiving, but of course, that never happened because we never met. I just took a friend home. And when I got home, she called and got all mad about that and said that she was waiting for me and wanted to go with me."

"Did she ever tell you that she was sexually assaulted?"

"She did. On one occasion, she said that her work had gotten broken into in the middle of the night and they were robbed and that she was sexually assaulted during that."

"Do you know whether that was true or not?"

"No, I don't know whether that's true. It didn't really make much sense to me because she didn't mention anything about it at first, and then it kind of came up later as 'Oh, I was sexually assaulted—oh, I was raped' is how she put it. But when she actually explained it, it was more of a sexual assault than a rape type of incident."

"Any other lies that she told you that stand out in your mind?"

"Not particularly. I mean, she had told me lies about talking to her ex-boyfriend. It almost seemed like she was trying to make me mad or trying to make me hate her. And I wouldn't make too much out of it, and then she would get mad about that and just kind of break down and admit that she wasn't actually telling me the truth."

"Were the two of you intimate at one time?"

"One time, yes." That wasn't exactly what I was asking, but close enough.

"Tell us what happened."

"I told her that I had had enough and was going to quit calling if we didn't meet. She gave in and told me where the motel was but that things weren't all like she told me. I drove down to North Carolina." He paused again but this time didn't continue.

"Airman, what happened when you got there?"

"Well, she sure didn't look like them pictures!" he exclaimed. I thought I heard several of the jurors snicker. "I was pissed. Ah, excuse me... but we ended up talking and I thought she was nice enough. She had a sweet voice. We went to a 7-Eleven and got a couple of bottles of wine and when we got back she let us into a room and, well, you know what happened next." Again, the goofy smile.

"Did she later tell you she was pregnant?"

"Yes, she did."

"Was that true?"

"No, not at all!" That pissed him off, I guess. "And that's not something you tell a man if it ain't true." I had to agree with him there.

"Based on what you know of Susan Jenkins, do you have an opinion as to whether she's a truthful person?"

"I very well do. She's not a truthful person at all!"

"Thank you, Airman. No further questions." I sat down.

Nora stood up and walked toward the witness. Adams stared at her wide-eyed, appearing mesmerized by her presence. "Just one question Airman Adams." He looked at her expectantly with that goofy look on his face. "You didn't kill anyone, did you?" Nora asked sweetly, her eyebrows raised questioningly.

Adams opened his mouth but no words came out.

CHAPTER FORTY-SIX

"THE DEFENSE WOULD LIKE TO call Sheriff Frank Mineo as its next witness."

Rarely do I call a law enforcement officer as a defense witness. They don't have much sympathy for someone charged with a crime. But I had no choice.

"Good morning, Sergeant Mineo, how are you?"

"Fine, thank you. Good morning to you."

"Where do you currently work?"

"At the Currituck County Sheriff's Department in Currituck County, North Carolina."

"And how long have you worked there?"

"Almost six years now."

"What are your duties?"

"Currently, I'm the supervisor of the Criminal Investigation Division for the department."

"And have you had several occasions to meet Petty Officer Miller during the last seven months?

"Yes, Sir, I have."

"Do you remember your first interaction with Petty Officer Miller?"

He nodded.

"Could you describe that for us?"

"Sure. I was sitting in my vehicle parked outside of the 7-Eleven filling out a report about a shoplifting incident. Mr. Miller pulled up beside me and asked for my help in finding someone."

"Excuse me. Do you remember approximately what month that was?"

"I'm not real sure about the month."

"Was it in the fall?"

"Probably late fall."

"Do you remember who he was looking for?"

"He said he was looking for his girlfriend, Samantha Stevens. He gave me an address of 131 Sea Haven Lane in Moyock, North Carolina. He said he was supposed to meet her down here that day but was unable to reach her on her cell phone. I told Mr. Miller that I wasn't familiar with a Sea Haven Lane in Moyock, North Carolina. I told him I didn't think there was such an address but that there were some new subdivisions being built, so maybe I was wrong. I checked with Central Communications and we couldn't find such an address. I then used my cell phone and called the number that Mr. Miller had given me as Samantha Stevens's cell phone.

"And what happened when you called?" I asked.

"I dialed the number and a female answered the phone. I asked if this was Samantha and she said yes. I identified myself as Sergeant Mineo with the Currituck County Sheriff's department and told her that I was assisting her boyfriend Joshua Miller, who was down here in Currituck looking for her. I asked her where she was. I'm not sure if she said Kill Devil Hills or Kitty Hawk. I know it was in Dare County, the next county over. And I told her that Joshua was looking for her and I gave him the phone so they could talk."

"How did she sound on the phone? Can you describe her tone of voice?"

"She sounded agitated or irritated when I mentioned that Miller was here looking for her."

"What did Petty Officer Miller do?"

"I let Mr. Miller use my phone. He walked away from me for a few minutes as they spoke. When he came back he gave me my cell phone, thanked me, and left."

"Describe his body language as he walked away."

"He just looked dejected. His shoulders were stooped and he shuffled away kind of like a whipped dog."

"Did you have another interaction with him a few weeks later? Do you remember when that was?

"Yes, Sir. That was Saturday December 4 at approximately—"

I interrupted. "Sergeant, how can you be certain of the date after so many months?"

"Because I logged it into our CAD, our computer-aided dispatch. That basically catalogs the fire, police, and EMS calls over a five-year period and keeps the dates and the times and describes what actions were taken."

"I'm sorry to interrupt you. You were getting ready to say, I think, what time this occurred."

"It was approximately quarter until two in the afternoon."

"Please tell us what happened."

"Mr. Miller walked into the station house approximately fifteen minutes before my shift began. He said he wanted to file a report of a sexual assault."

"Did you remember Petty Officer Miller?"

"I did. I think it was because I felt sorry for him the last time I saw him. I said hello and asked him if he had met up with his girlfriend the last time he was down when I helped him reach her. He told me that he didn't, that she was irritated that he had involved the police, and that she didn't like the police. She told him to just forget it, and so he said that he just went back to, I guess, Virginia."

"On that December 4, did he mention anything about a rape allegation?"

"Yes, he did."

"What did he say?"

"Mr. Miller told me that he had gotten in an argument with his girlfriend over the telephone the night before. He said he told her that he didn't think she really existed because of all the problems they were having trying to meet. He said he broke up with her. From my understanding, she called him back several times. The last phone call she told him that she had been raped."

"Was he trying to get her some help with that situation?"

"Yes, he was trying to file a rape report. Again, he gave me the Sea Haven Lane address in Moyock as her address. I checked to make sure. I thought it was the same address, but I wanted to make sure because this was a serious report that he was trying to make."

"And you actually did a thorough search for this address?"

"Yes, Sir, I did."

"Can you briefly describe to the jury the different searches you did trying to help Petty Officer Miller?"

"Well, he gave me the name of Samantha Lee Stevens with a date of birth. I believe it was June 5. I ran her name and date of birth to try to get a match for a driver's license or the type of car she drove. I didn't get a match. Then I had my communications people do a search of all fifty states. Again, no match found. He told me that he had gone to the 7-Eleven, I believe in Barco, which is on the way to Dare County. He had a picture of her on his phone, which he showed to the clerk. He said the clerk recognized Samantha and said he had seen her running in the area. Miller said she was an avid runner."

"Did you see those pictures on his cell phone?"

"I asked him if I could see a picture of her because I might be able to recognize her if she was a local. He showed me a picture of her on his cell phone."

"And how would you describe her?"

"She was very, very attractive. Thin build with long blond hair pulled back."

"And did you recognize that picture as someone who lived in the area?"

"No, I didn't."

"Did you tell him that?"

"I did. I told him that I didn't recognize her and that I'd been working the street for five years and had never seen that female running in the area. He then said she was a student at Old Dominion University. So I called ODU and spoke with a dispatcher named Hendricks from the ODU PD. I told him that I was doing a welfare check, trying to locate a Samantha Lee Stevens, and gave him the date of birth. He checked and told me there was no Samantha Lee Stevens that was a student at ODU. Then Miller told me that she lived in a house, her mother's house, which was off the road, you couldn't see it from the road. It was a long driveway. And that Samantha's mother had moved to Corpus Christi, Texas, and she was living in her mother's house. And so I also did a search of the Corpus Christi, Texas, area with no Stevens found in that area either."

"When you concluded your search, did Petty Officer Miller ask you for some additional assistance?"

"Yes. At that point, I sort of started wondering about the relationship—if he was even, in fact, dating a Samantha Stevens. He then said that her house had been broken into and that she had filed a police report. He wanted to know if I could research the police reports and find an address for her. I started wondering if he was actually in a relationship or if he was stalking this woman, if she even existed. I told him that that was confidential information and I couldn't give it to him."

"Did you express your concerns that maybe much of this relationship wasn't real?"

"I did. Before he left, I said, 'You know, Mr. Miller, this girl might be pulling your leg. No one knows her here in Currituck County, the address doesn't exist, and she's not a student at ODU.' I said, 'Are you sure about this girl? Doesn't this all seem a little strange to you?' He just shrugged and appeared to blow it off."

"Sergeant, that's all the questions I have. Thank you, Sir."

The Military Judge looked at Commander Dempsey. "Cross-examination?"

"Briefly."

Nora began slowly. "So Miller comes to you concerned about this alleged sexual assault of his girlfriend but gives you no details, correct?"

"Correct."

"At first, he seems very concerned?"

"Yes, Sir."

"But then when he leaves he's nonchalant about it all, correct?"

"Well, I guess. Yes, Ma'am. But I think he was pretty convinced about the situation the young lady was in."

"Thank you very much. No further questions."

I might have to rethink my position regarding law enforcement officers.

CHAPTER FORTY-SEVEN

IT HAD BEEN TEN DAYS since the trial started. We were all tired. Captain Johnson returned to the bench after giving everyone a few extra hours for lunch. "All the members have returned. Please be seated. Everyone else, please be seated. Commander Demarco?"

I rose. "The Defense would like to call Petty Officer Bill Holmes, United States Navy."

Commander Dempsey stood and began the preliminary questioning.

"Please state your full name, spelling your last," she asked sweetly. I'm sure she was the undoing of many an unsuspecting witness.

"My name is William Christopher Holmes, last name is spelled H-O-L-M-E-S."

"And what is your current rate, rank, and duty station?"

"I am an IS3 currently assigned to the US Central Command Joint Operations staff."

"Thank you very much, Petty Officer. Please answer any questions the Defense Counsel may have of you." Jesus Christ! I swear she batted her eyes. He was toast. I had to get my witness back on track.

"Good afternoon, Petty Officer Holmes," I said loudly.

He was still staring after Commander Dempsey. "Ah, ah... Good afternoon, Sir."

"Could you tell the members a little about your current job, what you do on a day-to-day basis?"

"Well, Sir, I'm a mobilized reservist. I'm part of First Phase Imagery Branch working in the Indications and Warnings Section. I'm currently working the war, basically. Mostly in Afghanistan is what I'm working on right now, Sir." Always good to wrap your witness in the flag if you can.

"So you're a mobilized reservist. What is your civilian profession?"

He suddenly became sterner. "I'm a police officer having worked for more than ten years in Florida, Sir." And it never hurts to bolster your witness's credibility.

"What positions did you hold within the police department?"

"I was a Division Commander with twenty-three officers working for me. Throughout my career I've worked in every division within our department from patrol, traffic, K9, special response team, criminal investigations, undercover narcotics, pretty much anything that needed to be done."

"Do you know Petty Officer Miller?"

"Yes, Sir. I attended C school with him last fall."

"Was that just before going to your current position?"

"Yes, Sir. I volunteered for mobilization and prior to going they sent me to NEC School for Imagery Analysts for approximately four and a half months. The day I graduated in March, I mobilized to the war zone."

"Did you get to know Petty Officer Miller very well?"

"In most training classes everyone's coming from different places, from different backgrounds, so nobody really knew anyone when we first got there. We had guys from all over the country. We introduced ourselves and found out a little about each other. At first, I really didn't know Petty Officer Miller. I just knew that he'd come from a ship and was a fleet returnee coming into the school as a cross rate. But as the class went on, everyone became more intimate with each other. We began to know each other better through social and group activities."

"How would you describe him?"

"The Petty Officer Miller that I came to know was quiet but funny when you got to know him. He was always willing to help out. Our class was broken up into three basic cliques: the older guys over thirty like me, the guys who were coming right from A school being new to the Navy, and some fleet returnees. I was in the older group, so I didn't necessarily hang out with some of the younger guys. Petty Officer Miller kind of bounced between all three groups."

"I understand you had a couple of significant interactions with Miller. Can you tell the jury about the first one?"

"Yes, Sir. At the beginning of class one day IS1 Foti, who was our course instructor, and IS1 Lambert, who was our class leader, were speaking to Petty Officer Miller. He was upset about something. I was approached by the two first class Petty Officers and asked if I could help Miller. They felt that because of my background in law enforcement, I could be of assistance. Miller had reported that his girlfriend, Samantha, had been involved in a serious auto accident the previous night and he didn't know how to locate her or what hospital she was in. They felt that with my background, I'd be able to get him through to other law enforcement agencies."

"Was this their idea or Petty Officer Miller's idea to seek help trying to find her?"

"I don't know who initiated it. I know they were not going to let him leave by himself."

"He was asking to leave?"

"Yes, but he was just too upset. He was beside himself."

"After you got the facts from him, what did you do?"

"I began researching on the Internet, looking for local area hospital contacts as well as contacts for local law enforcement agencies. Miller looked through the phone book doing the same kind of thing. We started making phone calls to see if there had been an accident involving this Samantha person."

"And did he let you hear any of the messages that were on his cell phone regarding this accident?"

"Petty Officer Miller played one message for me that was very garbled, very distorted, which he said was part of the problem. He was unable to get good phone messages. But it was a female basically saying, she never gave a name, that Samantha had been involved in an accident. I don't specifically remember what was said, but it confirmed to me that it appeared an accident had occurred."

"After the Internet search, what did you do next?"

"We didn't locate anyone named Samantha that had been involved in an accident. Petty Officer Miller told me that this girl would have been coming via a specific route from North Carolina to Virginia Beach. So we decided to retrace that route to see if there was any evidence of an accident within the past twenty-four hours. We drove south into North Carolina, stopping at several different locations along the way looking for any information about this woman. We stopped at a truck stop, at a mechanic's shop, and a post office. No one knew this person or had heard of any accidents or anything that resembled what we had been told."

"During the drive down to North Carolina, did you talk to Miller about his relationship with Samantha?"

"Yes, Sir, I did. He explained to me that he had been going out with Samantha for a short time but that they were very serious. He told me about how much in love he was with this girl and how important she was to him, how she was different from any of the girls he had dated in the past. He believed that this was the girl of his dreams."

"Petty Officer Holmes, in the ten years you've been a police officer, how many people have you interviewed?"

"Probably several hundred."

"Did Petty Officer Miller seem sincere to you?" You're not supposed to invade the providence of the jury; they decide whom to believe or not, but what the heck.

"Yes, Sir. He did. I believe he was very sincere in his feelings."

Now we were getting somewhere. "At some point he told you about his future plans, isn't that right?" You're not supposed to lead on direct, but if Nora was going to let me, it was okay with me.

"Well, I was somewhat suspicious of this. In my opinion, it was kind of an immature relationship, you know, young kids making rash decisions. Knowing that he was going to be out of school in the next few months, he was already making long-term plans with this girl, including his next duty assignment, which was going to be in London. So in my opinion, he was getting involved in a relationship that was going to end in a few months or it was going to get more serious and he's going to go overseas with her. He explained to me that the relationship had developed very quickly and was very serious, and in fact, she was going to drop out of college and travel to England with him when he completed school."

"At some point after going to all these places in North Carolina, I understand you received a telephone call. Tell us about that."

"Petty Officer Miller had some idea where Samantha lived. He had a street name. So we went looking in the general area where she might be. We drove around for a while but never found it. His cell phone rang while we were driving, and it was Samantha on the phone. We pulled over to the side of the road and they talked. He was very relieved. You could see his anxiety decreased significantly. He was just happy to talk to her. Obviously, I wasn't part of the conversation, but I could hear what he was saying. He asked her what happened, where she was, what was going on, how serious her injuries were, all that kind of stuff."

"At some point did he exit the vehicle?"

"Yes, Sir. During that conversation, they started talking about their relationship and he asked to be excused. He stepped outside to the side of the road so I couldn't hear the conversation. This went on for a few minutes. When he returned, he was very upset, not angry but sad. It appeared he had been crying, which took me back a bit. I asked him what was wrong. He said Samantha was trying to break off the relationship and he was trying to convince her otherwise. Apparently, they agreed, I guess, to talk later."

"What did you do then?"

"In light of him having talked to her and now being upset, I felt it best if we returned to the base. If he wanted to go visit her, he could go do it later on his own time now that he knew she was okay. So we started driving back. I actually drove because he was so upset. During the drive back, once again, there was more phone conversations and text messages back and forth between him and Samantha."

"And by the time you got back, what was the status of the relationship?"

"I'm not sure. But one of the conversations made me a little leery, actually. He was talking to her and telling her about all the effort he had gone to find her. At one point he said, 'I've even got a cop with me who is trying to help find you.' Immediately, on the other end of the phone, the conversation stopped. She just quit talking. She basically told Petty Officer Miller that she didn't want to talk to him while there was a law enforcement person present. Obviously, my hackles went up. I thought that was pretty hinky and it made me a little leery of her, very suspicious of why a person would do that."

"Did you express those concerns to Miller?"

"I did. In my opinion, based on what I'd heard of this girl and their relationship, I thought she was a scam artist. I thought she was just trying to get money from him, just from what little I knew. It seemed like she was definitely putting a scam on him when she didn't want law enforcement around."

"Did he listen to your advice?"

"He heard the words, but I don't think he took them to heart. He was reacting more with his heart than his head. He made a plan with her. After dropping me off, she was going to drive back here and stay at a friend's house off Dam Neck. He was excited. He said he was going to get her some flowers and a card or something. He planned to meet her later that evening."

"To your knowledge did she show?"

"Nope. I don't think she did."

"Over the next few weeks, did you get periodic updates from Miller about this relationship?"

"Yes, Sir. As you know, in a training environment you study for forty-five to fifty minutes and then take a break. During the breaks, the class has a little social time where we talk to each other, make plans for the evening, or whatever. When I would speak to Petty Officer Miller, he would give me updates about the relationship. Normally, our class did a lot of activities together. On weekends or after school hours, we'd study together or go to dinner, go to a concert at the beach, play football, stuff like that. So we were constantly asking Petty Officer Miller to join us and be a part of that. After he met Samantha, he wouldn't go out with us anymore."

"Did he say why he wasn't going?"

"Every time we planned some type of get-together, he was either talking to her or planning to meet. She was either coming to town or he was going to meet her. There was always some reason he wasn't able to hang out with the rest of us."

"You had a second significant interaction. Do you recall what happened?"

"I don't recall the date, but it was a Saturday morning in December. The reason I remember that is because, like I said, our class had social events every weekend and during Saturdays in Decembers there were college football games."

"Do you remember if it was early or late December?"

"It was within the first two weeks of December, before the Christmas break."

"Please continue."

"The class would get together and watch college football, play cards, just basically hang out together. From where my room is located in the barracks, I could look over the parking lot and see who was still there for the weekend; we all knew what everyone drove. On that morning, I was looking out the window to see who we could get together for the game. I saw Petty Officer Miller walking toward that strange-looking vehicle of his. I went out to invite him to come play cards and watch football. When I reached him, he was different, more withdrawn. He was upset. I asked him if everything was okay. He said, 'No, everything is not okay.' He then asked me if I could keep a secret. I told him under certain circumstances, yes, but under others, no. Then he told me that his girlfriend had been raped. I asked him what happened, where it happened, all that kind of stuff, trying to figure out the whole story. He told me that the night before they had gotten into an argument and broke up. She apparently went to a party and she left with two guys that she was acquainted with who were marines and then she was sexually assaulted by another marine. He wanted to help her, but she wouldn't tell him where she was."

"Did that seem like a credible story to you?"

"Sir, I was very skeptical. I expressed that to Petty Officer Miller. The events leading up to that and the different things I'd heard about this relationship and him chasing her around and every-thing made me very skeptical of this woman. First of all, I'd never met her. Everyone else in the class had girlfriends, wives, significant others who were part of the group and we all knew each other—how-ever, that's the one person we never met. Plus the fact that she didn't want him around. From my experience, if he was truly her love and the most important guy in her life, that's not normal."

"After you expressed your concerns to Miller, what did he do?"

"Again, he listened to what I said, but all he cared about was trying to find her. I tried to convince him that if she doesn't want to be around him right now, just let it go and she'll call him later. I told him to stay with us, you know, hang out. Spend the day with us, and if she calls, she calls, and he can go deal with it then. I tried to convince him to stay on base and hang out with the older crowd, basically."

"Petty Officer Holmes, you know about the charges that Petty Officer Miller has pled guilty to today."

"Yes, Sir, I do."

"Based on the amount of time you spent with him, do you think he can one day be a valuable member of society?"

"Petty Officer Miller has made a terrible mistake in his life, an absolutely terrible mistake. But I believe he can come back from this with a lot of work and a lot of healing on his part. He can come back from this."

"Thank you. Please answer any questions Commander Dempsey may have of you."

"Yes, Sir."

"Good morning, Petty Officer Holmes."

"Ma'am." He was starting to get all flustered again.

"I'm going to go a little bit out of order here, so I apologize. We may skip around a little bit, okay?" Again she smiled sweetly at him.

"Anything you say, Ma'am."

"In reference to that last question, whether you believe that Petty Officer Miller can come back from this terrible mistake he made. What is your understanding of what he's pled guilty to?"

He swallowed hard. "I believe it was murder, kidnapping, impersonating an NCIS agent, and obstruction of justice."

"And do you know the details of how he murdered Lance Corporal Williams and under what circumstances?"

"I've heard through the grapevine. I don't know the details other than I know a knife was used." He was looking down as he spoke.

"Did you know that Miller knew that Corporal Williams was going to be a father before he killed him?" She was no longer smiling.

"I found out Corporal Williams was going to be a father at his memorial service, Ma'am." Thankfully, he didn't directly answer the question.

"There is something I want to clarify for the record." She moved closer to him. "You said that you got to know him periodically throughout C school?"

Holmes only nodded. Dempsey didn't wait for an answer.

"And that he was kind of a go-between between the more senior people in the class and the junior people in the class."

"Yes, Ma'am."

"But my understanding is that he never really hung out with your social group outside of the classroom."

"Ah… I guess that's correct, Ma'am. Not much anyways." Wait a minute. I was beginning to wonder whose witness this was.

"In fact, you tried to set up, like you said earlier, social functions but he would never go, right?"

"We constantly tried to include him, yes. But he was always busy with something else."

"So beyond the classroom setting and beyond the one trip down to North Carolina with the accused and beyond that one conversation that you had with him out in the parking lot on the first or second week of December, you really didn't associate with Petty Officer Miller, did you?" Here she goes, I thought.

"Correct. Yes, Ma'am."

Dempsey started to bear down harder. "You really didn't know what he was doing on his own time, do you?"

"No, Ma'am."

"You only know what he conveyed to you, isn't that correct?"

251

"Correct."

"Petty Officer Miller looked up to you, didn't he?"

"I believe so. Yes, Ma'am."

"Why?"

"Probably because I'm older. He had expressed a desire to be in law enforcement at some point in his life." Oh shit.

Nora feigned surprise. "Explain that a little bit more, about his desire to be in law enforcement. Did he tell you what he had done in pursuing this interest?" Where was she going with this? But it was too late to object now.

"Petty Officer Miller, when we first met and during subsequent conversations, told me he had completed a private investigation course. I guess he took a course where he was going to get licensed. And that he was interested in, when he got out of the Navy, of becoming either a private investigator or some type of law enforcement officer."

"Why do you think he told you that?"

"Most likely trying to impress me, that's what I assumed."

"And with regards to tracking down this Samantha individual, he was getting frustrated, wasn't he?"

"Yes, Ma'am."

"Trying to find her and not being able to?"

"I believe so."

"What type of assistance did you provide him in trying to find her, outside of this trip down to North Carolina?"

"On one of the breaks in class, he asked me about detective work. Basically, he said, 'How do you go about finding a person, if they don't have a criminal record or anything?'"

"And this was in late November, early December, correct?" How could she know that?

"I believe so. Yes, Ma'am." Oh shit.

"So what did you tell him?'

"Well, he had several cell phone numbers for this Samantha and one of them was apparently registered to a guy. She was telling him stories about how she knew these different guys. I explained to him that in every state, they have a public criminal record system, and if you are an adult convicted of a criminal offense, there's going to be a record of it. I told him you can request a criminal history on any adult person. I told him to start there. I believe he went and did that."

"Why do you believe that?"

"It was probably a week or two later, during a break in class, he had a file with him with a lot of paperwork in it. I didn't get a chance to look at it. However, I think it had some information on the names Samantha had given him as well as some phone records and other things."

"And this is still in the late November, early December? Or at least before that conversation you had with him about this alleged sexual assault?"

"Yes, Ma'am. It was before that."

"Petty Officer Holmes, you stated that Petty Officer Miller had been dating this girl a while. Was it your understanding that he had actually met this young lady?"

"Ma'am, I assumed he had met this girl based on the conversations I had with him. There were always stories about them planning things. Honestly, Petty Officer Miller was not my priority, so I didn't completely follow his relationship issues. I had a lot of other things going on in my life. My assumption was that they had met. He never told me specifically that they did, but I'd always heard that they were going out. He was going to meet her. I assumed that those meeting occurred, but at no time did I ever concretely know that they did."

"Now, speaking of this meeting with Petty Officer Miller in the parking lot, when he told you he believed that his online girlfriend had been raped. He said he was going to do something about it, didn't he?"

The witness was silent. Before he could speak, she continued. "He was going to take matters into his own hands, wasn't he, Petty Officer Holmes?"

The witness sat back in his chair. "What he told me is that he wanted to report it. I explained to him the need for evidence in a sexual assault case. I said he needs to make sure she gets all the exams and make sure she gets to a hospital. And if all these different things were occurring, I told him he needed to make sure he contacted NCIS if the parties involved were military. He told me he would take care of that and he would contact NCIS even if she did not."

Nora started to bear down again. "But he gave you the clear impression that he was going to take matters into his own hands, did he not, Petty Officer?"

"He was angry. You could see he was upset about it."

"In fact, you warned him not to take matters into his own hands and to let law enforcement handle the situation, did you not?"

"Yes, Ma'am, I did."

"And you were not the only one who warned Petty Officer Miller about this Samantha chick not being who she really was, correct?"

"There was a lot of skepticism about this girl among our classmates, yes, Ma'am."

"And again, you were present when your classmates conveyed that directly to Petty Officer Miller, were you not?"

"I heard it in conversations. Yes."

"But he ignored that advice, didn't he?"

Again silence.

"And Miller's a rather intelligent guy, isn't he?"

"I would consider him very intelligent."

"No further questions, thank you." Nora turned daintily and returned to her seat. All eyes were still on her.

"Any redirect?" The judge was outwardly smiling at me.

"Yes, Sir." I stood and walked toward the witness. "In regards to when he came to you about the research he had done, you're a little uncertain on the dates, aren't you? Isn't it possible that the date could have been later on, perhaps in January?

"The only conversation I recall having with Petty Officer Miller after the Christmas break… I thought it was before the Christmas break." When Miller started becoming suspicious and began investigating Samantha was a crucial point. I couldn't concede it.

"Petty Officer, you are not 100 percent certain about the date being in early November, late December are you?

"I'm not a 100 percent sure on the dates, no, Sir, it's a range. My best guess."

"Thank you." I sat down. There was no recross.

One more witness and we were finished for the day. I needed to leave the jury with something memorable.

CHAPTER FORTY-EIGHT

"DEFENSE COUNSEL, PLEASE CALL YOUR next witness."

I stood. "Your Honor, the Defense would like to call, as our last witness of the day, Petty Officer Miller's mother, Mrs. Anne Davis."

Commander Dempsey stood to administer the oath. The two ladies locked eyes as the older woman approached the witness stand. Something passed between them.

"Please state your full name, spelling your last name."

"Anne Davis. D-A-V-I-S," she answered quietly. A light blue calico dress hung from her slight frame. She appeared lost in the big courtroom.

"Thank you, Ma'am. You may take a seat. I believe Defense Counsel has some questions for you." I could swear Nora mouthed, "I'm sorry."

I approached the podium, took a deep breath, and began. "Mrs. Davis, you are IS3 Miller's mother?"

This time, even more quietly, she answered, "Yes, I am." I could see the anguish on her face. I hated to put her through this. "Mrs. Davis, I know this is difficult, but you are going to have to speak up. That microphone is just for recording, it doesn't amplify." She nodded.

"Can you tell the court a little bit about your son?"

She began slowly. "He is my second son and his dad's, well, the person he considers his father, fourth son. His name was James Miller. I'm James's third wife, twenty years his junior. Joshua took

James's last name. Joshua was the ring bearer at our wedding. He sat in the front pew, grinning from ear to ear. He and James loved each other and were inseparable until the day he died…" Her words trailed off.

"May I approach the witness, Your Honor?" He nodded. "May the record reflect I am handing the witness a series of photographs, which have been previously marked, and published to the members, as 'Defense Exhibit Romeo.' Mrs. Davis, do you recognize the first picture?"

She turned it over in her small hands. She caressed the edges as a faint smile came to her face. "Yes. This is a photograph taken soon after Joshua's birth. Joshua's real dad is pictured as well as our son Bill." She again paused. "This would have been a Sunday judging from our state of dress. We dressed up on Sundays to go to church, so it would probably have been Joshua's first time going to church."

"Can you tell us a little bit about Joshua's early life?"

"He was a big baby, a big push, so to speak." She caught herself and seemed embarrassed. "He was kind of a surprise. As soon as we got the older one in school, Joshua came along shortly thereafter. It wasn't planned and caused a lot of problems with me and my husband at the time. He had just wanted it to be him and me. He started drinking." She paused. "And became violent." Her voice again trailed off. "We divorced shortly thereafter."

"Please look at the next photograph. Tell us about that picture?"

"This was after I married James. James loved Joshua from the start and treated him as his own son. Joshua's in the back of our pickup truck. We lived on a farm. We were clearing a piece of property, getting ready to build a house. I see a log pile in the back. James was retired, so we were always home together as a family."

"What did James do before he retired?"

"He had been in the communications business for fifty years. He first went into radio before television was even invented, that kind of gives you a timeline. When TV came along, he had his own television show back when TV was live. He eventually went into voice-over communication, and because of that, he was able to only work a few hours a week."

"And so you and Mr. Miller were able to spend the majority of your time at home?" I asked.

"Yes, the boys had the value of both of us there with them. And we lived in a small town so the church was important."

"Ma'am, please go ahead and flip to the next picture. Where was this photograph taken?"

"This was at Myrtle Beach. We really liked to vacation there. If we were lucky, we got down there once a year, a beach trip. Joshua didn't much like the ocean, but it was good to get away from the mountains. It was something different."

"And who is in the photograph?"

"That's me with Joshua on my shoulders and his big brother, Bill."

"Joshua has a huge smile on his face in that picture. Was that typical of him as a young child?"

"Yes. He was a happy child. A real nature child. Like I said, we lived in the country. We didn't have many children his age around and he was somewhat of a loner. He liked to go down by the creek and sit for hours."

"Please turn to the next photograph. It appears to be another family photograph. Does it hold any special memories for you?"

She held the picture up to her face to get a better look at it. "It does. This was the first house we built together and it was a good-sized house. But more than that, we built the lake, a barn, and had a pasture. We had chickens and ducks. A wild flock of Canadian geese used to come to our pond. Joshua there is barefoot. It was just the picture perfect family I had always wanted. I mean there was a lot of love between James and me. This was the second set of children he was able to raise and he was home. You know, giving them the care the other ones really didn't get a chance to have because he was working so much.

"So was his relationship with Joshua especially strong?"

"Yes, it was very special."

"What did he and Joshua do together?"

"Everything. Joshua was my husband's shadow. I mean, you know, splitting wood and gardening. He was a big gardener. I was a horseback rider, so, I mean, Joshua just did everything with him."

"Was there a particular trip that was special to your husband and Joshua?"

"My husband went to his fiftieth class reunion, if you can imagine that. And he took Joshua with him, nine years old, which was very unusual. He grew up in a small town in Mississippi, which didn't have a huge graduating class. In fact, it was such a small class, they had to put several years together for this reunion. He told everyone that this was his son. They couldn't believe it. They thought he was really his grandson. But he insisted Joshua was his son. It made the local newspaper."

"Turn to the next photograph, please. What is the moment captured there?"

"That's Joshua's first day of school and that's me saying good-bye. And of course, that's my baby, so it's hard to say good-bye on the first day of school." She began to cry.

"Mrs. Davis, do you need a moment?" She shook her head, so I continued. "Did Joshua enjoy school?"

"I remember he was really happy at that point, to find a group of playmates his own age because, you know, there wasn't many around."

"Did he develop any long-term friendships?"

"Well, not really. He just never seemed to have any long-term friends. He preferred being alone."

"His family life changed right before he turned ten, didn't it? What happened at that time?"

"Well, his dad had a history of heart disease. He had other heart attacks with his second wife. I married him knowing that. But I felt like it would be quality years, not necessarily quantity years. But when the day comes you never expect it."

"Can you describe the circumstances of that day?"

"Well, he came into the living room one morning and he just basically had a massive heart attack. He hit his head on the fireplace and there was blood everywhere. I was giving him mouth-to-mouth resuscitation. We were living in the log home at the time with ten-foot overhead ceiling and I glanced up and there was Joshua watching. I knew it was a bad thing to witness. I told him to go call 911 and run to the neighbors." She stopped for a moment. "I don't think he ever got over watching his dad die." She sighed.

"Did you get Joshua any counseling?"

She looked at me strangely. "No, Sir. We lived in the country. People don't go to counseling. We handle our problems the best way we can. I wouldn't know where to start with that."

I thought she was finished and began to ask my next question when she suddenly blurted out, "I wish we had gone to family counseling, you know, hindsight is 20/20. I think we needed family counseling, but at the time I didn't have a lot of money. Joshua withdrew, he became more solemn, and he kept things inside. Looking back, you know, it's a huge devastating thing in somebody's life, I don't care who it is. I'm sure he would have benefited from that." I knew she was now blaming herself for this tragedy.

"How did your family life change after IS3 Miller's father passed?"

"Our lives turned 180 degrees. All of a sudden, I had to be the primary caregiver and go from just being the nurturer, because his dad was always the disciplinarian, to doing both roles. All of a sudden, I was gone because I had to find a job. Joshua was left alone a lot and became more reclusive than he was before."

"Did his involvement in school change with his father's passing?"

"He was always smart. But after that, he kind of pulled back from his school studies. Especially through middle school, you know. I tried homeschooling. I put him in a special magnet school just to keep him interested in different things and tried to challenge him."

"At one point did you send him to live with his brother?"

"I felt, at that point, he needed a male role model and some male discipline in his life, so I sent him to Bill, his brother. You met Bill yesterday." I had prepped them both for their testimony and would have rather kept that quiet. "Bill had a family and children that were Joshua's age. I felt like Bill would be a good influence on him. I think he was sixteen when he went down there. Late fifteen—no, I think he was 16."

"And how long was he there for?"

"Three or four months."

"And then he came back to live with you before moving to Roanoke, Virginia, correct?"

"Yes. He lived with another family for a short time. He got a job as a cashier at a grocery store. Just in the three months that he was there, he had more commendations—you get these little pins, you know. He had more commendations than anybody in the history of the store in his short three months there. That's what their manager told me."

"When did you learn that he had made the decision to enlist in the Navy?"

"After that, he went to work right in the same shopping center washing dishes. He met a boy that worked in the restaurant who had been through the Navy and was talking to Joshua about it. He was telling him about all the benefits, the travel, and that you would be going to school and learning a trade and you know, it really—you could tell there was a world of difference between them. That boy was only a few years older than Joshua, and yet, because he had traveled and gone into a place with discipline, they were worlds apart. You know, very mature and together and here was Joshua washing dishes and looking for direction in his life. Shortly thereafter he decided to enlist."

"And how did he act after he made that decision?"

"It was the first time he really had direction in his life. You know, through his teenage years kind of bouncing around schools and school systems and this was the first thing he really liked and latched onto. His whole demeanor changed at that point."

"Please turn to the last picture in your set. What is that a picture of?"

"This was the trip that we made to Great Lakes. Bill and I went when Joshua graduated from boot camp. He was getting an academic award and we were really proud of him and wanted to be there for him. We took an extended weekend and we saw the sights of

Chicago. In fact, we had one of those hotels there right in downtown with those big buildings in the back. We were staying right down there and we were back together as a family. But the whole family had shifted, at that point, because Bill had direction, he was in school and Joshua now had a real direction in his life. From a mother's point of view it, was like a major ah-hah moment. Like my boys had gotten to this level and, you know, it was like launching Joshua out into the world. I was very proud of him."

"What were your expectations for his future?"

"Well, he picked Intelligence School. He was very interested in that. He said that he was going to be sent overseas and I was really pleased because I knew one of the best educations in life is to go out and see the world and to see how other people in the world live. When American kids travel out of this country, they come back with a new appreciation for American values and what we all take for granted here in this country."

"Did you have a chance to see him while he was stationed on board the ship?"

"Unfortunately, no. I wanted to but couldn't afford the trip."

"Did you see him when he returned from sea?"

"He came back a year later and was even much more grown-up. I think his heart was broken in a way because he had an unrequited love at one of the ports—a girl he really felt strongly for. And it just didn't work out."

"What was the next duty station he was going to?"

"He came back home for a short time, two or three weeks, something like that. Then he was on his way here to Dam Neck."

"While he was at Dam Neck, did you get to see him?"

"I visited him a few times. I live a five-hour drive from here, and because I hadn't seen him for so many years, I made it a point to get here if I could. I stayed at the Navy lodge which was cheap so I was able to stay a couple of nights at a time and visit him."

"Was he able to come home for Christmas?"

"He did, yes." She folded her hands in her lap.

"While he was home, was he going to have any guests join him?"

"He had told me a little earlier in the month—or maybe it was in November, I'm not clear when, that he had finally met a girl that restored his faith in women. He was really brokenhearted over that other one. He said he really loved this girl and she wanted to come meet the family. They were very serious about each other."

"Did he tell you her name?"

"He said her name was Samantha."

"Did he describe her?"

"Yes. He said she was very pretty. And blonde."

"Was that significant?"

"Well, yes. You see, I had had a psychic reading at the house a few months before, and I was told that Joshua was going to meet and fall in love with a blonde girl."

I saw the eyes of a few jury members rolling upward, so I quickly moved on. "Did you ever end up meeting her?"

"I talked to her on the telephone. At first she was going to be here for Christmas day but something happened—I'm not sure what. And then she said she'd be here the day after Christmas but never showed up. He sat all day at the airport waiting for her. At that point, I said to Joshua that I don't know if this is real. I said to myself that I'm going to keep an open mind. If she shows up, then I will believe in her, but she never came."

"How many hours did he spend at the airport?"

"From opening to closing, it was about thirteen hours."

"Mrs. Davis, you've been here all week, correct?"

"Yes." She looked at her clasped hands.

"And you've heard all the witnesses' testimony and learned what your son did. What is your reaction to that?"

She hesitated for a long time. I had met with her and went over the questions I was going to ask her on the stand. I did this with most witnesses; with some, I even made suggestions on how they might answer. I hadn't asked her this question. I wanted her unscripted answer.

"I think this is a horrendous human tragedy." She looked over my shoulder to the Williams family sitting directly behind me. "I want the entire Williams family to know that I have prayed for you

263

every night, every day since I found out this happened. My heart goes out to you, I will never be able to understand the hole this has put in your lives. I pray for Jonathan. I know his soul is in a good place." She looked at Jessica Williams, who was now crying. "I know what it's like to be a single mom. I just can't tell you how sorry I am for what you are going to go through." She took a deep breath and raised her head a little higher. "But I am also sorry for my family as well. It was one mistake, a huge mistake, that Joshua made in a moment of, well, I don't know… but it will forever haunt and affect his life and everybody's life concerned." She couldn't finish and lowered her head.

"Do you feel that the son you raised is still somewhere inside Petty Officer Miller?"

She looked up. "I know Joshua has a good heart. I know him intimately. He made a bad decision, made a huge mistake, but I still love him dearly and I know he has a good heart. I know he can still contribute to society. I know he can go into prison and do good. I know he can go and learn from his mistakes."

"Thank you, Ma'am. No further questions." I turned to Commander Dempsey.

Nora looked at me and then to the witness. She took a long time before she shook her head slightly. There would be no cross-examination, not even about the psychic. Nora was as emotionally drained as the rest of us.

Time to grab a quick bite to eat and prepare for tomorrow.

CHAPTER FORTY-NINE

It was Saturday morning. I had to finish my case today. It was time to move away from some of the emotional witnesses and call in a professional.

"The Defense would like to call Dave G. Butler." Colonel Butler, now retired, looked as if he could still complete the Physical Readiness Test in record time. He was short, only 5'8", with a wiry build. His hair was still close-cropped. He wore a brown tweed sport coat with arm patches and a bow tie that he tied himself. Damn, I wish I knew how to do that.

Expert witnesses are plentiful in military courts. If you can demonstrate a need for an expert in a certain area, the Government has to provide him. But they are a challenge. They are smart, well-credentialed, and expensive. And I have learned after many years in the courtroom that you can get almost anyone to say almost anything if you pay them enough. The trick is to make them appear as if they are not a "hired gun." They can be attacked on the amount they are charging for their time, their lack of actual hands on experience, the amount of time they spend testifying for one side or the other. The list goes on.

But as a defense attorney, they are oftentimes all you have. I once represented a sailor who was charged with murder after his girl-friend went missing. He claimed that after they had sex in the dunes, he went into the ocean to clean up. When he returned, she was gone. Her body was eventually found a few days later. One of the issues was how long she had been dead. We hired an expert in the gestation period of maggots. Interesting stuff!

"Sir, you are a retired Colonel from the United States Marine Corps, is that correct?"

"That's correct. Twenty-seven years."

"And were you also a Judge Advocate for a period of time in the Marine Corps?"

"Yes, Sir. I started off in the infantry. I was accepted into the law education program and became a Judge Advocate after that."

"Sir, I want to focus on the last job you held in the Marine Corps. Can you tell the members what that job was?"

"I was the President of the Naval Clemency and Parole Board for almost four years."

"As President of the Naval Clemency and Parole Board, what were your duties?"

He answered smugly, "The most obvious was that I presided over the Board whenever we sat to determine matters dealing with clemency and parole. I also made sure that all the packages were prepared that the members had to review and deliberate on before we voted on our cases. I also dealt with federal parole officers and was a liaison with the brigs."

"Sir, I want to focus for a few minutes on the process. Is there a regulation or instruction that governs that particular board?"

"Yes, Sir. SECNAV Instruction 5815.3J—which I helped to write." Butler was becoming a little arrogant, but there was nothing I could do about that.

"Can you tell the members how the Board of Clemency and Parole is constituted?"

"There are five sitting members of the board. All are Commanders or Captains, all are active-duty military. The President of the Board is a representative of the Secretary of the Navy. There is a Navy doctor, either a psychiatrist or a psychologist, that sits on the board, normally with a strong forensic background. There is a lawyer representing the Judge Advocate General of the Navy—it could be either a marine or a sailor. And then there are two line officers, one a marine, representing the Commandant of the Marine Corps, and one Navy, representing the Chief of Naval Operations."

"Currently, for a sailor or marine convicted and sentenced to life with the possibility of parole, when does the eligibility period for parole begin?"

"They would not be eligible for twenty years."

"Colonel, I'd like to spend a few minutes talking about the process for an individual who is applying for parole. Can you tell the members what that process entails?"

Colonel Butler shifted to the right so he could look directly at the jury. He said confidently, "The inmate fills out an application that he is given at the brig. Then everything that this individual has done is collected, both before and after his trial. The record of the actual trial is sent to us. We also get the brig progress reports, which include all the disciplinary reports since he's been in the brig. We get the psychological evaluations that were done and any treatment programs he's been in as well as how he's been doing in those programs, if he's been doing them at all. We review any education that he's completed both before and since he's been confined. We obtain recommendations from the unit he's assigned to at the brig, as well as the brig parole board and the recommendation from the CO of the brig. We also obtain any victim impact statements or any other correspondence that we've received. We take all that information and encapsulate it into a workable package that can be distributed a couple of weeks ahead of time to the board members so they have an opportunity to review it before we actually sit and deliberate."

"Can you describe the actual process of holding the board after you put the package together and distribute it?"

"Sure. Everyone reads the material before they get there. Then we go over the facts of the case so we can distinguish it from the other twenty or so cases we might be looking at that particular day. That's usually a pretty quick process. Then if there is a personal appearance in the case, if the individual who's up for parole has his appellate defense counsel, or his mother or his wife or somebody, we'll bring them in and listen to them. If there are any victims or families of the victim that decide to come, we'll listen to them. After all the personal appearances are done, then we sit down and we will begin deliberations. We go over the package in a lot more detail. We discuss it, and it can take, depending on the individual case, it can take a few minutes, or it could take a couple of hours to come up with what we think is the proper determination, and then we vote."

"Sir, you mention a number of items that go into the package that the board considers. Can you tell us some of the things that are important to the board and some of the factors you consider? And if some are more important than others?"

"All are important, and any one of them can be a showstopper. But probably the two most important aspects in the majority of cases are the treatment program and the disciplinary reports. If the individual is not following the rules of the brig, if he's continually getting in trouble, his chances of ever getting parole go down the tube. Likewise, if the brig determines there's a treatment program he should be in and he refuses or he goes and doesn't do a good job, that's going to hurt his chances of ever getting paroled."

"Can the Board request information in addition to what's been provided by the confinement facility?"

"Yes. The Executive Secretary and I go through every package, and if there's something that we feel is lacking or something that we think is a gray area, we will get back with the brig and try to make sure that's in the package, even if it means moving the parole board to another date. Likewise, the members have the package for at least two weeks. They will occasionally have a question on something and they'll shoot me an e-mail or give me a call. If I can find the answer for them, I will. If I can't, then I get with the brig and we'll get the answer for them. So they've got that prior to sitting down and deliberating on the case."

"Sir, is the concept of parole a right or a privilege?"

"Parole is not a right. It's something to be considered once you're eligible. The consideration doesn't mean you're going to get it. Not everyone who's eligible gets it."

"Sir, can you tell us some of the reasons why people are not given parole after they've gone through the process?"

"Well, it could be the heinous nature of the crime. It could be they have not made every effort to get treatment or successfully completed their treatment. It may be that they did not obey the rules of the brig and we don't think they're a good risk. Because one of the things we're looking at is whether this guy is going to be a risk to reoffend. Has he taken advantage of the educational opportunities in the brig? Now, we're not interested in getting them a college degree, but we do want them to have an education and training so that if they get out they can get a job. If they're employable, the recidivism rate is likely to be much less."

"I want to talk a little about the concept of someone being on parole. If someone actually receives that *privilege*," I emphasized the word, "and is granted parole, tell us about some of the constraints or limitations."

"Well, every case is different, but we do have conditions and stipulations. A federal police officer is checking up and supervising him on a constant basis. They're checking where the parolee works, where they live, checking their computers, the mail they receive, checking into whom their friends are, their bank accounts. They're looking at all these different things to see if everything is in order. We may say, 'No, you can't work there,' or 'You need to stop seeing that person,' or 'You need to close these bank accounts or credit cards,' things like that. We watch them very closely to make sure they are conforming to what we want them to do during the period they are on parole. If they're not, we can find that there's been a parole violation and, after due process, actually send them back to prison." Due process for a parolee—that was an interesting concept.

"Who provides input into the conditions that are placed on a parolee?"

"We routinely get recommendations from the brig's Commanding Officer as well as the person running the treatment program. But most of those decisions are made by our board. After we've drafted up the conditions of parole, it goes back to the brig. And if the brig CO wants to add something, he can. And once the individual reports to their parole officer, he can also add to the stipulations. They just cannot subtract from them without our permission."

"Sir, one of the things that you mentioned was the treatment programs offered and attended when considering parole. Tell us your understanding of the availability of such programs for a person assigned to a long-term facility such as Leavenworth."

Colonel Butler rubbed his hands together and leaned forward. "Sure. However, you must understand a person may not be sent immediately to Fort Leavenworth. There's been a downsizing there in the last five years. It went from a one-thousand-five-hundred-bed facility to a five-hundred-bed facility. It's not unusual for a person to stay at Charleston or Miramar or even Camp Lejeune or Camp Pendleton for up to three years or so before they go to Leavenworth. If that's the case, they would receive treatment at that Navy or Marine Corps facility first. Now at Leavenworth, they do have treatment programs that closely mirror the Navy's. But there are times when it's difficult to get someone in unless they've got enough time on their sentence. They look at everyone and kind of triage them. Those that are getting out first get treatment first. But generally speaking, there's an availability of treatment."

"Sir, I have no further questions at this time. Please answer any questions Commander Dempsey may have of you."

Commander Dempsey jumped right in. "What is clemency?"

I jumped right behind her. "Objection." Clemency was when one's sentence was reduced or forgiven. I didn't want the jury confusing the two concepts and thinking Miller might one day get off easy.

The Military Judge was apparently bored with my witness and had not been paying attention. He said, "I'm sorry, repeat the question please?"

"Colonel Butler, what is the typical type of clemency for somebody given a life sentence?"

"I'm going to sustain that." Undeterred, Nora took a different tack.

"Now, Sir, you mentioned that for the board members, this is generally a collateral duty, I mean, besides the President?" She smiled sweetly at him. I knew he was now in trouble.

"For the four board members, it's a collateral duty, yes."

"And during your tenure as President how many petitions did you review for parole?"

"I have no idea. It would just be a guess."

"Humor me, Colonel. Are we talking about hundreds or thousands?"

"Hundreds, probably, I would guess five to six hundred, that is a guess."

"And how much time did you spend reviewing a parole petition?"

"It varied greatly. A simple drug case doesn't get much time. A more complicated case may require several hours."

"And your board is located in Washington, DC, Sir?"

"Correct, at the Washington Navy Yard."

"Are all the members located in DC also?"

"DC or the surrounding area."

"And how often did the board meet?"

"We meet twenty-six times a year. Typically, every other week."

"And how long did you meet for?"

"We start about 7:30 a.m. and we end when we're done, typically between 11:00 a.m. and 1:30 p.m."

Shit! Dempsey stood there with her hands on her hips feigning surprise. "And then you're done for the day? Free to see the sites in DC?"

"Objection." I didn't even need to stand for that one.

Captain Jonson hated to but said, "Sustained."

She smiled sweetly again. "So your work is done all in one day?"

"Every other week." Nora let that answer sink in with the jury. I knew she was going to argue that these petitions didn't appear to get a rigorous review.

"Sir, you mentioned a number of items that you look at when you determine parole. Do you look at victim impact statements?"

"Absolutely."

She walked closer to him. "And you mentioned that the victims or their families are permitted to come testify?"

"That's correct."

"And who pays for the plane fare or rental car or gas money or meals or lodging or other travel expenses if the victims or their families want to come to DC to testify?"

Colonel Butler looked embarrassed. He stammered, "Ah, well… we don't have a budget for that, so I guess it would be at the individual's own expense."

"You guess?" Dempsey said sharply again, putting her hands on her hips.

I didn't want to object and draw even more attention to this obvious injustice in our criminal justice system, but if I didn't, Commander Dempsey would let the question hang in the air. "Objection."

She turned her head to the right so the jury couldn't see and smiled sweetly at me. "I'll move on, Your Honor." She moved even closer to the witness and started to bear down. I almost felt sorry for the marine colonel. "So a defendant who is given a life sentence can apply for parole at twenty years?"

"That's correct."

"And he can put in a request every year after that?"

"Correct, after twenty years."

"So a victim or his family that wanted to come and participate would potentially have to show up year after year after year if they wanted to say something to the board in person?" I know he wished she had moved on. And before he could answer, she added, "And at their own expense?"

"Yes," Colonel Butler acknowledged quietly.

"Now, Sir, there are situations where military defendants are in confinement but moved into the federal system, where your board would not have any cognizance over them, aren't there?"

"That's partially correct. Once the appellate process is complete and a discharge has been executed, the individual is no longer in the Navy or Marine Corps. At that point, they become eligible for transfer to the Federal Bureau of Prisons. Depending on the bed spaces and treatment programs, they might be transferred to the federal system. Once they're in the Federal Bureau of Prisons system, we would only look at them for clemency. They would fall under the US Parole

Commission for any parole." Commander Dempsey had done her homework as I knew she would.

"And the US Parole Commissions standards are generally more liberal, aren't they?"

Colonel Butler said sheepishly, "That's correct."

"And the Navy typically doesn't want to retain cognizance over a discharged individual, do they?"

"Once the discharge is executed and there's absolutely no possibility the individual will return to active duty, they typically want them to go to the federal prison," Butler said with resignation.

"So the likelihood of the defendant being transferred to the federal prison system is great?"

"There is a good chance it will happen at some point. Let's say, it takes twelve years to exhaust all the appeals and a discharge is executed. That doesn't mean that he would immediately be sent to a federal penitentiary. It might happen. But that could come at the thirteenth year or it could come at the thirtieth year."

"And, Mr. Butler"—she was no longer using his military title—"if the defendant is transferred, parole would be easier to get?"

"Yes. Truthfully, in my opinion, it's easier." I dropped my head slightly.

"There's one last thing I want to understand before I let you go." Nora paused for effect. "You said individuals are eligible for parole at twenty years, is that right?"

"Yes."

"And these include murderers, people who kill other human beings, sometimes for no good reason?"

"Objection."

"I'll withdraw the question. No further questions at this time," she said dismissively.

"Commander DeMarco, any redirect?" I had to say something.

"Just to clarify one point, Your Honor. Colonel Butler, there are many prisoners that are not paroled, correct?"

"Absolutely. Everyone's eligible, it doesn't mean they're going to get it."

"Sir, that's all for now." I wanted to have the last word, but Commander Dempsey was having none of it. She stood back up before the judge could say anything.

"Sir, statistics show that individuals that don't get parole are typically individuals that kill more than one person, correct?"

"Oftentimes that's the case, but there could be other factors. But that could certainly be a factor."

"And individuals that have a rape in connection with murder?"

"Sure, anything aggravating like that. It could also be that they simply continue to get in trouble when they're in the brig or they refuse treatment. Any of those factors can keep them in the brig or in the federal penitentiaries."

"And you mention that the heinous of the crime is a factor. Who determines what is heinous? Give us some examples of a heinous crime?"

"Clearly, anybody going to prison for a lengthy period of time has done something that's pretty bad. But there's murder, and then there's murder with torture, there's murder with multiple victims, there's murder with children, there's murder with other offenses, such as rape and things of that nature. We look at the whole picture. We don't just say, 'He's been a model prisoner for X number of years. Therefore, we're giving him parole.' We look at what he did to go to prison as well as what he's done since he's been in prison to try to come up with a determination or if he's truly repentant for what he's done and if he is a risk to society if we let him back out. So again, we look at all the factors, including the actual crime."

Nora clearly didn't like this witness. "Sir, the murder of an adult, is that considered a heinous crime for your purposes?"

"Certainly. But what I'm saying, I'm not trying to make light of this, but every man or woman is created by God, and we value their life individually and as a society. But there are other factors that we look at."

Nora simply glared at him and sat down.

"Any additional redirect?" The judge was clearly at the end of his patience and ready to end this sparring match.

"Sir, I just need to follow up on that last question." He waved me on. "Colonel, I think your answer was you couldn't answer Commander Dempsey's question in a vacuum, the murder of an adult. You need to be able to compare it to something. So let me just ask this question. I believe you said the board receives, as one of its exhibits, the record of trial, is that correct?"

"That's correct."

"Can you please explain to the members what a record of trial is?"

"It's a verbatim transcript of every event that takes place at the trial, including the motions and everything that's done when the jury's not present, and everything that's done at the appellate level. All that comes to the board."

"For example, if there was a stipulation of fact that was agreed upon and entered into evidence, would that be part of the record of trial?"

"That would be. Now realistically, the board members are not going to take the time to read a record of trial that might be two feet thick. That's part of the job of my office. We go through the record of trial, and we summarize it. And a summary of the record of trial could be as short as a page, or it could be as lengthy as eight or ten pages. Then we'll take extracts from that, maybe key witnesses or the closing arguments, and we'll put them in there so the members have it all to read. They'll have a good understanding of the case."

"Thank you, Colonel." I sat down.

The judge didn't even look at us as he darted from the bench. It had been a long week and one half. "This court is in recess," he said as he bolted out the door.

CHAPTER FIFTY

BACK ON THE BENCH, THE judge glared at me. "Does the Defense have any additional evidence to present?" He wanted this trial to end. Everyone did.

"Yes, Sir. At this time Joshua would like to make an unsworn statement."

An unsworn statement is a way for a military defendant to give his testimony to the jury without being cross-examined. It is not allowed in civilian courts. Most military lawyers rarely use it as they believe the jury will give it little weight since the client is not under oath. But how many clients lied while under oath? I couldn't let Miller take the stand and have Commander Dempsey cross-examine him, yet I had to find a way for the jury to get to know him.

As Joshua and I began to rise, Captain Johnson suddenly admonished me, "Counsel, may I remind you that in this courtroom your client is to be referred to as Petty Officer Miller. I've let you get away with it numerous times throughout this trial, but remember, this is a military court." Our battles were becoming more numerous. In chambers before and after court, I found it hard to remain respectful. I wanted to remind the jury whenever I could that the fate of a young man was in their hands. "Petty Officer" made Joshua appear more grown-up than he really was. I started to say something but realized now was not the time. The focus had to be on my client. I bit my tongue.

"Of course, Your Honor. My apologizes. May Petty Officer"—I paused slightly—"Miller take the witness stand?" I wanted present his testimony like all the others who had come into the courtroom. The judge would have none of it.

"No, he may not. Please have him make his statement from his place at counsel table. There's a microphone there." We were farther away from the jury than I liked, but maybe that wasn't a bad thing.

I motioned for Joshua to begin. I had no idea what he was going to say—he wouldn't tell me. Miller turned to face the twelve jurors who would decide his fate. He looked briefly over to the family to whom he had caused so much pain. Suddenly, Jessica Williams got up and bolted from the courtroom. Joshua looked stunned. He looked to his mother for help. She could give him none. He looked at me, a confused scared young man who didn't know how to handle life's strange twists and turns. He was shaking.

He took a deep breath and began. "Please bear with me. This is really difficult. I didn't want to do this so soon. I wanted to wait until tomorrow." It was as if he thought he could control the court proceedings. I couldn't imagine dealing with Judge Johnson if we had to hold court on a Sunday. "I've been writing my thoughts down on a piece of paper in my cell, but it hasn't come out quite right." He looked up and back toward the courtroom door before quickly looking back down at the sheet of paper he held in his hand.

"I have three things I'd like to say. Two portions I'm going to read, the other portion I don't need to read." He looked over at me. "Is it okay if I turn this way? Will it still pick me up?" he said, motioning at the microphone. I nodded for him to look at the jury and continue.

"With all that I'm about to tell you, please don't misinterpret it as an excuse for my actions but rather as an explanation for what I've done. Why Corporal Williams is dead, there is no excuse. There is only one reason and a very bad reason at that.

"After one month of talking with Samantha Stevens, I'd become frustrated with not being able to meet her. We poured our heart and souls out to each other, yet excuses kept coming up as to why we could never meet.

"When Samantha told me that she was raped, I became terri-fied. I was afraid for her well-being. I was adamant about her going to the police. Yet she refused. Samantha would say that the rape was her problem and not mine. She'd tell me to drop it but I wanted to protect her. I wanted to save her. But when I eventually tried to move on, she'd invent new stories of how she was being victimized. A break-in, being stalked by her alleged rapist, or receiving harassing phone calls. I didn't know what to do. I became so consumed with the situation that I went to the police for help. The police offered me assistance, but they couldn't locate a woman that didn't exist." Miller just shook his head. He continued.

"There were signs along the way, signs that told me I was being deceived, but I was too pig-headed to pay attention. Then there were coincidences that seemed to verify Samantha's story, and I believed in those coincidences because I wanted to believe in Samantha.

"We would all be better off today if I had just stopped to think or listen to others. Corporal Williams would be alive, his family much happier and not filled with this misery that I have caused them. Corporal Williams's wife, she would have never lost her hope and her child's father. His child would have a life that would include his father's love." Miller's hands were trembling as he gripped the paper tighter. His eyes started to moisten.

"I've lost people in my life to death but not from a murder. Not from a completely senseless and stupid death that could have been entirely avoided. Corporal Williams's death is a guilt that has never left me. And I couldn't live with it anymore. Now with having to witness the pain expressed by all his friends and family that guilt just weighs on me so much more. One of the reasons that caused me to confess was the disgust that I felt toward myself. And the fact that he was having a son." Miller's eyes moistened. "When Corporal Williams and I were talking, I learned about his family. I learned about his wife and his unborn child. It was his wife and child that I kept thinking about. In fact, I couldn't get them out of my mind. The thoughts of them kept tormenting me. Especially with her being pregnant with his unborn child. For her to never know what happened to her hus-band, and the little boy never knowing what happened to his father, was too much. Even after my confession, the guilt continues to haunt me. Whether in my waking hours or sleeping hours, it's something that will never leave me.

"One moment please." In the many months I had known Joshua, it was the first time I had actually seen him cry. Tears were running down his cheeks. He gathered himself and looked over at the Williams family. "I don't expect an apology to be able to fix this. There's nothing that I can do to make the situation any better or to ease your pain. No apology is going to bring Corporal Williams back. Perhaps in hearing my apology, you will one day recognize that I am aware of the disaster that I've created for all of you.

"So to all of Corporal Williams's friends and family members here today, I'm sorry that I've taken this very precious individual from your life. To Corporal Williams's mother and father, I'm sorry for taking your only son from you. To Corporal Williams's wife"—he looked again at the courtroom door—"I wish he could be here right now with you. I'm sorry for taking a piece of your soul and for taking a man that you loved. And there is no amount of sorrow I can express to Corporal Williams's son. I am truly sorry that you are never going to get to know your father's love." A tear fell onto the yellow legal pad he was reading from causing the ink to run.

"And to my family"—he turned toward his mother, who was softly crying—"I'm sorry for the embarrassment and pain that I've caused you and the shame that I've brought toward our name."

He laid the paper on the counsel table. He turned toward the picture of Corporal Williams that Nora had brought back into the courtroom in preparation for closing argument. "And most of all, to Corporal Williams, I'm sorry for the ridiculous mistake I've made. I've taken you from everything and everybody that matters to you the most. There is nothing that I will ever be able to do to make things better. To you I am most sorry."

Joshua turned back to the jury. What he said next surprised me. "Regardless of the punishment I receive, there's only one direction for me to travel and that is to move forward, learning from my mistakes. If you spare my life and send me to prison, I will rehabilitate myself, attend therapy, and utilize the education available. I will continue to take responsibility for my actions and not blame others. And perhaps, just perhaps, one day, I will have the chance to continue helping others. Hopefully, I will one day be a benefit instead of a burden. Perhaps one day I will earn the right to come back and enter society.

"That's all I have to say. Thank you for listening to me." Joshua sat down and stared straight ahead.

I sat at my counsel table for a minute, thinking about what Miller had just said. I looked at the jury. They were sitting back in thoughtful silence. Maybe he had gotten to them. Maybe he had gotten to them in a way I never could have.

I finally got up and walked over to the clerk, who was seated beside the judge. I entered into evidence the remaining documents, witness statements, pictures, and Miller's evaluations while on active duty.

I returned to my table and turned toward the judge. "Sir, the Defense rests."

I had one last task to perform.

CHAPTER FIFTY-ONE

THE JURORS CONTINUED TO STARE at me. I pressed on. "Trial Counsel asked rhetorically, 'What is a life worth?' There is no price you can put on a life. A life is priceless, everyone's life. There's no justification for what happened that night in those woods in eastern North Carolina—but there is a reason. And you've seen that reason. She took the stand.

"Members, think back if you will to the first time you were in love. In today's world, love is a very different concept than when you and I were growing up. The Internet has changed the rules of the game." I needed the jury to understand my client, even though I'm not sure I did. I switched topics. I would get back to 'Samantha' in a minute.

"Petty Officer Miller told you no apology can fix or restore the consequence of his actions. No apology can cure the grief he's caused the Williams's family. No apology can bring Corporal Williams back to life. He said, 'Perhaps in hearing my apology, you will one day recognize that I am aware of the disaster that I've created for all of you.'" I paused to look each juror in the eye. "If those words mean anything, that plea, that confession, if that acknowledgment means anything, and I submit it should, then Joshua's life has some redeeming value.

"The Military Judge will instruct that you are required to balance all the principles of sentencing. Five principles." I slowly counted them out: "The protection of society, the punishment of the wrongdoer, the preservation of good order and discipline, the deterrence of others, and the rehabilitation of the wrongdoer."

I walked slowly back and forth in front of the jury. "When you go back to deliberate, please examine how each of those five principles fit with the evidence you've heard and balance each of them as you are required to do. So let's examine them briefly together.

"The protection of society. As I said previously, if you believe Petty Officer Miller has no redeeming value, that he is a cold-blooded killer, that he was out there in those woods in eastern North Carolina just for the pleasure of killing, then kill him." Several of the jury members seemed to be taken aback by this—a good sign. I stopped for several seconds before continuing. "However, I don't believe that is what the evidence shows. Joshua Miller, before that night, had never been violent before. Something within him that night, something within him in those few moments, made him snap." I noticed a few jurors nodding slightly. Maybe it was wishful thinking on my part.

"When we talk about the next principle, punishment of the wrongdoer, think about what we're actually talking about. Trial Counsel said, 'Don't give Petty Officer Miller what he wants.' A minimum of twenty years in the Castle, the worst prison in the world, is certainly not something Petty Officer Miller wants. We all know what criminals experience in prison—eight-by-ten prison cells, no windows, the daily regimen they follow, the horrors of prison of which I will not speak. Who among us would want that? If Joshua doesn't conform, doesn't go to treatment, doesn't do all the things that he should do, then he will remain a prisoner for the rest of his natural life. At best, he only has the *possibility*," I emphasized the word, "of parole twenty years down the road. Trial Counsel said, 'Don't let the Williams family relive this tragedy.' No one wishes that on them. We sincerely hope that this trial brings them some closure. Commander Dempsey insinuates that the parole board will not do its job simply because it is a collateral duty. That they will take everyone convicted of murder and just let them slide on through." I made a gliding motion with my hand. "You know that's not the case. The board will have pictures of the crime, they'll have victim impact statements, they will have a whole range of evidence. So we hope the Williams family doesn't have to relive this event. And if the opportunity for parole should become available for my client"—I purposefully didn't want to personalize him this time—"there will be other alternatives for the Williams family to make their wishes known.

"I'll combine the next two principles, preservation of good order and discipline and deterrence to others. Certainly, someone in their twenties in a maximum security prison until they are in their forties, an age when most sailors are retiring with a pension, before even being considered for parole will help preserve good order and discipline with the troops and be a deterrence." I stopped and thought how stupid that sounded even to have to say it. "I guess that goes without saying." I saw some of the jurors nod and give me a brief smile, letting me off the hook.

"The last principle, I submit, is the most difficult one: the rehabilitation of the wrongdoer. I believe you can fashion a sentence that will benefit the needs of everyone: society as a whole, the Williams family's desire for justice and Petty Officer Miller. I submit that you can fairly balance the tragic events of January 1 with everything that has happened in Petty Officer Miller's life prior to that day. You have heard the aggravating evidence from the Government. For that short period of time, it was tragic. But you must look at the other evidence as well.

"During my opening statement, I asked you to examine three different periods of Joshua's life, no one period more important than the other, even the Susan Jenkins evidence. Whatever you thought of that, I was not trying to place undue weight on it"—the hell I wasn't—"but it was certainly something you needed to consider. I trust you understand that whatever was going on in that young man's life during that period of time, it was central to how he acted." I walked closer to the jurors.

"Let's talk about the first period of Joshua's life that we learned about from the testimony and letters of support from those who knew him best, his friends and his family. That is vital to understanding his makeup. Both families have their friends. The law doesn't allow you to give greater weight to one over the other. It's not a beauty contest. But it's something I'd ask you to examine.

"Joshua's mother testified to what he was like growing up. That he came from a loving family. He dropped out of school and tried to find himself. Joshua's father passing away was an important event in this young man's life. Maybe it was more important to his psychological makeup than we realize. You also had letters from other family and friends, Sherry Stewart, Marie Harrell, Nick Nelson. Everyone who knew Joshua said they were shocked.

"Ms. Stewart said Petty Officer Miller talked to everybody. She told you about her son with Down's syndrome. That Joshua would play with him. That Joshua befriended the one cat that nobody liked. Marie told you about when her son was in Iraq and she was feeling down, Joshua, shortly before these events, brought her a cookie to cheer her up. Nick Nelson, well, I guess Nick was always looked at as the computer 'nerd' we all knew growing up. But his one friend, the one person that befriended him, was Petty Officer Miller.

"That evidence gives you a picture of Joshua growing up. He was kindhearted and helpful. He wasn't a monster.

"You've also read statements from his shipmates, you have those in your binders, I won't belabor them. But the statements from people that knew Miller on board the ship, those he spent twenty-four hours a day with him, they also tell you about his personality. He was nonviolent, reliable, he cared about people. Lieutenant Marley said Joshua had a 'James Dean' type of personality, which may play into the second period of time I'd like to talk to you about.

"It appears that Petty Officer Miller always wanted to be the 'hero.' He wanted to protect the underdog. That appears to be part of his makeup." I wish I could have called Tanney as a witness, but that would have gotten us both in trouble. "That's why those seventy-seven days with Samantha, or Susan, are important. We all know that love is the most powerful of emotions.

"Certainly Susan didn't ask Petty Officer Miller to do what he did. But she did lead him to the night of January 1. And that's what's most important. Because without that connection, we would not be here today.

"You've heard about how Samantha led sailors on. You heard Airman Adams's testimony. What is most important is that Ms. Jenkins led Petty Officer Miller to believe that she was raped by three marines. And that they continued to harass her even breaking into her home. That she was in danger.

"Petty Officer Miller went to the police several times trying to do the right thing. Sergeant Mineo tried to help him. Petty Officer Holmes, a civilian policeman, tried to give him advice. He testified that Petty Officer Miller told him that he had found the girl for him. Holmes, who was a little older, thought it was an immature relationship, but Petty Officer Miller wouldn't listen. So Miller ended up trying to protect the young lady of his dreams.

"Examine the timeline in your binders. In December, after being told by Samantha that she was raped, he began looking for the marines. At some point in time, the unfortunate incident in the cafeteria occurred where Corporal Williams and Petty Officer Miller saw each other. Petty Officer Miller thought that Corporal Williams was involved and Samantha confirmed that. He went to interview Williams at the barracks. Remember, when Miller first questioned Corporal Williams, he left with conflicting emotions. There was no intent to harm anyone. When Miller returned at the end of December, knowing he had to get to the bottom of what was going on, the intent was just to scare Corporal Williams. You learned that from his confession. I'm asking you to put those events into context when determining whether this person is a monster."

I backed away from the jury and paused. I had to try and minimize the actual killing. "Even up until the moment this tragic event occurred, within seconds when the decision was made to…" I stopped. "Well, I can't explain why Joshua made the decision to do what he did. Why would someone who has been a good person his entire life all of a sudden snap?" I just shook my head. "It's a tragedy all the way around. But all the evidence shows that Miller's intent, even while driving down to North Carolina, was to scare Corporal Williams. Trial Counsel asked you to go back and think about how long five minutes is. We certainly hope, and I believe even the Governments medical evidence bears me out, that someone in that situation, under shock, would lose consciousness very quickly." I had to move on.

"That brings me to Petty Officer Miller's confession. Ask yourself, 'Is that something a hardened criminal would do?' Trial Counsel asked you to examine Miller's confession and whether it actually shows remorse. That's not fair to ask. We don't know Petty Officer Miller's emotional makeup. It's hard to gauge emotions from a mere piece of paper. As Joshua told you, he's had many a sleepless night. These tragic events are finally coming to an end for him. He had to have been on an emotional roller coaster. I believe the evidence shows that Joshua was trying to be as helpful as possible with his confession.

"Before you make your decision, I know you must be asking yourself, 'Is there any good in this man?' Please examine his confession again. Examine the actions he's taken since this event. I submit the feelings expressed show goodness somewhere in his heart. Joshua has pled guilty. He entered into a stipulation of fact that didn't require the Government to put on any evidence. He has no plea agreement. Joshua Miller comes before you knowing the consequences of his actions, knowing that the minimum sentence he will get is life imprisonment for at least twenty years. And life is life. Life imprisonment in the Unites States Disciplinary Barracks, Leavenworth, the Castle, is brutal.

"I also want to remind you before I sit down that there was some significant evidence that you didn't hear. There was no evidence that Petty Officer Miller is a sociopath, that he's psychotic, that he's got a mental defect, none of that. I almost wish there was an explanation for why he did what he did. But there is no psychological diagnosis that would hinder Joshua from successfully completing mental health treatment in the future.

"I also ask you to remember the testimony of Colonel Butler, even though it may only become relevant in twenty years. Commander Dempsey said, 'We have rules.' We certainly do and those rules were tragically broken. But we also have parole which is something that's developed over the last two hundred years in our criminal justice system. Criminal justice experts decided that parole was an appropriate piece of the puzzle—that's why it's allowed. And people who have taken another's life get a chance at parole. There's a reason for that. It serves as a vital tool in this whole process. Colonel Butler told us a little bit about the process and what they look for before parole is even considered. He told you that parole is a privilege, not a right. Someone has to earn it." My voice was beginning to fail me. I had to finish. I walked to the other end of the jury box and gathered my strength.

"Members, there's a parable in the Bible, John 8:3. It tells the story of a prostitute who is getting ready to be stoned for her sins. Jesus admonishes the crowd that has gathered, 'He that is without sin among you, let him cast the first stone.' Jesus was not arguing with the sentence. The prostitute was guilty in accordance with the laws of the time, the law of the land. The point of the parable is that you can't judge unfairly, you can't judge a person without knowing what he has gone through. We are all sinners.

"Certainly, the easy decision, the emotional decision, is to put Joshua to death. But I ask you to dig deeper within yourselves. Remember the promises that you made to me in voir dire. That you would consider all the evidence, both in aggravation and mitigation. All the evidence. I'm asking you examine all of it and then judge Joshua Miller fairly and compassionately.

"This is Petty Officer Miller's only day in court. If you have any doubts, I ask that you have them now because for him there is no tomorrow. Trial Counsel says, 'Don't give him what he wants.' Well, twenty years' minimum at Leavenworth is not what anyone wants. There are no winners in this case." I paused once again.

"I was trying to put twenty years into context for us, so I did a little research. Twenty years ago, gasoline was eighty-seven cents per gallon, there was no commercially available Internet, no cell phones, IBM hadn't built its first laptop. Twenty years is a long, long time. And that's just where it starts.

"Joshua should pay for what he's done. He should pay a significant price. Life imprisonment, life is life, and that is appropriate. But what I'm asking you to do is design a sentence where every day he has to get up and think about what he's done, where he has to get treatment and go to counseling, where he has to go to school, and he has to, somehow, make things right. He has to do all those things just to be able to step up to the plate." I was hoping I had some softball players on the jury.

"Commander Dempsey said I might ask for mercy, I might ask for compassion. Well, I am asking for that. But I'm also asking you to not to make the easy decision, make Petty Officer Miller work. Make him pay for what he's done. And by making that decision, isn't what you're really saying is 'I don't have enough information. I'm going to let the experts decide when the time is right.' You're certainly not saying that what Petty Officer Miller did was acceptable. You're certainly not giving Petty Officer Miller what he wants. You're not being disrespectful to the Williams family. You're simply saying 'I don't have enough information at this time.'

"I'm asking you to go back to the deliberation room and fashion a punishment that fits the needs of the Williams family, the Miller family, and society. That, I respectfully submit, is life imprisonment with the eligibility, one day, for parole.

"Thank you."

CHAPTER FIFTY-TWO

THE MEMBERS WATCHED ME AS I returned to my seat. I was tired both physically and emotionally. My body language showed it. I gazed over to the jury as I sat down. They also looked spent. The courtroom was silent.

Captain Johnson cleared his throat and began. "Members, the evidentiary portion of the trial has been concluded. I'm now going to instruct you on sentencing. I will provide a written copy of these instructions to the President of the Court for use during your deliberations." He paused as he put on his "Ben Franklin" reading glasses. It was the first time during the trial that he had used them.

"You are about to deliberate and vote on the sentence in this case. It is the duty of each member to vote for a proper sentence for the offenses to which this accused has pled guilty. Your determination of the kind and the amount of punishment is a grave responsibility requiring the exercise of wise discretion. Although you must give due consideration to all matters in extenuation and mitigation, as well as those in aggravation, you must bear in mind that the accused is to be sentenced only for the offenses for which he has been found guilty. A single sentence shall be adjudged for all the offenses to which the accused has been found guilty.

"The maximum punishment for the offenses for which the accused has been found guilty is death. You are at liberty to arrive at a lesser sentence based upon your own evaluation of the evidence presented with the exception that any lesser sentence must include the mandatory minimum term of confinement, which is confinement for the duration of the accused natural life with the possibility of parole after twenty years confinement.

"Our society recognizes five principles regarding sentencing of those who violate the law. These are, first, the protection of society from the wrongdoer; second, punishment of the wrongdoer; third, the rehabilitation of the wrongdoer; fourth, the preservation of good order and discipline in the military; and fifth, the deterrence of the wrongdoer and those who know of his crime and his sentence from committing the same or similar offenses.

"The weight to be given to any or all of these reasons, along with all the other sentencing matters in this case, rests solely within your discretion. Each type of punishment is separate and does not, by implication or otherwise, include any other type of punishment, with two exceptions that I will mention in just a moment.

"I will now briefly explain in more detail, the various penalties that may be adjudged by this court. This court may adjudge reduction to the lowest or any intermediate enlisted pay grade, either alone or in combination with any other type of punishment within the maximum limitation.

"A reduction carries both the loss of military status and the incidents thereto and results in a corresponding reduction in military pay. You should designate only the pay grade to which the accused is to be reduced rather than the rate or the rank.

"As a result of Article 58(a) of the *Uniform Code of Military Justice*, any sentence of an enlisted person in a pay grade above E-1, which includes either a punitive discharge or confinement in excess of three months, automatically reduces that individual to the lowest enlisted pay grade of E-1 by operation of law. This is the first exception to which I referred a moment ago. Notwithstanding the provisions of Article 58(a), this court may properly include an explicit sentence to reduction to E-1 or any intermediate pay grade as a part of any sentence if the court believes that such a reduction should be part of the sentence."

Captain Johnson paused as pushed up the glasses, which had worked its way down his bulbous nose. "As I've already indicated, this court may sentence the accused to confinement for a maximum duration of the natural life of the accused without the possibility of parole. The mandatory minimum sentence is confinement for the natural life of the accused.

"You are advised that a sentence of confinement for life without eligibility of parole means that the accused will not be eligible for parole by any official, but it does not preclude clemency action, which might convert that sentence to one that allows parole. By comparison, a sentence to confinement for life means that the accused will have a possibility of earning parole from confinement under such circumstances as are, or may be, provided by law or regulation.

"Parole is a form of conditional release of a prisoner from actual incarceration before his sentence has been fulfilled on specific conditions and under the possibility of return to incarceration to complete a sentence of confinement if the conditions of parole are violated. The exercise of parole, however, depends on several factors including but not limited to the length of the sentence to confinement, the nature of the crime, and the conduct of the accused during his period of confinement.

"In determining whether to adjudge confinement for life without eligibility for parole or confinement for life, you should bear in mind that you must not adjudge an excessive sentence in reliance upon possible mitigating, clemency, or parole action by the Convening Authority or any other authority. You should select the sentence that you believe best serves the ends of good order and discipline, the needs of the accused, and the welfare of society.

"In determining an appropriate sentence in this case, you should consider the fact that the accused has spent several months in pretrial confinement. The days that the accused spent in pretrial confinement will be credited against any sentence of confinement that you adjudge. This credit will be given by the authorities at the correctional facilities where the accused is sent to serve his confinement and will be given on a day-per-day basis.

"This court may sentence the accused to forfeit a maximum of all pay and allowances. Forfeiture is a financial penalty that deprives the accused of military pay as it accrues. Determining the amount of forfeiture, if any, the court should consider the implications to the accused of such a loss of income. Unless total forfeiture is adjudged, a sentence to a forfeiture should include an expressed statement of a whole dollar amount to be forfeited each month and the number of months the forfeiture is to continue. This court may adjudge any forfeiture up to and including forfeiture of all pay and allowances. The court is at liberty to arrive at any lesser figure or to adjudge a sentence containing no forfeitures at all.

"As a result of Article 58(b) of the *Uniform Code of Military Justice*, by operation of law, any court-martial sentence that includes either a punitive discharge or confinement for more than six months automatically results in a forfeiture of all pay and allowances due during the period of confinement. This is the other exception to which I referred earlier.

"Notwithstanding the provisions of Article 58(b) and without regard to whether this court includes a punitive discharge in its sentence, this court may properly include an explicit sentence to forfeit all pay and allowances or any lesser amount and duration of forfeiture as part of your sentence if the court believes that such a forfeiture of pay and allowances should be part of the sentence.

"This court may adjudge a punitive discharge in the form of either a dishonorable discharge or a bad conduct discharge. Such a punitive discharge deprives one substantially of all benefits administered by the Department of Veterans Affairs, and for that matter, the Department of the Navy.

"A dishonorable discharge should be reserved for those who, in the opinion of this court, should be separated under conditions of dishonor after conviction of serious offenses of either a civil or military nature warranting such severe punishment.

"A bad conduct discharge is severe punishment although less severe than a dishonorable discharge and may be adjudged for one who, in the discretion of this court, warrants severe punishment for bad conduct. In this case, if the court determines to adjudge a punitive discharge, it may sentence the accused to a dishonorable discharge or a bad conduct discharge. No other type of discharge or separation may be adjudged. Accordingly, you are not authorized to adjudge a dismissal or any type of administrative discharge.

"You should bear in mind that only matters properly before the court as a whole should be considered and in weighing and evaluating the evidence you are expected to utilize your own common sense, your knowledge of human nature, and the ways of the world. In light of all the circumstances in this case, you should consider the inherent probability or improbability of the evidence.

"Bear in mind that you may properly believe one witness and disbelieve several other witnesses whose testimony is in conflict with the one. The final determination as to the weight or the significance of the evidence and the credibility of the witnesses in this case rests solely upon you, the members of the court.

"You have the duty to determine the credibility, that is, the believability, of the witnesses. In performing this duty, you must consider each witness's intelligence, their ability to observe and accurately remember, in addition to the witness's sincerity and conduct in court.

"Consider also the extent to which each witness is either supported or contradicted by other evidence, the relationship each witness may have with either side, and how each witness might be affected by the sentence. In weighing a discrepancy by a witness or between witnesses, you should consider whether any discrepancy resulted from an innocent mistake or a deliberate lie.

"Taking all of these matters into account, you should then consider the probability of each witness's testimony and the inclination of the witness to tell the truth. The credibility of each witness's testimony should be your guide in evaluating testimony and not the number of witnesses called.

"The parties to this trial have stipulated or agreed, to the contents of 'Prosecution Exhibit IX, the Stipulation of Fact,' including its attachments. When counsel for both sides, with the consent of the accused, stipulate and agree to the contents of the writing, the parties are bound by the stipulation and the stipulated matters are facts and evidence to be considered by you along with all the other evidence in the case.

"Members, in selecting a sentence, you should consider all the matters in extenuation and mitigation as well as those in aggravation, whether introduced to you before or after findings, plus all the evidence you have heard in this case which is relevant to the subject of sentencing.

"Among the matters you should consider are the following: the accused age; the duration of the accused pretrial confinement; all the exhibits admitted into evidence by both the prosecution and the defense; that the accused enlisted evaluations indicate satisfactory performances as documented in 'Defense Exhibit T'; the accused's conduct in confinement as demonstrated in his brig records in 'Defense Exhibit E'; the medals and awards the accused is entitled to wear, as documented by 'Defense Exhibit B'; the lack of any previous convictions, or Article 15 *UCMJ* punishment; the character references offered by those that knew Petty Officer Miller; the witnesses' statements contained in 'Defense Exhibits F–Q'; the testimony of those witnesses that appeared live at this trial; and the accused's apology as contained in his unsworn statement.

"You should also consider the nature of the offenses of which the accused has been convicted which involve impersonating a US government official, kidnapping, obstruction of justice, and murder.

"You should consider the testimony of the Government witnesses including Dr. McDermitt, Sergeant Carlson, and Mrs. Jessica Williams. You can properly consider the impact that these offenses have had on her life.

"A plea of guilty is a matter in mitigation that must be considered along with the other facts and circumstances in this case. Time, effort, and expense to the Government have been saved by a plea of guilty. Such a plea may be the first step toward rehabilitation.

"The court will not draw any adverse inference to the accused from the fact that he did not elect to testify under oath as a witness. You are advised that an unsworn statement is an authorized means for an accused to bring information to the attention of the court and it must be given appropriate consideration. The accused cannot be cross-examined by the prosecution or interrogated by the court members or questioned by me with an unsworn statement, but the prosecution may offer evidence to rebut statements of fact contained in it. The weight and significance to be attached to an unsworn statement rests within the sound discretion of each court member. You may consider that the statement is not under oath, its inherent probability or improbability, and whether it is supported or contradicted by the evidence in the case as well as any other matter that may have a bearing upon its credibility. In weighing an unsworn statement, you are expected to use your common sense and your knowledge of human nature and the ways of the world.

"During argument, trial and defense counsel recommended that you consider a specific sentence in this case. The arguments of counsel and their recommendations are only their individual suggestions and may not be considered as the recommendation or opinion of anyone other than counsel.

"When you close to deliberate and vote, only the members will be present during your closed-session deliberations, and your deliberations should begin with a full and free discussion on the subject of sentencing. The influence of superiority in rank shall not be employed in any manner to control the independence of members in the exercise of their judgment.

"When you've completed your discussion, any member who desires to do so may propose a sentence. You do that by writing out a complete sentence on a slip of paper. The junior member then collects the proposed sentences and submits them to the president, who will arrange them in the order of their severity.

"You then vote on the proposed sentences by secret written ballot. All must vote. You may not abstain. Vote on each proposed sentence in its entirety, beginning with the lightest until you arrive at the required concurrence, which is three-fourths, or nine members.

"The junior member will collect and count the votes. The count is then checked by the president, who will announce the result of the ballot to the members. If you vote on all the proposed sentences without arriving at the required concurrence, you then repeat the process of proposing and voting upon the sentences.

"The second time around, if a member desires to do so, you may vote on all new proposals or proposals rejected on an earlier vote, but once a proposal has been agreed to by required concurrence, then that is your sentence. You may request to reconsider your sentence at any time prior to its being announced in open court, but after you determine your sentence, if any member suggests reconsideration of the sentence, open the court and I will give you specific instructions on the procedure for doing that. If that should occur, when the court is assembled, the president should announce that reconsideration has been proposed without reference to whether the proposed reballot concerns increasing or decreasing a sentence.

"As an aid to putting your sentence in the proper form, you may use the sentence worksheet. The worksheet is not intended to express any opinion either by me or by counsel as to what would be an appropriate sentence in this case, for you alone have the responsibility to make that determination.

"Captain," the judge said, addressing the senior member, "with regard to the worksheet, when you finalize your sentence, place an X at any applicable sentence element box, fill in any blanks, line through any and all unused portions, and sign the worksheet at the bottom.

"If during your deliberations you have any questions concerning sentencing matters, please open the court and I'll take those matters up with you. I would ask that if you do have such a question that you write it down on the question form that's been provided so that an accurate record of your question may be maintained.

"You may not consult *The Manual for Courts-Martial* or any other writing not admitted into evidence. Any instructions by me must not be interpreted as indicating any opinion on my part as to what would be an appropriate sentence in this case.

"In your deliberation room, you'll have all the exhibits that have been admitted into evidence. Please do not write on any of these exhibits, except obviously on the sentencing worksheet.

"In accordance with your best judgment, based upon the evidence that's been presented in this case and your own experience and general background, you should select a sentence that best serves the ends of good order and discipline in the military, the needs of the accused, and the welfare of society.

"Members of the court, you may now withdraw to the deliberation room. The court is now closed for deliberations."

The twelve jurors slowly rose as one, turned to their left, and entered the deliberation room. The door closed silently behind them.

CHAPTER FIFTY-THREE

IT WAS LATE SATURDAY EVENING. The worst part of any trial is waiting for the jury to return with its verdict. You are helpless. All the months of thinking about your case are over. All the preparation. All the planning. All the sleepless nights. The members were into their fifth hour of deliberations. Was that too long? Or too short? At least they were examining the evidence.

Any day in trial is a long day. Nothing in your life outside of that courtroom gets done. You don't pay bills. You don't exercise. You lose contact with friends and family. You are constantly on edge, never satisfied with your performance. You think of all the things you should have done differently, the questions you asked, or worse, the questions you didn't.

When you finally get home at night, you are too tired to eat, although you know you must. You grab a quick bite and then it's back to work. You organize the evidence presented that day to use later in the week during your closing argument. You prepare for the next day's witnesses. You can't sleep even though you are exhausted. You toss and turn in bed, trying to remember what you've forgotten. It's physically and emotionally draining.

And then it's over. And all you can do is wait.

After the jury retires to the deliberation room, you try to make small talk with everyone that comes up to wanting to know "How'd it go?" All you really want is to be left alone with your thoughts. You talk to your client and his family and try to prepare them for what might happen. You want to be positive, but you need to be realistic. How do tell a mother that her young son may be put to death?

I told Miller that when the jury returns and announces their verdict, he can't show any emotion no matter what happens. I've had clients whose knees buckled and they've collapsed right there at counsel table. I've seen wives faint and kids scream and run to hug their dad's leg before he was carried off to jail. It's a terrible time. And that time goes by ever so slowly.

Lawyers have all types of theories, as there are with most aspects of litigation, regarding the amount of time a jury spends deliberating. Some say if the jury comes back too quickly, your client is going to be found guilty, as the jurors didn't question the evidence. Conversely, if they are out for too long a period of time, there are questions and areas of reasonable doubt. Exactly what a defense attorney wants.

After so many years in the courtroom, you'd think I would have tried to stop figuring out what a jury will do. Intellectually, I realize that I will never know what's inside someone's head. Every juror brings different life experiences into the courtroom. Everyone's perception is different. But I still look for clues.

For instance, what does it means when the jurors return from the deliberation room and are filing back to their seats and they look at you? If they crack a smile, are you good? If they are looking down, are you in trouble? Maybe they're just making sure they don't trip over the chair in front of them.

The anticipation is great. When the jury goes out some attorneys go back to their office and try to work on their next case. Phones calls need to be returned; other clients have been calling wondering what's going on with their case. The jury can be out for hours or days. I have a hard time leaving the courtroom. I can't focus on anything, but what's going on behind those closed doors only a few yards away.

From my seat, I could hear the voices within. It sounded as if they were arguing. The bailiff sat in front of the doorway, not letting anyone in or out. Sometimes I go up to the bailiff and make casual conversation while actually trying to listen to what is being said inside the deliberation room. You can only catch a word or two, but anything is better than nothing. Some bailiffs catch on. No one yet has asked me to leave. Bailiffs and court reporters are a good source of information. If I want to know how I'm doing during trial or what the jury might be thinking about a particular piece of evidence, I ask them during a break.

The brig chasers, the guys charged with bringing Miller back and forth to the brig every day, were talking to my client. After all these months, they began to see each other for what they were, just young kids far away from home doing their duty, making mistakes and paying for them, their futures unknown. I didn't want to interrupt them.

There was a knock on the door. The bailiff jumped from his chair and opened it. He stuck his head in and then quickly withdrew. The jury had reached its verdict. He nodded to me and took off down the hallway to find the judge. A buzz immediately went through the building. Someone had to take the elevator down to the first deck to find Commander Dempsey. There was a flurry of activity. I didn't move from my chair.

After twenty minutes, everyone had gathered back into the courtroom. I hadn't said much to Miller. What could I say? We didn't look at each other. Perhaps we were afraid of what the other might see.

The judge entered from the side door and took his seat. He nodded to the bailiff, who opened the deliberation room door. The jury entered and quietly took their places behind their seats. They were looking down. The large courtroom was eerily silent.

"The court will come to order. All parties who were present when the court closed are again present. Members, please be seated. Everyone else, please be seated." He paused. "Captain Hagan, has the court reached a decision in this matter?

The Captain rose slowly as if the weight of the verdict was holding him down. "Yes, Sir. We have."

"And is your verdict accurately reflected on the sentencing worksheet?" The senior member only nodded. "Have you signed it at the bottom?

"Yes, Sir. I have."

"Please pass that to the bailiff. Bailiff, without looking at the worksheet, please bring it to me."

It took forever for the bailiff to traverse the ten feet from the jury box to the judge's bench. The judge slowly unfolded the paper, looked it over, refolded it, and handed it back the bailiff.

"The worksheet appears to be in proper order. Bailiff, would you please return this to Captain Hagan?"

The judge then turned slightly to look at me, almost sadly, I thought. "Accused and counsel, please rise."

We did as directed. I could feel Joshua rise unsteadily and grabbed his elbow to help him.

"Captain Hagan, would you please announce the sentence to the court."

Captain Hagan cleared his throat and began. "Intelligence Specialist Third Class Joshua Miller, United States Navy, it is my duty as President of this Court to inform you that the court in closed-session and upon secret written ballot, three-fourths of the members concurring, sentences you to the following: to be reduced to pay grade E-1, to forfeit all pay and allowances, to be discharged from the Naval service with a dishonorable discharge, and to be confined for the duration of your natural life without the eligibility for parole."

There was a gasp from the audience. I kept looking straight ahead. I couldn't tell from which side of the courtroom it came. I heard sobbing.

The judge instructed us to be seated, although his voice seemed far away.

Captain Johnson continued on, "Bailiff, would you please retrieve the worksheet and give it to the court reporter for insertion into the record." He turned toward the members and straightened up in his chair.

"Members of the court, you have now completed your duties and you are discharged with the sincere thanks of the court. Please leave all the exhibits behind. You may take your personal notes with you or you may leave those behind and the bailiff and court reporter will see that they are destroyed.

"To assist you in determining what you may discuss about this case now that it is over, the following guidance is provided: When you took your oath as members, you swore not to disclose or discuss the vote or the opinion of any particular member of this court unless required to do so in the due course of law. This means that you cannot tell anyone about the way you, or anyone else on the court, voted or what opinion you or they had unless I, or another judge, require you to do so in a court of law. You're each entitled to this privacy. Other than that, you are free to talk to anyone else about the case. You can also decline to participate in those discussions if that's your choice.

"Your deliberations are carried out in the secrecy of the deliberation room to permit you the utmost freedom to debate and discuss and so that each of you can express your views without fear of being subjected to public scorn or criticism by the accused, the Convening Authority, or anyone else. In deciding whether to answer questions about this case and, if so, what to disclose, you should have in mind your own interests and the interests of the other members of the court.

"Does any member have a question at this time?" The jurors were already gathering their belongings. "If not, you may now depart the courtroom and resume your normal duties."

The members of the court-martial withdrew quickly, their heads bowed. The judge nodded at both Commander Dempsey and me. It appeared he wanted to say something but then thought the better of it. He rose from his padded leather chair and started to exit through the side door to his chambers. Suddenly, he turned and instead came out from behind the bench and went over to Commander Dempsey. He looked her in the eye, smiled slightly, and shook her hand. He then turned to me.

We looked at each other for a moment. Neither of us moved to close the gap that was between us. He then extended his hand. I paused, then took the three steps needed to close the distance and shook it. He started to speak, but I cut him off. "It was a pleasure being in your courtroom, Sir." He seemed embarrassed.

"Commander. I wish you fair winds and following seas." A nautical blessing of good luck. I could only nod. He then gathered himself and left through the main door. I watched as he left.

When I turned back, Commander Dempsey had already collected her papers and was standing beside me. Our eyes met. She put down her briefcase and gave me a quick hug. "Michael, it is always a pleasure seeing you."

"You too, Nora."

"Come see me in DC?"

I smiled. "Sure."

"Promises. Promises." She smiled, winked at me, and quickly walked out the door. I returned to my chair. Joshua was still seated, staring straight ahead. His mother, seated two rows behind, had not moved. There were tears in her eyes. I did what she had asked me to do. What could I say to either of them that might provide some comfort? The MPs came up to us. "Commander DeMarco, we have to transport the prisoner."

I stopped them. "Give us a second." I looked at Joshua and he at me. So young, I thought. Was he a monster? I didn't know what to say. He spoke first.

"I just wanted to say thank you, Sir, for all you did." He paused, not sure if he should continue. Finally he did. "You saved my life." Again, a pause. "But I'm not sure that, in the end, you did me any favors."

With that, he rose and walked with the guards out of the courtroom and into hell.

CHAPTER FIFTY-FOUR

I WALKED ALONG THE BOARDWALK at the Virginia Beach oceanfront in an old Navy sweatshirt and shorts. The boardwalk is 2.8 miles long. I used to run it; now I just walk. I composed some of my best closing arguments in my head while running along the oceanfront. I've been fighting a long time—I'm not sure if I have any good arguments left in me.

There was a steady breeze blowing in from off the water. The salt air smelled clean. The waves were calm. I liked early mornings at the beach. Thank goodness the tourists had left for the season. No one yelling. No accents from faraway places. No tattoos on body parts that should be covered.

The adjacent bike path was empty. The air was turning colder. Even though most of the hotels were still open, no one was eating at the outdoor cafés. I found a place to sit under an empty awning and ordered a cup of coffee, black. There was a gas fire pit that warms me but only slightly.

I thought back to the many trials I've been involved in. Some lasted a day, others a month. You become close to the person you represent, you learn every detail of their life, and then they are gone. You rarely ever hear from them again. I can't remember many of their names. One case replaces the next, and before you know it, your career is almost over. And a good portion of your life. Litigation takes its toll.

Joshua Miller had been in Leavenworth for several months. The Williams family had forever lost a son. Susan Jenkins was back doing whatever hotel clerks do. It was only a year ago Miller reported to Dam Neck. Life can dramatically change in a short period of time. Joshua would be hard to forget. He hadn't written. I was expecting the inevitable Ineffective Assistance of Counsel motion. Maybe not, maybe this time I'd be surprised. But I doubt it. A prisoner has a lot of time on his hands. He has many voices in his ear, jailhouse lawyers abound. It's easy to "Monday morning quarterback" a trial. It never goes as planned. That's the nature of trial work. But you never let them see you sweat.

The waitress brought me my coffee. I watched the steam rise from the mug. I took a sip and then leaned back in my chair with my hands behind my head. What would the world would be like if everyone followed the law? Certainly, my world would be different. Why did I enjoy criminal work? Was it because the stakes were high? The adrenaline rush? The theater of the courtroom? I often told the young attorneys in the office a trial was like a play. It has to be well-scripted, well-rehearsed, every actor hitting his marks, knowing his part.

Did I really believe in the "system?" A system of justice where all are innocent until proven guilty. That guilt must be proven beyond a reasonable doubt as to each and every element of the crime charged. That the Government has the burden of proof and it never shifts. How many times had I said that? I could recite it in my sleep. Was the punishment awarded appropriate? Were all the defendant's life circumstances taken into account? Did we judge fairly? I questioned what I truly believed after all these years.

There were easier ways to make a living. I had turned down the job in Charlotte. Maybe I should still get out and go into civil practice, which was much less stressful. Maybe I could represent big corporations in hostile takeovers or go into personal injury litigation, where you're suing insurance companies and the only thing at stake is how much money your client receives. Sort of cheapens the process, doesn't it? Could I talk about 'negligence,' 'damages,' and 'mental pain and emotional suffering' all day? I have seen suffering and it wasn't from a whiplash. And the burden of proof by a 'preponderance of evidence' or 'more likely than not' just didn't seem fair—to either side. If I stayed in the military, there were many international law billets available. Maybe that was the way to go.

I finished my coffee and got back up to walk. What about society as a whole? How do people come to be in the circumstances they find themselves in? How one small, often careless, decision can affect the rest of their life. What was Joshua doing right now? A boy among men, in one of the harshest prisons in the world. How was he surviving?

I thought about all the young men and women who join the military for a better way of life. Most didn't have many opportunities in the small town where they grew up; most only wanted to see the world while learning a trade. Most, if not all, didn't realize what they were signing up for. Being yelled at by their Platoon Sergeant, Division Officer, or Department Head. Working twenty hours a day, seven days a week. Being gone for six months at a time and not being able to see their families or their children grow up. If you survived it, you were a better person.

Could the system be improved? Could it be fixed? Wasn't there a better way? I wondered. Too many questions to answer.

The sun was rising higher. It was time to go. I had done all I could for Miller and that would have to be good enough. At least that's what I told myself.

I got back in my car and drove to work. I had another trial starting in a few days.

ABOUT THE AUTHOR

DON MARCARI IS A TRIAL attorney with over thirty years' experience. After graduating from law school, he entered the Navy Judge Advocate General Corps, where his first trial became the basis for the movie *A Few Good Men*. He also represented the senior officer charged in the Tailhook trials, which became the basis for the movie *The Paula Coughlin Story* and the book The Mother of All Hooks: *The Story of the US Navy Tailhook Scandal*. Don has appeared on *A Current Affair*, *Unsolved Mysteries*, and *The Montel Williams Show*.

Currently, Don is the senior partner of a multistate law firm, which handles both civil litigation and military law. He has won numerous awards, including being named a Leader in the Law, Super Lawyer, and Top 100 Trial Lawyer and has received a preeminent rating by his peers.

In his spare time, Don is an adjunct professor of law, teaches legal classes at the local high schools, and coaches football. He lives in Virginia Beach and is the proud father of three wonderful children.